Lionfish

Nathanael Miller

This is a work of fiction. Names, characters, businesses, places,
events and incidents are either the products of the author's
imagination or used in a fictitious manner. Any resemblance to
actual persons, living or dead, is purely coincidental.

ISBN: 978-1-953475-07-7

Katrina

Sailors look at the stars as guides, companions, and inspiration.
You have long been one of the brightest stars and inspirations to me.

THE ADVENTURES OF THE
ACCIDENTAL DETECTIVE

...the Accidental Detective will return...

Janghwa Hongryeon jeon
"The Parable of Janghwa and Hongryeon"

Muryong and his wife had two daughters, Janghwa ('Rose Flower') and her younger sister, Hongryeon ('Red Lotus'). After their mother sadly passed, Muryong remarried, his new wife hiding a deep hatred of the girls.

The hateful stepmother began plotting against Janghwa as the younger woman planned her wedding. The malevolent stepmother had her eldest son frame Janghwa for unchaste behavior, then murder Janghwa after the young woman ran off in horror. However, as the young man pushed Janghwa into a pond to drown her, a tiger horrifically mauled him. Grief-stricken, Hongryeon followed her sister in death, drowning herself in the same pond.

For some years thereafter, every new mayor in the village would mysteriously die after a brief time. Finally, yet another new mayor took over. One night he woke up and saw the ghosts of two girls standing in his room. The mayor was frightened but asked the ghosts who they were and what they wanted. The specters told him no one had ever talked to them before, then demanded he expose the evil stepmother. The mayor solved the crime, executing the stepmother and eldest son for the murder of Janghwa. Muryong was spared when it was proven he was duped by the cruel woman's machinations.

Muryong remarried again. His lost daughters spoke to him in a dream one night, saying they were returning now that justice had been served. His new wife bore twin daughters, whom they affectionately named Janghwa and Hongryeon. The family lived in harmony, justice having found out those who treacherously committed murder.

> *--Janghwa Hongryeon jeon*, a Korean folktale from the Joeson era (1392–1897)

Table of Contents

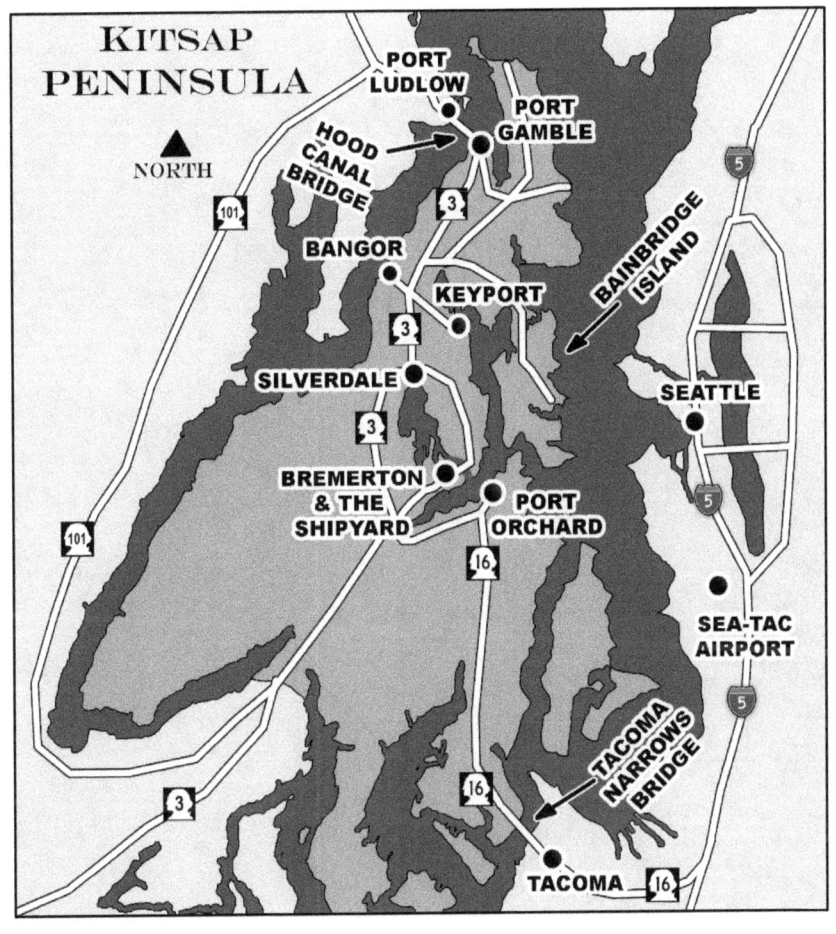

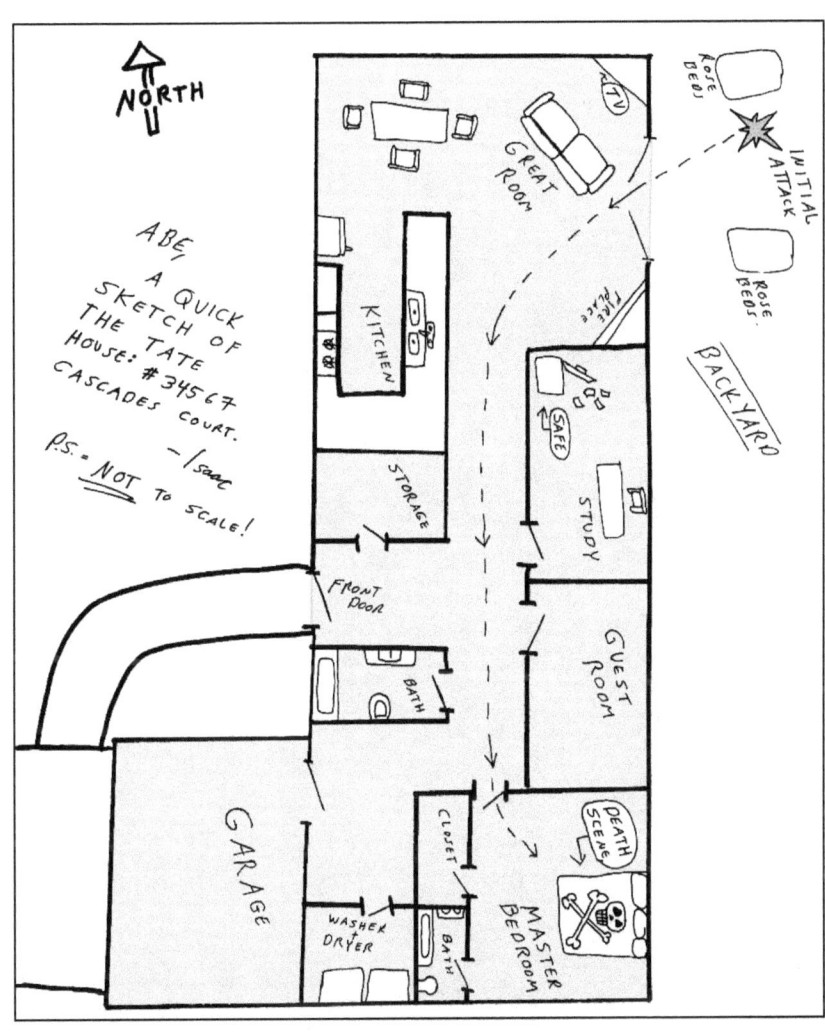

NORTH

ABE,
A QUICK
SKETCH OF
THE TATE
HOUSE: #34567
CASCADES COURT.
— Isaac
P.S. = NOT TO SCALE!

ROSE BEDS

INITIAL ATTACK

GREAT ROOM

TV

BACKYARD

ROSE BEDS

FIRE PLACE

KITCHEN

SAFE

STUDY

STORAGE

FRONT DOOR

GUEST ROOM

BATH

DEATH SCENE

GARAGE

CLOSET

MASTER BEDROOM

WASHER DRYER

BATH

1

Fo'c'sle
Chesapeake, Virginia
Thursday, December 6, 2018; 06:03 hours

The dawn was clear and cold, stars still shining even though the sun was sliding ever higher in the winter sky. The morning was perfect for saying farewell to a beloved family home.

Sarah Gray sat on the stairs, tears shining on her ebony face. Her eyes, redden with sadness, swept the now-empty, now-echoing house.

My babies grew up here, She thought, heart in turmoil. *My babies played here. My babies...*

"Balibte?" Abraham Gray tenderly laid a hand on her shoulder, the Yiddish expression for 'Beloved' bringing his wife back to the present, "You ok?"

"Oh, of course, I'm not, Abe!" Sarah began crying in earnest.

Abraham sat down next to her, wrapping his powerful arms around her. Even in the dim illumination of the single light in the foyer, his Caucasian skin and shock-white hair created a massive contrast to her dark skin and fluffy black afro.

"I'm...I'm sorry," Sarah said, regaining her breath, "Oh, Abe, I'm so sorry! I don't mean to be such a downer! We're supposed to be having a good time..."

"Sarah, we've lived in this house for over fifteen years. The girls grew up here, both had their Bat Mitzvahs *and* got married in the backyard," Abraham said, gently lifting his wife's face and tenderly wiping the tears from her cheeks, "We've written a *lot* of personal history here."

Sarah was shocked to see tears running down his face as well. She hadn't realized he had also been quietly weeping.

"It's not supposed to be easy," Abraham said, his voice softly compassionate, "I got to stay at the Norfolk Field Office for a good, long time. We put down roots here."

"And now we're moving," Sarah said, a shuddering rattle in her voice betraying her emotional fragility.

3

"And now we're moving," Abraham nodded, "Are you having second thoughts?"

"Yes," Sarah admitted, "But we made this decision together, the same way we made the decision for you to join NCIS together. They need you out west, and this'll be a great move for my business, especially as Liam's interested in combining our firms into a partnership."

Sarah sighed, wiping her nose daintily on a tissue, "It was so easy to decide to move that I guess I just didn't realize how emotional I'd be. It all just happened so *fast.*"

Abraham smiled, pulling Sarah's head down to his shoulder as he stroked her hair, "A few years ago I was trapped in a car with Isaac for a few hours, and I was required to listen to one of those *Doctor Who* audio plays he loves by that Big Finish company in Britain. There was this one character who had to decide to keep traveling with the Doctor, or else return to her home."

"I imagine the character was torn?"

Abraham nodded, "She was, indeed. The line that keeps coming to mind from her is, and I quote, 'The choosing is easy; it's the leaving that's hard.'"

Sarah snorted. Abraham glanced down, unsure if she was about to cry or laugh. When she remained quiet, he continued.

"It's going to be hard, Sarah," Abraham said, "But, we've got a good property manager, so the house will be here if we want to come back in a few years. And you're right; I *am* needed out west, and you've got a chance to take your firm to a new level. Besides, in the end, as much as I hate to leave, the house is just a building. *Home* is where *we* are. No one can take that from us."

"Thank you, Matok Sheli," Sarah said, using her favorite Hebrew term of affection for her husband, "I guess I just needed to cry out my goodbye. Still—"

Sarah's voice failed as affectionate laughter unexpectedly erupted through the sadness she'd been fighting, "Abe, I d have to say you've spent *way* too much time with Isaac if *you're* quoting *Doctor Who* now!"

Abraham smiled, gratified to see her mood lifting even as he gave a rueful chuckle, "I can't argue with that, Balibte!"

She rose, stepping into the foyer from the stairs while wiping a stray tear from her eye. Looking at the drop of water on her finger, she slowly, deliberately touched it to the doorframe.

"All I have to bless this house with are my tears," Sarah said, "But they're not all sad tears. Whatever the future holds…"

Switching to Hebrew, Sarah softly intoned the Birkat habayit, *"Bezeh ha shaʕar lo yavo tzaʕar. Bezot haddirah lo tavo tzarah. Bezot haddelet lo tavo bahalah. Bezot hammaḥlaqah lo tavo maḥloqet. Bezeh hammaqom tehi b'rakhah v'shalom."*

"Let no sorrow come through this gate," Abraham quietly placed his hand over hers, reciting the same blessing, but in English, "Let no trouble come in this dwelling. Let no fright come through this door. Let no conflict come here. Let there be blessing and peace in this place."

Hand in hand, they looked around the empty foyer.

"Goodbye," Sarah said quietly to the house.

"We had a great life here, didn't we?" Abraham asked, turning off the light while Sarah opened the front door.

"Yes, we did," Sarah said. Taking a steadying breath, she nodded, "Now, let's go have a good life out west."

Stepping into the cold dawn, Abraham locked the door. The frigid air shocked their lungs as they piled into their SUV, Sarah's Honda on a tow trailer behind the big Chevy. Sarah decided to let Abraham take the wheel while she continued to regain her equanimity.

Starting the engine and turning on the heater, Abraham slowly navigated down the driveway to the street.

Neither of them looked back.

ACCIDENTAL
DETECTIVE
MYSTERIES®

Prologue
Silverdale, Washington
Tuesday, August 7, 2018; 16:37 hours

The tragic day started out quite ordinarily, as tragic days always do. Young-Saeng Tate failed to show up for work for the second time in as many days. His colleagues in the Autonomous Engineering Department at the Naval Subsurface Experimentation and Development Command (NASED) in Keyport, Washington, contacted the local Kitsap County Sheriff's Office to request a welfare check.

Life happens, and the Tates were a notoriously private couple. There was no undue alarm over Tate's absence, even though he failed to return texts or calls. People assumed he had perhaps contracted norovirus or maybe food poisoning—the kind of illness that can wallop a person into incoherence in less than a day.

The Kitsap County police officers knocked on the door of the Tates' Silverdale home at 16:37 local time…only for the door to slowly creak open under their knuckles. The officers had barely registered this disquieting fact when the putrid stench of advanced putrefaction slammed into them. The olfactory linebacker was so powerful it physically knocked them back several steps.

Summoning backup before drawing their weapons, the two officers cautiously entered the quiet structure on Cascades Court off Ridgepoint Drive. The fair scent of cedars tried to waft about them, but the smell of death emanating from #34567 Cascades Court drove away the more pleasant odors. A few faces peered curiously through the windows of the other houses as the spectacle began to unfold.

Sweeping the house, the two officers cleared each room in a methodical manner that would have made their police academy instructors proud. The Grim Reaper's perfume was so thick they couldn't immediately identify its source.

They found what was left of Young-Saeng Tate in the master bedroom.

The mutilated body lying tied to the bed bore little resemblance to a human being, much less a handsome young man with a promising engineering career. In fact, the seasoned officers didn't even realize a body was in the bed at first.

Entering the bedroom-turned-charnel house, they were greeted by the horrid buzzing of a thousand angry flies. The black mat of insects rose from the corpse as one, a congealing dark smear in the air composed of carrion-eating insects gorged on a gory feast.

Once the cloud of flies ascended into the air, the police saw what could only be described as a macabre vision from the worst of slasher films. The young man's body, although severely disassembled by the mouthparts of 10,000 flies, had been thrashed and slashed with nearly surgical violence. The ghastly tableaux that had been executed when Young-Saeng Tate was executed defied comprehension.

Tate's unseeing eyes, frozen in a moment of eternal horror, glared skyward past the single rose in his mouth, its thorny stem shoved down his throat. Gelatinous cords stretched from what had been Tate's abdominal area to wrap around the ceiling fan over the bed.

The two officers, both grizzled veterans who'd seen more than their fair share of bodies mutilated by auto accidents and even bear attacks, groaned as one. The 'gelatinous cords' were Tate's intestines. Despite the decay, it was obvious someone had cut open Tate's guts with determined skill, pulling his intestinal tract out before hanging it from the ceiling fan, its ends still attached to his dead form.

The officers stared upwards in confusion. Tate's intestines were wrapped around the fan's blades and shaft as if the fan had been turned on and used to winch out the dead man's guts...

"Oh, shit!" One of the officers spit out through clenched teeth before both men reflexively gagged.

Despite a combined fifteen years on the force, the two officers found themselves overwhelmed by a scene far exceeding the worst nightmares of quiet Silverdale. They fled the horror to the fresh, clean air outside.

Kitsap County hadn't seen *anything* remotely like this in…well, ever.

The EMTs piling into Cascades Court were warned by the sick and stunned officers outside the house about what they would encounter. Mouths set, the medical personnel entered the structure, determined to fulfill their duties.

The backyard resembled a war zone. The Tates had been avid gardeners, with roses being their specialty. Deer fences were a requisite part of life in the Pacific Northwest for those seeking to keep peace in their gardens. Designed to keep the powerful ruminant mammals at bay, the strong mesh of the deer fencing around the rose beds had been violently ripped apart. Every rose bush was destroyed, but the other flower beds were intact and untouched. Dead and decaying rose bushes littered the yard just like the dead and decaying body parts littering the bedroom.

Investigators found a fire pit in the backyard (a common sight in the Pacific Northwest). However, inside the fire pit were the burnt remains of numerous photographs and other personal items. Most were charred to ash, but a few retained enough recognizable imagery to reveal the destruction of a wedding album and other personal papers.

Officers quickly noted three sets of footprints in the dirt tracked in from the backyard, through the house, and into the master bedroom. One set was quickly identified as Tate's. It both matched the tread of the shoes on his corpse, and its gait was shuffling and unsteady, indicating he'd been dragged while continually fumbling, trying to regain his feet.

The other two sets of prints, one larger than the other, were the only immediate clues available. All three sets were measured, photographed, and then cast in plaster.

The remainder of the house was immaculate. Chilled with anxiety by the rapacious nature of the murder, the Kitsap police swept the house again. Sealing each room with crime scene tape (in addition to the crime scene tape blocking off the house itself), they took care to ensure their documentation and evidence collection contained no errors.

Since Young-Saeng Tate was a civilian Navy engineer and his wife an active duty Navy officer, the Naval Criminal Investigative Service was immediately notified. Although committed in Kitsap County's jurisdiction, NCIS would be needed to assist with the investigation.

The first words to hit the airwaves merely mentioned a potential homicide in the usually quiet northwestern town…and then human ego intervened.

Jane Smith, an enterprising young intern at the sheriff's office, was given a look at the crime scene images by the helpful NCIS agent who provided photographic services. Seeking to prove her worth as a media source, she smuggled several prints and copies of the investigators' notes for delivery to *The Northwest Herald,* one of two small newspapers serving Kitsap County. The *Herald,* struggling through hard financial times, was desperate to get a leg up over its more successful (and ethical) rival, *The Kitsap Sun.* The *Herald* ran with the story, publishing several redacted photos in their print edition and making the uncensored versions available online.

Smith made sure to highlight the sections detailing the discovery of a ransacked safe in the study a few hours after Tate's body was found. Scattered 'Top Secret' documents were strewn about the floor, each photographed with loving precision by the NCIS agent documenting the scene.

Breathless with excitement at the scoop she just *knew* would cement her status as a highly valuable source (a potentially lucrative side gig), Smith collated everything relating to Project Lionfish, a Top Secret drone being developed at Keyport for the Navy and Coast Guard. Well, it *was* 'Top Secret' until *The*

Northwest Herald's headline the next morning efficiently set events in motion that would quickly overwhelm Smith's idyllic view of being the next 'Deep Throat:'

NAVY ENGINEER MURDERED IN SILVERDALE HOME

Top Secret 'Lionfish' Drone Motive in Young-Saeng Tate's Grisly Death

Navy engineer Young-Saeng Tate was found brutally murdered and dismembered in his Silverdale home yesterday. Sources close to the investigation provided documents indicating the assault occurred during the attempted theft of technical information relating to the Lionfish, a Top Secret autonomous drone being developed jointly by the Departments of Defense and Homeland Security...

The reaction was swift, sure, deadly, and politically inevitable.

Young-Saeng Tate was the (now dead) husband of Lt. Commander Delores Tate. In a rare move that puzzled investigators at the time, Young-Saeng had taken his wife's last name upon their marriage.

The Naval Base Kitsap public affairs officer was inundated with requests from as far away as Ireland and South Korea for information on the gory crime. He did his level best to deflect attention by referring inquiries to the Kitsap County Sheriff, but the issue refused to die.

Kitsap County Sheriff Denita Sigo discovered her Port Orchard parking lot had become a campground for media trucks when she arrived Friday morning. Getting out of her car, she was shocked, dismayed, and infuriated to catch a live broadcast being conducted in the early morning light.

"...so far neither Navy nor Kitsap County authorities have responded to any requests for information, but photos obtained through a source close to the investigation, while graphic, clearly show a violent home invasion and murder. Young-Saeng Tate, 36, was tied to his bed and violently killed, possibly *after* his body

11

was mutilated. Kitsap County officials are on the lookout for multiple suspects. It appears the victim was targeted over information relating to the Lionfish, a joint Army and Navy project developing a next-generation aircraft."

What the hell?! Sigo thought, *I know we had a leak, but, Jeez! There's no aircraft involved! These idiots can't even report the leaked information correctly!*

The reporter noticed Sigo. Nodding to his film crew, the three charged her, barely giving her time to shut her county SUV's door and get her hat on.

"Sheriff Sigo, Dan Keegan, News 23. Can you confirm that Young-Saeng Tate was assaulted during an attempt to steal classified information on the Lionfish project he was working on at Keyport?" Keegan rushed on, breathlessly trying to drown Sigo in a torrent of words. He apparently hoped swamping her with endless questions would frustrate her into making a revealing statement.

"Why has your office refused to release any preliminary conclusions to the public?" Keegan blustered on, "Is it true Mr. Tate had his intestines ripped out of his abdomen? What comment do you have on the coroner's speculation he was mutilated as torture before his death? Is there a serial killer in Kitsap County? What's your office doing to keep county residents safe?"

Sigo hitched a professionally friendly smile on her face, calling up every ounce of patience she had while also trying to recall every bit of media training she'd ever had.

"Well, good morning, Dan!" Sigo said, the stout woman straightening her uniform jacket and folding her hands casually in front of her, "Clearly, this is an extraordinarily violent crime. First off, all of us here in the department offer our deepest condolences to Mr. Tate's wife, loved ones, and friends."

Sigo saw Keegan was about to interrupt, so she headed him off at the verbal pass, "At this time, I can only say we have no evidence linking this to any other crime in Kitsap County. We're partnering with NCIS, and I'm grateful for their assistance. We did suffer an unauthorized leak from this department, and I've charged our internal affairs division to identify the person, or persons, who committed this serious breach."

Sigo excused herself, slipping into the building. She'd no sooner started checking her emails when Mary Graves, her secretary, popped her head into Sigo's office.

"Ma'am, sorry to bother you, but we've got another major problem."

Sigo sighed, leaning back in her chair, "This is the day for it, Mary. What's up?"

"Well, internal affairs identified our new intern, Jane Smith, as the person who leaked the information to the media. But…we just got a call from a unit responding to a vehicular accident up in Port Gamble. Jane was apparently hit in the head by a stray shot from a hunter. Her car swerved off the road into a tree. She's dead."

Sigo's jaw bounced off her desk in shock.

Could this day get any worse? She wondered in disbelief.

It did.

Despite her complimentary words, she was seething at the local NCIS office. For some reason she couldn't fathom, every agent except the special agent in charge of the Northwest Field Office was out of state on other cases. Even more infuriatingly, David Kerr, the special agent in charge, was none too forthcoming or friendly.

Working with that asshole is like pulling teeth! Sigo thought later as she left yet another pointless meeting with Kerr in his office on board the Bangor site of far-flung Naval Base Kitsap. Kerr told her—voice dripping with disdain—that he had several leads he was pursuing, and would backfill her later when he had time.

I'm going to raise hell about this! Sigo thought, getting back into her county SUV to leave the base, *This is my jurisdiction, and that Navy bastard has* no *right to try and run roughshod over my team's investigation!*

Sigo spent the weekend coordinating the efforts of her officers to conduct the investigation despite NCIS' wall of silence. She was surprised she didn't have gray streaking her hair from the stress of it all, especially when she saw Sunday's headline:

WASHINGTON STATE MURDER TIED TO RUSSIA
Sources Indicate Lionfish Drone Stolen for Sale to Russian Agents

Once again, Sigo was shocked by the lack of calls from NCIS, or even the FBI, at this point. She was sure such a revelation would have brought both bureaus down on Washington State like snow in January.

Monday, August 13th dawned with light clouds, the day slipping to a comfortable 75 °F before 'The Storm' broke at lunchtime.

Sigo had locked her office door to isolate herself during her lunch. She needed to clear her head after yet another stiff-armed response from NCIS, blocking her ability to get the names of Tate's Keyport coworkers so her team could begin interviewing them.

Turning on the TV, Sigo pulled a long draught of coffee into her mouth before the story flashing on the screen made her choke and spit the caffeinated beverage right back out.

"David Kerr, Special Agent in Charge of the NCIS Northwest Field Office, has made an arrest in the murder of Young-Saeng Tate, a Navy civilian engineer who was killed in Washington State earlier this month. In a statement released by Kerr, he identified Tate's wife, Navy Lieutenant Commander Delores Tate, as the prime suspect. Lt. Cmdr. Tate was arrested aboard USS *Gridley* in Bremerton today and taken into Navy custody."

"What the *hell* is that moron *doing?!*" Sigo yelled, nearly throwing her coffee mug at the TV.

Kerr's smarmy face suddenly appeared on the TV, addressing reporters outside Bangor's Navy Exchange.

"This has been a terrible tragedy for the Navy, and NCIS has been leading this investigation since the unfortunate death of Mr. Tate. We can now definitively say he died on Friday, August 3rd. Lt. Cmdr. Tate is currently undergoing questioning, but, so far, is denying allegations of her extramarital affair with a person of interest in Tacoma. Despite this, I'm confident we'll produce evidence to prove both she and her paramour planned and executed this horrific attack on her hapless husband in order to sell technology related to the Lionfish to America's adversaries abroad."

The national reaction was predictably explosive. Delores Tate was pilloried on every major news show that didn't bother to ask questions. Politicians piled on, decrying the toxic military culture allowing predators to thrive in the ranks. Pundits held up Kerr as a hero while snidely making not-so-oblique references to the lack of professionalism in the Kitsap County Sheriff's Office.

Oddly, not one feminist political group rose to the defense of Delores Tate.

Still, the whole thing began to look like a story that would engulf a few reputations and then die away...except for one somewhat peculiar senator who had a nasty habit of asking inconvenient questions. He'd seen more than one rodeo of egregiously incompetent investigations and false accusations in his day.

"Thanks for having me on today, Brett," Florida Senator Diego Alejandro said. Standing in the U.S. Capitol rotunda as crowds milled behind him, he smiled for the camera, "I know we're here to discuss the ongoing budget negotiations, but I'd like to make a comment regarding the tragic situation in Washington State. NCIS announced the arrest of Lt. Cmdr. Delores Tate in connection with the violent death of her husband earlier this month. Special Agent Kerr specifically stated Lt. Cmdr. Tate bore the 'bloody hand' that ended Mr. Tate's life. My question is this:

how could Lt. Cmdr. Tate be responsible for killing her husband on August 3rd when she was aboard her ship at sea over 500 miles away from Washington State that day?"

Chapter 1

Seattle, Washington
Thursday, August 30, 2018; 07:35 hours

"…turning now to the growing Oceanic Supply and Services Corporation, or 'OSSC,' scandal swamping Navy brass since 2016. Retired Navy Admiral Thomas Donovan, former Chief of Naval Operations, has been named as a person of interest by NCIS. OSSC and its CEO, Mitchell Forthnell Barrister St. John IV, locally known as 'Big Mitch,' are under investigation for allegedly bribing numerous Navy personnel with money, gifts, and prostitutes to steer Navy ships to ports serviced by OSSC…"

"Goooooood morning, Seattle! Tiny John in the Morning here on WAXE, your one-stop shop for news, entertainment, and sports! In traffic, ongoing construction's got I-5 North backed up into Tacoma. Big surprise, right? Moving on to local Navy news, Rear Admiral Skid Moore was indicted yesterday in the evolving 'Big Mitch' scandal and was relieved of command. Rear Admiral Arion Wren assumed command of Navy Region Northwest this morning…"

"…increasing clouds will keep Seattle's highs in the low 70s today with the usual scattered showers in the afternoon," The coiffed talking head on TV smiled blandly at the camera, his expression rather synthetic, "Adding to our ongoing coverage, the Navy announced charges yesterday against Lt. Commander Delores Tate for the murder of her husband, Young-Saeng. And, finally, in market news, the Neon Flamingo Group posted better-than-expected earnings following their acquisition of the faltering Ocean Adventure Cruises. The Dow Jones gained 0.2%, closing at 26,124.5…"

NCIS Special Agent Abraham Gray stumbled his bleary-eyed way out of the Pacific World Airways jet's cabin door. Nodding a tired 'thank you' to the flight attendant, he marveled at her stamina in the face of yet another overnight jaunt across the continent.

How in the hell *do flight attendants stay so damned cheerful?!* Gray wondered as his fatigued feet fretfully found their way through the jetway to the concourse. Smiling faces of several PacWorld employees beamed down from the requisite posters adorning the walls in the PacWorld wing of the Seattle-Tacoma International Airport.

Stopping to get a coffee from a Starbucks kiosk, Gray hefted his carry-on bag over his shoulder. Shifting his computer bag to his left hand, he gratefully grabbed the coffee with his right.

A tall man at 6'1", Gray was 52, but a thick neck under his square jaw alerted the observant to a muscular frame hidden by his impeccable blue suit, red tie, and American flag lapel pin. His blue-gray eyes, thick with sleep, peered foggily at the world from under a full head of thick, rich, and utterly shock white hair.

Better! Gray thought, savoring the first sips of the black coffee as the hot, sultry liquid warmed his insides. Seattle residents might be comfortable on a chilly morning, but Gray's body was acclimated to the stifling heat and humidity of Virginia's Tidewater region. He was freezing.

Next time I think about wearing a full suit on a red-eye, I'm going to have Sarah hit me upside the head. Hard! Gray thought. *From now on, I'm wearing casual clothes while flying!*

Distracting himself from the dreaded anticipation of baggage claim, Gray pondered the waves he was going to make back in Virginia. Norfolk International Airport TSA personnel had ignored his badge, NCIS identification, and orders (signed personally by Director Kirby Belk, no less). They did, however, try to arrest him for bringing a federally licensed firearm through security. The flubdub of bureaucracy gone mad almost cost him his flight.

Still, he was safely in Seattle and could now focus on getting his bags before facing The Problem at Hand.

Joining the early morning crush at the baggage carousel, Gray idly scanned a display of photos showing the dramatic growth of the Sea-Tac airport from the early 1960s to the present day. He had just reached the modern era when a buzzer sounded. The carousel clacked to life, disgorging passengers' bags with little mechanical courtesy.

Politely slipping past a knot of young men with ornately colored purple hair, Gray smiled to himself as he shot out an increasingly steady hand to grab his suitcase. Although wildly colored hair wasn't unheard of in Virginia, it wasn't as nearly prevalent a fashion choice as here on the West Coast. Gray found himself liking it. It made the crowd more interesting.

Bags in hand, Gray shaped a course for the arrival area to meet up with his ride…

…who was not there.

Gray checked his phone. Reviewing his text messages, he ensured he'd sent Kerr the correct flight number and arrival time—which he had indeed done.

So, where the hell is someone from the office? Gray fumed, already in a foul mood. Being unceremoniously plucked out of several ongoing investigations and packed off to the Pacific Northwest to clean up a growing mess grated on his nerves. He didn't appreciate being stranded at Sea-Tac on top of it all.

Dialing Kerr, Gray waited until his voicemail came up.

"You've reached the voice mail of Special Agent in Charge David Joseph Kerr, NCIS Northwest Field Office. Please leave a message and I'll get back to you when I can," Kerr's voice slithered from the phone.

"David, this is Abe," Gray said, forcing his voice to hide his irritation, "I'm at Sea-Tac. Where's my ride? You've had my itinerary for over a week now."

While preparing to slide his phone back into his pocket, Gray glanced up at a TV monitor. Shocked by what he saw, he dropped his phone.

"Damn!" Gray bent down, swiftly retrieving the device (the phone's screen was still intact; whew!), and returned his gaze to the TV. Inching closer, he rubbed his bleary eyes to ensure he was seeing the live broadcast correctly. Stepping even closer, Gray was able to hear the TV's sound over the morning bustle at Sea-Tac.

"I'm happy to say the Navy Judge Advocate General's Office has brought charges against Delores Tate," Kerr was speaking to a gaggle of reporters in front of the NCIS Northwest Field Office building. "This will bring a speedy end to a horrific crime sullying our beautiful community. A homicide, I might add, committed by a violent deviant, a sadistic individual intent on selling out her country for profit."

Turning on his heel before he lost his temper and punched the TV, Gray pulled his phone out and shot a text to his own boss, Charlotte Webb, back in Norfolk. By the time he finished the text, his anger had all but erased the fatiguing jetlag from his brow. Getting directions to the airport's car rental area, Gray set his firm jaw squarely on 'kill' and went to rent a vehicle so he could find out just what the hell Kerr was doing.

Digging the charging cable out of his laptop bag, Gray hooked up his dying phone to the car's power port, resuscitating the gasping device. He knew the drive from Sea-Tac to Bangor on the Kitsap Peninsula would take a couple of hours, but he expected to catch a nap enroute.

Instead, he punched in the Northwest Field Office's address into the phone's GPS, settled back, and began the trek across western Washington State.

Low, gray clouds scuttled across the sky, a solid curtain of thick moisture constantly threatening a rainy deluge. The traffic along Interstate 5 was intense. Gray was nearly sideswiped several times.

Jeez! He thought, *And I thought drivers on I-64 in Virginia were nuts!*

Sliding south from Seattle into Tacoma, Gray merged onto Highway 16. Leaving the congestion of the city, he rounded a bend into what could only be described as a picture-postcard fantasy.

The towering Tacoma Narrows Bridge loomed up out of the fog, a great steel sentinel standing guard over the land.

Although traffic was heavy, the landscape across the bridge morphed abruptly into the rural paradise of rolling hills, rocky ridges, and towering evergreens of the Kitsap Peninsula.

The landscape's serenity erased everything from Gray's mind. The beauty was hauntingly alluring, evoking thoughts of great mountains, ancient peoples, and legendary Sasquatches roaming the forests.

Gray's attention returned to the present with a metallic *thunk* as he passed through Port Orchard, rounding a hairpin turn along the water in Gorst, before shifting from Highway 16 onto Highway 3 North. The highway took him past the dead ships sitting in mothballs along the naval shipyard's inactive facility piers. Chief among these was the looming hulk of a decrepit aircraft carrier, the number '63' visible in faded numbers on the ship's island. Gray tried recalling the carrier's name, but was too busy staying in his lane.

Naval Base Kitsap had once been three separate bases: the Bangor submarine base, the Keyport torpedo station, and the Bremerton naval station. The bases were merged into the modern Naval Base Kitsap (or 'NBK') in 2004.

The Bremerton site was most famous for being the home of the massive Puget Sound Naval Shipyard, a yard rivaling the Navy facilities encircling Hampton Roads in Chesapeake Bay. Together, the modern Naval Base Kitsap's three sites created a unified naval hub just a shade smaller than the Navy presence in San Diego or Pearl Harbor. Only Naval Station Norfolk, the largest naval station in the world, exceeded these other facilities.

Continuing north into Silverdale, Gray hooked a left off Highway 3 and finally entered Naval Base Kitsap – Bangor.

Gray's temper was boiling by the time he drove past the Navy Exchange and found the small, understated NCIS building hidden in the woods behind the base theatre. Parking, he looked at his watch.

11:47. I'm starved, tired, and pissed off, Gray thought. *This is* not *the moment to charge in there with guns blazing. I need food.*

Locking up his car, Gray proceeded to hoof it back to the NEX complex. As expected, he found a Subway concession in the building between the NEX and the base Commissary.

Thank the Lord I beat the lunch rush! Gray thought, ordering a roast chicken sub on Italian herb and cheese bread along with a bottle of water. He needed to cool down while refueling his body. Settling down at an outside table to eat, he watched the growing throng of sailors heading into the shop for lunch. Gray breathed in the clean, brisk air. Marveling at the overtones of cedar dancing about, he finally began to understand just *why* Washington was called The Evergreen State.

"Special Agent Gray?"

Gray jumped, startled out of his silent fugue by a warm, rich voice falling on his ears from above. Swiftly wiping his mouth with his napkin, he looked up. A Navy chief petty officer with violently flaming red hair and a black badge embroidered on his green camouflage Navy Working Uniform's pocket, was staring at him.

The face was strikingly familiar, but it still took Gray a moment to place the man as he scanned the sailor's nametape: Fredriksen.

"Holy crap!" Gray smiled, rising as his memory shuffled the pieces into place, "Luke Fredriksen! How the hell are you?!"

"I'm great!" Chief Master at Arms Luke Fredriksen said, his smile widening. "Mind if I join you?" He asked, gesturing at the table with his own bag full of Subway,

"Please!" Gray shifted his lunch a bit to make room. The pale, elegant scent of cedar was now tinged by the unmistakably pungent aroma of tomato sauce emanating from Fredriksen's sandwich.

The big, muscular man, a dead-ringer for the stereotypical Viking, pulled out a metal chair and sat with surprising grace.

"Congratulations on making chief," Gray said, gesturing at the anchor insignia stitched onto Fredriksen's uniform blouse, "When did you pick up?"

"Last year," Fredriksen said, unwrapping his lunch, "I transferred here from Norfolk just before the results were announced."

"Nice!" Gray laughed, "Come out here for an assignment as a first-class petty officer, and end up getting advanced to chief!"

Fredriksen laughed, "Yep. The detailer was looking to transfer me again because there's a shortage of MA chiefs out at Pearl Harbor, but our CMC talked him out of it. I'm sure you've seen the news about the Big Mitch scandal and Admiral Moore getting relieved? Well, our security posture has increased because of that. Big Navy's worried some bad actors might try and take advantage of the bureaucratic chaos. With all the nukes stored here, that's a chance the Navy is *not* going to take!"

"Can't blame them," Gray said, taking another bite, "How do you like it out here?"

"Took a bit getting used to the weather and all, but I like it!" Fredriksen said enthusiastically, unwrapping his sandwich "So, what brings you out here? I haven't seen you or Chief Shepherd since the Bacon investigation aboard *Ponce* two years ago."

"Well, actually, Chief Shepherd is now just plain Mr. Shepherd," Gray smiled, "He retired last year."

"I know, I follow him on social media," Fredriksen said, "I've been following his travel blog. I'm jealous! Man, I need to take me a year-long road trip and see all 50 states when *I* retire, don'tcha know!"

Gray laughed, his foul mood ebbing in the face of good company associated with a wildly successful case back in 2016, "Are you with Naval Base Kitsap, or one of the tenant commands?" Gray asked, referring to the separate commands that occupied acreage on board Navy bases.

"NBK," Fredriksen answered, "Most of the MAs here are part of NBK. There's a small contingent of Navy MAs under the command of the Marine Forces protecting the nukes, but I can't really say any more than that. I'm sure you understand the security we have to maintain because of the strategic assets sited here, 'eh?"

Gray nodded, his hands wadding up the wrapper from his own demolished lunch, "I understand. I probably know more than you think I do, but I was just curious. My assignment won't require me to go anywhere near those assets."

"So, as I asked a minute ago in my own nosy way, what brings you out here?" Fredriksen smiled.

"Work, what else?" Gray said, sipping his water.

"The Tate fiasco, 'eh?" Fredriksen asked.

Gray wasn't surprised by Fredriksen's sagacity, "Got it in one, Chief. May I ask what brought you to that conclusion, though?"

Fredriksen shrugged a massive shoulder. The bones sliding around could have passed for tectonic plates.

"The last time I saw you or Chief Shepherd was in the middle of the Navy's *last* public embarrassment over a false prosecution," Fredriksen replied, wadding up his sandwich wrapper and stuffing it into a nearby waste bin, "Granted I'm pretty much just on the periphery of it all, but the Tate investigation smacks me the same way the Bacon investigation did back in 2016—a slipshod, shitty rush blaming the victim to cover the sorry ass of some high-up and incompetently narcissistic twit."

Gray laughed out loud, "Wow! That was nice! I never pegged you for such eloquent language!"

Fredriksen smiled, "I read a lot. And, like I said, I follow Isaac's blog. Read *his* writing enough, and his way of talking rubs off on you after a while."

Gray chuckled, then returned to the point, "Tell me about it! Anyway, mind me giving me some deckplate gouge on what your sailors think of all this?"

"Well, like that senator from Florida said, how in the name of John Q. Arbuckle could Lt. Cmdr. Tate kill her husband when she was at sea aboard *Gridley?*" Fredriksen said. "The *Gridley* was re-homeported from over in Everett to Bremerton two years ago to act as a testbed for some new tech, and they've been at sea almost as much as if they were on deployment. Every junior sailor I talk to can't understand why anyone would accuse Tate of murdering her husband when she wasn't anywhere near here."

"Interesting," Gray said, absorbing the information with renewed gusto, "I didn't know that about the *Gridley's* homeport. Until I flew in this morning, I honestly didn't realize just how spread-out this area is. I always thought Naval Station Everett was a whole lot closer to NBK, kind of like how stacked up everything is around Hampton Roads."

"A lot of people make that mistake," Fredriksen nodded, leaning back and crossing his massive arms, "I did, until I got here. Everett's two hours away on a good day because you either have to wait for the ferry, or drive down and take the Tacoma Narrows Bridge, and then get through Seattle traffic. That's why *Gridley* was moved to Bremerton; it puts her in better proximity to Keyport."

Gray's eyebrow twitched, "I assume you're not discussing anything that hasn't already been publicly released?"

Fredriksen nodded, "Oh, it's all public information. The only time non-nuclear-powered vessels are 'homeported' in the shipyard is for a long-term maintenance period. Otherwise, the shipyard and Bangor here are the homeports for the carriers and subs. *Gridley's* work as a test bed makes her a special case."

Gray glanced at his watch, "Damn, I need to get back over to the NCIS building. Chief, it's been great catching up with you. It's also good to know there's at least one person around here I can trust if I need help!"

Fredriksen rose as Gray stood up, "You know it. I've got a new cell; call me if you need me."

"Hang on," Gray fished out his smartphone, "Ok, shoot fire!"

Fredriksen provided his number, Gray's fingers adding Fredriksen's contact information to the device.

"Thanks, Chief!" Gray said, weariness creeping back into his blood thanks to his full stomach, "I have a feeling I'm going to need a few resources outside the normal NCIS lines if I'm going to clean up this crap show."

Chapter 2
Naval Base Kitsap – Bangor, Washington
Thursday, August 30, 2018; 12:17 hours

"You mind repeating that, Carol?!" Abraham Gray seethed, carefully enunciating each word through tightly clenched teeth.

"I'm afraid Special Agent in Charge Kerr has left for the day," Carol Keeters, Kerr's executive assistant, said tremulously to the face of the raging mass of fury standing in front of her. Wearing a black skirt, white blouse, and black blazer, her resigned, thousand-yard stare reminded Gray of a domestic abuse victim. Black shoes and a black hair band completed the monochromatic funeral-esque ensemble.

Gray forced himself to corral his temper, holding back the blistering rage boiling his blood. Keeters wasn't responsible for Kerr's behavior, and certainly didn't deserve to be the target of Gray's wrath.

"I just have to ask so I can tell my boss I did," Gray said, shoving his hands into his pockets to hide his clenched fists, "David *did* know I was arriving at Sea-Tac this morning, and that he was supposed to spend today briefing me on the Tate case?"

"Yes, sir," Keeters said, still worried about offending the man in front of her. Her poofy hairdo and old-fashioned horned-rimmed reading glasses added an interesting retro vibe to her sepulcher garb. "Here's a print-out of his calendar. You can see from the date/time stamp this was on his desk last week. I'm afraid I can't do anything else but say I'm sorry."

Gray took the paper from her without looking at it. Releasing a long, slow breath, he shook his head, "This isn't your fault, Carol. I'm sorry you're the unfortunate person getting caught in the middle. I appreciate everything you did to get my trip out here set up. When does David usually arrive in the morning?"

"He's always in promptly at 07:00 unless he has another appointment," Keeters said, a nicely manicured hand brushing her blonde coif out of her eyes, "And, as far as I know, he's got no appointments tomorrow morning."

Gray sighed again, screwing his self-control back into place. Not only did Keeters *not* deserve an ass-chewing, but Gray also needed to earn *her* respect as a professional ally.

"I know this is a long shot, Carol," Gray said, his voice continuing its descent back to a conversational tone, "But do you have *any* idea why he detailed every other agent to California, Utah, Nevada, and everywhere under the sun *but* here, leaving no one here but him?"

Keeters shook her head, "I don't have that information, I'm afraid."

Gray nodded again, hitching a smile over his features, "Well, again, I apologize for taking out my temper on you for something that isn't your fault. I'll go get settled in and see you tomorrow morning."

Gray left the base in a fog. He navigated on autopilot into Silverdale where he found the Viking Inn & Suites slightly uphill from Silverdale Parkway off Bucklin Hill Road and caddy-corner across a shared parking lot with an Oxford Suites. The Oxford Suites featured a waterfront bistro that Gray decided to try in a day or two after checking out the restaurant in his hotel.

Damn, this place is nothing but hills, ridges, and mountains! Gray thought, parking the car, *I always thought Georgia was hilly, but Georgia's flat as a pancake compared to Washington State!*

Gray checked in, receiving a room on the south side of the building with a balcony overlooking Dyes Inlet.

Unceremoniously dropping his bags onto the bed, Gray pulled the curtains back. Staring out over the inlet's still waters under a gray sky, he seethed while pulling out his cell phone, "Charlotte? Sorry to bother you so late; I know it's nearly quitting time on the East Coast."

"No problem, Abraham," The voice of Charlotte Webb, Special Agent in Charge of NCIS' Norfolk Field Office floated from the phone, "I got your text this morning. I've already signed off the paperwork for your rental car. So, what happened? Someone was supposed to pick you up and that field office was supposed to have a car for you."

Gray gave Webb a brief rundown on the morning's misadventures.

"You're telling me that son of a bitch *stranded* you and then left work *early?!*" Webb exploded so loudly Gray wondered if her voice would carry all the way from Virginia to Washington State of its own accord.

Webb sighed heavily, getting her temper back under control, "Ok, well, I'm sorry you're having to deal with that. I'll brief the director tomorrow, but, unfortunately, you're going to have to cope with the immediate situation on your own."

Gray chuckled, shaking his head, "Call me naïve, but I really wasn't expecting to find anything more out here than a badly handled case, not a field office in disarray being run by a man who's gone completely off the map!"

"Well, now you know why Director Belk sent *you* out there," Webb said, her tone indicating she was stating the obvious, "You've developed a reputation for cleaning up messes caused by other parts of NCIS."

"Tell me about it," Gray laughed ruefully, "Convincing you to let me bring Isaac in on the Symko case back in '99 seems to have started a trend in my career as the go-to guy for fixing things!"

"Can't say you haven't earned it," Webb said levelly, "I'll also let you in on a little secret: Kirby told me he's eyeballing you for some high-profile assignments after he was confirmed as our new permanent director earlier this year."

"Oh, good grief, no!" Gray face-palmed himself as he stared out over the water. He knew Mount Rainier was hidden somewhere in all those clouds, but the volcano was lost to the gray mists, "I appreciate the confidence—and I *do* mean that, by the way! But, well, I'm just a beat cop."

Webb laughed, "Abraham, to put it in somewhat poetic terms—and I freely admit this is Isaac's influence on me—you're trying to avoid a destiny greater than the one you dream of. Trust me, you won't get away from it. You're too professional and too honorable to let nitwits like David Kerr ruin NCIS' reputation! So, what's your next move?"

Gray shrugged reflexively even though Webb couldn't see him, "Well, if David wants to play this little power-trip game lording his rank over me, then I'm going to confront him with the reality that he does *not* know who *he's* dealing with."

"Oh?"

Gray nodded grimly, "Look, *I don't* aspire to be more than I am, but even I'll admit I've gotten very good at toppling the empires of bureaucratic thugs like David. We narrowly squeaked NCIS out of this kind of bad publicity two years ago with the Bacon case; I will *not* let David drag us through the mud!"

"Good. Call me if you need me," Webb said, "Otherwise keep me informed of your progress. Also, do you remember the conference call we had with Kirby when he cut your orders? He said he's got your back if you need to bring in any…outside help."

"Isaac's retired, and I am *not* bothering him!" Gray laughed, "Besides, I'm a grown boy. I can handle myself. I'll be in touch. Since David's being a dick, I'm going to head down to Port Orchard and see if I can start repairing relations with the Kitsap County Sherriff."

Denita Sigo shook out her black hair before pulling it once again into a tight ponytail. That accomplished, she leaned back in her chair, plunking her boots up on her desk and crossing her feet. Silently she studied the white-haired ghost of a man in the impeccable blue suit sitting across from her.

She had let him sit there for ten minutes now, neither saying a word. She telegraphed her rage with her eyes, but preferred to let the crushing weight of silence force him to speak first.

Maddeningly enough, he was the picture of calm. Legs crossed and hands neatly folded in his lap, he was content to let the silence grow. Sigo began to wonder how long she'd last in this staring contest of silence.

This is getting me nowhere fast, She thought, finally relenting.

"Ok, Mr. Gray, you win," Sigo said, carelessly conceding the match of wills to him, "And I'll give you props for actually coming to my office instead of summoning me to the base as if I were some kind of serf. So, for that bit of professional courtesy, I *will* ask you what you want instead of just telling you, and the rest of NCIS, to go fuck yourselves."

Gray smiled this time. Eyes closed, he chuckled ruefully, before opening them again and addressing her, "Sheriff Sigo, I can't blame you for your unhappiness over how you've been treated by my colleagues out here. I'm here to put things right. Here, this is for you."

Gray fished an envelope out of his inside jacket pocket. Passing it over to the sheriff, he sat back while she suspiciously opened it.

Shaking out the paper, she sighed, pulling her reading glasses out of their case and perching them on her nose.

To: Denita Sigo, Kitsap County Sheriff
From: Kirby Belk, Director, Naval Criminal Investigative Service

SUBJ: Requesting assistance for Special Agent Gray

1. *Sheriff Sigo, I have no illusions about the state of relations between you and the NCIS Northwest Field Office. I know Special Agent Kerr has not conducted himself in an exemplary manner, if you will pardon the understatement.*

I'm personally very grateful for the public show of cooperation you've maintained between our agencies, and I want to personally assure you I am taking steps to rectify the situation.

2. *Special Agent Abraham Gray has been dispatched from the Norfolk Field Office as my personal representative and fact-finder. He is also charged with re-opening the Tate investigation.*

3. *I realize you have no reason to do so, but I'm humbly asking you to provide him whatever courtesies you can as a favor from one law enforcement officer to another.*

4. *Thank you for your help. I know whatever you provide will be more than NCIS deserves, and I am personally very grateful to you and your team.*

> *Kirby Belk*
> *Director, Naval Criminal Investigative Service*

Sigo deliberately refolded the letter before returning it to the envelope on the desk. Looking up, she gave Gray the same piercing stare she used to crack suspects during interviews.

"If Kerr has gone so far off the map that you've been sent here, why doesn't Belk just fire him?" Sigo asked, her boots still on the desk.

Gray shrugged, "Politics, of course. Kerr's got some high-ranking friends in the Department of the Navy and the Justice Department, so Director Belk has to tread carefully through this minefield."

"You *do* realize Kerr illegally trampled all over my jurisdiction?" Sigo shot back, "The murder happened here in Silverdale, not on the base. Federal, state, local, and even tribal law states *my* office is the lead agency on the case."

"I won't argue that," Gray said, "And that's why I'm here. Our previous director allowed a great deal of malfeasance to grow inside NCIS. Belk was charged by the president, CNO, and even the U.S. Attorney General with fixing things. I'm here on his behalf to do that in this matter."

Sigo nodded, dropping her boots to the floor. Leaning forward, she pinned Gray to his chair with her gaze, "And I should believe you'll do things differently *why?* Seems to me your agency's got its head up its ass. What can you possibly say that I'd actually *believe?*"

"Not a damned thing," Gray shrugged, "I wouldn't believe a word I was saying if I was in your place either, Sheriff. However, I *do* have a job to do and I'm going to do it, regardless of your belief in my sincerity. If you and I can establish a cordial working relationship, it'll make my job easier, and, I hope, restore your faith in NCIS. However, I will complete this job one way or another."

Sigo fell silent, thinking. Studying Gray closely, she decided to trust her gut, "Ok, I'm willing to extend you a little rope."

"Enough to hang myself?" Gray smiled, his eyes twinkling with amusement.

"Or we use that rope to link up like mountain climbers," Sigo said, cocking her head and gazing keenly at Gray, "You decide which analogy will be more appropriate. So, what is it you want from me?"

Gray sighed, happily surprised the confrontation hadn't been more difficult than it turned out to be. He had too much else to do and wouldn't get very far without Sigo's help.

"I need to review, well, *everything* you've got because, frankly, you *are* the lead agency on this and…"

Gray trailed off, debating whether to finish the sentence.

"You don't trust Kerr will provide you with everything you need, do you?" Sigo finished the thought with incisive insight.

Gray nodded ruefully, "Correct."

Sigo nodded, "Ok. I'll give you a run-down before we head over to the coroner's office in Bremerton. Dr. Kellog's working late today, and he's pretty flexible about my people hitting him up at odd hours."

Sigo swung her legs back up, her boots again whumping down on the worn wooden desktop as she leaned back, hands clasped behind her head.

"The decedent's name is Young-Saeng Tate. He is…or, rather, *was,* a robotics and electronic engineer at NASED Keyport," Sigo rattled off, "That was one reason he was the youngest project lead in Keyport history—he smoked it in two highly specialized fields. The *one* interview I conducted myself was with Keyport's technical director. You're familiar with a technical director?"

"I am," Gray said, "The CO is in overall command of the facility, specializing in running the operational side. The technical director provides leadership continuity since the CO and other military staff regularly rotate. They're also an engineer, providing the commanding officer an 'inside reference' on engineering matters."

"Very good," Sigo said approvingly.

She's still gauging me, Gray thought sagaciously.

"Tate failed to report for work Monday, August 6th, and Tuesday, August 7th," Sigo said, returning to her narrative, "His supervisor contacted my office to conduct a welfare check on August 7th after he failed to return any calls or texts."

"His supervisor didn't send anyone to check on him first?" Gray asked, pulling a notebook and pen from his pocket. Flipping the notebook open, he began furiously writing in it, "Normally federal organizations, military or civilian, will reach out to their people first before involving local law enforcement."

Sigo nodded, her expression softening even further at Gray's insightful question, "I also asked him that. He told me the Tates were *extremely* private and preferred to keep knowledge of their home address to as small a circle as possible. Tate's supervisor was unable to go to his home himself, so, rather than give the Tates' address to someone else at Keyport, he called us."

"Very respectful of his employee's preferences," Gray said, "Also an interesting point about the Tates. Any idea *why* they were so obsessed with privacy? I mean, the fact he took his wife's surname seems significant. That's an unusual choice for a couple to make, both here and in Korea."

Sigo shrugged, "South Korea, to be specific. He and his two brothers were adopted by Nico and Stephanie Lýkos of Durham, North Carolina, when they were toddlers. Nico Lýkos was in the Air Force, and they were stationed in Seoul at the time. Young-Saeng spent his formative years growing up in California, Montana, and, finally, North Carolina after Lýkos left the Air Force and the family returned to Durham. Stephanie and one of the boys, Su-Jin, were in a nasty car wreck when the three boys were 13. Stephanie survived with severe injuries, but Su-Jin was killed."

"Wait, sorry," Gray said, looking up from his notebook, "All *three* boys were 13 at the same time? They were *triplets?*"

"Identical triplets, yes," Sigo said, eyebrows going up, "You weren't informed of that?"

"Nope," Gray said, anger flashing across his brow as he continued to scribble, "Thank you for that."

"No problem," Sigo said, "In case you're interested, Young-Saeng was born first, then Gippeum, and then Su-Jin. They were only separated by maybe ten or fifteen minutes. Like I said, Su-Jin died at 13."

Very interesting, Gray thought, the memory a friend flashing across his mind as he jotted down that new bit of information, "Please, continue."

"Young-Saeng married his high school sweetheart, Delores Tate, a month before she entered the ROTC program at the University of North Carolina, Raleigh."

"Did Young-Saeng attend UNC?" Gray asked.

"Yep," Sigo said, "Studied robotics and electronic engineering, earning a double master's in four years."

"Four years?!" Gray said, startled, "That *is* impressive!"

Sigo shrugged, "Apparently, the Lýkos boys were all geniuses. In addition to completing double masters' in four years, Young-Saeng spoke four languages and presented such a strong resumé

35

he locked up an open position at Keyport when Delores Tate got orders to the *Nimitz* a few years ago in 2010 when she was an ensign. Do you know the *Nimitz* is homeported in Bremerton?"

"I do know," Gray said, pen moving so fast Sigo was surprised the notebook didn't ignite, "Please, go on."

"From what little I was able to gather before Kerr ran me off the road, Delores spent the better part of five years on the *Nimitz,*" Sigo explained, "She did what I think you Navy folk call a 'back-to-back sea tour' by transferring from the *Nimitz* to the *Gridley* after the destroyer was moved here from Everett. You know about that homeport switch, right?"

"I do," Gray said, looking up from his notes, "And one of the things I need to find an answer to is the possible Lionfish angle. I saw the press hitting you with questions about that project and whether Tate's death was the result of technology theft."

"Yes," Sigo said, "Our newest intern, Jane Smith, leaked that information to the media. I can only guess it was an attempt to set herself up as a source, but, at this point, it's only a guess."

"Why? Did she pull a runner and disappear?"

"No. She's died recently."

Gray did a double-take, "Excuse me?"

Sigo sighed heavily, sadness washing over her face, "She was killed in a hunting accident up in Port Gamble the same morning we identified her as the leak. She was hit by a long-range rifle shot while driving. Accidents like this rarely happen, but they're not unheard of. Just last year we had two individuals killed the same way, one in Port Gamble and one outside Seabeck."

"I'm very sorry," Gray said, *"Please* forgive me for pressing this point, but I *do* have to ask—how sure are you that she was the leak?"

"Very sure," Sigo said decisively, feet still up and hands still behind her head, "She used the phone at her desk here to call *The Northwest Herald,* and she used her office computer to email them the material. She obviously ignored the paperwork she signed telling her all phone calls and all computer stations are monitored."

Gray shook his head, "Yeah, I've seen my share of servicemembers make that same dumb mistake in the Navy and Marine Corps. So, do *you* think the Lionfish project was part of this? Do you know why Young-Saeng had potentially classified documents in the house?"

Sigo shrugged, "I can't say. He had a safe in the study where he kept the material. The safe was cracked and crap was strewn all over the study. Whether Young-Saeng was allowed to have those documents at the house is something you'll have to find out. What I *can* tell you is that his body was mutilated like *nothing* I've ever seen before, and I've been in this business for over 30 years."

Gray sat back, looking confused, "Why mutilate his corpse after killing him? The time involved in what was done to his body is *not* something I'd think a suspect would risk."

Sigo's feet dropped to the floor with an ominous thud as she sat up, her back becoming rigid and her eyes cold, "Mr. Gray, I don't think his *corpse* was mutilated at all."

Gray took a moment to process that. Looking up slowly, his eyes grew wide in horror, "Wait…you mean to tell me—"

"I believe Young-Saeng Tate was *alive* when he had his intestines pulled out by the ceiling fan," Sigo interrupted, her face twisting into a mask of fury.

Chapter 3
Bremerton, Washington
Thursday, August 30, 2018; 17:21 hours

Gray's jawbone clattered on the floor as he absorbed the unmitigated horror of the crime scene photos in his hand. Sitting in the coroner's office, he felt his stomach heaving. Clamping down his self-control, he continued to sort through the case file Sigo had brought with them.

"Pretty gruesome, isn't it?" Dr. Richard Kellog asked from behind his desk, wearing blue scrubs, his hair spiking nearly straight out from too much coffee. Kellog's bloodshot eyes were still sharp and alert over the skinny man's stubbled face.

Gray couldn't find his voice as he sat back. Slowly, deliberately, he returned the photos to their proper folders, stowed said folders back into sequential order, and laid the whole pile on Kellog's desk.

Kellog and Sigo studied him.

Gray swallowed, forcing himself to gather up the shards of his shattered professionalism as he took out his pen and notebook from inside his suit jacket.

"Dr. Kellog, that was the understatement of the year," Gray finally replied. "I've been in law enforcement nearly 30 years myself, and this ranks in the top ten violent crimes I've ever encountered."

Sigo, sitting next to Gray in Kellog's office, suddenly reached over and put a comforting hand on his shoulder. She was surprised by how much she was taking to this new NCIS agent, "You ok?"

"I am," Gray answered, his face still gray, "I'll be fine. Ok…so…let me recap what you've told me, Dr. Kellog. The sheriff here told me—"

"Denita, please," Sigo surprised herself again by offering the familiarity. Something in Gray's manner, and his genuinely horrified reaction to the crime scene and autopsy photos, defeated the last of her defensiveness.

"Abe," Gray said, looking at her and smiling, "So, Doctor, Denita told me the basic timeline of the crime. I want to make sure I add your information correctly, so please offer any corrections to my notes—"

"Always happy to correct people," Kellog laughed, leaning back in his executive chair while crossing his legs. His voice was a cheese grater rasp made of equal parts cigarettes, coffee, and fatigue. Even so, there was a touch of good humor in it.

He's relaxing the more he sees Sigo...er, Denita, relaxing around me, Gray thought, *Ok, Abe, you've found your footing with these two. First down achieved. Now let's see if I can't get the ball a few more yards closer to the end zone.*

"Young-Saeng Tate was the victim of a home invasion by at least two people on Friday, August 3rd," Gray regurgitated what he'd learned, "Tate fought back, but the assailants overpowered him, tying him to his bed with household extension cords. They burned him with cigarettes and severely beat him before cutting through his abdominal wall. They used the ceiling fan to literally winch out his intestines. And you're saying this might have been done while he was alive?"

"That about surrounds it," Kellog nodded.

"What brings you that conclusion?" Gray pressed.

"The mutilations were done with *precise* anatomical knowledge," Kellog explained, "It's entirely possible to open the abdominal wall and remove the bowels while the victim is alive."

"I know; they perfected it during the Dark Ages," Gray nodded, a slight shudder running down his spine, "The practice was part of what the English termed 'Drawing and Quartering.' Amongst other tortures, the victim was disemboweled alive and forced to watch their entrails burned in front of them."

"You know your history," Kellog nodded approvingly, "The injuries inflicted on Young-Saeng Tate display a high degree of surgical expertise. No arteries or major veins were ruptured during the evisceration. The slashing of his throat is what finally killed him, but I admit there's no way to *definitively* determine if that was done before or after he was disemboweled. However, based on the injuries sustained, I *strongly* suspect evisceration while he was alive."

"I think they tried beating him to compel him to open the safe," Sigo said, "When that didn't work, I believe the assailants escalated to evisceration to force the issue."

"And you're positive there were two assailants?" Gray looked at Sigo.

"Two sets of unknown prints in the backyard. Judging by the size of the shoe impressions, one was a size 12 and the other assailant wore size 9 shoes, just like Young-Saeng. We initially thought there was only one assailant until my deputies realized the tread pattern of Young-Saeng's size 9 shoes were different from the tread pattern of the other set of size 9s."

"I'm convinced Young-Saeng fought back, and fought back *hard*," Kellog said, "From what Denita's people found, he was taken in the yard by complete surprise, but he fought like an alley cat before being overpowered and dragged into the house, where he again put up a struggle."

"We found notable evidence of a fierce struggle starting in the living room, then moving through the house to the bedroom," Sigo interjected. "Dirt tracked through the house showing Young-Saeng was dragged, but numerous pictures, vases, and other bric-a-brac in the living room and bedroom were shattered, knocked out of place, etc."

Kellog smoothly picked the story back up, "Young-Saeng's hands presented numerous defensive wounds, but the only DNA that I was able to recover from the blood and skin found under his fingernails and from hair follicles I found on his body was his own."

"Say what?" Gray did a double take.

"Young-Saeng had skin and blood under his fingernails, and some hair follicles on his body, but it all matched his DNA profile.

It's as if he scratched the living hell out of himself while trying to fight off his attackers," Kellog shrugged, clearly confused, "The other genetic material belongs to our unknown male, so that gives us something from one of the assailants, but those samples don't match anyone in any criminal database—our own, the FBI's, nada."

"And you also found the flower garden in the backyard destroyed?" Gray asked, looking back to Sigo.

"It was. They were known for their prize-winning rose bushes. The deer fencing was torn out and the plants were all trampled and ripped out by the roots," Sigo answered, but held up a cautionary hand, "Before you ask, we found no biological material on the plants other than Young-Saeng's blood as based on DNA evidence. The assailants used something thick to protect their hands from the thorns when they tore out the bushes."

"So, we have at least two assailants, one with size 12 feet and one with size 9 feet, intruding onto the property through the backyard," Gray recapped yet again, "Young-Saeng was taken by surprise, but got his wits about him and started fighting in the yard, and again inside the house. He was overpowered, tied down, tortured, disemboweled, and killed. You found blood and tissue under his fingernails consistent with defensive actions, and hair follicles on his body, but *most* of the DNA found was his own— including that found on the roses outside—while the other samples don't match anybody in any database."

Sigo and Kellog both nodded, but it was Sigo who spoke.

"That about covers it, Agent Gra...er, Abe."

Gray nodded, concluding his summation, "Young-Saeng was killed on Friday, but his body lay in the house—with the front door pushed closed just enough to look secure from the street, but in reality unsecured—and lay there until your officers conducted a welfare check four days later on Tuesday."

"Correct," Sigo nodded.

Gray looked down at his notes again, "And then last week *our* guy—David Kerr—announces he's arrested Young-Saeng's wife,

41

Lt. Cmdr. Delores Tate, for murder even though Lt. Cmdr. Tate was aboard USS *Gridley* over 500 miles out to sea."

"Got it in one," Sigo said, "In fact, Tate only learned of her husband's murder when the ship came back in on the 12th... assuming she really *didn't* have anything to do with the murder."

"That makes no sense," Gray said, more to himself than Sigo or Kellog, "The murder was discovered while *Gridley* was underway, yet no one contacted the ship or Lt. Cmdr. Tate?"

"David Kerr said that was his job," Sigo responded pointedly, "I suggest you take it up with him."

"Oh, I will!" Gray said, eyes flashing in anger before simmering back into jet-lagged fatigue, "Ok, it's late and I need to get some sleep. May I stop by your office tomorrow afternoon and get a copy of this case file, Denita? I want to compare your data with whatever our people have collected and analyzed."

"No problem," Sigo said, "You can have this material here. It's only a summary; the 'highlights reel,' if you will. I'll get you a certified copy of the whole shebang tomorrow, and I'll make sure you're given access to whatever you need going forward."

Gray nodded, sliding his notebook and pen back into his jacket, "I apologize again for how badly NCIS has handled things thus far. I'm very grateful that you're willing to give *me* the time of day. Just one more question—the Tates live in a pretty decent neighborhood, and your people noted the numerous security cameras on the neighboring houses. How did the assailants approach the Tate home undetected?"

Sigo stood, stretching her back, "Silverdale is riddled with hiking trails. There's one along the ridge that swings up behind the Tates' street. It'd be easy for an intruder to veer off the trail and gain entry to the Tate yard using the brush to prevent detection."

Gray rose, "I also noticed your people didn't say anything about the paperwork for this Lionfish project being strewn about the study in their initial reports."

Sigo shrugged, "Both officers said the study was untouched as they searched the house until finding the body and fleeing outside to await backup. When more of my people arrived, they went room-to-room, sealing every door to protect the scene. However, it was your man, David Kerr, who did the crime scene photography for me since one of my photographers is down with the flu and the others were unavailable."

"Say what?" Gray blinked in surprise.

"Yeah, Kerr actually did *one* good thing," Sigo shrugged, adjusting her Sam Brown belt and its myriad pieces of equipment, "He got to the scene about two hours after the discovery of Young-Saeng's body. He's the one who discovered the study had been ransacked. He'd been shooting the rest of the house—starting with the crime scene itself—and didn't reach the study for about four hours. When he saw its condition, he alerted me before going in to document it."

That's strangely helpful, considering how David's otherwise treated these people like crap, Gray thought. *Still, that means there's about a six-hour window between the discovery of the body and David discovering the study was ransacked. Weird...*

Gray returned to the Viking Inn & Suites. Needing time to think, he veered far out of character by ordering room service for a change. While waiting for his food, he shucked his jacket, hanging it on a coat hook before calling home to Virginia.

"Sarah!" Gray said gaily into his cell phone while loosening his tie with his other hand.

"Matok sheli!" Sarah Gray's merry voice floated across the continent, the Hebrew term of endearment rolling easily into Abraham's ears, "How was the flight?"

"Well, the *flight* was fine," Abraham said, standing at the glass doors to the balcony and staring out over the darkening Dyes Inlet, "The Virginia TSA was a bit of a crap show. I'll deal with that later; but, for now, obviously I'm here, safe and sound!"

"I'm glad," Sarah responded, and Abraham could hear her shuffling about, "I just got back from a late run to Kroger. Going to cook up some good, old-fashioned bar-b-que chicken tomorrow."

"I'm jealous; I've got room service sending up something that's supposed to be a hamburger, but we'll see when it gets here. I'm pretty sure everything I ordered is kosher, but I'm resigned to praying for forgiveness on the off chance the food isn't."

Sarah laughed again, "Well, just remember God didn't blast David to smithereens when he took the Bread of the Presence because he and his men were starving. I seem to recall high priest Abiathar *gave* him the bread. I don't think the Lord will smite you if you're forced to subsist on non-kosher food for a day or two."

"I hope not," Abraham, said, pulling his tie from his neck and throwing it behind him on the bed. Undoing the top button of his shirt collar, he cracked his neck, "I have no desire to be smited over food! Or is it 'smoted?' 'Smitten?' 'Smat?'"

"Smut?" Sarah's voice teased him.

Abraham chuckled before Sarah's voice turned serious, "How was the day?"

"Al hapanim!" Abraham cursed the day in Hebrew, "You would *not* believe the crap David Kerr's been up to out here! He stranded me at the airport, but—"

"That bastard did *what?!*"

"He stranded me at the airport," Abraham repeated, "But, to be honest, he inadvertently did me a favor. I got a rental car and drove over to the base myself. David then pulled a disappearing act, but that gave me a few hours to start rebuilding bridges with the local sheriff and coroner. Honestly, I thought the Bacon case was a crap show once Isaac and I got into it, but *this* makes that case look like some community theatre production of a low-rent murder mystery!"

"That bad, huh?" Sarah said. The sounds of groceries being shuffled had ceased. She was giving her husband her full attention now.

"Yes," Abraham affirmed.

"How much worse do you think this is gonna get?" Sarah asked, "It's spreading all over the news the same way the Bacon case did, and every politician *and* their Aunt Susans are clamoring for heads to roll."

Abraham sighed heavily, sticking his free hand in his pocket as he continued gazing out over the placid water, "Well, what I learned today complicates the situation even more. I don't know what David Kerr's thinking, but, if that idiot *wants* to destroy his career, he's doing a damned good job of it!"

"Matok Sheli, do you think this is going to be 'Isaac' bad?" Sarah asked gravely.

Abraham laughed a derisive snort, "Charlotte also mentioned him earlier today as well. This is an NCIS problem, and I'll be damned if I bug Isaac unless I have *zero* options left!"

"Well, he's not that far from you at the moment," Sarah said, "From what I saw on his blog earlier today, he was in Wyoming at Devil's Tower, and is now heading north. He should be in western Montana soon, if he's not there already. I *fully* respect you wanting to keep him out of this, but, if you need to throw a curveball at this thing, do what you have to do. Let's be honest, the fact you have as a 'secret weapon' is one of the reasons Belk sent you out there...besides the fact you're a holy terror when anyone screws up!"

"Hey, I'm sorry; I got so caught up in my own crap that I forgot to ask—how was your visit with the oncologist today?" Abraham switched subjects, face-palming himself for the oversight.

"Oh, don't worry about it! You've got more than enough on your plate. Anyway, still cancer free!" Sarah sang back, ecstatic.

"Even after twenty-five years, that's *still* great news to hear!" Abraham smiled.

"I'm just glad we had the girls early and didn't wait like we'd originally planned," Sarah said, "Not just because of the hysterectomy, but having the girls and you to think about gave me something to live for while fighting the cancer. But, I'm afraid I have to run; I've got a potential client in Iowa I'm interviewing with in fifteen minutes. I have to change for the video call."

"Iowa?" Abraham asked, impressed, "Sounds like your expansion plans are working!"

Sarah, a freelance cybersecurity consultant, had spent the last couple of years working to build her client base beyond the Eastern Seaboard.

"I know, right? Might even have a hit in Nebraska!" Sarah said, "You go eat your hamburger. And then catch some sleep before you go catch bad guys."

"I love you, Neshama!" Abraham said, "Good luck with the interview."

"Thanks! I'll talk to you tomorrow. Love you, too!"

The two parted ways, their digital connection fading into the ether.

Gray ate his dinner while watching the news. The burger and salad were surprisingly good, and he began to feel drowsy.

Still, better look at what I got from Denita again before I go rack out, He thought, setting the food tray on a nightstand before retrieving his notebook and the files Sigo had given him at Kellog's office.

He read over his notes again before rereading what he'd gotten from Sigo. The more he read, the more he found a peaceful night's sleep tiptoeing just out of reach. His mind was turning and burning as he tried to fit the disparate pieces of information into something resembling a semblance of order.

There's something *wrong here in all this,* He thought in frustration as darkness fell over the Pacific Northwest. *Something about this whole scenario is wrong and feels…I don't know. Not exactly 'staged,' but like something was organized after the fact to obscure the timeline...*

Chapter 4
Naval Base Kitsap – Bangor
Silverdale, Washington
Friday, August 31, 2018; 06:30 hours

Cloudy skies held court over a 64 ºF day. The local forecast had temperatures soaring to a positively tropical 70 ºF before the evening's cool returned the Pacific Northwest to the comfortable 60s.

Dressed in his favorite dark blue suit, red tie, and American flag lapel pin, Abraham Gray sat quietly in the reception area outside David Kerr's office. Carol Keeters did her utmost to appear she wasn't watching him, but she saw the agitation churning under the surface of his calm demeanor. Still, her subdued brown slacks and blouse helped her melt into the background as she nervously continued observing his behavior.

The lobby door blew open.

Keeters shot to her feet faster than a speeding bullet. Flying to the coffee mess, she poured the hot, black liquid into a porcelain mug bearing the U.S. Army Rangers emblem. Gray watched her fast hands stir in exactly two teaspoons of sugar and a smattering of cream as he rose to his feet.

So, David takes his coffee with cream and sugar, Gray thought. *Not like knowing that'll help me much…*

"Your coffee, Mr. Kerr," Keeters said, clearly on edge. This was a ritual she evidently performed daily.

"Oh, Gray, good to see you!" Kerr's plastic smile didn't reach his eyes, which remained coldly dismissive, "Sorry I wasn't able to help you out yesterday. Give me half an hour, and I'll squeeze you in."

Kerr grabbed the mug from Keeters' hand as if she were nothing more than a bookshelf. He then airily breezed past Gray like a yacht on the home stretch of the America's Cup.

Keeters rolled her eyes as she followed Kerr into his office, day planner in hand.

Gray slowly fell back into his seat as the office door closed behind the two of them.

I've got half a mind to bust in there right now, Gray fumed as the minutes slowly dragged on. *Nope. Patience...Patience...*

After thirty minutes had lugged on, Keeters opened the door, "Mr. Gray, Mr. Kerr will see you now."

She stood aside as Gray rose, picking up his briefcase and calmly strolling into the office as if he had not a care in the world.

Smiling smiled warmly at Keeters, Gray nodded, "Thanks again for the coffee this morning, Carol. It was excellent!"

Keeters flashed an uncertain smile at Gray while adjusting her horned-rimmed glasses. She obviously trusted him as much as she did Kerr...which is to say, not at all.

Gray heard the door shut behind him as he debated just how much of a pyroclastic flow to unleash on Kerr.

Hang on, Abe. This jackass outranks me, Gray thought fast, *Better play it a bit cool. After all, I* don't *have any information from* his *side.*

"Ah, Gray, sit down!" Kerr said, not rising, but gesturing to a chair across his desk.

At 5'11", Kerr was two inches shorter than Gray, and his dark brown suit hung on his wiry frame. Kerr's hair was still a nice sandy brown (or else he had it professionally colored), even though he was two years older than the 52-year-old Gray.

Gray approached the expensive mahogany desk, pulling back an expensive mahogany chair and settling into it while setting his briefcase by his feet.

Egotistical bastard, Gray thought darkly as he scanned the room.

Photos of Kerr from his Army Ranger days fairly papered the walls days along with numerous marksmanship awards. The bookshelf (also expensive mahogany) was littered with trophies extolling Kerr's proficiency as an Army sniper. Dozens upon dozens of photos in fancy gold and crystal frames showed Kerr posing with world leaders and even a few Hollywood starlets.

Three antique rifles were proudly displayed on a gleaming silver display stand atop the bookshelf. The stand itself had two photos of Kerr displayed in built-in frames.

Private firearms aren't allowed on U.S. bases, Gray thought, distracting himself. *But, then again, they* are *antiques. Might be authorized on this particular base. I'll have to look that one up.*

Gray's eyes settled on the ostentatiously fancy bronze-and-glass sign jutting up six inches from a marble plinth on Kerr's desk:

United States of America
Department of the Navy
Naval Criminal Investigative Service
Special Agent in Charge
David Joseph Kerr
Northwest Field Office
Honor et veritas

"I'm so sorry I wasn't able to meet you at the airport," Kerr said, his feet up on the desk as he scanned some documents while sipping his coffee, "I've been stretched pretty thin by cases in California, Utah, and Nevada that pulled all of my agents away. *And* the fallout from this Tate case has just been plain taxing."

"It's certainly taxing for Lieutenant Commander Tate," Gray said, crossing his legs and folding his hands in his lap, "Especially as you announced you'd arrested her on charges of homicide. A homicide, I might add, that took place here in Silverdale while she was underway aboard *Gridley."*

"Oh, that," Kerr said absently, not looking up from his papers as he talked, the tiniest of slurping noises coming from the continued sipping of his coffee. "Yes, I confess I was inaccurate on that note, and I'm sorry for the aggravation it's caused our *esteemed* new director. I should have said she was charged with *conspiracy* to commit murder."

Kerr finally pulled his feet off his desk, dropped the papers onto it, and looked at Gray for the first time, "I know why you're here. I got the head's up from Director Belk before you came out.

I'm sorry you're wasting your time, but there's nothing for you to do here."

"I'm afraid I don't understand," Gray said carefully, "You usurped authority from the local jurisdiction before making a highly ill-conceived arrest *and* making a patently false and inappropriate public announcement…and you say I'm wasting *my* time? You have to understand that contradicts everything I was briefed on at Quantico, and everything I learned from Sheriff Sigo yesterday, David."

"'Mr. Kerr,' please," Kerr corrected, his silky voice that of someone who knows their power—and wants to ensure everyone else knows it as well, "I believe team members must maintain a certain professional formality. Anyway, you've been given incomplete information at best, Gray."

"That's 'Special Agent Gray,' Mr. Kerr," Gray responded just as smoothly, "Since you wish to ensure proper professional decorum, I'm looking to you to set me the example by using *my* proper title. Sir." *Two can play this game, you twit!*

Kerr's eyes narrowed for just a second, the flash of irritation quickly replaced by another artificial smile. Gray saw right through it. Kerr was *definitely* not used to people holding their ground.

"No need for us to be so formal," Kerr said, backing down a bit, "But, sadly, yes, you're wasting your time. I confess to being a bit remiss in my comms with Quantico, but Sheriff Sigo and her cohorts have proven to be *woefully* inadequate in their efforts. I haven't seen *anyone* screw up a case this badly since Shey Cremer bollixed the Bacon case two years ago."

"Director Belk sent me out here precisely because *I* was the agent who cleaned up that mess," Gray said, watching Kerr's reaction.

Kerr blinked, surprise evident in his smug expression.

Ok, you dork, Gray thought, his face neutral but his mind racing, *You didn't do your homework.*

"Well, then, you're the best person to back-brief the director that I've got this one in hand," Kerr said quickly. Gray had the feeling Kerr was scrambling for a new approach as he continued, "I'll have Carol print you a certified copy of everything I've got on this case. You can pick it up tonight if you like. Once you read it over, I'll think you'll see why I've taken such drastic action. If I hadn't, this case would not only have been a media circus, but also a major national security breach."

"You *do* realize the director also sent me out here to find out why you emptied this office so abruptly?" Gray pressed, his soft, pliable façade beginning to drop away one piece at a time, "You've got fourteen drug-related offenses that you're sitting on. I know of two shoplifting cases at the Bremerton NEX you're not doing anything about because you've got nobody else around here, three domestic violence investigations, four—"

"I don't have to explain myself to you!" Kerr snapped, his fake joviality melting, "I'm sorry I couldn't meet you at the airport, but if that chapped your sensitive little ass, too bad! If I've had to detail all my agents out of state to cover cases with a higher priority than some dumb kid stealing toothpaste at the NEX, well, then, go blame Congress for not funding us appropriately! As it is, I'm meeting you today only as a courtesy, one agent to another, but this is *my* field office! You'll do well to remember that!"

"Are you finished now, *David?*" Gray asked casually, deliberately emphasizing Kerr's first name as he blitzed the senior agent with a very direct approach, "Because, if you're not, I'll go get some coffee to help me stay awake while you waste my time."

"What?!" Kerr snapped, jumping up, his chair rolling back three feet, "You son of a bitch! Where do you get off—!"

"Oh, go flash your badge somewhere else!" Gray snapped back, his harsh tone biting off the end of whatever Kerr had been about to say. He refused to rise, knowing his remaining imperturbably seated only wound Kerr up more, "I'm here as Director Belk's *personal* representative. I have the orders *and* authority to review not only the Tate case, but your office management, as you well know!"

Kerr's eyes blazed as Gray pressed on.

"Whatever mitigating factors there might be, you've put NCIS and the Navy into a *very* unfavorable light, and the director's not going to stand for it! You can either work *with* me, or else I'll brief the director tonight on this conversation and you'll be on your way back to Quantico so fast you'll think the Navy SEALs involuntarily extracted you!"

Kerr stared down at Gray who, in return, continued sitting quietly, staring back up with equal intensity.

Kerr suddenly resumed his seat, his face taking on its carefully sculpted smile again, "Special Agent Gray...Abe, if I may—"

"You may not," Gray said, his posture relaxing but his voice remaining as flexible as rigid steel, "'Abraham' is fine. Or 'Special Agent Gray.'"

"Abraham, then," Kerr responded as smoothly as any politician, "You're right. I do owe you an apology. I'm afraid my stress level has eroded my professional manners. Look, there's no need to get the director involved in this, not yet, at any rate. Look over my case files tonight. I think you'll find everything's in order, If I've made any mistakes, it was simply in being overly enthusiastic seeking justice for the deceased—and I *will* take the hit on that one without objection."

"I've never been one to jump to conclusions," Gray said, strategically giving a bit of ground and allowing his voice to soften back to a conversational tone, "And I understand better than most just how stressful high-profile cases can be. I also, however, don't appreciate being stranded at an airport."

Kerr stiffened, then blew out a short, frustrated breath. Gray had the distinct impression Kerr was about to explode on him again, but Kerr instead jabbed the intercom button.

"Carol! Get in here!"

Keeters popped into existence so fast Gray wondered if she had access to a space/time wormhole.

Oh, damn! Gray fought to keep his face straight, *That sci-fi crap Isaac loves is starting to rub off on me!*

"Yes, Mr. Kerr?"

"Why the *hell* didn't you have someone pick up Mr. Gray yesterday?!" Kerr stood, roaring so loud that Gray felt his hair follicles vibrating.

Keeters wore a long-suffering look. She was obviously accustomed to these temper tantrums, "Sir, you said you wanted to do that yourself—"

"If you want to keep your job, then do *not* contradict me, woman, and *especially* not when other people are in the room!" Kerr raged, slamming a hand on his desk, "Now start compiling a certified copy of the Tate case file for Mr. Gray!"

"By your command, sir," Keeters nodded, the most subtle contempt on her face as she exited the office.

"A bit harsh, don't you think?" Gray asked tightly, trying to control his boiling temper.

"That woman's a nightmare!" Kerr seethed, "She's never learned her place! But she *will* have all the material you need tonight. It should be ready around 17:00. Otherwise, I hope you have a good day. There's a great submarine museum just outside Keyport's main gate. Worth a visit."

Kerr proceeded to spin around in his chair, presenting his back to Gray as he fired up his computer in its expensive mahogany credenza.

Deciding a political advance to the rear would be in his best interest, Gray grabbed his briefcase, rose, and quietly left.

Keeters was nowhere to be found in the outer office. Gray could only assume she was down in the records room trying to gather up all material relating to the Tate case.

Gray headed back out to his car. Once inside, he pulled out his secure cell and dialed Virginia.

"Abraham," Charlotte Webb's comfortingly familiar voice emanated from the tiny speaker, "How's your morning been?"

"Well, I think I know why all the female agents here were sent out of state."

"Why's that?"

"David Kerr's a misogynistic bastard who treats women with all the respect of gum on the bottom of your shoe," Gray said tightly, starting the car, "He wasn't like this when I met him way back in the day, but, well, *now...*"

"That's him, all right," Webb's voice sounding grim, "He's turned into a nasty, chauvinistic piece of shit over the past few years. Well, most likely he was always a misogynistic pig but kept his true colors hidden until he was relatively untouchable. Hell, Abraham, he's had more complaints filed against him than Shey Cremer did before I was able to kick *him* out of NCIS."

"Let me guess," Gray said, wondering why in the world he'd started the car when he wasn't going anywhere yet. He switched off the ignition, "Powerful political friends?"

"Nailed it," Webb said, "He knows how to schmooze up to the right people, and he's developed a friendship with a certain congresswoman from Rhode Island."

"Let me guess, that's another reason why Belk sent me out here?" Gray laughed ruefully.

Webb laughed, "I don't doubt that was part of Kirby's reasoning. There's a lot more rot inside NCIS than you know. You and Isaac really started something last year!"

"I figured the dry rot was pretty bad after Cremer's ouster resulted in old Director Seldon getting fired. Crap weasels like Seldon don't get that high into power without an army of toadies supporting them," Gray ran a frustrated hand through his frustrated hair.

"And Kerr was one of Seldon's faithful toadies," Webb confirmed, "You and I—and Isaac—got some momentum going for the good guys, and Belk is counting on you to rattle Kerr's cage. If you'll pardon the chess analogy, your well-known ability to see 'sideways' through difficult cases, coupled with your current political capital, makes you the perfect knight to attack the problem from an unexpected angle. Kerr can't simply dismiss you, not with so many military and political leaders viewing you as *the* agent who 'saved' NCIS last year.”

"No good deed goes unpunished, huh?” Gray laughed sadly, "No worries. I'm on it. And don't worry—I'll watch my back. I'm getting a certified copy of the Tate files from Kerr's office tonight. He said something about Sheriff Sigo and her team being 'woefully inadequate,' but I've seen no evidence of that. I'm getting a full copy of her materials when I meet her for lunch later today.   My assessment might well change after I compare both sets of case files, but I honestly doubt it. I'll map out my next course of action once I do my homework.”

"Good plan,” Webb responded, "I've got to go; conference call for all the field office heads. Unfortunately, Kerr will be on it as well."

"Well, that's why you get paid the big bucks!” Gray laughed.

"True,” Webb said, "Listen, the shitstorm in the press is getting worse. If Tate's guilty, fine. But, if she's not, then you don't have long to act before she gets run through the meat grinder as a sacrificial lamb to the gods of political convenience.”

Chapter 5
Silverdale, Washington
Friday, August 31, 2018; 13:21 hours

"…turning to national headlines, Gippeum Lýkos, brother of Young-Saeng Tate, who was brutally murdered this month in Washington State, excoriated the Navy for allowing a known predator like Delores Tate to remain in the ranks simply because she's a female…"

"…while toxic masculinity makes up the great percentage of predators, women too can be deviants, and this Delores Tate was hip-deep in connection with agents from a major Asian adversary," The man on TV was thin, reedy, and his pinched face peered from behind owl-like glasses under bright pink hair, "Young-Saeng Tate was a brilliant engineer working on the Coast Guard and Navy's Lionfish project at Keyport in Washington State. Early reports indicate he discovered his wife's illicit activities and was killed before he could report to authorities her plans to sell the Lionfish drone…"

"…we're pleased to have Rhode Island Congresswoman Dana Cremer join us here in the studio," Declared the portly host, his moon-like face and expanding waistline suggesting a sedentary life largely spent in search of the next snack, "Congresswoman, thank you for your time. Before we get to your proposed legislation canceling all student debt, perhaps I could get your thoughts on the horrific homicide in Washington State?"

"Thank you for having me on, Brian," Cremer said, her delicately polished face flashing a thousand-dollar smile from under an elegantly coiffed pile of brunette hair, "I've been contacted by Gippeum Lýkos. He's seeking my office's assistance to compel Navy officials to bring this horrible, murdering woman, Delores Tate, to justice. Mr. Lýkos is grief-stricken at the death of his beloved brother, and expressed outrage that the Navy is stonewalling the prosecution of a woman who is a threat to national security…"

"…turning to news in the Pacific, Admiral Richard Roe, commander of the U.S. Pacific Command, denied any involvement in the growing 'Big Mitch' scandal swallowing up Navy personnel. Roe stated unequivocally he has never received monetary payments, gifts, or special consideration from 'Big Mitch,' CEO of Oceanic Supply and Services Corporation. Roe further stated that he only steered Navy ships to ports serviced by OSSC when operational needs required it…"

Abraham Gray scanned the crime scene. Signs of the forensic team's work remained in the scattering of fingerprint dust and evidence markers, but, otherwise, the house was as quiet as a sepulcher.

The bedroom had been cleaned, of course. Once the Kitsap County police and NCIS completed their work, the biological material had to be disposed of; otherwise, the Tate house would have become an active biological wasteland.

Gray looked up from the crime scene imagery in his hands to the deceptively serene sleeping space. The photos showing Young-Saeng Tate tightly secured to the bed, blood pooling on the covers and floor, and intestines stretching up to the ceiling fan, might have been from a different planet.

Gray's eyes returned to the pictures, studying the face of the dead man.

Tate's ghastly blue face screamed out unmitigated pain. Gray understood—and found himself agreeing with—Kellog's belief that Tate was alive when he was disemboweled. The man's look of pure horror loudly telegraphed his terrible final moments as his body was brutally disassembled around him.

Eyes leaving the photos again, Gray looked at the empty bed.

"Who did this to you?" He asked Young-Saeng Tate's ghost quietly, "You were way too clever to just go *quietly.* You've *had* to have left something to point me in the right direction."

"So, you talk to the dead too, huh?"

Gray jumped, "Jeez! Denita, you scared the crap out of me!"

Sigo stood outside the bedroom door, her uniform looking slightly worn after a long morning's hustle, "I'm sorry; I thought you'd heard me. Anyway, you talk to the dead too, huh?"

"My class's lead instructor at the police academy drilled into us that *all* investigators talk to the dead; some just don't realize it," Gray said, eyes returning to the room, "I was just about to head to the study. Care to join me?"

Sigo and Gray trooped down the hallway. A truly mismatched pair, Sigo was significantly shorter than Gray.

"This area was untouched by the attack on Young-Saeng," Sigo said as they traversed the immaculate passageway. "The fights he put up were in the backyard and in the great room. He must have been completely subdued by the time the assailants dragged him through this hallway because nothing here was disturbed."

Photos of Young-Saeng and Delores Tate adorned the walls. Several images showed them on a rocky beach, smiling during happier, more pleasant times. Others revealed photographic memories of the two hiking through a dreamscape of green forests, a shire where the *Lord of the Rings* might have been filmed.

"That's at the Hoh Rainforest," Sigo said, nodding to a hiking photo that caught Gray's eye, "Part of Olympic National Park. It's the wettest forest in the Lower 48."

Gray's eyes next found an image of Young-Saeng standing in a natty suit next to his wife on a ship's deck with an officer he guessed to be the captain of USS *Gridley.* Both men held a hand under each side of Delores' khaki collar, holding up her rank insignia for display.

"She put on lieutenant commander a month before the homicide," Sigo explained.

Gray's face quietly twisted with disgusted rage as he compared the smiling face of a young man excited by his wife's promotion with the ghastly death mask captured in the crime scene images.

They reached the study, Sigo pulling the "DO NOT CROSS" crime scene tape from the door so Gray could enter.

Stepping inside, Gray scanned.

The room looked as though it had been thrashed by a particularly violent tornado. The desk, obviously from a big box store, was capsized, a lumbering wooden freighter turned turtle by the gale. Its drawers were haphazardly scattered about the debris field, their contents littering the floor in a blast of secretarial shrapnel.

The three bookshelves were empty, their books thrown about the room by the suspects' hands. Several were torn apart, their pages crumpled on the floor like dead skin from a sunburn. Every photo in the room was smashed, even those left hanging crookedly on the walls. Gray noticed the photos were all of Young-Saeng and Delores.

"Interesting the assailants trashed *this* room and its mementos, but left the hallway intact," Gray said thoughtfully.

"And the great room," Sigo pointed out. "The only damage in the great room we determined to be a result of the struggle, not of deliberate vandalism."

"I see..." Gray said vaguely, studying the room.

The safe remained open, its contents vomited out during the breach. Gray knew the Navy had already collected all sensitive materials, and, fortunately, none of the Lionfish information was missing. By now, all that remained was the detritus of the Tates' lives.

Gray stared around, remaining quiet. Too many pieces of this puzzle didn't make sense. His mind shifted, shuffled, and slid the pieces around while his eyes continued recording data. Something was niggling at the nape of his neck, a tingling prickle of hair that alerted him that *something* was about to make sense in the bloody flood of two crime scenes.

Holy crap! Gray's heart leaped into his throat, adrenalin flooding his veins. Two entirely separate pictures clicked into place together like the missing pieces of a complex jigsaw puzzle. *I don't believe it, but* that's it! *That's what I've been trying to see!!*

60

"This was staged!" Gray declared, his voice that of a judge handing down immutable, immovable law.

"I beg your pardon?"

"Staged!" Gray said again with finality, his hand sweeping the room, "The safe was the target; the rest of this—the 'ransack the room thing'—is just a misdirection."

"Why do you say that?" Sigo asked, "My guess is our suspect ransacked the room to find the safe's combination."

"That type of safe is commonly used in the Navy, we also use it in NCIS," Gray explained, eyes still roaming the scene as he finally stowed the crime scene photos inside his jacket, "It needs a six-digit PIN code *and* the user's thumbprint to open. Even if Young-Saeng were so foolish as to store his PIN in this room, they couldn't open without him. Did you find any prints on it?"

"We did, and they were Young-Saeng's..." Sigo's face twisted as a revelation hit her, "Come to think of it, they were old. Smudged, like the safe hadn't been touched in a while, just maybe brushed up against while Young-Saeng and/or Delores moved about the room."

"Therefore, our suspect or suspects did *not* need Young-Saeng to open the safe," Gray said, his suspicion confirmed, "They had a means of bypassing the PIN code and thumbprint. And *that* points to a fantastically sophisticated and pre-planned safe-cracking operation. *Therefore,* they already knew what they wanted was inside the safe."

"I see why you said the rest of the room was likely ransacked as a diversion," Sigo nodded, cottoning on further, "I hadn't thought of that."

Young-Saeng was the target of the fatal attack, not the safe, Gray thought. *The safe was an afterthought they hit four days later, but why?*

"This happened during the six-hour window between Young-Saeng's body being found and Kerr discovering the study had been hit," Sigo sighed, "Which means whoever got in here is both a first responder *and* someone high enough up that *no one* would even notice them moving about the house undetected. This complicates matters greatly, you know."

"I've seen it before," Gray said, his mind racing back to the 1999 case in Spain where a Navy rear admiral abused his rank to move about freely and commit three murders. "It's a problem, but one I'm already chipping away at."

"Oh?" Sigo's eyebrows went up, "You've got an idea?"

"Not an idea so much as I've narrowed the field to 37 people once I eliminated you from the suspect list."

Sigo nodded, then froze when the import of Gray's statement smacked her upside the head.

"Eliminated me?!" Her head snapped up to stare indignantly at him, "You had *me* on your suspect list?!"

Gray smiled, eyes still mapping out the decimated room. He wasn't fooled by her words one bit; the tone in her voice betrayed the amusement in her heart.

"You damn well know I did, Denita," Gray said gently, "This breach in the study happened while *your* department had charge of the scene. You're the senior person, therefore *you* had the easiest opportunity to access the study without anyone paying attention."

"Ok," Sigo's voice was light, but she maintained her mask of righteous indignation, "So how'd you eliminate *me* so quickly, Mr. Genius?"

She needs to meet Isaac! Gray chuckled to himself before responding, "Video. I had the gang at Quantico pull an all-nighter scanning every piece of video footage from the security cameras around your building. During those six hours you never *once* left police HQ while coordinating the response to this homicide. Therefore, *you* didn't ransack this room."

Gray finally looked down at her, his face crinkling into a puckish smile, "Unless, of course, you preplanned the hit with accomplices. However, while that's theoretically possible, it falls outside the realm of probability based on your background. So, yes, you were on my suspect list."

Sigo nodded, but, before she could speak, Gray held up a hand.

"By the way, your indignant act needs work. Your voice gave the game away," Gray smirked in a good-natured way, "Especially as *you* did the same to me. I've gotten 58 notifications from various contacts that you've been running inquiries into *my* background, record, and movements."

Sigo's mouth fell open so far a steam locomotive could've used it for a tunnel. The shock crossing her face was complete. Closing her mouth with an effort, she blinked, then burst into a loud, cheerful laugh.

"Hot *damn!*" She slapped her thigh, "You *are* good! Still, just how in the *hell* did you get notifications about a *confidential* set of checks?"

"You said it yourself—I'm good," Gray answered, a puckish gleam in his eye.

The two turned to leave the room, Sigo restoring the crime scene tape across the doorframe.

"Nice!" Sigo chuckled again as they headed back down the hallway to the foyer.

"Denita, the fight and the bedroom are telling us one story," Gray said, shoving his hands in his pockets, "The study is telling us a separate, if potentially connected, story."

Gray checked his watch, "Damn, I've got to run. I'm meeting David for dinner here soon. Anyway, I think we've got two *separate* crime scenes here, not one contiguous scene. The fact the study was hit *days* after the homicide means it was a separate attempt."

"'Potentially related?'" Sigo asked thoughtfully, "I see what you mean. It's entirely possible the safe was hit by an entirely different set of people connected to my department after they realized the gold mine of classified information on the Lionfish in there."

"But, who in your department would've known what Young-Saeng was working on?" Gray wondered, "And how in the *hell* did they crack a safe needing two-factor authentication to open? No, I think an insider in the Navy—perhaps working at Keyport, but part of the local Navy-Marine Corps team—helped kill Young-Saeng before going after the safe."

Sigo sucked in a breath, "Oooh, boy. Crap. Well, at least that gives *me* an angle to run down. I'm going to start digging and see if any of our people—police or EMTs—had *any* kind of connection with the Tates. Your logic about the 'Navy-Marine Corps team' has a great deal of merit, but it's *my* responsibility to do the due diligence about *my* department's potential culpability in this."

"Good idea," Gray said, a deep breath shuddering its way into his lungs as he grimaced at the prospect of dinner, "In the meantime, I've got to go play nice with Kerr again!"

"Better you than me," Sigo grunted.

The Yacht Club Broiler was a dark, sedate place overlooking the waters of Dyes Inlet not a five-minute walk from Gray's hotel. The overcast skies continued to hide the mythic Mount Rainier everyone kept telling Gray dominated the horizon in good weather.

"So, you can see that case down at the Nevada National Security Site is too important for me to ignore," Kerr said, the remains of a lobster dinner cowering in fear on his plate next to a receipt for the check he had just paid, "And then the uptick in sexual assault cases in San Diego and Pearl Harbor demanded I detail the rest of my agents out of state. It's been a perfect storm, but I'm lucky that everything here in the northwest region has been mostly quiet enough for me to handle alone."

"Except for the Tate murder," Gray pointed out, dabbing the corner of his mouth with his napkin. Until quite recently a large piece of grilled salmon had adorned his plate under a small forest of grilled asparagus. Sadly, Gray's ravenous appetite ensured the quick extinction of the salmon and asparagus.

"Too true, Abraham," Kerr said breezily. His attitude and manner were relaxed and jovial, "Obviously, we can't discuss the details of anything here, but I wanted to give you an overview of the situation. I also figured I owed you a little more professional courtesy than I provided this morning. You obviously can't give the director a proper report if I'm acting like an idiot because I let my workload swamp me."

Gray smiled warmly, the low hum of the surrounding conversations a pleasant background noise, "We all have bad days, David. The Lord knows I've had my share. I try not to judge anyone after only one interaction, and the size of the case file box you provided certainly testifies to how hard you've been working on this one!"

Indeed, a locked file box big enough to use as an anchor for an ocean liner squatted at Gray's feet. Contained inside was a certified copy of everything Kerr had collected on the Tate case.

Kerr glanced at his watch as the kitchen doors clacked open, another meal zipping out to its recipient, "Damn! It's nearly 19:00 already! I'm sorry, Abraham, but I need to run. I've got a meeting with the Lion's Club this evening."

Gray rose along with Kerr, "No worries. I've got plenty of reading to do tonight. Hey, I know it's probably not a big deal, but do you mind if I use your secure video conference room as an office?"

"Sure," Kerr said, straightening his tie, "Anything I can do to help?"

Yes—go jump in Puget Sound! Gray thought, recalling Webb's text from an hour earlier telling him that Kerr had tried to co-opt part of the recent conference call to publicly complain about Gray's presence. Belk had just as publicly shut Kerr down, informing him quite plainly he was expected to work with Gray if he wanted a future in NCIS.

Still, nice to see you squirm a bit, you stuck-up zayin! Gray's face remained unreadable as the Hebrew curse slapped itself across Kerr's false smile.

"No, but thanks," Gray said easily, pulling a nondescript windbreaker on over his polo shirt. He'd traded his suit for more casual clothing before meeting Kerr for dinner, "Charlotte texted me from Norfolk. She needs to talk to me about a few of the cases I had to hand over to Carla Tenbold when I came out here. Easiest thing for the three of us to do is a video con Monday afternoon, and using that as an office will also just keep me out of your way."

Kerr nodded easily, "Always better to be face-to-face when you can. I'll make sure Carol has things set up for you. Well, I'll see you Monday afternoon, Abraham. I'm tied up Monday morning in meetings with some Seattle civic leaders. Again, my apologies for being such a yutz earlier. Call me if you need anything!"

The two agents shook hands before Kerr sped off. Gray hefted the massive file box, beginning the trek back to his hotel. He was glad the room had a well-stocked supply of coffee. He was going to need it.

I need another shower first, Gray thought, *I feel like I'm swimming in syrup from all the smarm that putz poured over me. Jeez, I just want to find out who killed Young-Saeng Tate, not play David's petty little political games!*

Chapter 6
Silverdale, Washington
Monday, September 3, 2018; 16:21 hours

"Helllloooo, Seattle! Tricky Ricky Ray here on WAXE with your drivetime drama! The National Museum of Brazil suffered a catastrophic fire yesterday. Early reports indicate over 90% of the museum's collection might have been destroyed..."

The TV anchor gazed solemnly into the camera, connecting with his viewers as he read the sad report, "The late Senator John McCain was laid to rest in Arlington National Cemetery yesterday. McCain famously spent five years as a POW in North Vietnam before entering politics..."

"...the Dow and the S&P 500 both enjoyed their strongest gains in August since 2014, and the NASDAQ's 5.7% was the best growth it's seen in August since 2000. Ocean Adventure Cruises gained 14 points with the launch of its two newest cruise ships, the *Ocean Voyager* and *Ocean Explorer,* the completion of both made possible by Neon Flamingo Group's acquisition of the formerly troubled cruise line. Minnesota's Fredriksen, Fleet, and Siphon Investment reported greater-than-expected earnings, but international investors wavered in the face of the sharp drop-off experienced by markets in India, increasing FFSI's investment liability in a new Indian powerplant..."

Charlotte Webb's ebony face shone brightly from the large, high-definition monitor mounted on the wall. Gray leaned back in a plush executive chair, enjoying the privacy afforded by the secure video conference room.

"Thanks for meeting with me so late, Charlotte," Gray said, appreciating the fact she stayed late in her Virginia office for the call.

Webb smiled, her white teeth glowing against her black skin, "You're dealing with David Kerr, Abraham. That alone entitles you to all the emotional support I can offer. The time of day doesn't bother me. I trust you gave Kerr our cover story?"

"Of course," Gray said, "And it's a neat one, at that. He won't question me getting up with you to 'go over' cases I handed off to others in Virginia. Incidentally, how *is* Carla doing with that domestic violence situation I gave her?"

"It's the typical mess," Webb said, looking into the camera. "The sailor in question was detained for assaulting his wife, but she was also detained for assaulting him, and then *both* were adamant the other had done them no harm and it was the neighbors lying about all the screaming and crashes from the house..." Webb trailed off, shaking her head in disgust.

"Gotta love those," Gray rolled his eyes, "A mutual destruction society."

"We've had a rash of 'mutual destruction societies' lately," Webb lamented, "But, back to the matter at hand. What have you been determined?"

"I've spent this past weekend going blind reading case files, but I did learn an interesting fact about Denita herself in the process."

"Such as?" Webb asked.

"She's the first full-blooded member of the Suquamish tribe to be elected county sheriff," Gray said, "And, as far as this case is concerned, well, Denita doesn't miss anything. Her files are impeccably organized and maintained; they're just as thorough as everything Kerr handed me from the NCIS office here."

"So hit me with the awful truth," Webb said darkly, "Because your body language and tone of voice are loudly telegraphing a major problem with this case."

"Is it that obvious?" Gray asked ruefully, pulling his notebook out of his blue suit jacket.

"Yes," Webb said, a wry smile curling her lip.

Gray smiled wanly, opening his notebook, "Ok, let me start with the incontrovertible facts I have first."

"Meaning you have a serious controversy on your hands," Webb said, a heavy sigh escaping her, "I see. Ok, go ahead with the incontrovertible first."

"Buckle up!" Gray said, glancing down at his notebook. Doing his best to keep it short, he gave Webb a précis of his findings, concluding with his thoughts on the breached safe and elimination of Sigo from the suspect pool.

Webb, however, locked in on an unexpected detail.

"There are no other forensic photographers in all of Kitsap *County?!"* Webb asked, shocked, "They don't have any other resources?"

"It's a lot more rural out here in Kitsap than you'd think," Gray glanced up from his notes, "As soon as you get north of Bremerton, well, Silverdale's a lovely little town, but it's *little.* The towns further north, like Poulsbo and Port Gamble, are even smaller." Gray said, before continuing. "The only local officers qualified in forensic photography were unavailable."

"Wow," Webb said, "I had no idea that area was so rural. Anyway, go on, please."

"David has training in forensic photography, so he volunteered to do the job," Gray continued. "He entered the house two hours after the body was found. Four hours later, upon completing documentation of the bedroom crime scene, he began documenting the rest of the house. That's when he discovered the study had been ransacked and the safe breached. So, that's a six-hour window during which someone ransacked the room while the house was full of first responders."

"Wonderful," Webb replied sarcastically, "So, what are you doing about the insider-threat angle?"

"Denita's working that right now for her department," Gray said, "She's the sheriff, so it's her place to do an internal search to see if she can link up any Kitsap County employees with the Tates. I've already hit up Veronica Bale for help on our end. She can run background checks on all the possible Navy and Marine Corps personnel from Quantico."

"Good," Webb nodded, "Now, fill me in on just how *Gridley* fits in with the Lionfish project."

Gray slid his notebook back into his pocket, "That's pretty straightforward. *Gridley* wasn't on the hook for any deployments between now and late 2019. That's the longest lead time of any Everett-based destroyer, so the Navy slid USS *Kidd* into *Gridley's* spot in the *John C. Stennis* Carrier Strike Group, and loaned *Gridley* to Keyport. *Gridley's* homeport was then switched from Naval Base Everett to Bremerton for the project."

"Really? A homeport shift within a local area?" Webb's eyebrows rose.

"Another thing I've discovered is just how freaking spread-out this whole place is," Gray said, "The Kitsap Peninsula's pretty compact, but Naval Base Everett's over two hours away, whether by ferry or car. It's not like the Tidewater area where we have so many assets located within a 45-minute drive of each other."

"Interesting. Well, anyway, back to *Gridley's* role," Webb said.

"Well, *Gridley* took the drone, or specific components, out to sea, usually with a Keyport engineer aboard, tested them, then brought them back," Gray shrugged, "The ship had tested the full Lionfish drone only four times before the homicide. The fourth test was underway while Young-Saeng was being killed."

"I know Delores Tate holds a Top Secret clearance," Webb said, "But did she have any *direct* interaction with the Lionfish?"

"She did," Gray confirmed, folding his hands in his lap, "She's *Gridley's* operations officer, so she was as hip-deep in testing the Lionfish as anyone else."

Webb blinked, "Therefore, she had as much access to the technology as her husband."

"Which *means* she didn't need to rob the safe in her own house—or kill her husband—if she wanted to sell the drone to our adversaries," Gray stated.

"And if she wanted to kill her husband, she *still* had no need to rob the safe," Webb said, leaning back in her chair and looking at her ceiling. "Do you think it's possible the homicide and the attempted theft were committed by two separate groups of suspects unrelated to the other?"

"Possible, yes, but not probable in my judgment," Gray answered. "The assailants had *intimate* knowledge of the Tates' routines, therefore it's logical to assume they knew about his work on the project and the safe in the house. Again, Delores could've killed her husband and stolen the Lionfish, but she's had access to the drone for a couple of years now. Hooking the two crimes together would be ridiculously foolish for a Navy officer trained in operational planning."

"Unless she was just stupid—and we've all seen that in suspects," Webb pointed out. "However, I get the feeling there's more going on here that makes you think otherwise."

"There is, and this is where the train *really* starts to go off the rails," Gray confirmed, "According to Kerr, Young-Saeng was a battered husband in an extremely abusive relationship. He's got numerous medical records from a local free clinic down in Bremerton documenting Tate's injuries. However, Denita got a look at the Tates' records from the naval hospital right as she began her investigation. According to them, Young-Saeng was in perfect health and showed no signs of *any* injuries."

"Say what?" Webb did a double take before recovering her poise, "I assume the timing of these records overlap?"

"They do," Gray ran a hand through his hair, "However, when *I* contacted the naval hospital today to start getting access to Young-Saeng's records, the hospital told me they'd suffered a cyber-attack. *Both* of the Tates' records were lost along with several hundred other servicemember and dependent records."

"Convenient," Webb said, her face betraying nothing, "What else?"

"I interviewed the CO, Technical Director, and Chief Engineer of NASED Keyport this afternoon. They all said Young-Saeng was the brains behind the recent breakthroughs in super-accurate GPS software enabling the Lionfish drone to self-guide through unknown waters. They also all gave glowing reports about *Gridley's* support, and about Lt. Commander Tate herself."

"Financial state of the suspect and deceased?" Webb asked, once again not betraying a smidgen of emotion.

Gray shrugged before rising to brew himself a cup of coffee from the Keurig machine in the corner of the room, "Well, much as with the medical records, which version do you want?"

"Beg pardon?" Webb's eyebrows twitched.

Gray snapped a pod into place, slipped a cup under the dispenser, and hit the button. The machine whirred happily.

"I mean that, depending on which agency we're talking about, I'm looking at two *completely* different pictures," Gray explained, "According to Sigo, the Tates were quite well to do. Each owned a 2017 Mercedes, and both cars were paid off. Neither was a gambler, but they like to go to Vegas to see the shows. Minor credit card debt, but nothing they couldn't discharge within a month if they wanted to. Between Delores Tate's salary and Young-Saeng's six-figure income, they were set."

"Ok," Webb said, "Now, what's the other picture, the one I'm assuming comes from Kerr's work?"

"You catch on fast!" Gray confirmed sarcastically as the Keurig sputtered and spat. Gray waited a second to let a stray drop fall into the mug, then lifted the hot, black coffee to his lips. *Man, I needed this!*

Turning back to the screen, he set his coffee on a coaster next to his papers before resuming his seat, "According to Kerr, Delores Tate was heavily in debt *and* having an affair with a man named William Smith. He's a barback at Baker Street Billiards, a pool hall in Tacoma. Delores Tate and the rest of *Gridley's* wardroom were in a pool league, and they often competed in tournaments at Baker Street Billiards."

"So, right there, we have a serious motive for her to sell the drone tech to a foreign power *if* her financial woes are real,"

Webb said, "Now, to summarize, you're saying the Kitsap County Sheriff's Office's narrative, and David Kerr's narrative, are 100% in opposition to each other regarding both medical and financial records?"

"That's what I'm looking at here, Charlotte," Gray said, "Oh, and one more thing."

"What?" Webb asked.

"Denita checked Delores Tate's credit cards this morning on a hunch," Gray said, "The hit that came back matched up perfectly with Kerr's information, but contradicted Denita's initial findings 100%."

"Is it possible she and her people made a mistake?" Webb probed, "Looked at the wrong person, misread the data; something like that?"

"Of course, it's possible, but, again, not at all likely in my opinion," Gray said, his hand unconsciously reaching up to straighten his tie, "Charlotte, someone initiated a retroactive hit job on Delores Tate."

"That would explain the discrepancy between Sheriff Sigo's and David Kerr's information," Webb nodded, "She started working the case several hours before he did; she might have gotten a look at the unaltered data before our person or persons unknown were able to screw with it. That would also fit the timeline of the sudden glut of public smears against Delores."

"Which means this is getting *way* bigger than any of us guessed," Gray said, "This case has elevated from a 'simple' murder investigation to something with major national security implications. We're dealing with someone, or 'someones,' who already cracked a high-security safe, hacked into some *seriously* hardened federal and civilian computer systems, and committed a particularly brutal murder."

"Agreed," Webb nodded, her face taking on a darkness that had nothing to do with her complexion, "This thing is escalating fast. I think we need to deploy more assets as rapidly as possible. Do you agree?"

"You stole my idea!" Gray laughed.

Webb looked thoughtful, "The easiest course would be to utilize local personnel. Did Kerr *really* send all his agents to other states?”

“He did, and he gave me his reasons over dinner Friday night,” Gray said, “He talked a good story, but it all just felt like smoke, mirrors, and misdirection to me. Question—just *how* many schmucks like Kerr did our 'esteemed' former director elevate throughout NCIS in the first place?!”

“Too many,” Webb said tightly, “And that's Kirby Belk's first line of attack—cleaning out Casey Seldon's political fungus.”

A loud pounding made both NCIS agents jump. Gray looked over his shoulder at his door, but it was Webb who rose.

“My end, Abraham,” Webb said, unsecuring and opening the door of her conference room in Virginia.

“Charlotte, Abe, I'm sorry to interrupt,” Carla Tenbold blew into the room like a squall line. A deceptively matronly-looking woman, many suspects underestimated Tenbold's level of physical training at their peril, “You both *really* need to see this!”

Tenbold sailed past Webb to a bank of monitors on the wall. Grabbing a remote control, she flipped on a TV news broadcast, hiking the volume up so Gray could hear it over the system in Washington State.

“…returning to our coverage of breaking events concerning the murder and espionage charges leveled at a Navy officer, we're joined in studio by Rhode Island Congresswoman Dana Cremer. Congresswoman Cremer, thanks for being with us tonight. During the commercial break, you said you had an announcement. Would you care to share it with everyone else?”

“Of course, I'm happy to, Anderson,” Cremer said, her face displaying a smug expression. She sat easily at the table on set, beige blazer unbuttoned to hang casually from her shoulders. Her hands were lazily folded on the table next to a coffee cup. “I've been in meetings most of the day with Senator Duryodhana drafting resolutions for the House and Senate to declare a vote of no-confidence in the rogue director of NCIS and calling on the president to reinstate former Director Casey Seldon."

"Now, that's interesting," The white-haired anchor responded, "I thought Seldon was removed due to several ethical violations, including squelching multiple sexual harassment complaints by female agents."

Cremer smiled, "No, Anderson, I'm afraid that's just propaganda ginned up by the president's radical base of racist, sexist reactionaries who want to drag us back into the 16th century. No, former Director Seldon was a man of sterling character who was unfairly targeted by a rogue Navy sailor."

"Congress is infamous for its lack of speed," Anderson commented, shuffling the papers under his hand (all were props; what he needed to know was shown on a teleprompter just out of the camera's field of view), "How much pressure can you put on a bigot like this illegitimate president with non-binding resolutions?"

"Oh, quite a bit, Anderson, quite a bit," Cremer said, a self-righteous smile crinkling her amber eyes, "When the full Congress of the United States adopts even a non-binding resolution, it sends a clear message that the American people will not tolerate the lawlessness this xenophobic, racist, and homophobic president presides over…"

Tenbold shut off the TV. Laying the remote control back on its stand, she turned, her round face burning bright red with indignation under her soft gray hair. *"That's* why I interrupted. You both needed to know what that bitch is up to."

"The president's already under a huge political strain, what with the false allegations of foreign collusion being leveled at him," Webb said, leaning back in her seat, a huge sigh of frustration escaping her, "This just might be one bridge too far if it goes through. We can't allow that."

"Excuse me?" Gray was alarmed, "Charlotte, I'm all for consigning Dana Cremer's political career to the ash heap of history, but we can't go meddling in the political process!"

"We can, Abraham," Webb swung around to peer directly into the camera at him, Tenbold standing behind her, "But not in any illegal or unethical manner. What we do is upend that bitch's flea-flicker play by solving the case *fast.*"

Gray blinked. Now and then Webb let slip a glimpse of her somewhat secret obsession with the National Football League.

"Congress *does* move slow, but Cremer's party controls the House," Webb continued in a deadly earnest tone, "And there're plenty of senators in the president's party that'll cross the aisle to put a knife in his back. Based on the berserker-level of hatred the opposition has for our current president, I'd say we have a week, *maybe* two tops, before Cremer and Duryodhana's resolutions can gain traction. Can you bring this one home in under fourteen days?"

Gray sat back, stunned. He'd seen his fair share of political vendettas and maneuvering, but *this* was sinking to a level he honestly never imagined possible, "Damn. Dammit all, I don't know. I just...don't...oh, fucking *shit!*"

Gray's fist slammed down on the table, his head dropping to his chest.

Webb and Tenbold blinked, but both remained silent. Tenbold had never once heard Gray curse before; Webb hadn't seen him frustrated enough to curse so vulgarly in English in fifteen years.

Gray, however, was not one to remain frozen by shock or indecision for long, "Fourteen days, huh?"

"At the max," Webb nodded, her unhappiness dripping across the internet.

Gray got up and began pacing. Webb and Tenbold could almost hear his mind whirring all the way over in Virginia. His face contorted into various expressions as he debated ideas within the privacy of his brain.

"Look," Gray said, turning back to the monitor, "Is there *any* way you could send Carla out here? Or Denny? Marjorie? Anyone at all?"

Webb shook her head, "Unfortunately, no. We've got too much going on here for me to spare anyone else at the moment."

"And Veronica's tied up in Quantico," Gray said, eyes dropping to the floor in confounded thought, "Dammit! I'm confident I can do this, but not in *that* time frame without extra help. Denita can only do so much; she still has a county to oversee."

Webb's face softened, "Abraham, I'm afraid you might have to make that phone call you've been trying to avoid."

Gray's head snapped up, eyes blazing with anger.

Webb headed him off at the pass, "You said it yourself—you need help to do this inside of fourteen days. I can't spare anyone else from this office, and Kerr's ensured you have no assistance on the deckplate there. Therefore, there's only one option left."

Gray sagged, "Charlotte, I spent *twenty years* trying to get Isaac *out* of the amateur detective business! I can't just about-face and call him back in now!"

Webb nailed Gray to the deck with her steely gaze, "So, you're saying your personal comfort level is more important than Delores Tate's life or protecting the security of the United States?"

Gray froze, mouth twisting before he managed to get out a jagged sentence, "You know what, Charlotte? There are times when I really hate you!"

Webb smiled as Tenbold rolled her eyes.

"Good," Webb said, "Then I'm doing my job. Now, the *big* question is availability. We're running against an unforgiving clock. Can you get Isaac there in time to be of any assistance?"

"Yes, I can," Gray said, feeling nauseous, "Isaac's in western Montana right now. Assuming he agrees, I can have him here within a day. Maybe two."

"I'll get the necessary paperwork done and send them to you via SIPRNet," Webb said, "Go to work!"

Gray knelt alone in his hotel room. He delicately sipped a ginger ale when not praying, trying to settle his stomach. His gut had revolted rather violently at the idea of making the call, and even a long conversation with Sarah hadn't done much to calm him. Desperate to find some inner peace, he affixed his yarmulke to his head, draped his prayer shawl around his shoulders, and knelt before the Lord.

The *one* person he had privately vowed to never call upon was now the *one* person he needed.

The hours ticked by, Gray remaining in deep prayer.

He had a job to do, and he was duty-bound under oath to use any and all legitimate means to complete it. Webb was right; he had no other choice if he hoped to finish the job in time. Sighing, he rose, removing the shawl and yarmulke. Locating his phone, he began mashing buttons.

Abraham Gray was determined to unleash the Accidental Detective.

Chapter 7
Elkhorn, Montana
Monday, September 3, 2018; 15:12 hours

Retired Navy Chief Petty Officer Isaac Shepherd was lost in the past.

He wasn't over-much concerned; after all, he *had* intentionally traipsed into the Old West. Carefully poking around a long-forgotten ghost town, he was happily ensconced deep in the mountains of western Montana. Surrounded by a score of derelict wooden buildings, the retired sailor steadily uncovered the secrets of Elkhorn.

Established in 1872, Elkhorn was fueled by the local silver mines' rich production of the precious metal. The mines had already begun playing out when an 1888 Diphtheria outbreak killed off many of the town's children. The final blow to Elkhorn's prosperity came when railroad service ended at the end of the 19th century. Elkhorn began to contract, finally being abandoned in the 1970s.

A few hardy souls still made their homes in this obscure corner of the western Montana mountains, but Elkhorn itself was as dead as the Old West frontier it once marked.

In other words, it was exactly the kind of place one would find Isaac Shepherd happily getting lost in.

Today, a small part of Elkhorn constituted the smallest state park Shepherd had ever encountered in his life: two whole buildings. Gillian and Fraternity Halls stood side by side, relics of a bygone age protected by the Montana state government. The rest of the forgotten town was slowly falling into the attic of history.

Somewhat shaggy hair, far more salt than pepper, was contained under a relatively new round-rimmed cowboy hat Shepherd whimsically named *Montana*. Appropriate, considering he'd bought the chapeau back in Bozeman. His beard, a verdant gaggle of steel gray fur sprouting from his face, had only been grown out since the previous (and preposterously cold) January. He'd shaved it briefly in the spring to attend a friend's retirement from the Navy, but then retired his razor once more. Like his hair, the beard was scraggly, evidence of his determination to stray far from Interstate highways and civilization. He preferred trundling along back-country roads exploring small towns and deep-diving into local history as much as he could during this year-long Grand Tour undertaken to see all 50 states (and a bit of Canada).

Hiking boots crunching over the old wooden floor, Shepherd's bulky, barrel-chested form exited Fraternity Hall. His feet shaped a course up the hill towards the town's cemetery. Adjusting his camera belt on his waist before pulling off his bifocals, he blew a piece of dust off one lens. Replacing the spectacles, his sea-green eyes once again brought the world into sharp focus.

Reaching boot hill, he explored the quiet community of the long dead for a time before stopping short, amazed by something he hadn't expected to find.

A wooden grave marker from 1886 that's been sitting out here for over 150 years…and it's completely intact!

Pulling out his camera, Shepherd photographed the grave marker before kneeling down to read it. The syntax was a bit jumbled, as if the parents of the deceased child took a pre-existing marker and added the child's name to it, but Shepherd was able to make it out.

Elisya Stevens, Shepherd quietly read, *Born 1886, died in April 1898. Damn. Only, what? Twelve? The kid missed the 1888 Diphtheria outbreak by a good mile, but she still died at 12. Childhood mortality was* way *higher back then, but, still, I wonder what happened?*

Getting back to his feet, he surveyed the cemetery again. A tombstone with a lamb carved atop it caught his attention. Lambs were a common motif on children's tombstones from the late 18th century until the early 20th century.

Yep, another little one, Shepherd nodded to himself, crouching down to read the carved marble stone: *Thomas John Willey, son of J. & E. A. Willey, died May 3, 1890. Aged 3 days.*

"Three *days?!*" Shepherd was startled, "The Willeys must have had some money to afford a big marble stone for a 3-day-old baby. Jeez, though. Talk about tragic!"

Rising to his feet, Shepherd completed his tour of Elkhorn's boot hill before heading back toward the town's skeletal remains.

Finding a good tree, he pulled Albert the Crab out of a pocket of his cargo pants. Albert, a small, toy plush crab, had been a security object for Shepherd for years now. Shepherd couldn't leave the house unless his bodyguard, Albert, was hidden in a pocket or his backpack.

Recently, however, Shepherd had found a new, public identity for the red crustacean: Albert the Traveling Crab. Shepherd was quite the ham, and loved being in photos, but found himself recoiling from selfies early that summer. Watching his fellow tourists ignore the grand vistas of the Maine coastline, instead obsessing over the perfect selfie spot, inspired Shepherd to do something different.

Thus, Albert had come out of hiding. Although Shepherd did occasionally have his photo taken here or there (his mother would've killed him otherwise), Albert was now the public face of Shepherd's Grand Tour USA. Albert had happily taken on the new responsibility with gusto (Albert was a very easy crab to work with!).

"Come on, buddy," Shepherd said, perching the toy crab in a tree with the looming forms of Gillian and Fraternity Halls in the background, "This should make a good Instagram photo. And then I'll set this thing up on timer and get one of me to send to Mom and Pop."

Albert waited serenely, patiently posing while the retired Navy photographer got the angle just right.

Shepherd snapped the photo before reaching up to retrieve Albert and continue a conversation he'd been having with the crab for nine months now, "I guess I did block most of it out for 20 years, but ever since talking to Aidan and Linda about that first case back in '99, man, Albert, it's been on my mind a *lot.*"

Sliding Albert back into the cargo pocket on his pants leg, Shepherd kept up the monologue.

"Still, I did tell Aidan that I was close to a decision whether to keep playing detective or not. Can't tell you *why,* but I have the weirdest feeling I'm about to make that decision."

Now, that *was a funny way to put that!* Shepherd thought, his hiking boots crunching on the gravel in front of Gillian Hall. Pulling his camera belt off his waist, he unhitched a small tripod from it, rigging up his Nikon so he could do a self-portrait on Gillian Hall's front porch.

"I don't know, Albert," Shepherd began talking to the toy crab in his pocket once again, "I've got absolutely *nothing* empirical to base this on. It's just a…just a feeling in my bones. I do know I've needed time away from all the dead bodies to think, and this trip has certainly given me that."

Well, Knucklehead, Shepherd thought wryly to himself, *You've been away from dead bodies 'long enough' if only you* don't *count that little dust-up you helped the sheriff solve down in Kentucky back in January. You never know when to quit!*

Setting the timer, Shepherd's long legs swiftly strode to Gillian Hall's aged wooden porch. Leaning on a post and setting *Montana* at a jaunty angle, Shepherd waited for the shutter's timer to go off.

Still, Shepherd thought, *Nearly twenty years of playing amateur detective on top of my regular duties in the Navy was quite a way to spend my young adulthood. I've got a lot to be proud of, but it came with a lot of emotional baggage, too. I don't think burying the baggage with the bodies was a good idea, though. Bodies stay buried; baggage keeps coming back from the grave until you actually* deal *with it!*

The camera snapped its shot. Glancing at his watch, Shepherd was surprised to find it was nearly 16:00.

I'm retired now. Maybe I ought to try and stop using military time...

He'd been exploring Elkhorn since 7:00 that morning—and *that* was after making the hour-long drive from his hotel in Whitehall up into Big Sky Country's mountainous region.

"Damn!" Shepherd said, gathering up his camera gear, "I need to get going!"

Shepherd fished his key fob from his pocket and clicked the button, unlocking his small, blue SUV, affectionately christened *Sarah Jane.* Named for a favorite *Doctor Who* character, she blinked her lights at him while disengaging her locks.

Pulling Albert out of his pocket and setting him in front of the shifter, Shepherd loaded up his gear before taking one last look around. He wanted to etch Elkhorn into his memory.

The drive back to Whitehall's tiny limits was less than 50 miles, but the narrow, winding roads forced him to drive slowly for a good ways. It was either that, or else risk a head-on collision with a member of the large cattle population in the area (or possibly even a moose).

Stopping to grab a sandwich from a local burger joint once he was back in Whitehall, Shepherd hightailed it to his hotel.

"We're back, Happy!" Shepherd announced to his teddy bear as he burst into the room.

Happy Bear, an old, red, tatty, and very tubby teddy bear, happily looked up from his place on the bed. Apparently, Happy had been napping comfortably.

"Thanks for fluffing the pillows for me, Happy!" Shepherd laughed, carefully setting his camera gear down. "Ok, got some work to do, so I need to get my butt in gear, guys," Shepherd said, setting Albert on the nightstand next to the bed.

One fast shower later, the former Chief Mass Communication Specialist woofed down his dinner while downloading his photos to his laptop.

The photo captions didn't take long, nor did the two-page blog column. Reading it aloud several times, he edited it down from a cacophony of competing clauses to a coherent choir crooning the complex tale of a lost mining town in the Montana mountains. Satisfied with the written version, he set up the portable webcam, mic, and lights. Pulling a decent polo shirt on over his boxer briefs, he activated the lights, turned on the camera, and began filming.

"Hello, and welcome to another episode of Travel Log here on Sparks TV! I'm Isaac Shepherd. Lost amongst the western Montana mountains, Elkhorn embodies the tale of a mining boom town gone bust…"

The video only took ten minutes to film.

Not bad; I usually don't get it on the first take like that! Shepherd smiled. He'd edit the video later. The web connection here was too slow for him to upload a video, blog column, and photos. However, he was far too experienced in media production to put off getting the video filmed and column written, lest his impressions and ideas fade with time.

Shepherd rose and went to brush his teeth. It was past 23:00 and he was pooped.

Funny how much I've been thinking about what I told Aidan and Linda back in January, Shepherd thought, shucking his shirt and pulling back the covers on the small hotel bed. Happy Bear was already in bed and settling down for the night.

In a way, telling them was almost as difficult as living through it was. But, then, until I told them about it, I never really thought about it. Just kept it buried, and that's no way to live free.

Sitting on the edge of the bed, Shepherd settled his CPAP mask on his face before swinging his feet up. Lying back, he wrapped an arm around Happy Bear. Albert the Crab settled down on the nightstand to keep watch.

The CPAP machine quietly hummed, the steady stream of air ensuring Shepherd continued breathing through the night.

Shepherd ebbed restlessly into sleep, visions of Old West buildings morphing easily into snippets of lighthouses in Maine with Martha, his former stepdaughter, who had spent most of June and July with him exploring New England.

Sunlight glinted cheerfully on azure ocean waters as cowboys thundered by, their horses' hooves barely rippling the water's surface while New England fishing boats chugged past. Sliding deeper into the realm of dreams, Shepherd's mind left the waking world far behind...

...until The Beep pinged through the room, demanding immediate attention.

Shooting upright, Shepherd's arm swiftly pulled the mask from his face before swinging down to shut off the CPAP machine. Snapping on the bedside lamp, his eyes and ears began scanning the room for the source of the unexpected sound.

The Beep chirped again, emanating from his computer bag.

Shepherd stared dumbly at the bag, trying to figure out just what he had in there that would *beep.*

The camera's on the charger, Shepherd thought, *The computer's on the desk. The only thing left in that bag are some USB cables and...*

And the Bat Phone.

The Bat Phone was an old, but specially hardened, cell phone Abraham Gray had given Shepherd years earlier to provide a secure line of communication during their adventures. Although he habitually kept the software updated, Shepherd hadn't *used* the Bat Phone since...

Since 2016 during the Bacon case, Shepherd thought, *What the hell is it beeping for now?!*

Realizing the easiest way to answer that question was to get up and answer the dumb thing, Shepherd slid out of bed. Pulling a shirt back on over his boxer briefs to ward off the chill, he retrieved the bag, his mind already running in high gear.

Excavating the phone from the depths of one of the inner pockets involved a terrific fight against the clutches of two greedy USB cables, but Shepherd successfully liberated the device. The LCD screen lit up as he flipped the phone open.

A text message demanded his attention.

"Abe?!" Shepherd stared dumbly at the sender ID.

Pulling out the desk chair, Shepherd sat down while opening the message:

Silverdale, Washington. Come at once if convenient.

"What the hell…?" Shepherd reacted, but his surprise doubled when a second text popped into the phone as he watched.

If inconvenient, come all the same.

Shepherd read the location again: Silverdale, Washington.

"Abe, what the *hell* are you doing in *Washington State?!*" Shepherd blurted out aloud.

Spinning around in the chair, Shepherd opened up a browser window on his laptop. A news search of Navy issues in the Pacific Northwest didn't take long.

Damnation! Shepherd thought, stunned into disbelief, *I know I went 'off the grid' and stopped obsessing over the news a month ago, but how in name of John Q. Arbuckle did I miss* all this?! *Still, why did they send Abe out there from Virginia?*

Pulling away from the stories, he opened another window to begin plotting a route to Silverdale.

And then stopped. The seconds clicked by, turning into minutes, as he engaged in a fiercely contended debate with himself.

I could just say 'no' and walk away, One side of Shepherd told himself, *Abe wouldn't begrudge me that at all.*

No, he wouldn't, Another part of his mind piped up, *But would that be the* right *thing to do?*

Shepherd sat there, listening to various voices in his head argue the issue.

Well, I did tell Aidan back in January I had the oddest feeling I was going to face a resolution to this question sooner than later,

Shepherd thought sardonically as the debate raged on in his brain, *I just didn't expect 'sooner' to be this much sooner!*

Like an eagle cresting turbulent storm clouds, Shepherd's decision broke free into the brilliant light of clarity. In a way, he realized he'd always known the decision; he just needed time to get there on his own.

"Screw it," Shepherd said, looking at his reflection in the mirror over the desk. A contented smile brightened his features as he finally arrived at the conclusion he knew he'd reach eventually, "I *am* the Accidental Detective, and it looks like there's a monster stalking the countryside again. Time to put the Grand Tour on hold for a bit!"

Returning to the abandoned laptop, he began plotting the route.

Ten hours by car, but it's nearly 1:30 in the morning now, and I've been hiking all day, Shepherd thought, *I'm in no shape to get up early and drive that far safely. Better tell Abe to expect me Wednesday.*

Grabbing the Bat Phone, Shepherd's finger slid the miniature keyboard out from the underside of the phone. Mashing the tiny buttons, he sent his answer into cyberspace.

I'm on my way. ETA Wednesday afternoon.

Shutting the Bat Phone, Shepherd laid it on the desk before sagging back to bed. Slipping his CPAP mask over his face and turning out the light, Shepherd laid back, content with his decision. This time he slid gently into the world of dreams...

He was standing on the flank of a great, somnolent volcano, the summit arcing far above his head into a sapphire sky. Below his feet, magnificently broken mountains cascaded away.

A full, rich female voice caught his ear. Turning, he saw a woman in a gray robe looking out over the grand vista, her feet lost in a raging sea of colorful wildflowers. Her face was shrouded under the robe's hood, yet, somehow, Shepherd knew she was speaking to him.

"From birth, through death and renewal, you must put aside old things, old fears, old lives," The woman said, the rich tones of her smooth voice dancing in the clear alpine air, "This is your death, the death of flesh, the death of pain, the death of yesterday."

She held out her hand, proffering something in her grasp. Shepherd tried to see her face, but the eternal folds of her hood prevented him from observing her features.

Sighing, he extended his hand to her. She placed something long and cold in his palm. Looking down, he saw she'd handed him a magnifying glass mounted on a curved piece of elk antler that served as a handle.

Turning, she gazed out to the horizon, "And so, it begins."

Chapter 8
Silverdale, Washington
Wednesday, September 5, 2018; 17:22 hours

"…turning to national news, Derecho Aviation reported a cyber-attack on their corporate network. A Derecho spokesman said the attempted breach targeted the Derecho development office in Bremerton, Washington, where Derecho is working with Seagull Electronics Alternatives to develop the A.I. software for the Navy's next-gen carrier-based interceptor, the YF-114 Tomcat II. Derecho said the attempt was thwarted by the company's tough security protocols…."

"…Emirates flight 203 made an emergency landing in New York this morning after declaring a medical emergency. Multiple passengers fell sick with fever, coughs, headaches, and other flu-like symptoms during the flight. The plane and its passengers were quarantined by the FAA pending an investigation…"

"…on Capitol Hill, Congresswoman Dana Cremer of Rhode Island accused Florida Senator Diego Alejandro of misogynistic anti-Hispanic bigotry after the senator criticized Cremer's plan for mass amnesty for illegal immigrants. The senator, whose own parents fled political oppression in Cuba, responded while talking to WTXT News:

"If the good congresswoman from Rhode Island is indeed serious about stopping human trafficking, then I'm sure she'll join my efforts to secure the southern border. Once she takes some time to research the issue, she'll see just how many women and children are raped, abused, and otherwise exploited by the drug cartels and coyotes, and that doesn't include the abuse suffered by men…"

Shepherd was introduced to MOD Pizza by his friends in Ohio during the previous Christmas holidays. He thoroughly enjoyed the eatery's industrial look and relished the personalized pizzas they concocted behind the counter.

He was thus excited when Gray texted him to meet up at the MOD Pizza located in The Trails, a newly developed shopping area in Silverdale off Greaves Way.

Shutting down *Sarah Jane's* engine, Shepherd deactivated and stowed his GPS unit before picking up Albert. Sliding the crab into the side pocket of his cargo pants, Shepherd opened the door and stood up for the first time since stopping at a rest area just inside the Washington State line several hours earlier.

Stretching each limb with all the grace and concentrated intensity of a cat after a long nap, Shepherd's eyes swept the scene. Sunset was still about two hours off, but the angled light already pouring through the emerald evergreen trees created an ethereal ambiance. The temperature was in the mid-70s, and the air was briskly crisp compared to the heavy, humid air he was accustomed to back on the East Coast.

Man, no wonder they call this place the Evergreen State! Shepherd arched his back as he marveled at the sea of firs, cedars, and other evergreens stretching to the mountainous horizon.

Reaching into the SUV, he grabbed a new—but already well-worn—blue field jacket. He'd recently retired the old green one he'd worn for most of his active duty career, carefully stowing the tired, threadbare garment in one of his footlockers with other Navy memorabilia. He'd found this new jacket while staying with his folks in his hometown of Niceville, Florida. He'd spent one Sunday afternoon sewing a small Navy chief anchor patch above the jacket's left breast pocket while he and his dad watched NASCAR.

Locking up *Sarah Jane,* Shepherd started towards MOD Pizza. His eyes peered through bifocals perched above a still-grizzled steel-gray beard as still-disheveled salt and pepper hair (about two-thirds salt, one-third pepper) rolled out from under his hat in a discombobulated wave that nearly smothered his ears.

A light breeze bearing the combined scents of various food from different eateries wafted through that discombobulated mass of hair. The tickle of hair on his ears reminded him how long it'd been since he'd had a haircut.

Ahead of him stood one wing of the swanky strip malls making up The Trails. This particular complex housed a Chipotle, a dentist's office, an AT&T store, and MOD Pizza. Stomach suddenly rumbling, Shepherd increased his pace.

One hand already grasping the cold metal handle, he was about to enter when his gaze latched onto the reflection of a man sitting at an outdoor table with his back turned. Something about that hunched back was familiar...

Turning, Shepherd studied the seated figure briefly. Sitting at an outdoor eating area under a lighted torch (Shepherd realized dozens of these torches dotted the outdoor area), the man wore an impeccable blue suit, and a flutter of shock white hair could be seen peeking above the bent-over neck.

Shepherd blinked, smiling in amused recognition, *Man, he'll never change!*

Shepherd took one step toward the figure when a leaden weight unexpectedly crashed into his stomach. Butterflies hatched, beginning an unpleasantly giddy dance in his stomach as he stopped in his tracks.

The sudden combination of trepidation and excitement was not something he'd expected. Granted, he and Gray hadn't seen each other in person in nearly a year, but they *had* collaborated over numerous video conferences wrangling together a textbook Gray was developing.

Seeing Gray sitting just a few feet from him, in a land far removed from where they'd parted a year earlier, threw Shepherd into a surprising state of insecurity.

No, I'm not afraid, I'm just feeling sorry for Abe! Shepherd realized, his hand falling from the door handle. *He spent twenty years trying to get me out of the detective game, and now he calls me back in.*

Shoving his hands in his jacket pockets for a moment, Shepherd stared at Gray's back as Gray stared down, evidently studying his phone.

The news reports of the Tate case are bad enough, but this situation's got to be a freaking dumpster fire of epic proportions for Abe to ask me *for help after all those years trying to get me to stop playing detective,* Shepherd thought, *I'm happy to see him, but calling me in must have ripped out his liver!*

Still, nothing was gained by delay. Having said goodbye to each other in eastern Virginia the previous September, the two men were about to say hello in western Washington State this September.

The inevitable was now inevitable.

A quote from *Richard II* began snaking through Shepherd's mind. He and his former stepdaughter, Martha, had listened to numerous Shakespeare plays while touring New England, and his bear-trap memory permanently filed multiple quotes from the Bard. The trip with Martha had allowed them to continue bonding while affording his ex-wife and her new fiancé a bit of time to develop their romance further.

Shepherd swallowed his emotions back down before quietly approaching the silent figure.

"My crown I am, but still my griefs are mine. You may my glories and my state depose, but not my griefs; still am I king of those!" Shepherd quoted in a clear, ringing voice.

Abraham Gray shot to his feet in surprise, whirling around so fast one might have thought he'd been spat out of a small tornado.

Blue-gray eyes blinking, Gray beheld the apparition in front of him. Shaggy hair, unkempt beard, pants with dirt-stained knees, and dried mud caked on the hiking boots were just part of the ensemble draped over the man in front of him. A blue field jacket hung dusty over a disheveled T-shirt while a mildly pungent whiff of earth, moss, and sweat permeated the late afternoon air.

Isaac Shepherd appeared for all the world like a reclusive mountain man come to town for a rare visit (or the stereotypical wild-haired, grizzled bearded veteran; either one).

"You look like hell," Gray said stupidly, his own emotional state launching itself off the charts of reasonable comprehension.

"Yeah, sorry about that," Shepherd ruefully looked down at his decidedly dirty state. "I've spent the past few weeks off the grid. I wasn't expecting to return to civilization for a while yet."

The two men locked eyes again, and the dam finally broke. Joyful laughter overcoming all challengers, they roughly embraced in a collision that could have sunk a small cargo ship. The two friends held each other for a moment before separating again. A small cloud of dust rose from Shepherd's jacket as Gray patted his shoulder.

Gray discreetly hid his cough.

"I can't wait to hear all about it, Isaac," Gray said, forcing away another cough, "I've been following you online. Have to say, you're making Sarah and me jealous! Yeah, sure, we've been to Europe and all, but Sarah's never been west of the Mississippi River, so you're giving her ideas—and making my future a living hell!"

Shepherd and Gray shared another laugh before finally catching their breath.

"Damn, it's good to see you again, brother!" Shepherd said, "I've missed you."

"I've missed you, too," Gray admitted, unable to keep the sadness out of his voice even as his smile dimmed, "And I'm truly sorry I had to interrupt your road trip for *this.*"

"Don't be sorry," Shepherd said firmly, "To steal a line from Captain Kirk, I assume the odds are against us and the situation is grim?"

Gray dropped his head, chuckling. *Lord help me, but I actually miss his unholy penchant for quoting movie lines at the most wildly inappropriate moments!*

"You could say that," Gray looked up, unknowingly providing Captain Picard's actual response to Captain Kirk in *Star Trek: Generations.*

Shepherd smiled, sliding slightly into paraphrase mode, but continuing the quote as a private joke with himself, "Well, most people would say I'm an irrational, illogical human being for taking on a mission like that. Sounds like fun!"

"Isaac, you don't know the half of it," Gray said, shaking his head in warning. Disbelief etched his face into a mask of confusion, "This is…well, you're just *not* going to believe it."

"Before we get down to business, let's get some food," Shepherd said, gesturing at the door to MOD Pizza. "I'm starving. After we're done, you can catch me up a bit before I head over to Port Ludlow."

"Port Ludlow?"

Shepherd nodded, "It's over on the Olympic Peninsula, about 30 minutes away. My friends Liam and Maria Gumataotao live there. You should remember them—you met them on Guam back in '05."

"I do remember them," Gray nodded, "Sarah's been mentoring Liam since he started his own cybersecurity business. You're seeing them tonight?"

"I talked to them today on the road," Shepherd said, "They're letting me stay with them. It's a hell of a lot closer than my brother A.J.'s place over in Seattle."

Gray smiled, "I'd forgotten one of your brothers lives out here. But, and I hope this doesn't piss off your friends, you're staying here in Silverdale at the Viking Inns and Suites. I need you close, not half an hour away. I already got you a room down the hall from mine, and NCIS is covering the tab."

Something tripped a warning bell in Shepherd's head, "The look of your voice and the tone on your face is somewhat alarming, Abe."

Gray chuckled, finally shoving his phone back into his pocket, "As I said a minute ago, Isaac, you are *seriously* not going to believe this. There's more at stake than you know, but you're right. Let's eat and get you settled in."

The two entered the boisterous restaurant, its dining area nearly full and its noise level just this side of a jet engine running on high power. Gray used his government travel card to pay for a large mushroom pizza and two drinks. The pair filled their cups before finding a vacant table in the corner next to the plate glass windows overlooking the scenic parking lot.

"I've always been amazed by how easily you eat in a place that prepares pork on the same counter as everything else," Shepherd said, sipping his unsweet tea. At 45 years old, his barrel-chested build didn't need any excess sugar expanding it.

Gray smiled, shrugging as he swallowed a gulp of soda, "I do my best, but I've got to be realistic. Either I hit the high points—like simply not eating pork—or else I starve until I can get to my hotel and make a peanut butter sandwich." Gray blinked in surprise watching Shepherd, "Hey—why the earplugs?"

Indeed, Shepherd was discreetly inserting two small, custom plugs into his ears.

"Legacy of the traumatic brain injuries I earned during my Navy adventures," Shepherd sighed, "Noisy places like this have started giving me, well, the docs call it 'sensory overload events.' I get a headache in the *bones* behind my ears and then I just start shutting down from the overload. Doc recommended these when things get too loud so I can stick around and not have to leave early."

Gray nodded sympathetically, "Do you need to go somewhere else? This place *is* pretty noisy."

"Hell no!" Shepherd smiled, putting the earplugs' tiny case back in his pocket, "MOD Pizza rocks! Besides, I'm good. Oddly enough, the earplugs make it easier to hear *you* since they block out the ambient gibberish."

The two men could not have made a greater contrast if they tried. While no one stared at them, many of their fellow diners couldn't help but be struck by the smoothly polished man in the blue suit and the raggedy vision of a man who looked for all the world like he lived on the streets.

"…so, Martha discovered lighthouses aren't quite as boring as she thought once we got into Connecticut," Shepherd said, "She got enthused after she started hearing some lighthouse ghost stories. Well, that, *and* finding out many lighthouse keepers were, in fact, women. That girl's going to have a great career in music, but I think she might also start writing books about true-life ghost stories. They're like candy to her!"

"Her and you both!" Gray said, eyes twinkling, "Hey, jumping subjects, what was that quote you said when you got here? Sounded like Shakespeare."

"It was. *Richard II,*" Shepherd answered, "Martha's on a Shakespeare kick. She and I listened to at least half a dozen Shakespeare plays in the car, and we must have watched Kenneth Branagh's *Henry V* on DVD at least once a week. She was determined to memorize it."

"That's a stretch," Gray laughed.

"Not really," Shepherd shrugged, "My brothers and I had *Star Trek II: The Wrath of Khan* memorized by the time we were 13. All you need are two helpings of good memory, fifteen thousand spoonful's of repetitive viewing, and a soupçon of obsession. One thing the three of us always shared was a love of dorking out over science fiction and superheroes, even when they were obsessing over sports and I was doing photography for the school newspaper."

"Gray!" The server at the counter shouted over the roiling din, sliding their pizza into a box.

Laughing Gray rose to retrieve their food. Returning, he laid the box on the table while Shepherd cracked his knuckles.

"Not counting a few dried apricots, I haven't eaten anything since 11:00 this morning, in Idaho," Shepherd said, "My stomach is gnawing on my backbone!"

The two men paused, each taking a moment to say a quiet grace.

Gray leaned back, letting the hot pizza cool a bit, "So, how far along are you on your Grand Tour?"

"Ahead of schedule, actually," Shepherd said, also content to let the pizza cool down a smidge, "After I dropped Martha off back in Virginia in early July, I pretty much knocked out everything east of the Rockies and in Canada."

"Did you ever find your great-great-great-grandparent's grave?" Gray asked, intrigued, "You mentioned in a blog post you wanted to go look after you and Martha found your great-great-grandparents' grave in Rhode Island."

"I found the graveyard," Shepherd said, a bit sad, "It's located in the cemetery of St. John the Baptist Parish Church in Roxton Falls, Quebec. Sadly, there're large sections where the old wooden markers have rotted away. Took a bit of digging, especially as I don't speak French and had to be coddled by some very sympathetic Quebecers, but I learned the last of the Shepherds left Roxton Falls over a hundred years ago, long after *my* branch of the family went south to Rhode Island."

Shepherd took a sip of his tea before continuing, "With no one to maintain the grave markers, they deteriorated, and I didn't have time to go through the old cemetery records to track down the exact location. That's something I'll have to do in the future."

Gray reached out, pulling a slice from the pizza, "I'm sorry. It must have been frustrating to be so close, yet still not find the actual graves."

"It's rare, and I mean *rare,* for wooden grave markers to last unless they're in an extremely dry climate," Shepherd said, grabbing a slice, "I actually found a couple in a Montana ghost town called Elkhorn, but that's the exception. Although Elkhorn gets more rain than Roxton Falls does, it's at a far higher—and therefore drier—elevation. The drier air preserves wood pretty decently."

"So, what's been your favorite place so far?" Gray asked, liberating another piece of pizza from the box.

"You *would* have to ask that!" Shepherd shook his head, leaning back in his seat. Another small cloud of dust poofed up from his jacket. "I *really* fell in love with Montana. Devil's Tower in Wyoming was freaking unbelievable. I think Martha and I could *both* happily settle in Portland, Maine. I don't know, Abe. It'll take a while for me to sort *that* question out!

"What's your deadline? November?" Gray asked before biting off another mouthful.

"Yep. My brothers and I's birthday is on November 8th, so that'll be the day I cross the state line into our native Texas—which will be state #50," Shepherd said, wiping his hands on a napkin before pulling another slice from swiftly-disappearing pizza.

"I saw you went to Hawaii with your folks in April. How's your grandmother?"

"Fading," Shepherd said, sadness etching his face, "She's pretty physically fit for a woman in her low 90s, but the dementia is taking its toll. It took her about three hours to remember me, and several times she thought Pop was Grandpa. She's in a good assisted care facility, and she's happy, but time and age are catching up to her."

"I'm sorry," Gray said consolingly, "My mom had dementia. I know the road your family is on."

Shepherd looked wistful, "Thanks. It's not easy."

Gray sighed, then shook his head, "Changing subjects to be a bit more cheerful, how are you getting to Alaska? Driving?"

"Flying out of Seattle, actually," Shepherd answered, a sly smile on his face, "That's why I was in Montana. I was going to hit Idaho, then head over to Seattle and stay with my brother there for a week before flying up to Anchorage to stay with my buddy, Hazy Payne, and his wife."

"Hazy still running that backcountry air service?" Gray asked.

"Mmm-hmmm," Shepherd nodded while he chewed. Bradley 'Hazy' Payne and Shepherd had known each other since their first Navy assignments back in 1998.

Swallowing, Shepherd took a sip of tea, "Glacier Air Pilots, or GAP. He's got twelve pilots working for him now. Since I shifted rudder to come here for this case, I'll fly up to Alaska when we're done. Then bounce back down to stay with A.J. and his family for a week before I start down into Oregon and lands further south."

Shepherd blinked, realizing something, "Hey, dude, I'm sorry! I forgot to ask—how was Sarah's oncology check-in?"

"Excellent," Gray smiled, leaning back, "Still cancer-free. Since it's been over twenty years, they told her she only needs to see her primary care doctor."

"Yeah," Shepherd said, again wiping his hands on his aggrieved napkin, "But, she'll insist on seeing the oncologist every five years or so anyway, right?"

Gray laughed, "She will, indeed! Sadly, she still wrestles with the fact she couldn't give me a son in addition to our daughters since she had to have the hysterectomy and chemo right after Rachel was born. It breaks my heart that she struggles with that because all *I* care about is that we *do* have children!"

"I know, old friend," Shepherd said, "It's not a rational thing, but we both know that 'emotional reality' and 'objective reality' don't always jibe—especially where parenting instincts are concerned."

"She always dreamed of watching her husband play ball with his boys *and* girls the way her father did with her and her brothers," Gray said, "She loved growing up that way. We *did* talk about adopting when the girls were still little, but we both agreed it wasn't feasible with her health in question for those years. Hell, I almost couldn't take that job in Spain because of her health issues, but she got medical clearance, and so we went. And then we met *you.*"

"And your life's been an exciting adventure ever since!" Shepherd laughed, "Personally, I'd hate to *not* be here. For one thing, I'd be bored silly if I weren't around. After all, I *am* the most extraordinary person I know. Good thing I'm so damned humble…"

Gray groaned, rolling his eyes in affectionate amusement at the old joke as they polished off the last of the pizza. Policing their table, they dumped their plastic cups into a recycle bin and consigned the pizza box to its fate in a rubbish bin.

"Come on, Mr. Humility, let's get to the hotel and get you checked in," Gray said wryly, straightening his tie, "I'm sorry to chuck you into the deep end, but we've got an early day tomorrow. I recommend you rack out after you peruse the case file summaries I'm going to give you."

"Sounds good."

"Oh, by the way, nice work in Kentucky!" Gray said.

Shepherd was startled, "Say *what?!* How in the *hell* do you know about that?! There wasn't *any* kind of federal involvement in that one!"

Gray laughed, thoroughly enjoying the rare chance to blindside the hyper-intelligent, quick-witted Shepherd, "The sheriff called Charlotte while you were helping him. You've got a genuine reputation in law enforcement, you know. He wanted to verify he had the *real* Accidental Detective assisting him, not some poser."

Shepherd laughed, "I know I have a rep, I just didn't expect it to precede me into tiny Kentucky towns! But, yeah—that was an interesting one. Like finding a needle in a haystack—or, rather, a body in a haystack since that's where the corpse was stashed!"

Chapter 9

Silverdale, Washington
Thursday, September 6, 2018; 06:00 hours

Gray stepped into the bustling marble lobby of the Viking Inn & Suites.

A convention must be getting set up to start, He thought, watching the bevy of busy beavers bustling busily about setting up seating and tables in the bright ballroom off the lobby.

An inordinate number of people wearing expensive suits and trailing expensive luggage stood impatiently at the check-in desk. With his own precisely pressed dark blue suit, brick-red tie, American flag lapel pin, and perfectly styled white hair, Gray fit right in.

Glancing at his watch, he was just wondering where the hyper-punctual Shepherd was when he spied a tall silhouette wearing a round-rimmed cowboy hat near the doors. The cut of the man's jib against the early morning light coming in the broad glass windows was instantly recognizable.

"Isaac!" Gray called just loud enough to be heard over the crowd.

Shepherd turned, stepping away from the window. As he moved, the backlighting faded and the lobby's overhead lights illuminated him.

Gray's eyes popped in surprise at the transformation Shepherd had undergone since the previous night.

The shaggy, salt-and-pepper hair had been severely cut back. Shepherd had shaved the sides close, leaving enough length to blend seamlessly with the now-neatly trimmed steel-gray beard.

Shepherd wore his familiar old brown corduroy sport jacket, but it was settled over a spiffy blue polo shirt. A white undershirt peeked out of the polo shirt's collar, creating a triangle of white fabric against which rested another staple of Shepherd's wardrobe—a small, round pewter necklace of an owl.

Stylish khaki pants encased his long legs, tapering down to a pair of brown leather cowboy boots, which clicked rhythmically on the tile floor as Shepherd walked over to the stunned Gray.

"Abe?" Shepherd asked, pulling the hat from his head. Even the top of his hair had been trimmed and shaped back to a reasonably civilized length, "You ok? You look like someone just stepped on your pet frog."

"Ah, no…I mean, yes. Yes, I'm fine," Gray said, laughing at himself, "I'm sorry. I just didn't expect you to clean up quite so much…or so fast. We got here pretty late yesterday; when did you have time to slip off to a barbershop?"

Shepherd laughed, "I didn't; I've been carrying electric clippers for a while now. I just hadn't *used* them for a month or two since I was off in the wilds. Took a while to clean up the mess in the bathroom, but I wasn't about to inflict *that* on the hotel's housekeeping staff!"

"Nice boots!" Gray said, looking down.

"Thanks," Shepherd said, "Got them in Dodge City, Kansas. Still getting used to them, but, so far, they're the only shoes I've had in years that fit so well I don't need orthotic inserts. For boots with a rigid sole, they're surprisingly comfortable to wear for long periods."

"Good!" Gray said, "Well, come on. There's an IHOP and a Starbucks down on the corner. Let's get breakfast, and I'll start bringing you up to speed. Trust me, there's at least one individual I need to warn you about. He's going to go ballistic once I introduce you, so I need you to be prepared."

"Dude, he won't be the first member of NCIS to get a professional wedgie up his butt when he sees me," Shepherd pointed out.

"Not like this," Gray said heavily, "David Kerr is a special piece of work."

* * *

"I WILL *NOT* ALLOW THIS…THIS UNQUALIFIED *HACK* TO INTERFERE WITH THE CASE!" Kerr roared, his voice so loud the office door rattled on its hinges. Kerr had bolted to his feet when Gray introduced Shepherd, his desk chair skidding backward from his eruption.

Shepherd sat quietly, legs crossed and hands folded in his lap. Content to merely observe the drama, he shifted his gaze to Gray, almost as if he were watching a tennis match.

"This man is no 'hack,' David!" Gray responded sharply, rising to his feet to meet Kerr face-to-face, "And, forgive me for pointing this out yet again, but my authority comes straight from the *director!* Frankly, you don't have a say in this matter!"

"This raging jerkoff has no business interfering with a federal investigation, and you know it!" Kerr bellowed, his face purple with abject rage. His finger stabbed the air in Shepherd's direction, "I don't care what you say, I will *not* allow my case to be jeopardized by some amateur asshole!"

"It's not your case, it's *mine,*" Gray snapped back, hands on his hips, "And while Isaac's qualifications might not have been conventionally obtained, you know full well he's assisted us on countless investigations over the past twenty years!"

"Just because he got lucky in Virginia helping you people out of your shortcomings doesn't mean I'll let him sully the reputation of *my* field office, Gray!"

Shepherd kept his mouth shut, tamping down the myriad of colorful responses his brain suggested. He preferred instead to study Kerr's body language. The man's reaction to his presence wasn't exactly unexpected, but he couldn't get past the impression Kerr's violent verbal vehemence was *seriously* out of proportion to the moment.

Letting his eyes scan the office, he noted the numerous awards from Kerr's Army Rangers days. Shepherd had researched Kerr a bit the night before. The man had been one of the Rangers' top snipers during those early dark days in Iraq back in the early

2000s. Kerr was repeatedly praised for his cool, icy demeanor under pressure.

The Silver Star alone testified to Kerr's glacial calm and steely nerves—especially considering he'd been awarded it after returning to the Middle East following a lengthy stay in the old Walter Reed Army Medical Center. The convalescence had been required after Kerr sustained multiple injuries in an IED attack in Baghdad.

So why is he reacting like a panic-stricken schoolboy who didn't do his homework? Shepherd wondered.

Scanning the desk, Shepherd noted its lethally clean efficiency, broken only by the ridiculously flamboyant name sign, traditional in-box, and a small plastic case of breath mints.

Eyes shifting upward, Isaac noted the three antique rifles proudly displayed above a bookshelf crammed with legal books and pictures of Kerr with various important and famous people. The décor and cleanliness screamed of a man who was cool and methodical—and full of himself.

And yet, here he is throwing a temper tantrum, Shepherd thought once again, still analyzing Kerr's unexpected behavior, *Shey Cremer is the only other NCIS agent I ever saw throw a tantrum about me, but* he *didn't scream, much less pound his desk like a spoiled toddler.*

"You have *no* idea who you're crossing, Gray!" Kerr screeched, "I have friends in Congress and the media that'll crucify you for bringing in some motherfucker whose dick is probably the size of a breath mint!"

"Well, now you know why your mom's breath is so minty fresh every morning," Shepherd said genially.

Kerr and Gray's argument crashed into the loudest silence Shepherd had heard in a very long time.

"What...did...you...say...?!" Kerr, overcoming his shock, turned slowly, growling dangerously at Shepherd.

Gray was staring at Shepherd, eyes bulging in abject surprise.

"Oh, I'm sure you heard me," Shepherd responded lightly. Since his retirement from active duty, the last vestiges of intimidation by government authority figures had evaporated. "I'm quite aware you're not happy with me being here, but I *am* here. We'll get on famously as long as *you* stop trying to assert yourself by the size of your cock."

Gray's face was a sickening gray color as he tried to process Shepherd's strategically ruthless counterattack.

Shock rendered Kerr entirely speechless.

Shepherd took advantage of Kerr's discombobulation to press his point home. Still sitting comfortably and casually, he cocked his head slightly to one side, "I'd also advise against you threatening Abe or myself with that 'media card' you mentioned. If you have any idea who *I* am, then you know *my* media contacts are *way* bigger than yours, just like my cock."

Gray rammed his brain back into gear, forcing his eyes away from Shepherd, "David, I'm sorry you're unhappy, but this is how things are. Isaac's here as my special consultant. You've deployed all your agents to other states, meaning you have to work all your local cases alone and can't offer me any assistance. Since Isaac was in the area, NCIS doesn't have to spend the money detailing someone else out here from Virginia."

Kerr's throat rattled dangerously, but Gray cut him off.

"We'll stay out of your way, don't worry," Gray said, regaining his poise, "But I need help if I'm going to bring the Tate case home properly. I appreciate you letting me work out of the small conference room. So, with introductions now made, we'll get out of here and go to work."

"You're going to be very unhappy you brought this…person…into this, Gray!" Kerr seethed venomously.

Gray shrugged, "I sincerely doubt it, but I hope you have a good morning nonetheless! Come on, Isaac."

Shepherd rose, turning to follow before stopping as if struck by a thought. Holding out a small, plastic box, he offered it to Kerr.

"Breath mint?" Shepherd asked, the picture of serene innocence.

"GET OUT!" Kerr screeched.

Calmly following Gray out of the office, Shepherd threw one last wink at Kerr before closing the door behind him. He was sure he heard Kerr once again slam his fist on his desk in anger.

Carol Keeters stared at the two men, frozen in shock. Kerr's voice had penetrated the office door, allowing her to hear every word he'd been shouting.

"I…ok…" Gray stammered as the two stood for a moment, struggling to find his voice, "Isaac, come on! Are you *trying* to start a fight?!"

"Abe, relax," Shepherd said firmly, while giving Keeters a reassuring smile, "I was curious as to how he'd react. His behavior towards me was *way* over the top—even by old Shey Cremer's standards. I mean, come on! The man reacted to me with all the panic of a desperate proctologist diving back in to retrieve a lost wedding ring!"

Gray flinched in spite of himself, a certain set of muscles down south on his body clenching hard as the picture penetrated his brain. Shaking his head to (unsuccessfully) erase that mental image, Gray looked back at Shepherd, "And how in the hell did you just *happen* to have a box of breath mints in your pocket at that precise moment?!"

Shepherd smiled puckishly, holding up the box of candies, "It's his. Swiped it off his desk when I stood up. Seemed like a good way to end the interview."

Keeters broke into a delighted laugh, the ringing sound driving the last hint of tension from her shoulders.

"Oh gevalt!" Gray ran a hand over his face as he turned, leading the way down the hall deeper into the field office building.

The two men entered the breakroom to make a cup of coffee. Gray rummaged through the cupboards to find a box of coffee pods for relocation to their shared conference room-turned-office.

Shepherd tossed the breath mint box onto the counter next to the coffee machine.

"Look, Isaac, I know you're not active duty anymore, but there's still a level of professionalism and decorum you need to maintain!" Gray admonished tightly.

"Oh, good grief! Abe, chill out, would you?!" Shepherd snapped, "I am *not* some naïve waif blundering around like a bull in a China shop! Besides, I just told you that there *was* a method to my madness. To be honest, I'd have thought my lengthy silence during Dr. Doom's tirade would have tipped you off to that!"

"Just remember that *I* still have rules I have to follow…and I still have to work with these people once you're back on your trip," Gray sighed, pouring himself a cup of coffee, "Still, I must concede that you *do* have a point. What did you conclude about David?"

Shepherd eyeballed Gray hard, clearly tempted to keep arguing his point, but instead shifted rudder to a different course, "For a man whose professional reputation was founded on a cool head and glacial nerves, Kerr's wound up tighter than a cheap watch. Granted his political protection has largely evaporated, but he reacted to *me* with a level of personal vitriol that makes little sense, seeing as he and I never met before today."

"I agree, and that both worries and confuses me," Gray said, sipping his black coffee while Shepherd poured cream into his cup, "I know I'm a threat to his political position—he was one of former Director Seldon's cronies, after all. But you're right—as soon as I said your name, he lit up like a firecracker. His reaction was *way* out of proportion to even what I expected."

"Exactly," Shepherd said, "He's behaving as if he has a *personal* vendetta against me. I mean, he's got a *Silver Star* for cool-headed actions in *direct combat,* and yet he's *completely* losing his crap over a special consultant."

Gray shook his head, finally allowing a chuckle to bubble up, "I have to admit, as many times as I've seen you verbally take someone down, I *was* caught off guard by your vulgarity! Usually, you're a bit more refined."

Shepherd laughed as he followed Gray out of the break room towards their conference room-turned-office, the box of coffee pods tight in Gray's hand, "Abraham, you forget that *I* learned how to be a sailor on a *flight deck!* I know a whole *hell* of a lot more colorful 'Navy-isms' than you can imagine!"

Entering the small conference room, Gray shut the door. Tossing the box of coffee pods onto the table by the Keurig machine, he beckoned Shepherd over to the safe. Gray began punching in a code on the keypad above the fingerprint reader.

"Ok, enter any six-digit PIN," Gray instructed, "When the light flashes yellow, enter it again, then press your thumb to the reader plate. When the light flashes green, your PIN and thumbprint will be recorded, and you'll have access to this safe."

Shepherd followed directions. The tiny computer controlling the safe's lock beeped, whirred, flashed, and finally granted him access. With a hefty metallic *clunk!* the safe popped open.

"Fancy!" Shepherd said, "The only safes I had access to when I was active duty used old-fashioned manual tumblers. I feel like I'm in a James Bond movie!"

Smiling in amusement, Gray reached in, pulling a hefty file folder from the safe. Gesturing Shepherd to the conference room table, he began disbursing the contents of the folder.

"Badge identifying you as a special consultant with full access to all relevant parts of this building," Gray said, "Here, give me your visitor badge and put this on instead."

Shepherd complied, removing the visitor badge that had been clipped to his jacket and replacing it with the access badge.

"Here's a certified copy of the letter naming you a special consultant signed by Director Belk himself," Gray said, handing a piece of heavy vellum paper to Shepherd. "You're authorized to request the same levels of access and information a badged agent can. However, you don't have the authority to detain anyone, nor make any arrests. I also can't issue you federal authorization to carry a weapon; I'm afraid you're subject to local state law on that one."

"No problem there," Shepherd said, "I prefer to rely on my rapier-like wit, anyway. Besides, you and Sarah still have my guns in your safe back in Virginia, and I ain't spending the money on a new 9mm just for this investigation."

"Can't argue with that," Gray smiled, "Sit down and get comfortable. Let me get you up to speed before we go meet Sheriff Sigo at 13:00."

Shepherd pulled out a chair, "Hold up a second—what about clearances? My security clearance is inactive now."

"Already covered," Gray said, pulling another massive pile of folders and material from the safe, "Your Top Secret/SCI clearance has been reactivated and updated."

"Top Secret/SCI?!" Shepherd was startled, "Abe, I haven't held *that* level of clearance since I ran the print shop at the Office of Naval Intelligence for a year, and *that* was, what…twelve years ago? I've only had a Secret clearance for most of my career. How'd you get my clearance reactivated without me doing a new SF-86 form, interviews…you know the drill."

Gray settled himself into a chair, a mischievous smile playing across his square-jawed face, "Isaac, the *director* of NCIS himself approved you as a special consultant. Do you *really* think he can't get you the clearance you'd need?"

"Good point."

"I contacted the FBI's Behavioral Analysis Unit once I was handed this assignment. That's the report they sent me," Gray handed Shepherd a hefty report.

Shepherd took the weighty tome.

TATE CASE PERSONALITY ANALYSIS

COMPILED BY

**FBI SPECIAL AGENT SHEY CREMER
BEHAVIORAL ANALYSIS UNIT**

Shepherd cocked an eyebrow at the name of the author, but otherwise nodded and set the report aside, "Thanks; I look forward to reading it!"

Gray laughed sympathetically, "Now, seeing as you were up late last night cutting your hair and researching David Kerr, can I assume you also gave a bit of thought to the case itself?"

"I did," Shepherd nodded, sipping his coffee, "I scanned the crime scene reports you provided. You're right; Sheriff Sigo is no slouch in the paperwork department. Her case files provided a very vivid description."

"So, anything strike you right off the bat?" Gray asked.

Shepherd sipped his coffee again. Replacing his cup, he leaned forward on his elbows, fingers steepled.

And Mr. Spock is once again on stage! Gray smiled fondly.

"This whole crime strikes me as *personal,*" Shepherd said, his voice smoothing out as he ramped up, "The level of violence—and the fact the attack was *in* the Tates' home—it was designed to inflict the maximum possible level of both physical *and* psychological pain. At least one of our suspects bears a pathological hatred for the very existence of one of the Tates, if not both of them."

Gray cocked his head as Shepherd continued.

"My gut instinct is that Young-Saeng Tate was *the* target, and Delores Tate is being set up as the fall guy…or fall girl, to be more linguistically precise," Shepherd said, "Of course, I could be wrong. Delores Tate could be the actual target, and Young-Saeng was tortured and killed in the marital bed to torment *her.* However, I don't think that was it."

"Why not?" Gray sipped his coffee.

"The roses," Shepherd said, fingers still steepled as he looked at Gray, "Young-Saeng was the rose guy. Delores Tate loved gardening, but she preferred cultivating annuals. The fact a *rose* was shoved into Young-Saeng's mouth post-mortem was a *very* personal and intimate act of desecration. The suspects also took

110

the time to *violently* destroy Young-Saeng's rose beds outside, but left the other flower beds alone."

Shepherd shifted in his chair, "Abe, I think this was aimed at Young-Saeng personally, and I think the campaign against Delores Tate is a distraction."

"And the Lionfish?"

"I believe the Lionfish was a crime of opportunity our suspects took advantage of, or else just a misdirection to confuse us. The fact the Kitsap police originally found the Tates' study intact, and then it was vandalized later after the police were on the scene—leads me to think it was...."

Shepherd shrugged, ramping up to his conclusion, "Abe, the campaign against Delores Tate is misdirection, but I also have the oddest feeling the Lionfish angle is just a red herring, too; the sequence of events is just too fishy for me to come to any other conclusion!"

Gray did his best to ignore the horrible puns. Reactions only encouraged Shepherd, and he certainly *didn't* need encouragement!

"You got all that from reading the summary files last night?" Gray asked instead.

"I did, so take it all with a grain of salt," Shepherd said.

"Interesting," Gray nodded, impressed.

"How so?"

"Well, first of all, I fully agree with your assessment of the Lionfish angle," Gray said, "I'm also convinced it was a crime of opportunity—if not an outright misdirection—the suspects took advantage of when it presented itself."

"You *do* realize what that means?" Shepherd's eyebrows went up.

"Yes. Someone in local law enforcement or local emergency medical services is involved," Gray said heavily. Shaking his head, he pointed to the report next to Shepherd, "The FBI got that report to me after I arrived, meaning it took them over a week to come up with an opinion that largely matches what *you* just laid out after only one night studying some file summaries."

"Score one for me!" Shepherd said lightly, "So, how do you want to play this?"

"I think we'd best play this as subtly as we can…even though getting *you* to do anything subtle is a tall order!"

Shepherd smiled, "Touché! Go on."

"I want you to focus on the actual murder," Gray said, "I'll handle the Lionfish angle. It'll raise a lot fewer questions if *I'm* the one going on board Keyport and *Gridley* to poke around the technical side of things. The Navy recovered and accounted for all the Lionfish paperwork in the Tate house, but that doesn't mean our suspect or suspects didn't photograph it or make copies of the digital files while they had access. The big dogs in the intelligence community are on that one already, but it'll help us greatly if I can get us some more gouge on the Lionfish itself."

"And you might just shake loose a few new leads in the process," Shepherd nodded thoughtfully, "Well, we've got a few hours until we meet with the sheriff. Let's go to work."

Gray began pulling out crime scene photos and enough paperwork to have felled a small forest.

"Ok, I'll get you up to speed before we break for lunch," Gray said, "After that, I'll drive you back into town so you can get your car. We'll caravan down to Sheriff Sigo's office in Bremerton, then split up after that for the rest of the day."

"Sounds good, Fred! I *love* splitting up and looking for clues as long as Scooby Snacks are involved!" Shepherd's eyes twinkled.

Gray's eyes rolled. Taking a deep, calming breath, he pushed away thoughts of demonstrating his sidearm, focusing instead on the case at hand.

Chapter 10
Port Orchard, Washington
Thursday, September 6, 2018; 13:33 hours

"…turning now to the Tate Murder in Washington State, Gippeum Lýkos, brother of the slain Young-Saeng Tate, demanded the Navy prosecute Tate's wife, Delores, for domestic abuse and murder. This comes as Lýkos also announced the death of his and Young-Saeng Tate's adoptive parents, Nico and Stephanie Lýkos. The Lýkoses were found dead in their Durham, North Carolina, home two days ago, their deaths attributed to chronic heart disease by the medical examiner…"

"Illinois Senator Justin Duryodhan introduced a non-binding motion to censure NCIS Director Kirby Belk. Speaking from the Senate floor, Duryodhan had this to say:

"Delores Tate was a known domestic abuser who has ties to questionable foreign nationals, yet the Navy disregarded this out of some misguided idea that Delores Tate's gender prevented any threat of legal ramifications. This political opportunism resulted in the death of a brilliant Navy civilian engineer and potentially compromises our national security…"

"…the entertainment world was stunned by the loss of actor Burt Reynolds, who passed away earlier today. Reynolds cemented his status as a leading man with the thriller *Deliverance* in 1972 and rocketed to superstardom playing the Bandit in the 1977 action/comedy *Smokey and the Bandit…*"

"Dr. Pounder will see you this afternoon, Isaac," Denita Sigo said, hanging up her phone before leaning back in her chair and plopping her booted feet back up on her desk, "If you can be there at 16:15, Dr. Pounder'll have some time available. She's normally pretty guarded, what with protecting patient privacy and all, but, since you're an NCIS consultant, *and* because I made the request, you shouldn't have any difficulty learning what you need."

"Swell!" Shepherd said, crossing his legs as he shifted his weight, "I appreciate the effort!"

"You can thank Abe," Sigo said pointedly, "I've never had an easy working relationship with David Kerr, but these past few weeks made me begin to question *all* NCIS agents. Abe has restored some of my faith."

"He has a habit of doing that," Shepherd laughed, playfully popping Gray on the shoulder with his fist. Gray rolled his eyes as Shepherd went on, "I understand your office suffered a loss a couple of weeks ago as well?"

"One of my interns was shot and killed up in Port Gamble," Sigo nodded heavily, "We think she was hit in a hunting accident. A stray bullet nailed her in the head while she was driving."

"Abe said she was the one who leaked your files to the press," Shepherd said, "Do you have any indication her death was connected to the Tate case?"

"No," Sigo said, "What makes you say that?"

Shepherd shrugged, "The timing of her death in proximity to her leaks caught my eye. I'm probably just being paranoid."

"He's good at that!" Gray laughed, standing up, "Ok, I have to run. I've got a meeting on board Keyport in forty-five minutes."

Shepherd glanced at his watch, "I've got one with Delores Tate in a few myself. After that, I'll drive over to the clinic and meet with Dr. Pounder. Tate's got a civilian lawyer, right?"

"Correct," Gray said, "And she's extremely hostile, so watch your back. I'd strongly recommend you *don't* unleash your unrestrained wit right off the bat. Discretion is often the better part of valor, along with sometimes putting a cork in your humor."

"Ok, Dad," Shepherd quipped, his voice carrying the slightest hint of irritation as he stood. Reaching out to shake Sigo's hand, he smiled, "Denita, thanks for your help."

Returning his handshake, Sigo dropped her booted feet from the desk and stood, "Isaac, it's been a pleasure. Sgt. Boothe will meet you out front and escort you over to the corrections facility. One last thing—I actually *have* heard of you, but, to be honest, it wasn't anything good. Still, most of those opinions came from David Kerr, and I'm learning his judgment is not the most reliable."

"I'm not surprised," Shepherd shrugged, straightening his brown corduroy sport coat, "Nor can I blame a lot of NCIS personnel for being unhappy the way I used to waltz in. I wasn't exactly the most graceful of amateur detectives."

"I think a more accurate description is that you're about as subtle as a hand grenade in a barrel of oatmeal," Gray said, eyes twinkling.

"Hey, that's *my* line!" Shepherd laughed, "Go come up with your own!"

The desiccated skeleton that was Navy Lieutenant Commander Delores Tate rattled through the door into the interview room, bones clattering underneath sagging skin that was itself largely hidden under sagging red prison coveralls. The dark circles entombing her eyes were so glaringly stark they looked like some goth teen had spilled black eyeliner all over Tate's face. The slack-jawed expression marring her visage was but a darkly ironic parody of a human face.

In short, the woman looked like hell. Shepherd noted the vacant expression in the dull, plastic eyes peering from Tate's emaciated skull. She moved robotically, as if on autopilot.

Behind her, Amanda Pile towered in her power suit consisting of a burgundy skirt, burgundy flats, light burgundy blouse, and, finally, a dark burgundy blazer that wrapped her body in a neon sign proclaiming her force of personality. Even her briefcase was burgundy.

Someone ought to tip her off that she's not nearly as adept at carrying off that look as Margaret Thatcher was, Shepherd thought, keeping his face straight as he rose from the bare metal chair he'd been waiting in.

"Commander Tate," Shepherd nodded a kindly and, he hoped, disarming greeting as Tate was directed to a seat opposite Shepherd, "Thank you for agreeing to speak with me. I am so sorry for the loss of your husband, and, while it's a grotesque understatement, I can only say I know this is a very difficult time for you."

Tate didn't acknowledge Shepherd's comment.

She's almost catatonic, Shepherd thought, mildly alarmed. *Shit. She's been through the wringer so bad I don't think she knows I'm here right now.*

"What do you want, Special Agent Shepherd?" Pile snapped impatiently, "I want it on record that my client is meeting with you against my recommendation. I told her the only NCIS person she should speak to is that Gray asshole since he's in charge of this farce now."

Two thousand witty, biting, and sarcastic retorts zipped across Shepherd's mind, but he forcibly talked himself off the ledge.

She's on our side, He reminded himself, *And, truth be told, she has every right to be hostile.* Someone *with a great deal of power is targeting her client.*

"I understand your feelings, Counselor," Shepherd said, holding out a hand to her, "And I truly do sympathize. To use a ridiculously inadequate verbal shorthand, something is rotten in Denmark, and the commander here seems to be the target of at least part of it. I'd be worried if you *weren't* enraged by it all."

"Spare me your insipid platitudes, Agent Shepherd!" Pile snapped, refusing to shake hands, "This case has been railroaded into the mud by myopic twits like you and the other NCIS assholes out to blame my client for an offense she never committed."

Shepherd dropped his hand, an affable smile remaining on his face, but his temper percolating uncomfortably.

Stay cool…stay cool…stay cool…

116

Still, a *little* humiliation might just cool her jets long enough for him to get past the rocky introductions.

"Again, I understand your concerns, Counselor," Shepherd said, straightening his bifocals, "One minor note of correction, however. I'm a civilian special consultant brought in to review the case, not an agent. Reading Special Agent Gray's request for this interview in detail would've clued you into that not-so-obscure fact."

Pile's mouth dropped open in shock.

Shepherd ignored her, sitting down and folding his hands on the table. His eyes met Tate's, the level of pain and confusion in the disgraced officer's vision breaking his heart.

"Commander, please allow me to properly introduce myself," Shepherd said easily. "My name is Isaac Shepherd. I'm a retired chief petty officer currently engaged as an objective special consultant to review your case. Special Agent Gray believes there's a conspiracy out there aimed against you."

Pile dropped her briefcase. The interview room briefly resounded with its thumping impact on the floor before the lawyer hastily bent down, scooping it back up.

Shepherd ignored her.

"I'm here as a personal representative of NCIS Director Kirby Belk," Shepherd continued, "I have to advise you that I am *not* a law enforcement officer. I'm simply a Navy retiree with specialized training and previous experience enabling me to act as a special consultant. I promise *nothing* except that I'll do my utmost to get to the bottom of this. I'm not a magician or a lawyer; just a consultant."

Pile finally sat down next to her client, her face as slack as Tate's, "You're not...you're not an agent? But David Kerr said—"

"I'm sure Special Agent Kerr misspoke by accident," Shepherd smoothly deflected, "He's under a great deal of pressure at the moment."

Tate still hadn't spoken, but her face had taken on a slight resemblance to that of a living human being.

Pile shook her head, as if trying to clear her thoughts, "Wait, let me get this straight. *Special Agent Gray* brought you in? On behalf of the NCIS *director?"*

"That's correct, Counselor," Shepherd confirmed before returning his gaze to Tate.

"You…" Tate's voice sounded hoarse, like two steel rasps grinding together, "You…believe me…?"

"I do," Shepherd said, "My sole objective is The Truth with a capital 'T.' Having reviewed all the case evidence, I firmly believe that capital 'T' points towards your innocence."

Tate looked at Pile. Shepherd was gratified to see the lawyer's fire-and-steel persona softening into a human countenance of compassion as she met her client's eyes. Laying a gentle hand on her arm, she smiled lightly at Tate.

"Let's see what Agent…, I'm sorry, I mean, what Mr. Shepherd wants to know."

"So…you were a chief?" Tate's dull, grief-torn eyes finally seem to focus on him.

"I was, indeed," Shepherd nodded. "Believe it or not, I understand much of what you're going through right now."

"How can you?!" Tate's eyes flashed with blazing anger, the first emotion Shepherd had seen from her, "You're not sitting in here being accused of killing…of killing…your own…husband!"

Tate suddenly rose, leaning on the rickety table with quivering arms as her voice spiraled upward into a hysterical wail, "You haven't been lied about all over TV! You don't have everyone you care about being harassed by the media and Navy authorities! *You aren't facing spending the rest of your life in this shithole with asshole guards and freaks fucking themselves with toilet brushes in the goddamned cell next to you every fucking night!"*

Tate collapsed onto the metal table, sobs erupting from her with volcanic velocity. Pile laid an arm across Tate's shoulders as the officer wept. Tate's wrenching cries echoed around the concrete room like a sonic tsunami, ringing in Shepherd's ears.

Shepherd waited quietly, fighting back an emotional storm. The problem with being an empathic person meant Shepherd experienced the emotional pain of others with startling clarity.

Taking a breath, he forced himself to stay in the 'now.' Once Tate had calmed down and blown her nose, Shepherd took a breath.

"Commander, I *did* sit in your place once, long ago. I was falsely accused of murdering my own shipmates back in '99 and nearly railroaded into prison by some very powerful people, including an admiral," Shepherd explained, "Special Agent Gray apprehended the real killers and got me out of that mess."

Pile flinched in surprise, knocking her briefcase off the table. It hit the deck with a sizable *whump!*

"Commander, may I ask you some questions now?" Shepherd asked, seeing that Tate was calming down.

Tate glanced at Pile. Pile nodded approvingly before reaching down to retrieve her briefcase again.

"I know you've been through this at length already, but I have to do my job properly," Shepherd said, noting the corrections officer outside the interview room door was staring in, apparently on edge after Tate's emotional breakdown.

"Go ahead," Tate said, her voice still raspy, but carrying the oddest note of hope this time. She reached up, brushing her lank hair out of her eyes. Shepherd imagined her hair possessed a lustrous sheen when properly cared for.

"I've reviewed Agent Gray's interviews with your commanding officer, XO, wardroom, etc.," Shepherd said, deliberately using the information to calm Tate's jangled nerves, "Your captain has nothing but great things to say about you. Same with the XO. Both declare you're a model officer, and both expect you to take command of a ship in a few years. Frankly, everything *everyone* aboard *Gridley*—officer and enlisted—says about you indicates you're a thoroughly professional naval officer at the top of her game."

Tate's eyes cleared a bit more as she took in the first accolades she'd heard about herself in weeks.

Shepherd pulled a notebook and pen from inside his jacket, "We *are* in a non-secure facility, so I'll keep my questions about the Lionfish project pretty nonspecific. Was it normal for Young-Saeng to bring paperwork home?"

Tate nodded, "It was. *Gridley* was the test bed for the Lionfish, but the safe in our study was all his. Even though *Gridley* was testing the drone and its components, my clearance didn't authorize me to see much of its development details. You remember how all that works, don't you?"

"I do," Shepherd said, "A clearance only allows you access if your job requires you to have access. Did Young-Saeng work from home a lot, or just occasionally?"

"It was kind of a 50-50 thing," Tate said, her energy level low again, "He'd often work from home like a lot of engineers, so the study was set up as a secure office for him when he needed it."

"Do you know of any data breaches, or other security threats, that compromised, or threatened to compromise, the Lionfish?" Shepherd asked, pen flying over the pad using a personal shorthand he'd developed during his days racing to take notes at Florida State University.

"No," Tate shook her head.

"Ok, thank you for that! Now, moving on to another aspect of this investigation…I have a meeting later this after with a Dr. Donna Pounder, director of a free clinic here in Bremerton," Shepherd said, "Dr. Pounder says she treated your husband numerous times for injuries consistent with domestic abuse, and—"

"I *never* fucking hurt him!" Tate roared, nearly shooting to her feet again.

"Delores, calm down. He's not accusing you of doing so," Pile said, shooting an evil look at Shepherd, one that said he'd damn well better *not* make such an accusation.

Shepherd remained unfazed. He simply continued his sentence as if nothing had happened, "…and yet I believe Young-Saeng's records from the naval hospital indicated no such injuries ever happened. Unfortunately, a data crash at the hospital wiped out his records. Do you have any idea how such a discrepancy could have occurred?"

"N-no, but we have a spare copy of his and my medical records," Tate said, a tear slipping down her emaciated face.

"Say what?" Shepherd was startled.

"We made a habit of keeping an updated copy of our medical records," Tate explained.

Pile looked askance at Tate for a moment, but then her expression softened again. Looking back to Shepherd, Pile took a breath, "I'd recommended Delores keep that under wraps because I intended to drop it like a ton of bricks on that asshole's...on Kerr during discovery when this goes to trial."

Shepherd remained quiet, waiting patiently.

Pile resigned herself to Tate's disclosure of the medical records' existence. "The Tates kept a copy of their Navy medical records with their tax records and mortgage paperwork in a safe-deposit box at the Navy Federal Credit Union branch in Silverdale."

Shepherd didn't react outwardly. There was still one potential hurdle...

"Commander," Shepherd looked at Tate, "How recent are these copies? If they're more than a month or two old, I'm afraid that won't help us in the present."

"Young-Saeng picked them up from the Bremerton Naval Hospital two weeks before he..." Tate choked on a sob.

Only two weeks before the murder! Shepherd was silently jubilant, *This could be our first hard evidence against Kerr's narrative!*

"With your permission—and with your counselor present, of course," Shepherd nodded at Pile, "May I photocopy those medical records? If so, I'll get the necessary paperwork to Ms. Pile by this afternoon, tomorrow morning at the latest."

"I'll make and hand off the copies to you," Pile cut in, her voice dangerous, "I'll be damned if more of my client's

paperwork 'mysteriously' vanishes in a conveniently timed data breach. I'm quite aware someone is also trying to create a fictitious picture of Delores' financial affairs!"

"That's another reason I agreed to take this case," Shepherd responded casually, using the opening to further disarm Pile's arsenal, "The convenient timing of the data breaches affecting the commander's medical *and* financial history are just too coincidental to be real, in my opinion. The fact that we have a recent copy of the *Navy's* medical records will also go a long way in establishing the falsity of the financial accusations."

Pile looked over to Tate, "Delores, this is your decision, but I recommend you agree to this request."

"As long as you make the copies, Amanda," Tate said before turning back to Shepherd, "Ok. You can have them."

"Thank you," Shepherd said without hesitation, "If y'all can excuse me for a moment, I need to make a phone call so we can get that moving. Please give me a moment."

"Sure," Pile said after Tate nodded her assent.

Shepherd left the room. Tate and Pile sat quietly until he returned a few moments later.

"Counselor, you'll be getting the formal request from Carol Keeters, senior executive assistant at the NCIS office, within the hour. Now," Shepherd turned his attention back to Tate, "I understand you and Young-Saeng kept to yourselves. Y'all never had anyone over to your house, Young-Saeng never attended any command functions with you; even his coworkers at Keyport largely didn't know you lived in Silverdale. Y'all have no social media presence at all. No Facebook, LinkedIn, Instagram…nothing. Why not? Why so private?"

"We thought it was safer that way."

"Safe from what?" Shepherd asked. Noting a particular twitch in Tate's eyebrow, Shepherd had a hunch, "More to the point, safe from *whom?"*

Tate's mouth clamped shut. Looking away, she shook her head.

"Commander," Shepherd said, calling upon his best firm, but fair, 'chief petty officer voice' from his Navy days, "Commander, I need to know what *you* think if I'm going to be of any help at all. *Who* were you and Young-Saeng trying to hide from?"

Tate looked at Pile, who nodded encouragingly.

Tate swallowed, apparently coming to a decision. She looked up, fully meeting Shepherd's eyes for the first time.

"Gippeum. He's been trying to kill Young-Saeng ever since he killed their other brother when they were kids."

Chapter 11
Port Orchard, Washington
Thursday, September 6, 2018; 14:32 hours

"Why do you suspect Gippeum?" Shepherd asked calmly, betraying no surprise, shock, or disbelief. In fact, he was rather proud of himself for *not* dropping his pen in surprise.

Hell, it ain't like I haven't seen family kill family before, Shepherd thought, waiting for Tate to answer.

"You don't seem phased by my client's accusation, Mr. Shepherd," Pile said.

"I've seen worse, believe me," Shepherd said to Pile before returning his attention to Tate, "Commander, your brother-in-law has been all over the news leveling accusations at you. I'm assuming you have more to base *your* accusation on than simply being pissed at him."

"Young-Saeng, Gippeum, and Su-Jin are—were—identical triplets. All three were adopted by Nico and Stephanie when they were infants," Tate's voice clawed its way out of her emaciated throat, "The Lýkos were stationed in Korea at the time. The birth parents were destitute and couldn't afford to raise triplets, so they gave them up for adoption. After Nico retired from the Air Force, they settled back in Durham. I went to high school with the two boys who survived. That's where I met them."

"If you don't mind, please tell me what happened to the third brother, and why you suspect Gippeum," Shepherd asked. From Tate's expression, he realized she was used to people dismissing this particular item out of hand. However, he stared hard at her, his body language telegraphing just how seriously he took her beliefs.

"Their third brother, Su-Jin was killed in a car wreck when they were 13," Tate said, her voice firming up a bit as she realized Shepherd was indeed truly listening to her, "Their mother, Stephanie, was badly injured, but survived. The brakes failed, and the investigators suggested the vehicle was sabotaged, but they had no suspects. Well, none they bothered to look at because they were so fucking caught up in their own ideas."

"So why do you suspect Gippeum?" Shepherd asked, gently redirecting her back on topic.

Tate sighed, "By the time we were in high school, we all *knew* Gippeum had done it because of the things he said, and the things he didn't say, if that makes any sense. Before the crash, he had been under the car 'examining' it, but Young-Saeng caught him coming back into the house with brake fluid all over his shirt. Their parents didn't believe Young-Saeng for a second. The next day he *begged* his mother and Su-Jin not to go run errands, but they did and the brakes went out."

"That's pretty compelling at face value," Shepherd nodded, "But I suspect you have more than that?"

"During high school and college, Gippeum continually made snide remarks he played off as sarcasm that he was already halfway to inheriting the Lýkos' small estate. Whenever someone mentioned Young-Saeng would get half, Gippeum always smirked and said that Young-Saeng might not live long enough to see it."

"That *is* interesting," Shepherd nodded, notes spilling from his pen into the notebook, "I'm going to run that one down. What else can you tell me about how the boys grew up."

"Their parents seemed to become increasingly frightened of Gippeum as they got older. We were all afraid of him as we got older. He was just never quite…quite right in the head," Tate said, shrugging, "But he seemed to get away with everything he did. Muffin, the Lýkos' golden retriever, was found dead and skinned in the backyard. Gippeum joked he wanted to see 'how she worked,' but denied killing her. Money would go missing from Mrs. Lýkos' purse, and the next day Gippeum would magically have some new electronic gadget or expensive clothing item. The Lýkos stopped having company over whenever Gippeum was home because guests would always 'mysteriously' get sick."

"Wow," Shepherd shook his head in disbelief, "I'm surprised he didn't just freak people out from the way you describe him."

Tate sighed again, her form sagging into itself a trifle, "Sometimes he did, Chief. Kids at school were always staying away from him because he was just…he just gave off this weird, creepy vibe. But around adults—it was like he shifted into a whole other personality that was charming and fun and witty. It was like living in a *Twilight Zone* episode; all the kids knew he was a fucktard of a freak, but all the adults seemed convinced he was a complete little angel."

"I've seen that psychology before," Shepherd said, pen still moving at warp speed across his notebook. Shaking his head slightly to refocus his thoughts, he inhaled a deep breath, then looked back up, "Let's move on to the boys' education."

"All three boys were flat-out geniuses," Tate said, "Su-Jin died when they were 13, but Young-Saeng and Gippeum were accepted into Mensa when they were fourteen. You know Mensa—that genius club?"

"I am familiar with them, yes," Shepherd said, not mentioning his own brothers were members, even though he wasn't interested in joining the organization.

"We attended Fire Ridge Polytechnic High in northern Durham," Tate said, "It's a technical school for gifted students to prepare them for STEM careers."

"Go on," Shepherd encouraged.

"I'm gifted, but I'm not on Young-Saeng and Gippeum's level," Tate said, "There's a reason Young-Saeng was the youngest man to ever lead a major research and development project at Keyport."

"Do you think Gippeum was jealous?" Shepherd asked.

"Gippeum is a complete *psychopath!*" Tate snapped, the acid from her voice burning holes in the metal table, "When Young-Saeng and I started dating in high school, Gippeum tried to impersonate his own brother to bang me—and this from a man who was actually gay! *That* incident nearly resulted in *me* being arrested for an alleged sexual assault until Young-Saeng provided proof Gippeum was lying. Not only did their parents not do anything, but they also kept the police out of it!"

"I see," Shepherd nodded, intrigued. *She says he's gay, but used a pretty convoluted scheme to try and bang her. Either he's bi, or else he's such a psycho he'd bed someone just to put a trophy on his mental wall...*

"Gippeum could always figure out how to destroy somebody if he wanted to, whether because he didn't like them or just because he thought it'd be funny," Tate said, "He could hack into a database and fuck up your entire life—finances, school records, whatever. He once got in and destroyed Young-Saeng's grades in physics. Never got caught, be we knew it was him from his endless boasting. Young-Saeng was only saved because Gippeum, although smart, was inexperienced. He neglected to wipe the backup server."

Tate shook her head before continuing, "He's a master manipulator. He...he just knows how to *get* to people. Gippeum got their parents so convinced I was a predator that I was nearly arrested again when I was 17. Young-Saeng and I had to stop seeing each other until we were both in college. As soon as we graduated, we eloped and got the hell away from that maniac!"

Tate shook her head, "Most people never believed us about that *mi-chin-nom* once they met Young-Saeng."

"Beg pardon," Shepherd held up a hand, "Me-chin-*what?*"

"Sorry, Chief," Tate said, "It's a Korean expression. 'Roughly translates to 'crazy bastard.'"

"I see," Shepherd nodded, "Please, continue."

"Well, because they were identical, everyone assumed Gippeum would be as compassionate as Young-Saeng...or else that Young-Saeng was just as...as *evil* as Gippeum," Tate said miserably.

"I know the problem," Shepherd said, "I have two brothers— and we're identical triplets as well. All three of us keep having to remind people we're only identical in appearance, not personality. Now, I'm guessing you and Young-Saeng became so well-guarded to keep Gippeum as far away from you as possible?"

"Yes," Tate said, bloodshot eyes glistening with new tears, "Young-Saeng had *zero* illusions about his brother. That *mi-chin-nom* could talk his way out of *anything.* Young-Saeng knew how to keep our location and movements off the radar, but we always lived in fear that his brother would find us. Young-Saeng even took my name when we married to help keep our location secret."

"You said before that Gippeum tried to kill Young-Saeng when they were kids," Shepherd's eyebrows went up, "Could you elaborate on that?

"Sure. He tried to drown Young-Saeng in the pool when they were toddlers," Tate explained, "Gippeum said he was curious about what happens when you breathe water. He later hit Young-Saeng with the family car when they were 16. Said he 'accidentally' hit the accelerator instead of the brakes. Young-Saeng suffered a broken femur from that 'accident.'"

"Ouch!" Shepherd flinched involuntarily at the image of the largest, strongest bone in the human body being snapped in two.

"Oh, it gets better, Chief Shepherd," Pile said, picking up on Tate's use of Shepherd's old rank, "Go on, Delores."

Tate nodded, "A boy at Fire Ridge High had been harassing both Young-Saeng and Gippeum our sophomore year. That little fuck was a straight-up asshole, but he didn't deserve to die. About a month after the bullying began, he took a drink from his water bottle during the chemistry class he shared with Young-Saeng and Gippeum, and died violently from an extreme overdose of water hemlock poisoning."

Shepherd did his best to prevent another flinch from twitching his form. Early the previous year, *he'd* nearly been poisoned by a suspect who tried to use water hemlock on him. Tragically, another sailor had died instead, with Shepherd witnessing the whole gory scene.

Tate was still talking, "Just before that happened, Gippeum had gone to the cabinet where they stored their things to get a drink from *his* bottle. There just happens to be a pond near the Lýkos' house where water hemlock flourishes."

Tate's breath was coming faster now as she recalled the traumatic memories, "Somehow, though, the police 'investigators' didn't even *talk* to Gippeum, even after being told by numerous students—and Young-Saeng himself—that Gippeum had *repeatedly* made open threats to kill that bully."

"And their parents did nothing?"

"I told you, Chief—I think the Lýkos were *terrified* of Gippeum," Tate said, her eyes flashing in anger, "It really started after the dog was skinned and Su-Jin was killed. Those people *knew* what kind of monster that *mi-chin-nom* was, but they were too fucking scared to *do* anything!"

"I see," Shepherd nodded, intrigued. *Even if Gippeum doesn't have anything to do with* this *murder, he's still a raging psycho!*

"I'm sorry to be blunt, Commander," Shepherd looked up from his notes, "I have to ask—do you have any specific, hard evidence Gippeum committed *this* current atrocity?"

Tate deflated with a visible sound of dried leaves being crushed underfoot.

"If I did I wouldn't be in this shithole, but that *gesekgi* has set me up again," Tate said, shoulders falling to the region of her abdomen.

"Another Korean expression, I assume?" Shepherd asked.

"Yes, sorry. It means 'son of a bitch,'" Tate explained.

"Fitting," Shepherd raised a single eyebrow as he jotted down the expression.

"I think he's going to win everything this time," Tate said despairingly, hopelessness filling up her broken voice, "He's already killed my husband. Now he's out to destroy me. He won."

Shepherd's heart was breaking as he watched Tate fall apart again, the sobs echoing around the small room. Pile put an arm around Tate's shoulder again as she sobbed for a few minutes before regaining her composure.

"Commander," Shepherd said, shoving his empathy aside and focusing on the job at hand, "I'm very sorry I have to ask this, and please forgive me for being blunt, but how do you respond to the allegations of an extramarital affair with a William Smith over in Tacoma?"

"You mean that asshole bartender at the pool hall?!" Tate nearly laughed hysterically, "Yeah. Right. Even if I did cheat on Young-Saeng, it wouldn't be with a dick who wants to get into the pants of every woman in the state!

"I see you don't have a high opinion of him," Shepherd said wryly.

Tate fell into a fit of disbelieving laughter so staccato in its intensity her spittle flew across the table, spattering Shepherd's glasses.

"That asshat gave *two* of my junior sailors chlamydia back in June!" Tate said, finally recovering herself, "And that was just *Gridley!* Last year he accused a female officer on *Nimitz* of rape! The only thing that saved *her* was the sex tape they'd made showing it was all consensual. The only reason I know Smith is because my pool club meets at Baker Street Billiards where he works. That cocksucker isn't *half* the man Young-Saeng was!"

Shepherd casually took off his glasses, subtly wiping the lenses. Replacing them, he glanced at his watch, "Unfortunately, I have to head to my other appointment. Commander, I'm very grateful for your time, and I am so sorry for your loss. For what it's worth, you have my word that Special Agent Gray and I both are proceeding under the assumption you're innocent *unless* proven guilty by the evidence in court."

Isaac Shepherd had peered into the abyss of human evil as many times as the average person changes socks in a year. He might have been horrified, enraged, and saddened by what he saw, but he was never disturbed. He could stand in the middle of a crime scene and make corny jokes about lending a hand while holding a plastic bag containing the victim's severed appendage.

He could easily deliver dumb quips in the face of violent adversaries threatening him with a firearm.

The Bremerton Free Clinic, however, stirred up the one weakness his stomach always suffered from—people struggling with barely a medical resource to call upon.

The clinic, housed on the first floor of the old King Textile Building on Park Avenue and 6th Street, provided medical support to the poor and underserved in the Bremerton area. The waiting room screamed of despair and desperation with people who were homeless, drug addicts bearing railroad tracks up their arms, and women who were clearly domestic abuse victims trying to hide the bruises on their downcast faces.

The sea of broken humanity was overwhelming. Shepherd tried his best to disappear into the floor in the back corner of the dimly lit waiting room.

The King Building itself was a bizarre collision of worlds. The old structure's upper floors housed the local offices of Seagull Electronics Alternatives and Derecho Aviation. The engineers and technicians made their way to their floors via a separate lobby and elevator added to the historic structure back in the early 1980s. There was no denying the clashing contrast of their suits and ties with the rumpled clothes of the poor and indigent entering the ground floor through the 19th-century textile plant's original doorway.

I'm no fan of socialized medicine, Shepherd thought, *But there's got to be a better way than what we're doing now...*

"Mr. Shepherd?" The nurse at the front desk called quietly, "Dr. Pounder will see you now. Tiffany here will escort you back to her office."

Pulling his thoughts back to the present, Shepherd pulled his 6'4" frame from the chair, his legs hefting him forward. Stepping gingerly through the sea of dilapidated humanity, Shepherd was aghast to see several women—each holding either an infant or small child—recoil slightly in fear as he passed by, his large body clearly a symbol of masculine evil to the poor mothers.

God, I'd love a chance to spend a few minutes in a soundproof room with men who think it's cool to beat up women. I have a hammer I'd like to introduce to their faces...

Refocusing his thoughts, he reached the receptionist's desk. Tiffany was a small-boned Asian woman wearing faded blue scrubs. She looked at him as if he'd run over her mother. He greeted her pleasantly, but she simply jerked her head, indicating him to follow her. He allowed her to guide him back through the labyrinth created by the haphazard renovations done on the King Building throughout the years.

Erected in 1892, the structure originally housed King Textiles and Fabrics. The historic building retained the tile floor and overhead pulleys from the earlier century that had once been attached to belts powering the factory's equipment.

The clinic itself was funded by the non-profit Rose Percy Foundation, 'funding' being a barely adequate term. Like many nonprofits, the foundation relied heavily on private donations to supplement the foundation's trust, but finances were always like walking a tightrope.

The clinic was appropriately clean, the medical equipment gleaming with sterile beauty, but it was all second-hand. A third of the overhead lights in the hallway were either out, or else flickering toward their demise. Shepherd suspected the chipped linoleum floor was the original from 1892, but it was as yellowed from age and abuse as were the formerly white tiles lining the walls.

The hallway smelled of antiseptic and alcohol, but the ancient stains along the corridor evoked the smell of stale cigarette butts and laborers from a bygone age sweating under oppressive conditions.

Shepherd assumed the upper three floors housing Seagull Electronic Alternatives and Derecho Aviation were in better shape. However, down here, the decrepit hallways reeked of a building largely forgotten by most of the city's busy residents, if not by time itself.

Thank God they at least adhere to sterilization standards! Shepherd thought. *All this place needs is a little blood spatter to look like a bad remake of* Hellraiser!

Tiffany knocked on a threadbare wooden door. The door creaked, sounding like it was one step away from falling into splinters. Poking her head in, Tiffany finally spoke, "Dr. Pounder? Mr. Shepherd is here to see you."

A muffled voice responded, leading Tiffany to step back, glaring at Shepherd as she said, "Go in, but be quick about it. Dr. Pounder still has several patients to see."

Shepherd stepped past Tiffany into the old office. He was again struck by the contrast of the cleanliness of everything compared to its ancient age. The door creaked wearily again as Tiffany left, closing it behind her.

Dr. Donna Pounder rose to greet Shepherd...and rose and rose and rose.

Pounder was the tallest woman Shepherd had ever met. Towering at least half a head taller than him, he guessed she clocked in at an altitude of 6'9" tall.

Finding clothes must be a nightmare for her! The thought involuntarily raced across Shepherd's head.

"Mr. Shepherd," Pounder said holding out her large hand, her soprano voice was surprisingly delicate for such a large woman. Shepherd had expected a baritone.

"Doctor, thank you very much for your time," Shepherd said, taking her hand. Her hand enveloping Shepherd's, he nodded up to her, "I know you're busy, and I promise to keep this as short as possible."

"Thank you. Please, sit," Pounder gestured to the wooden chair across the desk from her. It looked like it was made around 1780.

Shepherd sat, fighting to keep a look of shock off his face as he realized he still had to look *up* at Pounder even after she returned to her seat. He reckoned she got reactions like this all the time, and he was determined to be the exception.

133

"I understand you're here to discuss Young-Saeng Tate," Pounder said.

"I am," Shepherd nodded, "Before we begin, did you receive the authorization paperwork from the county clerk, ma'am?"

"I did, and I will do my best to comply," Pounder said, "But, you have to understand our mission here includes protecting patient privacy. Most of our patients try very hard to stay under the radar, and some are hiding in fear for their lives. I understand Young-Saeng was murdered, but I have my own guidelines to follow, so please be advised I can only assist you in the most narrow limits allowed by law."

"I fully understand, and I appreciate your position," Shepherd said, noting the dark circles under Pounder's eyes and the slightly uneven haircut. She was exhausted and overworked, even by nonprofit standards.

"May I ask what your involvement in this is?" Pounder said, picking up her coffee mug and draining it. "You're not an agent or police officer. So, who are you?"

Keep it short, you long-winded jackalope, Shepherd thought sternly to himself.

"I've assisted NCIS—and specifically Special Agent Gray—numerous times over the past twenty years," Shepherd said, "I have a specialized level of training and field experience that enables me to approach difficult cases from a unique angle."

"So, you're saying NCIS is incompetent?" Pounder asked pointedly, her eyes locking onto Shepherd's eyes. "Based on my interaction with the first agent on this case—that David Kerr—I find it suspicious the new guy has to call in an outsider."

Shepherd effected his most disarming smile, "For the most part, NCIS performs their mission superbly. Unfortunately, there are times when NCIS personnel can fall short of standards, and it appears David Kerr has done so on this occasion. That's why Special Agent Gray engaged me; he believes an 'objective outsider' will help restore trust in NCIS' credibility."

Pounder nodded, satisfied, if not happy, "You sound like a public information officer talking to the press. So, what is it you want to know?"

Shepherd shrugged, amused that his background in Navy public affairs showed through so clearly, "Well, I need to know *your* observations about Young-Saeng Tate. What I need to get is an idea of…well, any hunches you might have had about his situation, any 'gut feelings,' things like that."

"That's an unusual line of questioning for a detective," Pounder said, folding her hands on her desk.

"I'm an unusual detective," Shepherd said lightly, then caught himself, "I'm sorry if that came off as flippant. Years of experience have taught me to listen to hunches, gut feelings, instincts, etc. I've had more than one case where a gut feeling provided the lead that ended up being the offender's downfall."

"I see," Pounder sighed, "Well, for one thing, Young-Saeng was far more talkative than most of my patients."

"Talkative?"

Pounder nodded, "You have to understand, Mr. Shepherd, although we serve *all* indigent people in the area, most of our patients are *not* very talkative. Many suffer from various addictions, and many call the streets their home. Many of the women here are battered by abusive husbands or boyfriends. And most men we see are reticent to admit they're being physically abused, whether by a woman or another man, so the few who *do* come in usually lie about the root cause."

"I understand," Shepherd nodded, "When I was in the Navy, I had a number of sailors who were abuse victims as well, but would often defend their abuser. I also found that the few male victims I had were usually the most vociferous in their declarations refusing help. Broke my heart *and* drove me around the twist because I couldn't do anything to the abuser without the victim's cooperation."

"Exactly, you *do* get it," Pounder said, relief washing her face like cool, clear water, "Young-Saeng would openly tell me about

Delores Tate hitting him at home, or threatening him quietly when they were out at dinner or something. I recall one story before last Christmas when he and that fuc…that wife of his were at her command holiday party."

Sounds like someone trying to establish a narrative… Shepherd's notebook and pen were out in a flash. He looked up expectantly at Pounder, waiting for her to go on.

Pounder sighed, "Apparently, he'd been talking to one of her female shipmates, and that b…woman…got jealous. She took Young-Saeng outside and told him he was going to get the, how did he put it? Oh, yes, she was going to 'beat the shit out of him for acting like a man-whore.'"

Shepherd kept his face neutral, "I take it Young-Saeng came in the next day presenting physical injuries consistent with a beating?"

Pounder nodded again, leaning forward and placing her elbows on her desk, "He said he was able to sneak in here on his lunch hour. He had bad bruising on his back and arms—including bruising that was caused by a hand forcibly gripping his upper arm. I tried to get to set Young-Saeng up with some sort of assistance to get him away from that monster, but he said he loved her and knew she could change."

"I'm always surprised every time I hear something like that," Shepherd said, "And yet it's such a sadly common statement by abuse victims that I'm surprised I'm surprised by it."

"Me, too," Pounder replied, voice numb with sadness.

Shepherd adroitly hid just how much he was reeling under multiple mental blows landed by the discrepancies between Pounder's and Tate's stories. He felt like he had just landed on an entirely separate planet.

"You said that was last Christmas," Shepherd said, getting them back on track, "What else can you tell me?"

"This past July 4th weekend Young-Saeng came in with a fractured ulna in his left arm," Pounder said, her teeth beginning to clench in anger, "He said he fell off a horse during a riding accident, but he also had a black eye. I'm sorry, but you don't get a fist-shaped black eye by hitting a rock. His injuries were escalating fast, but Young-Saeng was trying to protect that bitch who was hurting him!"

Something about Pounder's sudden emotional outburst triggered a revelation in Shepherd's mind.

"You told him he was in mortal danger, didn't you, Doctor?"

Pounder's eyes widened in surprise, "Actually, yes. Yes, I did. How did you know?"

Shepherd deflected, "Just a guess. What was his response?"

"I told him that the abuse had gone from bruising and sprains to broken bones in only *six months,*" Pounder breathed hard, voice wavering under the threat of an imminent emotional eruption, "I told Young-Saeng he needed to get out of that house because she was going to kill him. But he said she was just under stress, and he was going to try harder to be supportive of her. He wouldn't listen to anything I said!"

Pounder lost control, slamming a hand on the desk and shooting to her feet. Spinning on her heel, she walked over to a bookcase and stared at nothing.

"Mr. Shepherd, he couldn't break the cycle! I tried, God I tried so damned hard!" Pounder's voice broke, a sob escaping her. "I *swear* I did everything I could, but he wouldn't listen and now he's dead!"

Chapter 12
Silverdale, Washington
Thursday, September 6, 2018; 17:17 hours

"...South Korea's Gae Dokkaebi Industries Technology announced the deaths of founders Jung-Hoon and Hae-Won Chul today. The Chuls founded GDI Tech in Seoul in the late '70s. Living in squalor, the pair made their living repairing radios and other electronics for U.S. soldiers stationed at Camp Stanley, slowly building their company into a global powerhouse over the past fifty years. The Chuls were two of the wealthiest South Korean citizens by the time of the dot-com boom in the '90s…"

"…South Korea is still mourning the loss of two of its most powerful tech moguls, the husband-and-wife team of Chul Jung-Hoon and Chul Hae-Won. Although the founders of GDI Tech have been living reclusively since 2015, their globe-spanning technological empire operates in 27 countries. Rumors have circulated for several years that the Chuls were in search of an 'heir apparent' to take over as CEO and COO. GDI Tech's announcement of a new, hand-picked CEO and COO boosted company stocks significantly…"

"…Rhode Island Bishop Archibald Cremer faced renewed scrutiny today after disgraced former priest Judas Arnold was found dead in his Utah residence by officers attempting to serve him with a subpoena for a lawsuit from another former altar boy the defrocked priest is accused of molesting," The TV anchor's face might have been a plastic mask for all the expression he showed, "Cremer is accused of intimidating victims after the alleged abuse came to light in 1983 before the Vatican defrocked Arnold in 1985. The bishop's office released a statement asserting this is a politically motivated attack on his niece, Rhode Island Congresswoman Dana Cremer…"

* * *

The fast-fading light lit up the distant Olympic Mountains. The jagged peaks of the range were a stark, dark silhouette against the orange light splashing across the Washington sky. Soaring to nearly 7,000 feet in elevation, the twin peaks of The Brothers were the most captivating scene for those drinking in the Olympics' grand vista.

Mrs. Jill Nash was most helpful. Shepherd had found her puttering in her front garden next door to the Tate house when he arrived. Nash was breathlessly eager to discuss the case—and talk about her sizable herd of cats—as the scent of cedar slipped around them in the cooling evening air.

She and Young-Saeng had spent many hours talking about the cultivation of roses and cats. Nash said Young-Saeng would spend hours talking roses, but always declined to discuss anything else. She also said he enjoyed listening to her recount the adventures of Mr. Butterworth, Bigsby, Princes Pearl, Queen Elizabeth, and the rest of her feline family.

Shepherd had been hard-pressed to politely extricate himself from Mrs. Nash's enthusiastically energetic ebullience and the convention of the cats congealing around their feet, but he *was* able to finally escape her rambling. Still, the verbal tsunami had been worth it because he came away with a more complete picture of the Tates' life. Nash's description of the affectionate, playful relationship between Young-Saeng and Delores certainly belied the visions of broken bones and violent threats Pounder described.

Now standing in the quiet bedroom where death had partied hardy mere weeks earlier, Shepherd's eyes glazed over. His memory took control of his mental screen, overlaying photos of a handsome young man lying dead and mutilated on the marital bed, his frozen face a ghastly mask of terror liberally mixed with excruciating agony.

Shepherd was tired. His brain felt stretched, taut, and exhausted. He needed sleep. Even back in his active duty days, he made a point of taking at least ten minutes to shut his eyes and defrag his brain after lunch. Today's whirlwind adventures had prevented that. Still, the coffee he'd consumed a couple of hours ago remained effective, allowing his synaptic network to keep firing on all cylinders.

"Talk to me," Shepherd asked Young-Saeng's ghost quietly, "Which way do we jump? Be Janghwa and Hongryeon for me; help me prove that he did this to you."

"Who's Jane-away and Hungry Jean?"

Shepherd jumped, "Jeez! Abe, you scared the crap out of me!"

"Chill!" Gray said cautiously, holding his hands up in a disarming gesture, "It's only us."

A flaming head of red hair was visible just over Gray's shoulder.

Shepherd dropped his arms. Retrieving his skin and bones, he re-articulated his skeleton before zipping up his epidermis back up over it.

"Dammit, Abe, don't *do* that!" Shepherd's chest heaved as he caught his breath.

"I'm sorry I'm late, but the bloody rental car broke down," Gray said, smiling as he recalled Sigo accidentally startling *him* in this same room only days before, "Company's towing it, but they won't have another one for me until tomorrow. I was lucky enough to run into Chief Fredriksen here, and he gave me a lift."

"Who?" Shepherd straightened his sport coat.

"That'd be me," Fredriksen said, his large frame stepping from behind Gray, his flaming hair and piercing blue eyes brilliantly contrasted against the dark hallway behind him, "It's good to see you again, Isaac!"

Shepherd blinked, "Luke! I didn't realize you'd been sent out here. I know I sent you a charge for your charge book when you picked up chief, but, still, let me congratulate you in person!"

Smiling broadly, Shepherd held out a hand.

Fredriksen's massive mitt gripped Shepherd's somewhat smaller hand. Both men were the same height, but, whereas Shepherd was a barrel-chested veteran, Fredriksen's body bulged with the rippling steel of a chronic weightlifter. The sailor was in civvies, but the blue polo shirt stretched over his frame bore the Naval Base Kitsap logo and his belt buckle sported an emblem proclaiming 'NBK Chiefs Mess.'

"I ran into Abe right after he got here," Fredriksen said, shaking Shepherd's hand while he spoke, "Decided to check up on him and found him outside the NCIS building with a dead car. He told me he needed to meet you here, so I gave him a lift. I wanted to see you again anyway."

"Well, it's always good to see a friendly face," Shepherd said warmly, "Especially after the help you gave us during the Bacon case. Are you involved in this investigation?" Shepherd gestured over his shoulder at the room.

"No," Fredriksen shook his head, "Other than giving Abe a lift, I'm just being nosy."

Gray noticed Fredriksen had yet to let go of Shepherd's hand, and that he'd casually laid his free hand on Shepherd's shoulder. The big MA's eyes were firmly locked onto Shepherd's peepers. Gray cocked a single eyebrow up, intrigued by the interplay between the two men.

Shepherd laughed, "Far be it from *me* to castigate a man for being nosy, considering I haven't kept my nose out of things that didn't concern me for 20 years!"

"Well, at least you do it with style, 'eh!" Fredriksen laughed, still holding Shepherd's hand, "And it's a nice nose, too, dontcha know!"

Shepherd laughed, eyes twinkling, "Thank you! It comes in handy for sniffing out trouble!"

Gray coughed, "Sorry to break up 'old home week,' gentlemen, but I'm afraid we do need to get to work. So, who *are* Jane-away and Hungry Jean?"

Shepherd laughed, "No, Janghwa, as in 'shzang-a-way' and Hongryeon as in 'hong-ree-in.' Korean names. *Janghwa Hongreyon jeon* is an ancient parable I came across while researching Korean culture. Short version: evil stepmother has her two stepdaughters killed. The girls' ghosts finally convince

141

the local mayor to expose the crime and execute the stepmother and her son, who helped in the crime. There's more to it, of course, but that's the gist."

"Ah, the old 'evil stepmother did it' thing!" Fredriksen laughed.

Gray noted that, while Fredriksen finally let go of Shepherd's hand, he kept his other hand on Shepherd's shoulder and held the retired chief's eyes for a few beats more before redirecting his gaze to Gray.

Shepherd nodded, "Pretty much. The 'evil stepmother' trope isn't confined to just Western culture. The story struck a chord because that's how Abe described examining a crime scene to me a long time ago when he was training me—that we're trying to listen to ghosts."

"Interesting perspective," Fredriksen nodded, finally releasing Shepherd's shoulder.

Gray gestured around the room, "Well, if Young-Saeng *can* give us any help, we certainly need it. Someone gutted him like fish and used the ceiling fan to winch out his intestines, probably while he was alive and watching. We're just lucky the fan didn't spark and catch fire when its motor eventually burnt out. Would've destroyed what few clues we've got."

"Have you 'heard' anything?" Fredriksen asked, intrigued that both Shepherd and Gray seemed to be talking about listening to ghosts literally as well as figuratively.

"In a way, yes," Shepherd said, "But it's…I've got some ideas knocking about up here," Shepherd tapped the side of his head, "It's like hearing voices in the hotel room next door. You can *hear* them, but you can't quite get what they're saying into focus. I know who did this, but I *can't* see how to prove it yet."

Gray cocked his head, "Wait a minute there, Sherlock. What do you mean know *who* did it? There's still a few thousand things we don't know, not the least of which is reconciling the contradictory narratives created by Sheriff Sigo's investigation and David Kerr's work."

142

"Oh, those contradictions are bigger than you know, Abe," Shepherd said, his voice heavy with a 'this is going to get worse before it gets better' tone, "But those contradictions don't alter the reality that I *know* who did this...well, I know *one* of the two 'whos' who did this. The big question is how to prove it."

Gray's eyebrows hit the ceiling with an audible thump while Fredriksen's jaw bounced off the floor.

"Hang on, Hercule Poirot," Gray said, disbelief etched across his face, "I'm still trying to catch you up. You've got an ID on one of our suspects *already?"*

"Yeah, but it's not some great leap of Sherlock Holmsian logic, Abe," Shepherd said, waving his hand dismissively, "Once I brief you on what I learned today in Bremerton, you'll see it too. But, unless you and I can overcome a *massive* forensics hurdle, the 'who' will skate off Scott-free."

"Can I ask a question?' Fredriksen ventured.

"Sure," Gray said.

"Was Tate tortured to extract the data to open his safe like they said on the news?" Fredriksen asked.

"We don't believe so," Gray answered.

"Why not?"

"The safe was cracked four days *after* the murder...and inside a six-hour window between the discovery of Tate's body and the completion of crime scene photography, Luke," Gray explained, "Therefore, the safe was not part of the murder, but was cracked as a separate, if related, crime. The attack on Tate was apparently a personal hit, and we believe the torment inflicted on him was for the amusement of the suspects."

"You're telling me the suspects tortured and disemboweled this guy with surgical precision just for *fun?!"* Fredriksen said, his face blanching as if he was about to throw up, "That's disgusting!"

"Tell me about it," Gray said, nodding, "Anyway, the safe was *not* a target during the murder. It was opened *days* later, and only *after* first responders were already in the house."

"I spoke with Mrs. Nash next door when I got here—at extreme length," Shepherd's eyes twinkled.

Gray rolled his own eyes, "I know all about the 'extreme length' of talking to Mrs. Nash. Sheriff Sigo said one of her officers was trapped in Mrs. Nash's house for four hours during their interview with her. Mrs. Nash insisted on showing every photo of every cat she'd ever owned while talking about her relationship with the Tates. I managed to keep *my* conversation with her short enough to just hear the tales of Muffy, Spot, Lexington, and 'The Purrrfect Mrs. Molly,' but that was still 45 minutes of my life devoted to cats and only 15 minutes devoted to an interview."

"I see you've met her!" Shepherd laughed, "Still aside from the stories *I* got of Tippy, Mr. Cuddles, Sam The Genius, Flaky Dave, and Princess Puffiness, Mrs. Nash provided me a wealth of detail on how the Tates interacted with each other. According to her, they were affectionate, jolly, relaxed…everything you'd expect a happy couple to be."

"Did she witness anything on the night in question?" Fredriksen asked.

"No," Gray and Shepherd answered in unison. Looking at each other in surprise, they both released a chuckle before Gray went on.

"Mrs. Nash said she was up late that night watching 1951's *Rhubarb,*" Gray said, "She didn't hear anything unusual."

"Most of these houses don't have central air conditioning," Fredriksen pointed out, "So I'm guessing her windows were open. Even with the TV on, she didn't hear anything? I mean, Tate was attacked first in the backyard before they dragged him into the house."

"Whatever happened outside was fast and quiet," Gray shoved his hands into his pockets, "They got Tate into the house before torturing and murdering him. After the homicide, our suspects returned to the backyard, trashing every rose bush Young-Saeng cultivated."

Gray glanced around the room before continuing, "They then re-entered the house to stuff one rose down Young-Saeng's throat. Mrs. Nash's TV is located on the far side of her house from here, so the bulk of her house and the bulk of the Tates' house shielded her from hearing any noise."

"I don't suppose you got lucky and got any blood off the thorns?" Fredriksen asked.

"The only blood we found is Young-Saeng's," Gray said, "Perfect match in blood type and DNA. Our killers were careful. *Very* careful."

"There *are* walking trails all over the Ridgetop area, but I'm surprised the killers were able to get up into the yard unseen by anyone," Fredriksen said, "They had to have surveilled this place and planned this attack for weeks, if not longer. Assuming what I've been able to learn is accurate, they came during a perfect window to catch Young-Saeng outside, but all the neighbors *inside.*"

"Spot-on, Luke," Shepherd nodded, impressed, "They executed the execution perfectly."

Gray rolled his eyes as Shepherd went on, "Still, *that* level of surveillance means an *extensive* investment of time…and *that* means we're dealing with at least one professional here."

"I know we can't rule anything out at this point," Gray said, "But, I have the distinct impression at least one of our suspects only realized *after* the murder a technological gold mine was in that safe."

"And they cracked a *safe* during a six-hour window while the first responders were *in the house?*" Fredriksen's eyes popped in surprise.

"Exactly," Gray said, "Which itself points to one of the first responders being responsible for the safe, if not the murder."

Fredriksen groaned, glancing at his watch, "Well, it's getting late, and I'm chairing a duty section leader meeting early tomorrow to coach my first classes through some watch bill issues."

"Yeah, we need to go eat and get back to the office, anyway," Gray said, leading the other two toward the front door. "Thanks for your help today, Luke."

The three exited the house, Gray turning to secure the door and re-string the crime scene tape. Night had fallen, the obsidian sky obliterating the forms of the Olympic mountains. Light clouds wafted overhead in the cool breeze. A cat zipped by underfoot.

"Not a problem," Fredriksen said, holding out a massive hand to Shepherd, "Isaac—do you still have the same phone number you had back in Norfolk?"

"Yep," Shepherd nodded, shaking Fredriksen's hand.

"I had to get a new phone. I'll shoot you a text so you have my new number," Fredriksen said, eyes glinting brightly in the darkness, "Let's meet up for dinner when you have a moment."

Gray's eyes narrowed ever so slightly as he again noticed the ever-so-slight way Fredriksen's eyes narrowed as he talked to Shepherd—while still holding onto his hand.

"Sounds like a plan," Shepherd said, his voice genial and easy, "Good luck tomorrow. Oh—you *do* know the difference between an active duty chief, and a retired chief, right?"

"No, what is it?' Fredriksen asked, finally letting go of Shepherd's hand to fish his car keys from his pocket.

"Happiness!" Shepherd said, chortling.

"Nice!" Fredriksen laughed, giving Shepherd a small wink.

"Hey, Luke," Gray caught Fredriksen's attention, "I know you don't need reminding, but I do have to caution you that everything we've discussed tonight is confidential."

"Understood," Fredriksen nodded genially while looking at Shepherd, "Ok, you two be careful. Night!"

Gray's mouth twitched.

Fredriksen hopped in his car, a 2015 Ford Mustang GT that was nearly as red as his hair. The car roared to life, its lights painting the Tate house in a vivid glow before Fredriksen carefully backed out of the drive, slowly drifting down Cascade Court towards Ridgetop Road.

Shepherd pulled his keys out, popping the fob's button to unlock *Sarah Jane.*

"That car has nearly as much muscle as he does," Shepherd said, "But I'll take *Sarah Jane* any day of the week and twice on Sunday! You'd be surprised just how smooth this baby is at 110 miles an hour over backwoods roads in Montana…not that I'd know, of course!"

"Riiiiiight," Gray said, opening the passenger door and getting in, "Man, that guy is *totally* into you, Isaac!"

"Hmmm? What do you mean?" Shepherd asked, pulling his door shut and snapping his seatbelt into place.

"What do you mean, what do *I* mean?" Gray asked incredulously, clicking his seatbelt into place as Shepherd started the engine, "He was checking you out the *whole time!"*

"He was just being friendly, especially now that he's also a chief," Shepherd said dismissively.

"Isaac, *that* was a bit more than friendly," Gray said, his incomprehension at Shepherd's obtuseness growing, "Come on, man; he asked you out!"

"You think he's gay?" Shepherd queried, his eyes on the road as he began to drive to Ridgetop Road, "Abe, he was just being nice. I mean, he *did* help us out with a pretty big case a couple of years ago. He's just excited to see us again."

"He's *happy* to see me again, yes, but he's *excited* to see *you,* my friend!"

Shepherd shook his head, "I think you're reading way too much into things."

"I am not," Gray said definitively, "Give it some time."

"Oh, come on!" Shepherd laughed openly at Gray's assertion, "Abe, he's just being friendly!"

Gray dropped his head in defeat, "Isaac, I don't understand you sometimes. Well, actually, *nobody* understands you most of the time. For a man who's a genius at working out psychology and reading human behavior, you sure can be *dense!"*

Chapter 13
Silverdale, Washington
Friday, September 7, 2018; 06:15 hours

The day was already cloudy with temperatures reaching the upper 50s. Shepherd found the weather refreshingly brisk and energizing. His upbringing had largely landed his family in tropical zones due to his father's Air Force career, so he was accustomed to heavy, wet air that did its level best to dissolve one's skin.

The dry, cooler Pacific Northwestern air was a wonderfully agreeable change.

I guess I shouldn't be surprised, Shepherd thought, sipping his coffee in the NCIS building's small conference room, his brown leather western boots resting on the table as he leaned back, perusing a statement from one of Kitsap's police officers. His thoughts, however, strayed down a different road.

The docs did *tell me the heat stroke I suffered back in '05 on Guam during the* Pacific Blaze *incident wrecked my body's ability to properly regulate temperature, and I'd probably really start noticing it when I started pushing 50...*

Shepherd smiled to himself, laying the statement back down on the table, *Guess I've only got a few more years before I hit the point where past injuries will combine with age to make life...more interesting.*

"These copies of the Tates' medical records are great," Gray said, examining the material. Tate's lawyer, Amanda Pile, had delivered the records to Shepherd at the Viking Inns & Suites earlier that morning.

"It certainly provides us our first concrete break in this case," Shepherd said. *"Now* we have physical evidence from the Navy itself that Young-Saeng wasn't a battered husband. There's an impostor in play here, meaning there's only one person it could be."

"I know; we'll get to that in a minute," Gray said, holding up a finger while still reading the medical files, "We still need to trace back the cyberattack on the hospital servers. Same with the financial data. Since we now have positive proof the 'Young-Saeng' at the free clinic was a pretender, we can also undercut the credibility of the financial records. It's not enough to protect Lt. Cmdr. Tate in court—yet—but we're on the right track."

Gray put down the records, sitting back upright and rubbing his eyes. Picking up his coffee, he sipped the steaming brew gingerly, "Before we go further on this track, let me ask—how familiar are you with the Lionfish project?"

Shepherd dropped his feet from the table while straightening his brick-red collared shirt. Thinking for a moment, he absent-mindedly tightened his sleeves above his elbows. Possessing arms as long as an albatross' wings usually meant he couldn't find sleeves that fit without spending a small fortune in big and tall men's shops. So, he usually just bought shirts off the rack that fit his wide shoulders and rolled the sleeves up. Problem solved.

"I know it's some kind of super-secret-squirrel underwater drone, but that's about it," Shepherd answered, wondering for the two-millionth time how the NCIS agent kept his hair perfectly styled without any visible product shellacking it into place. "I've been meaning to ask you about that, but we've been running pretty hot and heavy trying to get ahead of that congressional cow, Dana Cremer."

Gray snickered, "You should hear what Charlotte calls her."

Shepherd's eyebrows shot up, his voice fraught with sardonic wit, "Wait, are you telling me that Charlotte Webb, Norfolk's Special Agent in Charge and the *epitome* of high professionalism, speaks ill of an elected official in foul language?"

Gray laughed out loud, "Oh, *hell* yes! You forget that Charlotte grew up in the backwoods of eastern Tennessee. The Ku Klux Klan burnt crosses on the front lawn of her family's farm. That woman can swear in ways that make everything *you* learned in the Navy look like a class in Edwardian elocution!"

149

Their laughter echoed off the soundproof paneling for a brief moment before they recovered themselves.

"Ok, let's start with the high points," Gray said, settling back in his chair, "This is all Top Secret and above, so it stays in this room. The Lionfish would *still* be under wraps if it weren't for the leaks in this case…and that means the DoD and DHS classification officers are working overtime declassifying what's gone public while protecting what hasn't."

"I've been struck by just how much information the Navy's been able to *prevent* from going public," Shepherd noted, "You forget; I was in public affairs. *Trust* me; it takes a *lot* of creatively clever thinking to keep the media from *realizing* you're guarding a major story. That told me a *lot* about how advanced this thing must be."

"It's a truly amazing piece of technology," Gray nodded, "The Coast Guard approached the Navy for assistance in developing an autonomous underwater drone that could search independently for mariners in distress during adverse weather conditions. Say a freighter is foundering during a hurricane. Normal Coast Guard assets certainly can't conduct search-and-rescue operations in that kind of weather—"

"But an autonomous drone sailing underwater could search by staying *beneath* the worst of the storm," Shepherd cottoned on.

"Bingo, as you like to say," Gray nodded, "To pull that off, they needed an artificial intelligence and autonomous navigation system far more advanced than anything today, so they partnered with the Navy here at NASED Keyport."

"Let me guess, the Lionfish then grew in scope," Shepherd said flatly, knowing where this was headed.

Gray nodded, picking up his coffee and taking a sip before continuing.

"You guessed it," Gray said, putting the mug back down on a coaster, "The Lionfish evolved into a modular platform that can conduct autonomous search operations—even carrying life-saving equipment to deploy until manned rescue operations can be conducted. However, this modular approach means the drone can also carry surveillance systems, weapons, anything the Navy, Coast Guard...hell, even the Marines might need."

"Ok, but here's the $64,000 question," Shepherd said, "So what? The Navy's been working on autonomous underwater drones for years now. Why is Lionfish such a big deal?"

"The 'so what' is the guidance system and A.I. developed by Seagull Electronics Alternatives and Keyport engineers—led by Young-Saeng," Gray said, cocking his head to one side, "The breakthrough they achieved in hyper-accurate self-navigation and location accuracy is about ten years ahead of North Korea, Russia, even China."

"How hyper-accurate is 'hyper-accurate?'" Shepherd asked, leaning forward a bit to rest his elbows on the table.

"*Gridley* deployed the drone for a full-on navigation test just *hours* before the Tate murder," Gray said, "The Lionfish was sent to search for a target 250 miles from the ship."

"Whoa!" Shepherd's eyes popped in surprise, "Over *two hundred miles?!*"

"Did I neglect to mention the ridiculously efficient storage batteries Keyport also invented for it? Oh, sorry about that," Gray said. "Anyway, the Lionfish came to within three inches of the target's center after a 250-mile trip, before navigating back to *Gridley* precisely on schedule."

Shepherd leaned back, stunned. Letting out a long, low whistle, he nodded, "Wow! That would certainly give our sea services a real swim fin up in the world!"

"So, you can see why the Navy and Coast Guard are up in arms about this," Gray said, his voice grave, "We can*not* allow our adversaries to get ahold of this kind of technology. Imagine what Iran could do with this. Or China. Whatever the original motive for killing Young-Saeng Tate was, our suspects might very well be scoping the international black market for a buyer right now."

"Any idea how they cracked the safe?" Shepherd asked, picking up his coffee cup to take a sip.

"None as of yet," Gray said, running a frustrated hand through his hair, "The computer controlling the safe's tumblers recorded it was last accessed a week *before* the murder."

Shepherd shrugged, his own frustration bubbling up for a moment, "That's the *one* thing Gippeum couldn't have done, even if he'd forced Young-Saeng to give up his PIN number. They might be identical, but even identical twins and triplets have unique fingerprints. The safe still wouldn't have opened for the brother."

"I have to admit that Gippeum Lýkos killing Young-Saeng and framing Delores is logical, but there's just no way to build *that* into a trial-proof case, not on what we have now," Gray said, tapping in frustration.

"Only an identical twin could fool Dr. Pounder," Shepherd said, "The good doc's records identify a man *identical* to Young-Saeng with actual broken bones, contusions, etc. However, Young-Saeng's *Navy* records show a man in perfect health. Logically, Gippeum is the only person on the planet who could successfully execute such a deception."

"Except for the fact he was one of the first people Sheriff Sigo looked at," Gray threw up his hands, "There's *no* record of Gippeum Lýkos being out here at all. No flight itineraries, no witnesses who saw him on a plane or bus, no rental cars, nothing. In fact, during the time of the murder, he was in the Outer Banks at Nag's Head, North Carolina, with a friend, Matthew Murgatroyd." Gray finished.

Shepherd coughed and choked on his coffee, fighting not to spit it all over the table.

"Matthew *Murgatroyd?!*" Shepherd got himself under control. Setting his coffee back down, he cleared his throat, "Really?!"

Gray smiled, "I had the same reaction. But, yes, really. Murgatroyd and Lýkos were renting a beach house. They apparently spent several days there," Gray held up another report. "I even have cell tower records showing Lýkos' cell phone pinging along the Outer Banks and his debit card being used to buy food and some souvenirs in local shops."

"No." Shepherd said flatly.

"No?"

"No," Shepherd repeated, "That makes no sense. A person wearing a disguise, even prosthetic appliances and make-up, could probably fool most everyone, but not a *doctor* doing a *physical exam.* And there's zero evidence Dr. Pounder is part of a conspiracy."

"Isaac, I'm not discounting *why* you believe your theory so strongly," Gray sighed, "But we have to follow the *physical* evidence, and the only physical evidence we have firmly places Gippeum Lýkos three thousand miles east while his brother was being murdered."

"But it *has* to be the brother," Shepherd said, his voice betraying a hint of doubt. "I did some checking, and Delores Tate was right. Both brothers were in Mensa. Gippeum has advanced degrees in chemistry, quantum mechanics, and engineering. One of his books, *The Dynamics of an Asteroid,* even hit *The New York Times* Best Seller list and was noted for being accessible to the lay public, not just academics."

Shepherd shook his head, his expression firming back up with confidence, "Abe, he's got the brains to pull it off, and, assuming Delores Tate's right about him being a psychopath, he'd have the psychology to pull it off. It *has* to be him."

"Isaac, I understand, I really do," Gray said emphatically, "Unfortunately, my hands are tied by the available evidence."

"I'm not arguing with you; I *do* concede the current physical evidence we currently have doesn't stack up at the moment," Shepherd held up a hand, "My gut tells me I'm right, so I'll—"

"It doesn't matter what your gut tells you," Gray interrupted, "Without physical evidence, I just can't go on a theory."

Shepherd stared at Gray for a moment, exasperated. When he spoke, his voice was tight with impatience.

"I know that, Abe. We've been doing this for twenty years now. I *was* going to say that, while we're pursuing more conventional leads, I'll make it one of *my* projects to work out *how* he's pulling it off."

"Sorry; I didn't mean to be so dismissive," Gray said, looking contrite, "We're interviewing William Smith today—you know, the man Delores Tate is alleged to have been sleeping with."

"When and where do we meet him?" Shepherd stood, stretching.

"He agreed to meet us at Baker Street Billiards where he works," Gray answered. "He'll be there at 10:30 with the other staff, prepping for the place's opening at 15:00."

Gray shifted again, hooking one foot over the other beneath his chair, "It's over in Tacoma, about 25, maybe 27 miles one-way, and rush-hour over the Tacoma Narrows Bridge can be just as backed-up as rush-hour traffic over the Hampton Roads Bridge-Tunnel in Virginia. That alone makes the appearance of her having a sneaky, extra-marital affair all the more plausible."

Shepherd nodded, "You're right. The drive time *alone* would provide great cover for an illicit affair."

"As to the Lionfish, I want to get a better read on what the intelligence community might be saying about it," Gray said, "I really don't want to do this, but my options are running out. Can your friends, Aidan and Linda Stavenger, discreetly—and I mean *discreetly*—look into it?"

The Stavengers, a dual-Air Force couple Shepherd had gone to high school with, both commanded intelligence squadrons on board Wright-Patterson Air Force Base in Ohio.

"No can do this time," Shepherd sighed, "Linda is on emergency leave in Florida. Her grandmother had a stroke last week."

"Oh, man!" Gray's face was stricken, "That's awful!"

"The woman *is* 103, so it's not like she didn't have a full life anyway if the worst happens," Shepherd said, "But Aidan's also taking leave so he can wrangle their five boys. He obviously can't work *and* haul The Horde around to all their extracurricular activities by himself. He'll be offline for at least another five or six days."

"Damn," Gray thumped a frustrated hand on the table.

Shepherd held up a hand, "Don't get your anchor chains fouled up, old friend. I still have a few cards to play. I'll hit up Steph and Diego in D.C. Steph's pretty well settled on the D.C. Circuit, and Diego's now the chairman of the Senate Intelligence Committee."

"Good for him!" Gray said, impressed.

"There was some reshuffling in party leadership, and he got that committee chair in addition to remaining on the Senate Armed Services Committee. I'll see if they can get us any gouge on the Lionfish."

"Excellent!" Gray smiled, "Hell, it was Stephanie's research that rumbled 'Aaron Seeley' back on *Ponce* in 2016 and revealed he was CIA. We can use their help right now, especially since the 'Big Mitch' scandal's sucking the oxygen out of most resources NCIS and the FBI can field."

"Well, we're also not without local help."

"Denita's already giving us everything she can," Gray pointed out.

"No—my buddy from Guam, Liam Gumataotao, over in Port Ludlow, remember? I was planning to stay with him and Maria until NCIS provided me that lovely suite down the hall from yours."

"That's right!" Gray's memory kicked in, "I forgot! Sarah's been mentoring him! You think he'll be willing to help?"

"You know it," Shepherd smiled, "I'll talk to him soon as I can. Now, onto breakfast. It's nearly 7:30 and I'm Jonesing for something really bad for me. Liam recommended a place called Elmer's up in Poulsbo. He said it's kind of like a local Pacific Northwest Denny's. You fly, I'll buy?"

Gray smiled happily, "Done and done! After that, we'll meander over to Tacoma and see what Mr. Smith has to say."

Chapter 14
Tacoma, Washington
Friday, September 7, 2018; 10:30 hours

"The 'Big Mitch' scandal plaguing the Navy's Pacific Command took another turn today when it was announced that Admiral David E. Jones, Commander of the U.S. Atlantic Command out of Norfolk, will be taking over Pacific Command immediately. Several military analysts suggest this assignment all but guarantees Jones' ascent to Chief of Naval Operations…"

"…in related military news, the resolution, introduced by Illinois Senator Justin Duryodhan to censure NCIS Director Kirby Belk was blocked by Florida Senator Diego Alejandro. Alejandro condemned the resolution as an attempt to falsely accuse Belk of the illegal and unethical actions his predecessor, former Director Caleb Seldon, is currently under investigation for…"

Shepherd found the drive to Tacoma a singularly mesmeric experience. He'd been too focused getting on to Silverdale the other day to admire the scenery much. The long, winding path south along Highway 3 was a collision of Navy nostalgia and scenic wonders that took his breath away.

Puget Sound Naval Shipyard came into view as they sped along with the morning traffic.

"What carrier is that over there?" Gray asked, jerking his head to the left as he drove, "The one in mothballs? I've been wracking my brain for days, but I can't place her."

"*Kitty Hawk,* CV 63," Shepherd said, "She was decommed in 2009. Fun fact: the first model ship I ever had was a little snap-together replica of the *Kitty Hawk* my dad built for me in 1975 when I was four. About three years later my brother Josh busted it in half playing with a slingshot in the house. He ended up getting the whoopin' of his life. I still miss that little model."

Gray smoothly swooped along with traffic into the hairpin turn in Gorst where he shifted from Highway 3 to Highway 16 South, which would eventually take them into Tacoma. Vast swaths of Highway 16 were surrounded by vast tracks of woodlands, an ever-so-slight mist giving the more distant trees a spectral look.

The two sped through Gig Harbor, finally approaching the famous Tacoma Narrows Bridge. Gray slid over to the right, entering the toll booth. Upon paying, he rolled up his window and proceeded to merge back into traffic.

"I think I remember seeing something on the History Channel about the first bridge collapsing during World War II," Gray said.

"1940, actually," Shepherd answered as the newer span of the two-span bridge approached, "It was called 'Galloping Gertie' because of its unexpected oscillations. Engineers didn't have a great deal of experience with the aerodynamics of a structure in an area with high winds like this place experiences, so they built the bridge too light and thin. It was torn apart by 40-mile-per-hour winds only four months after it opened."

"Any casualties?" Gray asked as the tires hit the bridge's pavement.

"Sadly, one dog," Shepherd said, "The 'old' span over there—the one running west today—was completed in 1950. Locals called it 'Sturdy Gertie,' in contrast to 'Galloping Gertie.' The eastbound span we're on now opened in 2007. There's no toll on the old span because it's been paid for. The only tolls are on the eastbound span. Liam and Maria joke that it costs them an 'admission fee' to get to the rest of the state whenever they go on a road trip."

Gray chuckled as the deep, epic slopes of the Narrows dropped far down into the waters of Puget Sound below. He never ceased to be amazed by the sheer volume of obscure information Shepherd somehow managed to vacuum up with such ease.

"I was hoping to see Mount Rainier," Shepherd said, looking out his window, "But, Liam told me not to get my hopes up this time of year. Too cloudy."

157

The rest of the drive went quickly as Gray followed the smoothly dictated directions emanating from his GPS device. Getting off Highway 16, they navigated through the twists and turns of western Tacoma until finding a massive brick-and-concrete building squatting on the corner of South 19th Street and South Sunset Drive.

"That is one *ugly* building!" Gray said firmly as he parked. Shutting down the engine and undoing his belt, he felt inside his jacket to make sure he had his pen and notebook. Opening his door, he stepped out of the car, shaking his head, "Looks like a fall-out bunker from the old Soviet Union!"

"Brutalist architecture," Shepherd said, his face crinkling in dislike, "Grew out of the modernist movement and hit its heyday in the 1960s. Thank God it started fizzling out in the '70s."

"Isaac, I know I've asked this before, but I'm going to ask it again," Gray said, hands on his hips as Shepherd came around the sedan to join him, "Just how in the *hell* do you know all this crap?!"

"Simple…I'm brilliant," Shepherd said off-handedly, one eyebrow rising puckishly. "Seriously, I don't know. My brothers and I just have this way of finding stupidly obscure, out-of-the-way trivia. And remembering it."

Oy Gevalt! Gray thought, shaking his head.

The building was a stolid confection of gray concrete members with red brick filling in the voids. Evidently, some long-gone architect thought the bricks would spruce up the structure. Instead, they created an accurate approximation of a decrepit prison from a third-world country. The top two floors appeared to be residential units while Baker Street Billiards occupied the entire first level.

"Ok, don't go charging in there leveling accusations," Gray cautioned, "And don't jump on everything he says. Wait for the conversation to develop a bit in case further context sheds new light on a statement he makes."

Shepherd's head snapped around, his face twisting in an exasperated mask, "I *have* done this before, and *sometimes* even without *you.* I mean, I *did* solve a splendid little murder down in Kentucky back in January all by my widdle self!"

Gray looked chagrined, but tried to inject a bit of humor to ease the tension. "If you keep acting like a child, you're going to end up in time out, young man!" Gray said, smiling apologetically.

Shepherd's eyes still glowed with irritation, but he took a breath, his frame relaxing a bit, "Only if I get to have my teddy bear with me!"

Gray smiled, "Ok, let's go."

The heavy iron door, its paint faded and covered in old graffiti, clanked open when Gray knocked. Showing his badge, he introduced himself and Shepherd.

"Yeah, Billy said yous was commin,'" The weathered face behind the scraggly beard said, "He's at the bar. Go on in, but don't order nothin'. We can't serve shit until we open, or the owner'll skin us alive."

"I appreciate the warning, but we're good," Gray said amicably, leading Shepherd into the pool hall. The fluorescent lights shone brilliantly as the small staff scurried about the building.

The place effectively duplicated every other pool hall Shepherd had visited. The vast floor was crammed with pool tables, each surmounted by a light fixture wrapped in an ornate glass hood bearing an advertisement for beer, spirits, sporting teams, etc. Rows of flat-screen TVs papered the walls while neon signs, again advertising beer, hung dark and deactivated. The smell of alcohol, both domestic and imported, perfumed the air.

Gray and Shepherd found William Smith hunched over, pulling glasses from the dishwasher hidden under the bar and hanging them in the racks overhead. Smith was thin, his skin sallow and his eyes slightly yellowed. Shepherd had no desire to find out what had given Smith's eyes such an unhealthy color.

"Mr. Smith?" Gray flashed his most disarming smile, "I'm NCIS Special Agent Abraham Gray. This is Isaac Shepherd. I appreciate you taking the time to speak with us."

Smith's eyes narrowed as they scanned across Gray's face, but widened in shock when he saw Shepherd. Smith almost immediately returned his face to a neutral setting, but Shepherd had seen the man's surprise.

Not expecting two of us...? Shepherd wondered.

"My lawyer said it'd be better to talk to you than tell you to go to hell," Smith snapped, his plain face taking on an ugly character, "Delores was leaving that fucker for me, but you lot threw her ass in jail first. What do you want?"

Gray and Shepherd exchanged glances as Gray pulled out his notebook and pen.

"You maintain you were having an affair with Delores Tate," Gray said, "She, however, denies it. Why would she do that if she loves you?"

"Because her stupid-ass husband is dead and everyone thinks she did it," Smith bit off the end of his words, "Just like in the movies, everyone blames the wife!"

Shepherd stood quietly, hands in his pockets as he studied Smith. His face might be plain and sallow, and his eyes might be yellowed, but he was by no means unattractive. In fact, with something other than a ragged, pudding-bowl haircut and his stubbled neatly shaved, the man would have been almost handsome.

He noted that Smith's eyes kept flicking towards him even as Smith angrily spoke with Gray.

He's afraid of me, but not of Abe? Shepherd wondered.

"Where did you and Delores engage in your dalliances?" Gray asked, dragging Smith's eyes from yet another furtive glance at Shepherd.

"Dally-what?!' Smith asked.

"Hookups," Gray responded, "Where did y'all meet for your hook-ups?"

"My apartment down the street a ways," Smith said, but Shepherd noted yet another glance his way.

"Forgive me for pushing this," Gray said, his voice guaranteed to drive Smith up the wall with its inoffensive concrete slam of facts, "But she carpooled here with her shipmates from USS *Gridley*. None of them gave evidence she ever stayed with you."

"They're lying to protect her ass!" Smith sneered, "That bitch told me she loved me! She even paid extra for her 'shipmates' to play longer so she and I could go bump fuzzies at my place!"

Another odd glance at Shepherd.

I can't put my finger on it, Shepherd thought, *But I swear that man recognizes me, but I'm also positive we've never met...*

"Delores leveled some serious accusations against you," Gray went on, "Including accusing you of sexual harassment against other sailors."

Testing his theory, Shepherd took a small, seemingly casual step forward. Smith's eyes briefly darted his way before returning to Gray.

"She's lying!!" Smith said, his voice nearly squeaking as he reflexively threw another glance at Shepherd.

Yep, he's definitely *reacting to my presence, not Abe's,* Shepherd thought. *But I need a bit more evidence...*

"She said some pretty horrible things about you, and yet you're still saying she loves you?" Gray pressed as gently as a concrete block dropping on a watermelon, "That doesn't make any sense."

"I don't care nothing what makes sense to *you!*" Smith snapped, sweating now. His eyes quivered as if he was forcing himself to keep them on Gray, "Everything was fine until her husband was killed and you people threw her in jail! She wasn't even here...she was at sea when the dumb jerkoff was snuffed!"

"Do you have any cash register receipts showing she paid for extra time?" Gray pleasantly hit Smith across the conversational face. "That would certainly back up your assertions of the affair."

"My lawyer told me if I talked to you it'd be a show of good faith that would help me in court!" Smith sneered wildly, his speech speeding up out of control. The man was losing his cool and clearly wanted to get out of the interview. "I talked to you.

I'm done. That bitch said she loved me and now she's trying to fuck me over! Get the fu—"

Shepherd pounced.

"Liar!" He belted out loudly, 'covering' it with a grand, theatrical fake cough.

Smith jumped so hard his spleen was left on the bar. Skin turning milky white with pure terror, he scooted several feet away with surprising speed.

"I am *so* sorry!" Shepherd pretended to clear his throat, again playing up the theatricality of his actions, "I got something caught in my throat! I just couldn't swallow all that!"

Gray looked daggers as Shepherd's face melted back into its bland, pleasantly vague smile.

Smith was gripping the bar with white knuckles, his frame trembling. Tiny drops of sweat were flung from his skin by the violence of his quivering.

Yep, that nozzle is terrified of me, but why?! *He and I haven't met before today.*

"Well, I think that about wraps it up here, Special Agent Gray," Shepherd said amicably, earning yet another enraged look from his pissed-off partner. "Mr. Smith, thank you for your time! You've been most helpful. I do hope you have a *great* morning!"

Shepherd deliberately overplayed his wave to Smith, using his large frame to frame the movement in a comical, almost slapstick fashion. Turning, he loped off towards the front doors, his towering form easily sliding around the pool tables until he sauntered out of the building.

"Isaac, you're an idiot!" Gray raged at him once he caught up to him at the car, "What in the living hell do you think you were doing?! You just fouled up an interview! What's gotten into your thick skull?!"

Shepherd's fist clenched, quivering with barely restrained rage. Choosing his words carefully, he spoke slowly and exceptionally clearly—always a sign of extreme anger.

"Abraham, there was a time *not* that long ago when you gave me the benefit of the doubt. This is now the *third* time in two days you have spoken *at* me as if I'm some dimwitted idiot!" Shepherd growled, enunciating each word with deliberate precision, "Do you think retirement turned me *stupid?!*"

Gray put his hands on his hips, his eyes on his shoes as he fought to contain his temper, "No. I don't think it 'turned you stupid' or anything like that."

"Then what turned *you* stupid, Captain Blinders?!" Shepherd spat back across the hood of the car, "Or did you *not* notice that Smith reacted in abject, outright, plain, old-fashioned *terror* when he saw *me?!* Not you, *me!* I've never met that fool, yet he was acting like I decapitated his cat! Your interview was over when he told us to get out, and *you know it.* So, I took the opportunity to test my theory and I was right. He's *terrified* of me for some reason, and that can't be a coincidence!"

Gray looked off to the side, annoyance filling his face, but a wisp of embarrassment was starting to make itself known.

"So, tell me, Mr. Genius Federal Agent, why?" Shepherd raged on, voice rising to a deep bellow that was just this side of outright shouting, "Why is a bar back who's clearly lying about everything afraid of a man he's never met? Well?! I'm waiting!"

Gray stopped short, realizing in horror that not only was Shepherd correct in his assessment; but that he, Gray, had indeed missed Smith's behavioral cues.

"You're right," Gray said, embarrassment turning to humiliation as he unlocked the car, "I was too focused on my line of questioning, and I missed some important observations. I'm sorry."

"Listen, if you don't want my help, tell me now and I'll get back on the road, but I'm not going to spend the next few days having my ass chewed by a man treating me like a recalcitrant seaman who can't make morning Quarters on time!" Shepherd commanded, "You asked me here to help. You know how I operate, so stop jumping down my goddamned throat before I lose it!"

Sucking in a breath, Shepherd opened the passenger door. Settling himself into his seat, he spent the drive back to Silverdale in silence, calming down.

Gray, wisely, let him be for a while before venturing to repair the damage.

"Isaac, again, I'm sorry," Gray said as they sped north back on Highway 3 into Silverdale, "I honestly don't know what's wrong. I'm just...I'm just off-balance in a way I can't put my finger on, and I don't have Sarah here to talk to like I'm used to. It's not like I haven't been on remote assignments before, but there's just something that's got me...bugged. But, you *are* correct about Smith's behavior, and that adds another wrinkle to this mess."

"Thank you," Shepherd said, his anger abating, "I appreciate the apology very much. Look, I know we're on a tight timeline here, what with Wonder Bitch over in Washington trying to screw your director up the aft like some demented alien butt-hugger parasite—"

"Now *there's* a picture I'll never get out of my brain," Gray muttered.

"But, dude, come on. This is *me.* We've been through murder, terrorists, and Hampton Roads traffic together. If you need to talk, I'm here," Shepherd said, compassion washing away the remnants of his temper, "Just like you used to tell me—don't Lone Ranger it, ok?"

Gray didn't answer, but the side of his face told Shepherd he was wrestling with something pretty hard.

"Isaac, if I can figure out what's got me wrong-footed, I *will* take you up on that offer," Gray finally said, "For the moment, I...I just don't know. Something's just...not quite right."

"I've had seasons in life like that myself, old friend," Shepherd said.

The NCIS building was in the same place where they had left it earlier that morning—behind the Bangor NEX complex.

Which is good, because if it moved, it'd mean the Cascade volcanoes had blown us all to hell! Shepherd thought with amusement as the two men entered the building.

"Mr. Gray, I'm sorry to bother you," Keeters ran up to them from where she'd been talking to the building's receptionist.

"Carol, *please,* call me Abe," Gray said, sharing a distressed glance with Shepherd. "What's up?"

"Someone is waiting to see you," Keeters said, clearly discombobulated by whatever situation had landed on her desk, "I just had him taken to the conference room. There's a Chief Fredriksen acting as escort until you take over. He brought the visitor from base security to our office."

"Thank you very much, Carol," Gray said, wondering why Keeters was so flustered, "Well, Isaac, let's go meet our visitor."

The two passed through the bulletproof door into the Northwest Field Office's depths.

Kerr was leaving their conference room.

"Go take over!" He barked at a Master at Arms who'd been waiting outside.

"Has Mr. Magician here pulled a rabbit out of his hat and solved the case yet?" Kerr spat at them as he passed by.

"Hey, you ought to run over to Walmart," Shepherd said lightly, "I think there's one over in Poulsbo, right? Anyway, you should go check it out."

"Why?" Kerr snapped.

"They're having a sale on personalities. You could get a working model for cheap!"

Kerr snarled, stepping into his office and slamming the door so hard the pictures in the hallway rattled.

"He's in a good mood," Gray said, rolling his eyes as they headed down the corridor. Reaching the conference room door, he turned the handle, "I swear, that man is driving me around the twist! I'll take an honest bigot like Shey Cremer over an entitled political flunky any day!"

165

The two men stepped into the conference room before crashing into a startled, shocked halt. The apparition of a dead man sat serenely in a chair at the big table, his confident smile radiating up at them. Behind him stood the hulking form of Luke Fredriksen, his green 'digicam' uniform and his bright blue eyes contrasting with the pastel browns of the room.

Shepherd kicked his mind back into gear. This was no ghost materializing before them. This was a real, live, flesh-and-blood, human being wearing the face of a man he'd come to know through photos of a particularly violent crime scene.

Gippeum Lýkos sat peaceful and quiet, his smile pleasant, but his eyes as cold as a burning iceberg.

Chapter 15
Silverdale, Washington
Friday, September 7, 2018; 12:37 hours

Gray was the first to recover his voice, "Mr. Lýkos...this is an unexpected pleasure." Gray said before glancing up at Fredriksen, "Chief, thanks for all your help. We'll take over; you can head out if you want."

"Thanks, Mr. Gray," Fredriksen nodded, before holding out a hand to Shepherd, his smile brightening ever more slightly, "Isaac, give me a shout later!"

"Thanks, will do," Shepherd smiled pleasantly, shaking Fredriksen's hand before the MA left the room. He threw a small wink at Shepherd as he departed.

"Well, *someone* seems to have a suitor, Mr. Shepherd," Lýkos said in a softly sarcastic voice filled with an undercurrent of deadly venom, "Assuming, you're astute enough to recognize the opportunity and intelligent enough to pursue it. Sadly, I doubt your level of perspicacity is adequate to the situation."

Shepherd's mouth fell open, dumbfounded. He could only stare back blankly, his brain on lockdown.

Gray shook his head, feeling as if he'd just been caught on the periphery of a bunker-buster bomb demolishing an outhouse.

"Mr. Lýkos, what brings you to Washington State?" Gray asked, pulling out a chair and sitting down as casually as his surprise would allow.

"Why, the murder of my brother and the horrible campaign to protect that predator wife of his, of course," Lýkos responded without looking at Gray, his eyes still locked on Shepherd's.

Lýkos' mannerisms were graceful to the point of being nearly effeminate as he shifted, crossing his legs and folding his hands in his lap. He wore brown slacks and an expensive tan Oxford button-down shirt under a black high-end fleece vest. Brown leather loafers encased his feet.

"Are you all right, Mr. Shepherd?" Lýkos asked in a searingly silky voice, "Your current facial expression resembles a dead halibut."

Isaac closed his mouth. Swallowing hard, he shook his head as if to clear it, "Forgive me. I was…you caught me off guard."

"I can tell," Lýkos said dryly, a sly smile crinkling his eyes as he rested one elbow on the table, his chin gracefully resting on one elegantly extended finger.

"Mr. Lýkos," Gray said, "First, allow me to extend my deepest condolences on your loss. I understand your parents passed away last week, as well."

"Tragically, yes, my parents recently passed," Lýkos said, finally deigning to look at Gray, "They were both chain smokers, and I'm afraid it'll be ruled that emphysema is what took their lives."

Gray blinked in surprise, *That's a strange turn of phrase…*

"As to my brother, the man was a low-IQ buffoon who jumped into the bed of every woman he could find," Lýkos said with all the emotional energy of a three-day-old corpse, "However, despite his low moral standing, he *was* my brother, and I'll not rest until his killer is properly chastened for his death."

"That's pretty cold, Mr. Lýkos," Shepherd said, his face unusually pale, but his sea-green eyes still bright, "From what we've learned, your brother was quite a brilliant man, and pretty dedicated to his wife."

"I imagine the same could be said by those loyal to Brandy Sniffer, but you know perfectly well she was a tramp whose behavior led to her tragic end on the *Ponce* two years ago," Lýkos said.

Gray blinked in surprise again, *How the hell does he know about that?*

"Loyalty usually blinds us to the truth about those we 'love', Mr. Shepherd," Lýkos was saying, "More often than not, loyalty is often more a hindrance, if not an outright threat, to our capacity to see the truth of a situation for what it truly is. I'd have thought a man of your abilities would understand that by now."

"My abilities are not in dispute at the moment, Mr. Lýkos," Shepherd said, shoving his hands in his pockets, "What *is* in dispute is whether your brother was killed by your sister-in-law or an as-yet-unknown set of assailants. So far, the evidence is inconclusive at best."

"Of course, it is," Lýkos said, "And that's why I'm here. I believe my presence will help quickly conclude this case and return you to your little road trip. Your photography is top-flight, but I sadly find your travel blogs quite pedantic. You spend far too much time attempting to entertain the lowly educated masses instead of seeking to apply critical theory to your subjects."

"Well, always nice to have another follower," Shepherd replied weakly. He still felt as wrong-footed as a man with only a left leg trying to put on a right shoe.

"I suppose I should be grateful you took the time to come here and assist on this case," Lýkos said, his eyes narrowing as he lowered his hand from his face, demurely uncrossing his legs, "Even though I fear your lack of observational skills will leave you missing yet another opportunity to establish a potential relationship."

Gray watched the interplay between Shepherd and Lýkos with morbid fascination. He had the oddest feeling some kind of intellectual conflict was being enacted on a level far beyond his comprehension.

From the look on Shepherd's face and his uncharacteristic inability to deliver a sharp retort, Gray realized his partner was completely off form as the blows rained down upon him.

"Mr. Lýkos, uh, Gippeum," Gray said, attempting to regain control of the room, "I do appreciate you coming out here from North Carolina."

"Oh, it was no trouble at all," Lýkos said, still looking at Shepherd, "I had some personal business to attend to on this coast, so it was not inconvenient to come here and put right this awful situation."

"What personal business do you have on this coast?" Shepherd asked, "Now that your brother is dead, I mean."

"Collecting his remains and burying him with our dear parents, of course," Lýkos said, his voice betraying not a scintilla of grief, "A man with a reasonable level of intelligence would have worked that out. I'm beginning to understand why you never joined Mensa like your brothers."

Shepherd's eyebrows shot into his hairline, "Beg pardon?"

"I've known your brothers for many years now," Lýkos said coolly, still ignoring Gray, "Not very well, of course. Like you, they demonstrate a decidedly uncouth populist bent to their thinking. However, despite such shortcomings, both *are* exceptionally intelligent men. It is such a pity you didn't inherit the same level of mental acuity they possess. Such a debilitating reality must severely strain your relationship with them."

"Gippeum," Gray said, again trying to establish some semblance of control, "It speaks very well of you to have come out here for your brother's remains."

"Special Agent Gray, please, let's not pretend things I obviously don't feel," Lýkos said, looking over at him, "I stopped liking my brother a long time ago. He displayed a self-destructive trend in his relationships from the time we were teenagers after our other brother, Su-Jin, died. The fool threw his life away in a misguided marriage to a woman who abused him and finally killed him. I'm here out of a moral obligation I believe I have, but let's not pretend I'm here out of some deep love for a man who shared my DNA but little else."

"I appreciate your honesty," Gray said, "It's refreshing. I'm used to people proclaiming familial love to the heavens above right after beating the crap out of their spouse."

"I'm sure you are," Lýkos said, "I prefer to avoid such inane mundanities. You know very well from my body language alone there was no love lost between Young-Saeng and I. My time is

170

too valuable to be wasted lying about it. Nor am I jealous of his supposed 'successes,' unlike Mr. Shepherd here."

Shepherd shook his head, "I...wait, what?"

Lýkos smiled sweetly again, the way one does before twisting the head off a child's doll.

"You've spent most of your adult life playing detective while you were active duty in the Navy. Your brothers went to the Naval Academy, but you enlisted instead. It truly saddens me to see just how desperate you have been all your life to get attention by engaging in a self-destructive game playing the hero. Really, Mr. Shepherd, you must learn some self-respect...and even self-forgiveness for being the intellectual runt of the litter."

Gray swore he could feel a cerebral shockwave hit him after that last barb.

Jeez, this man has it in for Isaac!

Shepherd was again silent. He just stared, his face still slightly pale, but his eyes narrowed, "Mr. Lýkos."

"Gippeum. Please," Lýkos smiled politely.

"Mr. Lýkos," Shepherd's voice was hardening as he struggled to find his footing, "You could have contacted the local police, or even the nearest NCIS office, if you wished to get in touch with us. And yet, here you are after making a trans-continental trip. What do you want? Why are you *really* here?"

"Are you hard of hearing, Mr. Shepherd?" Lýkos sighed, looking for all the world like a teacher taking pity on a particularly dim-witted student, "As I already stated, I'm here to collect the remains of my later brother."

"And?"

"'And' what?" Lýkos inquired, "Are you suggesting I'm here for some nefarious purpose? Are you suggesting I'm here to cover up a crime scene? What basis would you have for such an accusation? I was in the Outer Banks with a friend when my dear, delusional brother was murdered."

Lýkos rose gracefully, shaking his head with false sympathy, "Special Agent Gray, I can see your, um, *partner*...is not operating at full capacity. I'm sorry for coming in at such a bad moment. Perhaps you should get him some coffee. Or maybe a milkshake. Something tells me he is accustomed to simple things. I'm sure that would restore his spirits."

Gray's shock was so paralyzing that he didn't even think to rise for a moment.

"Ah, yes, well," Gray stammered, finally standing, "Allow me to escort you out, Mr. Lý…Gippeum. Isaac, I'll be back in a moment."

Gray returned in less than five minutes. Shepherd was still standing where he'd been when Gray and Lýkos had departed.

"Isaac?" Gray asked, concerned, "Are you ok? I've never, *never* seen you so off-balance like this. Well, not in a long time."

Shepherd shook his head as if he were coming out of a dazed trance.

"What? Sorry—what?"

Gray grew more alarmed, "Are you ok?"

"No. Yes…yes, I am, sorry," Shepherd looked as if he'd just experienced a very large explosion in his washing machine, "I'm…I wasn't expecting…where in the *hell* did that *gesekgi* come from?!"

"Guh-sek-*what?*" Gray asked, confused.

"Sorry. 'Gesekgi.' It's Korean for 'son of a bitch," Shepherd explained, "I picked it up from my interview with Delores Tate. She's not overly fond of that man."

"I'm not surprised," Gray said, "Look, this is going to be uncomfortable, but I have to ask for the sake of proper due diligence—*do* your brothers know him?"

"I have no idea," Shepherd said testily, "Mensa's got something like 145,000 members worldwide. Maybe they do, maybe they don't. I'll have to ask A.J., and maybe give Josh a call over in Pittsburgh tonight. Why?"

"Well, if they do, then you have a personal connection to the brother of a murder victim you're investigating…a brother you happen to think is the murderer," Gray said, "That could be insinuated as a conflict of interest in some quarters."

"You're right, of course," Shepherd said, too distracted to notice Gray's surprise at his response. Gray had fully expected Shepherd to argue with him. Instead, Shepherd went on, still staring at the table, "This really *could* create an awkward appearance. I honestly don't think so, but Charlotte should know so she can be ready to handle any backlash that might arise."

Shepherd remained immobile, his gaze on the table while a tiny bead of sweat wound its way down his temple. Gray's eyes widened when he noticed Shepherd's left hand had clenched so tightly into a fist that a thin line of blood seeped from where his fingernails dug into the skin of his palm.

"Now, are *you* ok?" Gray put a hand on Shepherd's shoulder, forcing him to physically turn around so they could make eye contact, "Isaac, for God's sake, relax! You're as uptight as a long-tailed cat in a room full of rocking chairs occupied by over-active knitters who drank too much caffeine!"

Shepherd's eyes widened in surprise before he choked and broke into a spluttering laugh, "Wh—what?! Where...?"

Gray smiled, shrugging, "I stole it from you. Figured it would be a good way to get that brain of yours back in gear. Dude, what *happened?* I feel like just had a front-row seat to a squadron of B-52s carpet bombing a kid's sandbox."

"That's nothing," Shepherd said, checking his hand. Fortunately, he'd only given himself a small scratch. "I feel like *I* was the sandbox being carpet-bombed. Have to admit I didn't see *any* of that coming...or coming and coming and coming."

"Sit," Gray ordered. Shepherd sat, Gray taking a seat next to him, "Ok, well, we've just met Gippeum Lýkos and he clearly does *not* like you any more than William Smith does."

"I noticed," Shepherd said, his voice as dry as desiccated sand, "We have two men involved with this case, and both of them apparently would prefer me to take an early exit from the rest of my life. Coincidence?"

"Of course not," Gray said firmly, "I'm not nearly as good at statistics as you are, but even *I* can tell you the odds of this are *way* too high for it to be a fluke."

"Agreed," Shepherd said, nodding.

"So, what *did* just happen?" Gray asked, "I haven't seen you off your game in years. I'm used to *you* verbally outflanking and flattening the other guy."

"Abe, I can't quite describe it," Shepherd said, "It's…it's like in chess when your opponent makes an aggressive move you didn't even know was possible, and you spend the rest of the match getting clobbered, never quite being able to regain momentum."

Gray nodded, sympathy etching his face, "I get it. I imagine that's an extremely unaccustomed feeling for someone like you to have. Probably a bit frightening too."

"What do you mean, 'someone like me?'" Shepherd asked, voice sharp as a Ginsu knife.

"Isaac, relax and put down your guns," Gray admonished, "You and your brothers are geniuses. On top of that exceptional level of native intelligence, all three of you are incredibly quick-witted. Once you developed some self-confidence as you got older, well, I honestly can't think of *one* time where I saw you verbally or intellectually outclassed."

"Ah."

"'Ah,' yes," Gray, said nodding sagaciously, "Isaac, you're usually the one who's three steps ahead of the rest of us. Looks like today was the first time in a long time you ran into someone who's your equal. You're not used to being on the intellectual defensive, and it's got you over a barrel. Happens to the rest of us mortals quite often."

"Jeez, you make it sound like I'm some Olympic-standard egomaniacal twit who thinks he's better than everyone else," Shepherd grumbled.

"You know that's *not* what I mean!" Gray said emphatically, his voice taking on a slight edge, "Isaac, I'm stating *fact*. It's been

174

years since you've encountered a full-on intellectual *equal.* You're not at *fault* for that; it's just…it just *is.* But you've met him now. That means you'll be better equipped next time you run into the dork."

Shepherd nodded, "I…yeah. You're right. Thanks."

"Any time," Gray smiled, "Oh, one more thing, just for the record."

"What's that?"

"You *are* an Olympic-standard egomaniacal twit!" Gray laughed, "But, at least you're a *nice* Olympic-standard egomaniacal twit!"

Chapter 16
Silverdale, Washington
Friday, September 7, 2018; 14:01 hours

Recognizing Shepherd needed to get away from NCIS to regain his equanimity, Gray insisted they go to lunch over in the village of Keyport.

Keeters had recommended Keyport Mercantile and Sandwich, a small, local eatery on the waterfront of Keyport's tiny marina. The place was a combination old-fashioned general store and sandwich shop. Locals regularly patronized the general store half, while locals and Navy personnel from NASED Keyport kept the sandwich trade a true breadwinner.

The two men kept their conversation to neutral subjects as they munched until Shepherd's phone beeped.

He pulled the phone from his pocket, checking the text, "It's Stephanie. Hey, Abe—any chance we could set up a video conference in 30 minutes? Steph and Diego are at her office and want to get online to discuss what we need. Steph's office has an encrypted secure line."

"You contacted them already?" Gray said, surprised, "Damn, you're fast. Sure. I'm done if you are. Have her send the number to my SIPR email."

The large flat screen monitor blinked, burped, belched, and finally begat a grainy image that jerked, jumped, jiggled, jangled, eventually settling into a coherent picture.

"Good afternoon, oh Knight of the Woeful Countenance!" Federal Judge Stephanie Limbani chortled, her dark skin cracking into a bright smile from her office in Washington, D.C.

Next to her, the swarthy, slightly scarred, but handsome, face of Florida Senator Diego Alejandro twitched into a befuddled expression.

"Steph, are you *ever* going to get some new material?" Alejandro asked, pretending to be exasperated.

Gray looked curiously at Shepherd, "Care to fill me in?"

Shepherd glanced over, "About what?"

"'Knight of the Woeful Countenance?'" Gray asked, "What's that all about?"

Limbani looked shocked from across the continent, "He never told you?!"

"Told me what, Your Honor?" Gray asked.

"He sang the part of Don Quixote when our senior class did *Man of La Mancha,*" Limbani said, "He's always been tilting at impossible windmills anyway...as I'm sure you know!"

Gray chuckled while Shepherd rolled his eyes, "I thought you played baseball and worked on the school paper your senior year. I know you did a *little* theatre work, but just as a stagehand."

Alejandro laughed, "Nope. He sang Don Quixote, and I was Sancho."

"How the hell did you find time to win the high school state baseball championship *and* play the lead in a musical while playing photographer for the school newspaper?!" Gray asked Shepherd incredulously.

Shepherd shrugged, "I used to be a bit of an overachiever."

"'Used to be'?!" Alejandro, Limbani, and Gray all exclaimed in unison, three pairs of eyebrows rising in disbelief.

Limbani shook her head, "Isaac, saying you were a 'bit' of an overachiever is like saying the wreck of the *Titanic* is a little bit damp."

"*Anyway,*" Shepherd laughed, "Diego, you remember Abe, don't you? Y'all met on Guam back in '05."

"How could I forget? He came out for that Sumay Strangler dork, and then we all got caught up in the *Pacific Blaze* incident," Alejandro said, pointing to the scars making one side of his brown-skinned face resemble a pirate movie's lead actor, "I got these when those assholes blew up the damned ship!"

"Tell me about it," Shepherd said, pointing to his temple, "I've got scarring just above my right ear from that gun going off next to my head."

Alejandro grimaced, "I'm surprised you didn't lose any hearing."

"Say that again; I couldn't hear you!" Shepherd cupped his ear, pretending to be hard of hearing.

"Isaac, you're a dork!" Alejandro said, laughing before turning his turned his attention back to Gray, "Anyway, Abe, it's good to see you again!"

"You too, Senator," Gray smiled, "I'm not sure *any* of us got out of that incident completely intact. I wound up with two broken ribs and a dislocated shoulder when the shockwave from that blast hit the cutter *Galveston Island.*"

"Abe, I don't believe you've had the pleasure of meeting Stephanie," Shepherd said, pulling them back on topic. "Judge Stephanie Limbani of the D.C. Circuit Court, NCIS Special Agent—and piano player extraordinaire—Abraham Gray!"

"That's right!" Limbani nodded, "Isaac's told us you play a mean set of ivories! When are you going to start a YouTube channel or something?"

Gray looked askance at Shepherd, but smiled, "Isaac's been riding me for years to do that. Let's just say I'm considering it. Now, first off, Your Honor, I'd like to thank you both for taking the time to jump online with us today."

"No," Limbani said forcefully, but kindly, *"First off,* it's Stephanie, or Steph, and he's Diego. Abe, you earned first-name rights a long time ago. So, what can we do for y'all?"

"Are you two following the Tate investigation?" Shepherd asked, standing up to remove his brown corduroy sport coat. Walking over to a peg rail on the wall, he hung it up. Tightening the roll on the sleeves of his brick-red shirt, he returned to his seat, "Abe and I need some help outside of NCIS to sort some of this out."

"Outside NCIS?" Limbani asked, "May I assume this has something to do with Wonder Bitch and her lackeys making trouble on Capitol Hill?"

"Partly, Your Hon…er, Stephanie," Gray said. It would take him a bit to relax into first names. Still, Limbani, Alejandro, and Shepherd had been friends since 1986, and the two *had* aided them on several cases before.

"It's also partly because there's a truckload of dry rot festering inside NCIS," Gray continued. "I got sent out here because our local special agent in charge was deemed 'untrustworthy' due to both his staffing decisions and his handling of the Tate case."

"You're thinking his allies inside NCIS will taint your evidence," Alejandro said. It wasn't a question. "I see your problem. So, what can we do?"

Gray quickly outlined the two vastly different narratives they'd uncovered regarding Young-Saeng Tate's murder.

"What we need right now is to get some high-altitude analysis on the Lionfish angle," Gray said, "There's every reason to fear our suspects are already seeking a buyer. The Navy recovered all the paperwork Young-Saeng had brought home, but that doesn't mean our suspects didn't copy any of it."

"And you need this investigated without Wonder Bitch throwing more obstacles in your path," Limbani said, "I'm tracking."

"You *really* don't like Dana Cremer, do you?" Gray couldn't help but ask, a twinkle in his eye.

Limbani replied by staring coldly through cyberspace at Gray, "Abe, Dana Cremer is the venereal disease of Congress."

"Ouch!" Gray sat back, startled by Limbani's vehemence.

Limbani took a breath, "There are a *lot* of very decent people in Congress, despite what news outlets might portray. However, Congress also attracts some of the most corrupt people imaginable. Dana Cremer was already a bitch when I got here in 2016, but when Diego and I got some dirt on *her* to protect Isaac after he got that jerkwad brother of hers fired from NCIS last year, I just…she's just…"

Limbani trailed off, always a sign of deep rage.

Alejandro piped up, "Anyway, we'll be happy to help, but it might take us a bit. I only became the Senate Intelligence Committee chairman two weeks ago. I'm still getting read into all the various agencies I'll be getting briefings from."

"I know," Shepherd said, "Normally I'd throw this to Aidan and Linda, but with Linda back in Niceville seeing her grandmother and Aidan having to ride herd on The Horde—"

"And just *why* do you keep calling their kids that?!" Limbani demanded.

"Have you *met* their kids?" Shepherd's eyes twinkled, "I mean, come on. Even though those five boys are well-mannered, polite, and studious, they have all the energy of nuclear-powered chimpanzees chugging espresso!"

Limbani laughed, but then turned serious, "Hey, wait—did you get Linda's email this morning?"

"No," Shepherd's heart dropped into his stomach, "Please don't tell me Granny Darha died."

"Last night," Diego said, his voice sad.

"Damnation!" Shepherd thumped the table unhappily. Looking over to Gray, he said, "Granny Darha lived in Tampa, but she spent a lot of time in Niceville with Linda's family. She was a surrogate grandma to all of us growing up."

"Damn. Man, I'm sorry," Gray said, his face sympathetic, "It's hard when the adults you grew up with start passing away."

"She was 103," Alejandro said, "And she was in Niceville visiting Linda's folks when she had the stroke, so, at least she wasn't alone. But, yeah…I guess *we* all just took one more step into being the grown-ups."

Limbani was looking at the notes she'd taken during Gray's summary, "Let me get us back on track because I have to hear a case in 20 minutes. I don't know how much good *my* contacts will be in this one, but I'll do what I can. Still, I think Diego will a lot more effective here."

Alejandro nodded, "When do y'all need a response?"

Gray shrugged, "We need to get a read on this as fast as possible. I know this is asking a lot, but is there *any* chance y'all could have something by Monday afternoon, Senator…er, Diego?"

"Consider it done," Alejandro said. "I'm not promising *War and Peace,* but I can have something for you by then."

The three Niceville High School alumni continued sharing the quips and inside jokes springing from such a long friendship for a few more minutes. Gray sat quietly, following along as best he could while being amused at how cluelessly they'd conversationally pushed him to the side.

Saying their goodbyes, Limbani reached forward, popping a button on her remote control. The screen blinked and went dead, the call ended.

"Well, *that* was a new one for me!" Gray said, blowing out his breath and leaning back in his chair.

"What was?"

"That's the first time *I've* personally asked a federal judge and a senator for help investigating a crime!" Gray laughed.

"Well, you never forget your first time," Shepherd couldn't resist, "I just hope we were gentle enough for you!"

Gray snorted, but otherwise ignored the double-entendre. Instead, he got up and walked over to a whiteboard where he and Shepherd had scrawled a hasty timeline.

"I know you're going to talk to your friend, Liam, about doing some digital skullduggery in regards to the hospital cyberattack and the financial records we think were altered," Gray said, hands on his hips, "But, I wish I could have Charlotte and the Norfolk team deal with that angle."

"Me too, believe it or not," Shepherd said sympathetically, "I know Liam's helped us before, but that was when he was a cop back on Guam. I'd rather depend on an established ally when it comes to the cyberattacks, but, still, Sarah trusts him."

"Sarah doesn't trust easily or quickly," Gray agreed, "She's almost ridiculously vigilant about protecting her professional reputation, so the fact she's been mentoring Liam since he started up his firm means a lot. I trust Sarah's judgment, so that means I have to trust Liam…but we'll still—"

"—trust, but verify," Shepherd cut in, "Of course. We can start building up our confidence level tomorrow."

"Tomorrow?"

"We're having dinner with him tomorrow night, remember?"

"We are?" Gray asked, his face blank.

"Oh, crap!" Shepherd smacked himself on the forehead, "I'm sorry, I forgot to tell you! He and Maria invited us over for dinner tomorrow night. That'd be a good time to talk to him. Also, I'm going to see if they'll let me invite A.J. That way I can ask him if he and Josh know the *gesekgi*."

"Wow," Gray said, "You *really* don't like Gippeum Lýkos, do you? The last time you talked like *that* was when Melody Rhyme murdered two people aboard the *Dwight D. Eisenhower.*"

"You had to feel it too, Abe," Shepherd's voice was mired in a tone that liberally mixed one-part disgust with two parts alarm and one part sheer disbelief, "That man is just…just *evil.*"

"Are you sure you're not still unsettled because he got the verbal drop on you?" Gray asked carefully.

"Of course, I'm pissed off about that!" Shepherd dismissed the suggestion with an irritable wave of his hand, "No one likes being beaten at their own game. But you *were* right; I'm not used to running into someone who *can* best me. No; I'm talking about *him.* He's a walking incarnation of pure, undiluted evil."

"Any ideas yet on how he pulled off being on the East Coast and West Coast at the same time?" Gray asked hopefully.

"Not yet, but I'm working on it," Shepherd said, pointing to a small pile of books neatly stacked on the floor behind the chair he'd taken to using. Gray realized the books were all discourses on genetics and genetic theories.

Shepherd noticed that Gray noticed the subject matter of the books. "Genetics are one idea I'm running down, but there's also another angle I'm exploring. You see, the *gesekgi's* written a few physics textbooks and teaches quantum mechanics at the University of North Carolina at Chapel Hill. However, the kind of money he'd need to pull this off is *way* beyond a university salary, even for a tenured professor with a Ph.D. like him. If I can't find a way to use DNA evidence to nail his ass, uncovering the money trail might nail him for us."

"How in the *hell* do we use forensics to differentiate between identical triplets...well, 'twins' now since the third brother died years ago," Gray said, thumping his fist against the wall.

"I'm working on it!" Shepherd reassured Gray, "I'm going to become an expert in DNA theories and genetic forensics in the next 72 hours."

"Ok, I've got another interview aboard NASED here in 45 minutes," Gray said, looking at his watch, "I'll be done by 16:00 at the latest. Then you and I are going to catch the ferry and go to Seattle for dinner."

"We are?"

"We are," Gray nodded emphatically, "We've been running at full military power ever since you got here. We both need a few hours to slow down and clear our heads. You might be an unpaid volunteer consultant, but I've got enough per diem to feed an army, so we're going somewhere nice. Meet me in the hotel lobby at 17:00, ok?"

"Done and done!"

Chapter 17

Seattle, Washington
Friday, September 7, 2018; 18:52 hours

The great metal manatee of the Seattle Ferry lumbered across Puget Sound, its bow aimed toward the Seattle skyline. The wide, plodding craft's gleaming green and white livery glistened under the gentle misting of salt spray as its bow pushed aside the dark water.

Night had descended. The Pacific Northwest was moving into a time of late sunrises and early sunsets known as 'The Big Dark.' The air was a mild 64° F, but most of the ferry passengers stayed inside the warm and warmly lit cabin. The bright flying saucer of the Space Needle and the colorful light show of the waterfront area weren't enough to entice them out on deck. They lived here, after all. They'd seen it all a thousand times before.

Only one lone passenger remained out on the weather deck, his footing as steady as any mariner's. An experienced sailor, his sea legs were sure, and he enjoyed the sway of the deck under his feet. His innate love of the restless water soothed, but could not mute, the turmoil in his heart.

I'm glad I already made plans to see Bob in November after the Grand Tour is over, but this just sucks!

"Isaac?" Abraham Gray said, exiting the cabin and heading over to stand by Shepherd's side.

Shepherd had been agitated and quiet ever since they met in the hotel lobby. The drive to the Bainbridge Island Ferry Terminal had been oddly silent because the usually irrepressible Shepherd had been deeply repressed.

"Isaac?" Gray said again, laying a hand on Shepherd's shoulder, "Hey, it doesn't take Hercule Parrot to see something's wrong."

Shepherd sadly smiled at the familiar gag. Gray had accidentally mispronounced the name of Agatha Christie's most famous detective a couple of years earlier, and Shepherd had laughed himself silly over the mistake. The blunder had since become a running joke between the two.

"I'm sorry, Abe," Shepherd softly spoke, his voice just loud enough to be heard over the hissing fizz of the ferry's wake, "I got an email from Bob Wilson this afternoon. He's another one of my old high school gang."

Gray nodded, "I remember. He flew out to Guam back in...what? '99? 2000?"

"It was in early 2000," Shepherd said, "His wife had died, and he left his son with his folks so he could fly out and get some downtime. Hazy Payne, Cody Rupp, and I took him to Paris with us for a week."

"That's right," Gray nodded, "He was talking about moving to Tampa for a new job as a fire investigator so his son would have more resources in the Tampa school district after his wife passed away. What happened?"

"Well, he's been retired for a few years now," Shepherd said. "He was at a firefighting symposium on Staten Island on 9/11."

"That's right," Gray nodded, "You told me they rushed to assist the response efforts. Didn't he stay in New York helping clean up The Pile for a couple of months?"

"He did, and he's fought multiple respiratory illnesses ever since," Shepherd said dully, "Three years ago he developed lung cancer. The shit's moved into stage 4. He's still got a couple of years, but the odds of a long life aren't looking good."

"Damn, Isaac. I'm sorry," Gray said, taking in the heavy news.

Shepherd's head dropped momentarily before looking back up at the approaching city, "It's ironic since it's been nearly twenty years, but Bob'll be the first person I *actually* know who was killed by 9/11...even if it took about twenty years to happen. Still, he's been working with John Stewart and a few others to get Congress off its ass to permanently fund the James Zadroga 9/11 Health and Compensation Act."

"John Stewart—*The Daily Show* comedian?" Gray asked.

"That's him. He's been advocating on this issue for years. I just hope Bob lives long enough to see it through. All Bob ever wanted to be a firefighter and save lives."

"Well, he's making a difference with this effort in Congress," Gray said, "Even though he's…"

"Dying. You can say it," Shepherd sighed, "I mean, I know we still have a couple of years at least, but…*dammit!* I hate goodbyes."

The ferry lightly bumped its blunt bow against the Seattle Ferry Terminal's dock. Gray and Shepherd joined the disembarking throng flooding through a cattle chute of passageways built from wood and scaffolding. The terminal was undergoing massive renovations, causing the passengers to be shunted through temporary walkways out to Alaskan Way.

"I imagine this crowd is off the chain during the summer months," Gray said, noting that Shepherd's mood was gradually improving.

"So where are we going to eat?' Shepherd asked, zipping his blue field jacket partway up and planting *Ike,* his older round-rimmed cowboy hat, on his head.

"No idea," Gray shrugged, plopping an Atlanta Braves ball cap on his head, "But this is the Seattle waterfront. South of here are the stadiums, so I'm betting if we go *north,* we'll find something."

The evening chill was countered by the vivacious energy giving life to Seattle. Even though summer was over, Alaskan Way was still full of tourists drawn by the Pac Northwest's stunning beauty. The two men passed small eateries, souvenir shops, and several buskers working the sidewalks with their various talents.

"Okay, I've never seen *that* before!" Gray laughed, nodding at a group of bicycle taxi drivers dressed as famous comic book characters such as Iron Man, Spider-Man, and Batman.

"Reminds me of buskers I've seen in Time Square. I doubt they've been licensed by Marvel and DC Comics, though!" Shepherd said, finally smiling, a light chuckle rumbling up from his belly.

"And who is this fine fellow?" Gray said as they came upon the bronze statue of a portly man feeding bronze pigeons outside of Ivar's Fish Bar on Pier 54.

Shepherd glanced at a small information sign, "This is Ivar Haglund. Oh, he's the founder of this place," Shepherd pointed to Ivar's, "Hmm…says he started by opening an aquarium on the waterfront, but when he started making more from his guests eating at his snack bar, he shifted into restaurants. Cool character!"

"I didn't realize Nordic peoples had been such big settlers here, but that explains the Scandinavian influence I've noticed in this part of the country," Gray said as they began moseying north again.

"Kid Canaveral?!"

Shepherd's head jerked around so fast it nearly parted from his neck. Gray, long trained to react when Shepherd reacted, whirled around to find himself looking at two Isaacs, both with glowing green eyes and neatly trimmed steel-gray beards.

"Son of a rabid terrier!" One of the Isaacs—Abraham Gray's Isaac, specifically—exclaimed before laughing, "Space Cadet! What the hell are you doing *here?!*"

Gray's brain kicked his common sense back into play. He wasn't looking at some rip in the space/time continuum spitting out an alternate-universe version of Isaac.

Idiot! Gray quietly laughed at himself, *That's one of Isaac's brothers!*

"Hey, hey!" The brothers embraced, laughing heartily.

"I was going to call you!" Isaac said, "Abe, you remember my brother, A.J.!"

"Good to see you again!" Gray said, shaking A.J.'s hand, "How's Josh? Is he still coaching with the Steelers?"

"He is, indeed," A.J. replied, returning Gray's handshake with frightening enthusiasm, "Offensive coordinator. Where the hell did you two come from? And why you didn't tell me you were in my city, Isaac?!"

Isaac shoved his hands in his pockets, "Ah, well…I'm not on holiday right now. Abe needed an assist."

A.J.'s face fell so hard it nearly cracked the sidewalk, "I thought you gave up this stupid detective crap when you retired. No offense, Abe," A.J. shot a dismissive glance toward Gray.

Gray did his best to keep his face neutral.

"Retired from the Navy, yes," Isaac said, just now realizing a small group of young adults huddled behind A.J., "As to the rest…well, dude, we need to talk. And I mean *seriously* talk. But not here. You've got people with you—can we meet tomorrow?"

"I'll do you one better," A.J. said, turning to his entourage, "Charlie, Doug, Lydia—go on back to Port Angeles. I'll catch you up on Monday; my car's still at the terminal on Bainbridge Island."

"Will do, Mr. Shepherd," Lydia nodded, "See you Monday morning!"

Lydia turned. She, Charlie, and Doug wrangled the rest of the students up, herding them south toward the ferry terminal.

"Port Angeles?" Isaac asked.

"We're doing a study on the thermal hot springs in the Olympics for a couple of weeks, so we're staying out there."

"I thought the Olympics were built by uplift, not volcanoes?" Gray asked, "That's what the 'welcome to Seattle' video on the plane said, anyway."

A.J. nodded, "They are, but there's a small thermal system, meaning groundwater is being heated by magma. It's a tiny possibility, but we're investigating whether we might be looking at an emerging volcano in a few million years."

Gray sighed, shoving his hands in his pockets, "Well, at least that gives me time to update my will!"

A.J.'s face grew serious again, "Okay, Isaac, just *what* in the hell is *so* damned important you're playing detective again?"

"What's so damned important is murder," Isaac said, "And you and Josh are both persons of interest in this one, so don't go being your usual dismissively stupid self. We need to talk. For real."

The deathly pallor overtaking A.J.'s face testified to the shock value of Isaac's words.

"Uh…so, what are you two doing over *here* tonight?" A.J. asked.

"It *was* supposed to be a dinner away from the case for a few hours," Gray said, "But Kid Canaveral's right. We need to talk, and the sooner the better."

Isaac gave Gray an exasperated look at the use of the nickname.

"Okay…" A.J. nodded, "I know a pretty good place called The Crab Pot up on Pier 57—the same pier with the big Ferris wheel. Great seafood and just noisy enough that we can have some privacy if that works for you two."

"So, 'Kid Canaveral?'" Gray asked after the three had ordered.

The trio was seated in a section so loud with gregarious guests a spy satellite with an ear trumpet couldn't have eavesdropped on them.

"Josh, Isaac, and I were on a big space kick back when Pop was stationed at Andrews Air Force Base in the late '70s and early '80s," A.J. said, "We built a mission control out of shoe boxes, construction paper, and our space shuttle and rocket toys. We must have been, what, bro…Six? Seven?"

"Seven when we started, I think," Isaac leaned back, allowing their server to refresh his glass of unsweet tea.

"We all decided we needed code names," A.J. smiled, taking his salad from the server, "Isaac's Kid Canaveral, I'm Space Cadet, and Josh is Martian Boy."

"And *you* are most certainly *not* allowed to get any mileage out of this one, Abraham! Shepherds only!" Isaac laughed heartily.

Gray laughed, studying the two members of the triplets that sat next to him. They truly were the definition of identical. Each man's beard was trimmed to nearly the same length, differentiated only by the specific pattern of dark hairs mixing with the gray ones.

Whether by design or accident, both brothers also had their more-salt-than-pepper hair cut nearly the same. Were it not for the different clothing and glasses frames, Gray might have thought he was seeing double.

"Isaac just grew out his beard," Gray said, "Is yours a recent addition, as well?"

A.J. nodded, "Actually, yes. Josh also grew his out. We both realized how good *we'd* look after seeing Isaac's photos, so we grew them out. My wife loves it!"

"Looks like you started a trend," Gray said to Isaac.

"Not to split hairs, but yes," Isaac said.

"We could comb through the details of Josh and I's decision to follow Isaac's example, but I don't want to brush off what y'all needed to talk to me about," A.J. replied.

Gray loosed an agonized groan. Rubbing his temple with his hand, he shook his head, "Don't tell me all *three* of you love stupid puns?!"

"Well, we *do* have our dad's sense of humor," A.J. started.

"He wants it back," Isaac continued.

"But we're keeping it!" A.J. finished cheerily, sharing a puckish smile with Isaac as Gray leaned back, face-palming himself.

"Ok, now, look, bro," A.J. turned serious over his ranch dressing, "Why are you doing this stupid shit again by playing detective? No offense, Abe."

"None taken," Gray replied, once again forcing himself to *not* roll his eyes.

"I changed my mind," Isaac said tightly, "You can lecture me later. Right now, Abe and I need to know if you or Josh know Gippeum Lýkos from Mensa."

A.J. nearly spit out his mouthful of salad. Barely choking it down, he paused as their server reappeared.

A.J. continued clearing his windpipe of lettuce as a cup of steamy, creamy clam chowder was set down before Isaac. The server asked them if they needed anything else.

"No, we're good, thanks!" Gray said affably.

The young man flipped his tray up in a fancy way before disappearing back into the crowd.

"Oh, crap! You're part of the *Tate* investigation?!" A.J. finally asked.

Jeez, they even have the same twitches in their eyebrows! Gray noticed, *I wonder if Josh does too?*

"Space Cadet, Abe and I *are* the Tate investigation," Isaac said tightly, "And it's a bigger mess than you can imagine. Now, your reaction was rather epic, so just how *well* do you know that Lýkos asshat?"

"Ah, I see you've met him," A.J. said with zero sarcasm, "He's been at a few Mensa conventions that Josh and I attended over the years. I'm a year away from getting my Ph.D. in volcanology, not psychiatry, but even *I* can tell you that asshole is a pure psychopath. He's a cold-hearted, dangerous bastard."

"We could tell," Gray said lightly, "We spoke with him in person this morning. He showed up in Silverdale unexpectedly."

"What do you know about him?" Isaac pressed, "He named-dropped you and Josh during our interview. This puts me in an awkward position since I'm supposed to be the 'objective independent consultant'...but it also means we have some valuable insight into the man. I'll risk the conflict-of-interest charges later. Right now, we're running down a particularly violent murder. So, spill it."

A.J. looked upset, "Just so you know, Mom and Pop are going to be *pissed* you're still playing detective instead of getting a job and acting like you've finally grown up, bro."

Isaac cocked his head to the side. Gray knew that look; Isaac was winding up a sockdologizer of a comeback.

"Interesting you say that since, out of the three of us, *I'm* the one who's retired *and* financially independent at 45. You and Josh still have a few hundred grand in student loans to pay back, last time I checked. Or am I mistaken about whose long-term career planning proved most financially advantageous?"

Gray did his best to keep his face straight instead of laughing at the shocked, hang-dog expression twisting A.J.'s features. He could see A.J. had never considered the strategic wisdom of Isaac's life choices.

"So, what *do* you know about this *gesekgi?"* Isaac pressed.

"This what?" A.J. asked, confused.

"Korean for 'son of a bitch,'" Gray supplied before seeing their server approaching with their meals, "Hold up a minute, guys."

Platters laden with freshly steamed shellfish, fried clams, slabs of salmon, and roasted vegetables formed a small mountain range across their table. The Shepherd boys dived into the shellfish; Gray accosted the salmon. The vegetables thought they were safe until three forks mercilessly began spearing numerous members of their tribe as their server left.

A.J. began speaking once they had filled their plates, "I met Young-Saeng—the nice one—a few times. I'm not sure if Josh met him. Young-Saeng was quiet, but, damn, that man was *brilliant!* Those brothers might even be smarter than the three of us, Isaac. I'm pretty sure they'd rate over 200 on an IQ test."

"Where do you three clock in at?" Gray asked, intrigued.

"Pretty damned high," The two Shepherd brothers said in unison before returning to their conversation.

Gray rolled his eyes.

"Spill it, Space Cadet," Isaac directed for a second time.

A.J. nodded, "Ok, ok. Young-Saeng had a decency about him, but Gippeum can be charming, winning, and even flirtatious; then turn cold as a snake. Classic psychopathic narcissist, lacking empathy, conniving, manipulative…the works."

"Do you have any biographical data on the two of them beyond your experiences?" Gray asked as he cut into his salmon steak.

192

"Young-Saeng told me a bit one time at a conference," A.J. said, "We were attending a forum on the potential use of robotics for geological investigation."

"That certainly cuts across both his field and yours," Isaac said.

"Young-Saeng said they were triplets," A.J. shrugged, "All three were born in Seoul, but the family was living in abject poverty, so their parents put them up for adoption through a Catholic charity."

"I knew about the adoption, but not the Catholic angle," Gray said, "Please continue."

"The third brother died in a car wreck when they were 13," A.J. said, "Young-Saeng wouldn't say more than that. But he did tell me he'd been doing some genealogy. This must have been…let me see…" A.J. munched a shrimp while he thought, "Good grief, that was last summer, just before you retired, Isaac. Wow, time flies! Anyway, Young-Saeng told me he'd found their birth parents running an electronics company in South Korea."

"Anything else?"

"No," A.J. said, shaking his head, "We were chatting during a break, and they called the forum back to order right about then. So, that was about it."

"Anything else?" Gray asked.

"Only that Young-Saeng made it a point to *never* be at a Mensa function if Gippeum was there," A.J. said, "He'd only say they had a difficult relationship, but I could tell it was more. *Way* more. You could see it in his eyes whenever Gippeum's name came up. Young-Saeng was terrified, *horribly* terrified, of his brother. I never could find out why, though. He refused to talk about it."

Chapter 18
Seattle, Washington
Friday, September 7, 2018; 21:13 hours

Following the uproarious feast, the three men slowly made their way south along Alaskan Way. Deliberately leaving the Tate case behind, they kept their conversation confined to neutral subjects, such as A.J.'s upcoming dissertation on Mount St. Helens. The change in subject was a welcome distraction after Isaac broke the news about Bob Wilson's cancer to A.J. Although not part of Isaac's friend group in high school, A.J. and Josh had grown up knowing Isaac's friends even as Isaac had known theirs.

"The volcano is just not where we'd expect it to be," A.J. continued rambling about Mount St. Helens as they slipped past a knot of revelers exiting Elliott's Oyster House, "The system is located significantly west of the rest of the Cascades arc. My dissertation won't reveal any explosive revelations—all puns intended—but I'm confident my exploration of the microfractures spidering through the surrounding crust might contribute to one day figuring it out."

Gray stopped by a souvenir shop, "If I don't pick up something for Sarah, she'll kill me. She's always wanted to visit Seattle."

The shop turned out to be rather large. The trio lost themselves in the racks of T-shirts, magnets, stuffed animals, puzzles, and snow globes with miniature Space Needles nestled inside. Half an hour later, they rendezvoused at the entrance, ready to head back to the ferry terminal.

Gray did a double take. A.J. and Isaac had each purchased small, stuffed killer whales with 'Seattle' embroidered on their sides. A.J. was carrying two of the fuzzy toys.

"Josh'll love this!" A.J. was telling Isaac.

"Odds are that'll end up in his office!" Isaac laughed.

"Wait, all *three* of you collect stuffed animals?" Gray asked, disbelief etching his face.

"Yeah, duh!" Isaac and A.J. said in unison, both displaying identical expressions of incredulity at Gray's question.

"Ok, sorry!" Gray laughed, "I just thought collecting stuffies was Isaac's hobby."

"Being born in Texas, we're all Dallas Cowboy fans," A.J. said.

"Ok. So what…?" Gray asked curiously.

"Well, Josh is the offensive coordinator for the Pittsburgh Steelers," A.J. answered, "He's got a big ole' Dallas Cowboys teddy bear on a shelf above his desk. Everyone—even the head coach and owner—have to look at it when they walk in to see him!"

Gray began laughing hard. Recovering his breath, he looked at Isaac, "Yeah…Josh is *definitely* your brother!"

The three enjoyed a leisurely stroll back to the ferry terminal. Their timing was good; they only had to wait ten minutes for the next ferry to Bainbridge Island. The large craft was largely empty that time of night, so they had no trouble finding seats to relax in while enjoying the slow ride across Puget Sound.

"So… exactly what time *did* you park this morning, Space Cadet?" Isaac asked, trying to keep an amused smile off his face.

"Nine," A.J. said, irritation turning his face into a dour mask.

"Yeah, I'm pretty sure your battery is as dead as Disco," Isaac said, mouth twitching as he fought not to laugh at his brother's plight.

A.J.'s pretty little blue sedan sat forlornly in the Bainbridge Island Ferry Terminal parking lot. The aggrieved machine's dying headlights feebly emitted a desultory glow as the last of the battery's juice drained away.

"I've got a rental," Gray shrugged apologetically, "Unfortunately, it didn't come with jumper cables."

Isaac shook his head, "Dude, it's an hour-and-a-half round trip to Silverdale and back. Just crash in my hotel room tonight. I'll give you a jump tomorrow morning."

A.J. quietly snarled an undistinguishable curse or two before looking up, "Thanks."

"Do you also use a CPAP machine as well?" Gray asked A.J.

"No," Isaac groused, "This nitwit is the only one of us three *without* sleep apnea."

Gray's cell phone rang. He stepped away to answer it.

A.J. laughed, his sour mood breaking, "Well, at least now I'll get a firsthand look at how you play detective, Isaac!"

"You think you're joking, but, sadly, you're not,' Gray said, voice tight and his face rigid.

Isaac knew that expression, "Oh, for crying out loud! Let me guess—we've got another dead body, don't we?"

Gray nodded, "That was Sheriff Sigo. Delores Tate is dead."

"Son of a *bitch…!*" Isaac's face morphed into a mask of pure rage.

A.J. found himself extremely discomfited by Isaac's rapid change of mood. He'd never seen his brother look so angry before.

Gray nodded, his countenance hardening with fury, "She was shot by a long-range weapon while walking in the prison yard. We have to get down to the Kitsap County jail *now.* A.J., I'm sorry, but I'm afraid you're stuck with us for a while. Let's go; it only happened about half an hour ago!"

The drive to the Kitsap County Jail down in Port Orchard took an hour. Contrary to the movies, Gray had no portable flashing red light to stick atop the roof of his rental car, so he had to be mindful of the speed limit.

Still, he *might* have violated a few local speed laws…

"Ok, look, bro, this is a crime scene, so do *not* touch anything, and do *not* go anywhere unless Abe or I tell you to, ok?" Isaac turned, addressing A.J. in the back seat, "Understand?"

"I'm not an ignorant fool, Isaac," A.J. replied testily.

"I'm not saying you are," Isaac responded firmly, "But this is *not* something you're remotely accustomed to seeing or dealing with. So, please, *please,* just this once, do me a *huge* favor and listen to me, ok?"

"Whatever," A.J. rolled his eyes at his brother's hen-pecking caution.

196

Gray and Isaac locked eyes for a minute, the unspoken look between them communicating a great deal...but then the moment passed.

Gray smashed the brake pedal down, locking up the antilock brakes. The car jetted into the parking lot outside the correctional facility, Gray expertly steering it into a free slot. An armada of police vehicles was stuffed into the limited space, their flaring lights casting ghastly, dancing shadows as Gray and his passengers disembarked.

The Kitsap force was already familiar with Gray and Isaac, but A.J.'s presence caused a bit of consternation. Fortunately, Sheriff Sigo was waiting for them and ran interference at the first checkpoint.

"Damn!" Sigo exclaimed as the three men surrendered their metal objects (the only exception being Gray's badge). "And you said there are *three* of you? Isaac, please tell me your other brother isn't in the state?"

"Pennsylvania," Isaac grinned, serenely allowing a guard to pat him down.

A.J. shivered as he was searched for contraband after handing over his car keys and pocketknife.

"Thank heaven for small favors," Sigo planted her hands on her squat hips, looking up at Gray and the two Shepherds. Her own Sam Brown belt was secured in the checkpoint's storage area, but the lack of weapons didn't diminish the air of authority she exuded, "Short version: due to the chronic depression Delores Tate was suffering, the psychiatrist recommended she take an extra walk in the exercise yard for 15 minutes before lights out at 22:00. She was outside with a guard when...well, come and see."

Turning, Sigo addressed A.J.

"I need you to stay inside of the blue lines," Sigo ordered, "That'll keep you out of arm's length of the cells. If anyone throws something at you, let *us* handle it. Don't talk to any of the prisoners, and *do not* respond to them in *any* way. Avoid all eye contact. Most of these inmates are pretty low-threat, but we have to maintain consistent standards throughout the facility."

The three followed Sigo through the thronging corridors. A.J.'s face grew increasingly pale as heavy prison doors clanged shut behind him and thick prison glass increasingly separated him from the rest of the world.

The low-security wing of the facility put A.J. in mind of the sort of sterile maze one usually sees in pharmaceutical commercials. The tile gleamed so white it almost hurt A.J.'s eyes, and the smell of antiseptic was itself strong enough to wipe out a few hundred bacterial colonies.

There were no smells of urine, feces, or sweat echoing off the gleaming tile walls and floor, nor cries of distress wafting through the air like a demented odor.

The stark, hard, brilliantly lit environment had no soft edges or plush carpets to help dampen sound. Voices and footfalls carried without interruption, bouncing back and forth mercilessly in a self-perpetuating audio cacophony assaulting A.J.'s ears. He began to breathe heavily as he realized he couldn't tell where the footfalls were coming from anymore. Was he only hearing their footsteps, or were those the bootfalls of guards on the other side of the building mixing with their own?

How the hell is this not *bothering him?!* A.J. thought, looking at Isaac's calmly strolling form ahead of him.

A violent *BANG!* crashed through the ice-hard corridor, causing A.J. to jump so hard he nearly took out an overhead light.

"Just a cell door over in the other block," A guard told A.J. after seeing him jump, "Nothing to worry about."

"Easy for you to say," A.J. muttered, too shaken up to be embarrassed.

"This is why it's usually kept perfectly silent in a correctional facility after lights out, A.J.," Isaac said over his shoulder. "Even the guards are locked in at night because there's just no way to stop sound from echoing around here like a grenade blast."

A.J. found the sterile, echoing rigidity of the prison far more alien, unwelcoming, and frightening than anything he and Josh had experienced during their plebe year at the Naval Academy.

He shivered as he continued following Isaac and Gray.

Although he studiously avoided eye contact, A.J. *was* a Shepherd boy. His eyes might not be as keenly trained as Isaac's, but his skull housed a brain just as quick on the uptake. The lights in the cells had also been illuminated due to the breach in security, affording A.J. the chance to surreptitiously study the inmates around him.

Women ranging from beautiful to broken down sat forlornly in their cells. Most women were alone simply because the rural nature of Kitsap County meant the inmate population was not overlarge, but a few did share their cramped quarters with a cellmate. A.J. noticed that most of the inmates watched them with varying degrees of interest or hostility. Some, however, simply stared at them silently through eyes glazed over with fatigue after being suddenly awakened.

Passing by Central, the eyes of multiple guards beadily watching them, A.J. glanced again at Isaac. He was still shocked his brother was relaxed and unfazed as they strode along. *Jeez...he's actually* used *to this shit!*

The labyrinth finally ended, only one more door separating them from the prison yard—and the crime scene.

"A.J., stay here," Isaac said quietly, "Crime scenes are...well, not pretty. You don't need to see what's out there. If we're longer than a few minutes, I'll get someone to take you somewhere to wait."

Isaac turned, following Gray and Sigo out into the prison yard. A.J. watched the yard's floodlights spill over the back of Isaac's blue field jacket before curiosity got the better of him. Catching the heavy door, he slipped through.

"The chain-link fence certainly didn't provide any kind of obstacle," Gray was saying as A.J. surreptitiously approached the group, "Still, I think we can safely conclude the shot came from

199

above the fence based on the spatter pattern. There's plenty of places up in those hills a marksman could have been positioned."

"Agreed," Sigo said, "I've already got a team up in the hills, but, even with the K9 unit, they're just poking around in the dark. I doubt they'll find anything before sunup—and that's assuming our shooter left anything to find."

"Impact damage concurs with your assessments," Isaac said while crouched over the flattened form of the formerly living naval officer.

Delores Tate lay sprawled on the asphalt as if some great dog had picked her up and shaken her so violently her head split open, then dropped her unceremoniously in a puddle of her own blood and brain matter. The pool was thick and goopy, reflecting the harsh prison yard lights with a sickeningly burgundy flair. Bits of white skull and pinkish gray brain lay in a fan past her towards the prison building, marking the trajectory of the shot.

"The entry wound is well above the right temple," Isaac was saying, hands kept firmly at his sides since he had no gloves on, "Seems to be a slightly fore-to-aft hit. From what I can see, the exit wound is pretty ugly. Blew off nearly the whole left side of her face."

"Crap!" Gray swore, slapping a hand on his thigh in a rare public show of frustration, "This stinking mess just keeps getting worse!"

"Tell me about it!" Sigo seethed, "You realize what this means, right? It means I've got *another* leak in my goddamned department!"

"Not necessarily, Denita," Isaac replied, still crouched over the body, "It's possible this facility was externally surveilled, just like the Tates' home was. Clearly, Delores was murdered by the same freakazoids that killed Young-Saeng. Our assassin—or assassins—could have been given inside information on Delores's schedule, or been watching this place for a few days to determine her routine."

"Or both," Gray cautioned, "We have to look at all three possibilities. Denita, the officers who were out here—how close was the sound of the gunshot to the fatal impact?"

Sigo looked surprised, "I don't know. I'll have to ask them. Why?"

"That'll help us get a rough idea if the killer was close, or took a *seriously* long-ranged shot," Gray said, "It's not much, but that data might help narrow down both potential suspects *and* where you should place your search teams. After all, if the shot came from a ways off, then we can determine pretty quickly our shooter is a highly skilled marksman, not your run-of-the-mill thug."

"As if there's anything run-of-the-mill about thugs!" Isaac stood with difficulty. His knees, injured two decades prior, groaned out in a deep, bone-shaking ache while cracking like old-fashioned Pop Rocks candy. The joints did *not* like crouching in squats anymore.

A.J. finally got a good look at the body—and blood and brain matter and skull—of Delores Tate.

Gravity had already begun pulling her skin into a deathly sag. Tate's arms and legs were sprawled in a manner that reminded A.J. of the last time he'd seen some frat boys and sorority girls passed out around the University of Washington's campus following a football game. However, the shattered head mercilessly pulled A.J.'s attention back to the present.

Tate lay on her back, her head twisted to one side. The right side of her head showed a tiny, neat hole just above the temple.

The pool of blood under her body was strewn with shattered bones and crumbled pieces of brain matter looking like so much rotten cottage cheese. The blood and moist tissue debris twinkled under the floodlights. A.J. realized he was looking at part of her jaw—with the teeth still in it.

"Abe, are there any known rogue sharpshooters in the area NCIS knows about?" Isaac was asking when the searing sound of vomit crashing onto concrete yanked his head around.

A.J. was throwing up with remarkable violence. A weak gurgle that might have been language bubbled out of his mouth between the rapid-fire shower of shellfish emerging from his stomach with stunning rapidity.

"You stupid, stinking *idiot!*" Isaac cursed, sprinting to his brother, "I *told* you to stay inside, you dumb ass!"

"S—sorry!" A.J. finally managed to get a few words out between the tectonic heaves of his stomach, "I just…wanted to see…"

"You *moron!*" Isaac bellowed so loudly his voice echoed off the concrete prison walls several times. He jumped backward to keep another wave of vomit from splattering his shoes. Turning, he saw, well, pretty much everyone staring at them. Corralling his temper, Isaac forced himself to unclench his fists. Assaulting his brother in front of half the Kitsap County Police Department was not a particularly wise idea.

"Can you walk?" Isaac demanded, his voice icy with barely restrained fury.

"Y—yeah, I think so—" A.J. started to say.

"Come on, you insegrevious *idiot!"* Isaac barked acidly, grabbing A.J.'s arm with a level of violence that shocked A.J. into coherence, "Let's get out of here before you contaminate the whole goddamned crime scene any further!"

The midnight hour was nearly upon them when Gray finally turned up in one of the lounges for the corrections staff. Isaac was standing, arms crossed, his face screwed up in rage as his brother sat on a couch. A.J.'s face was pale as he held a cup of water in his hand.

"Isaac, we're done here for the night," Gray said, his own eyes giving A.J. a sharp look, "Let's get back to Silverdale."

A.J. looked up at Isaac, "Bro, you've been standing there for an hour. Just say it."

"Abe, close the door," Isaac ordered.

Gray obliged, his own eyes burning holes into A.J.'s visage.

"I've been waiting for Abe to get here so you could hear from a *professional* just what you might have fucked up tonight, Mr. Genius!" Isaac spat, "Abe, care to illuminate?"

Gray's temper had been on a high boil...but seeing Isaac's volcanic rage cooled his anger just a bit. Not much, mind you, but a bit.

"A.J., first off, the *only* reason you were let in the building was as a courtesy to Isaac and me," Gray said, his voice sharp, "You were allowed in because it was *believed* you'd respect the directions of *all* personnel involved in this situation...most *especially* your brother. He told you very clearly to stay inside!"

A.J. wilted, which was saying something seeing as he'd spent over an hour vomiting up everything he'd eaten for the past week.

"Sheriff Sigo was two seconds away from throwing all *three* of us out on our goddamned asses!" Gray snapped, his temper still so riled up that he fell into a rare use of public cursing, "I had to do a *lot* of very fast talking to preserve her cooperation! She's already had a *shitload* of crap dumped on her by NCIS. It's taken a *lot* to earn her trust, and now you nearly blow it all because you were *curious?!*"

"I—" A.J. started to sputter, but Gray interrupted mercilessly.

"I don't want to hear it!" Gray bit A.J.'s head off venomously, his temper boiling back up, "Look, I know full well you and Josh think you two are some pair of super-duper, high falutin' elites because you're Naval Academy ring knockers, but, you know what, Andrew?"

A.J. just stared, waiting for the blow.

"You're an ignorant little *putz!*" Gray snapped, the acid in his voice scorching the paint on the walls. "You know *nothing!* I don't care how much of a big shot you are in your clean little academic circles; *this* is the *real world,* and you've made yourself *nothing* but an embarrassing liability! You need to get your fucking head out of your ass *and grow up!*"

Gray stopped himself. A.J.'s head had dropped, his gaze on the floor.

Looking at Isaac, Gray gave a 'your turn' gesture to him.

"Look at me, Andrew," Isaac ordered, still so angry that he forgot to react to Gray's uncharacteristic use of foul language.

"I can hear you," A.J. said, his head still lowered as he set his cup back on the table.

"That was *not* a request!" Isaac reached down, grabbing A.J. by the collar and hoisting him to his feet in one fluid, rage-filled motion. A.J. nearly lost his balance, but Isaac maintained his grip, bringing his brother's face within inches of his own.

"Look. At. Me. Andrew." Isaac seethed through clenched teeth.

Gray watched, suddenly ready to leap to A.J.'s defense if Isaac completely lost his temper.

Satisfied that A.J. was now meeting his eyes, Isaac released his grip. A.J. stumbled back a step but maintained his footing…and eye contact with Isaac.

"A woman—an *innocent* woman—was *murdered* tonight, and every bit of that freaking prison yard is full of potential evidence *you* might have just fucked up by throwing up all over it!" Isaac's voice spat out like boiling cobra venom, "Someone's *already* brutally murdered a man in his *own bedroom*…and they now took out his wife! I don't *play* detective, you hubristically sanctimonious prick! I *am* a detective, so check your self-righteous elitism at the door, or I swear *I'll* break your goddamned jaw myself next time!"

Seeing A.J.'s look of abject shock, Isaac throttled back a bit. Taking a breath, he closed his eyes.

Collecting his thoughts and calming down a little, he swallowed, opened his eyes, and met A.J.'s gaze again.

"Andrew," Isaac's voice was still hard as steel, but he reduced his volume to something near conversational levels, "There's a whole *world* of monsters stalking the quiet countryside outside your little pristine bubble of faculty meetings and staff lunches."

Isaac put his hands on his hips before continuing, "It's people like Abraham and I who prevent those monsters from turning your precious, pretty little ivory tower into an unholy tower of terror! So, from now until the sun explodes, you will do *exactly* what we tell you, no more and no less! Do. You. Understand?!"

"I do," A.J. said, a feeling of shame creeping over him.

"You better be *real* clear on that," Isaac growled dangerously, "As I said, you're in *my* world, and this is *no* game! In *this* world, people get hurt, and people die!"

Glancing between the burning eyes of his brother and the coldly angry eyes of Abraham Gray, A.J. swallowed, nodding vigorously.

Chapter 19
Port Ludlow, Washington
Saturday, September 8, 2018; 17:14 hours

"…Gippeum Lýkos released a statement earlier today condemning the murder of his sister-in-law, Delores Tate, who was shot in the Kitsap County Jail while being held on charges of murdering her husband. Lýkos' lamented the shooting because, 'this ugly, horrible woman has escaped the justice she so richly deserves for the death of my poor, love-sick brother…'"

"…continuing with military news, Admiral David E. Jones assumed command of U.S. Pacific Command in Pearl Harbor earlier today. The Navy hopes Jones' record of integrity will help reform the Navy's image after the long-running 'Big Mitch' bribery scandal, a scandal still impacting naval careers…"

"The aerospace and defense sector saw growth in its valuation after Derecho Aviation unveiled the first depiction of the new YF-114 Tomcat II next-gen interceptor being developed in conjunction with the Navy. The Navy announced the YF-114 prototype will make its first flight by June of next year…"

"…the visiting New York Yankees trounced the Seattle Mariners 4 – 2 at Safeco Field today…"

"Isaac, he is a *total* stud!" Maria Gumataotao gushed quietly, her round, cheerful face surmounting a jigglingly round figure as she eyeballed Luke Fredriksen, who was over in the TV room with A.J., "If you let him go without a fight, I'm going to hit you upside your thick skull!"

Isaac took the lid off the pot of chicken adobo. Seeing it simmering, he lifted the pot off the stove, placing it on a hot pad Liam set out on the floating island. Although it had been years since the three had cooked at the Gumataotao's former home on Guam, they'd fallen back into the routine easily enough.

"I'll consider myself warned," Isaac responded dryly, the savory smell of the adobo calling up memories of swaying palm trees and warm nights on a tropical island.

"Bro," Liam said, his face serious, "Don't be an idiot. I know you're here working right now, but this case won't last forever. You *better* go out with him before you leave the state!"

"Or else what?" Isaac raised an eyebrow.

"Or else I'll hold you down while Maria noogies you!" Liam laughed, the enticing odor of fresh dinner rolls joining the olfactory symphony.

Maria lifted the finadene sauce off the stove, "Dinner!!!"

Fredriksen and A.J. popped to attention from where they'd been studying the Gumataotao's fish tanks in the TV room. Scurrying with the fervor of starving men, they appeared in the kitchen as if by magic.

The five gathered around the floating island while Maria said grace. Once the prayer was finished, a free-for-all erupted as the gathering piled their plates high with food before happily landing on the dining room table.

Fredriksen made a deliberate point of sitting next to Isaac.

"This is a gorgeous little town!" A.J. was saying, "My family and I've never really explored Port Ludlow."

"Started out as a logging town," Liam said, dismantling and devouring a piece of chicken, "Mid-19th century, I think. But, today, Port Ludlow's a...oh, what's the term, Maria?"

"A lot of people call us a 'bedroom community' for Seattle," Maria said, "But that's not accurate. We're a community of retirees and people who largely commute to Silverdale and Poulsbo."

"Moving out here from Seattle must have been a big change," Fredriksen said, scooping rice onto his fork.

"Not as bad as you might think," Liam said, "We didn't want to go back to Guam, but we both wanted a quiet little area. Maria's got her garden and volunteers at the veterinary clinic over in Port Hadlock. My work in cybersecurity is all remote, so it works out."

"This might be a nice little town to settle down in after retirement," Fredriksen said, glancing at Isaac with the most subtle of sly expressions. "What do you think? Get a little house out here and spend the rest of our lives watching the sunrise over Mount Baker?" Fredriksen said, referring to one of the prominent volcanic peaks in the Cascades.

"I owe you one for helping us on this case, Liam," Isaac said, dismissing Fredriksen's comment with the laugh of the innocently dense. "Abe and I are about ready to bang our heads into a tree if we can't get more hard evidence of the attack on Delores Tate's identity. The medical records I mentioned earlier are a start, but we *have* to get some traction on obtaining proof her finances were also targeted."

"Well, the fact you've obtained copies of both the Tates' Navy medical records is a big help," Liam said, "Besides the obvious value they hold as evidence of a cyber hit, they give *me* a solid foundation to start working on the problem."

"How so?" A.J. asked.

"Not to get too deep into *Star Trek*-like techno-babble," Liam ladled finadene sauce into a side bowl, "It gives me a starting point by showing me how the Naval Hospital system was accessed. Cybercriminals are criminals; their modus operandi rarely change. By seeing *how* the attack on the Naval Hospital was conducted, I've got a reference point to use in examining the financial records."

"You still trying to figure out how to use DNA analysis to differentiate between identical twins—well, technically triplets since there was a third Lýkos brother once upon a time," Fredriksen looked at Isaac.

"I am," Isaac said, "I think I'll have read everything on planet Earth about genetics before I figure it out!"

"Oofda! That's a tough nut to crack, all right. Still, don't sell yourself short, Isaac. You've cracked tougher questions before."

Fredriksen laid a hand on Isaac's shoulder, squeezing it slightly while giving Isaac a gentle smile followed by the merest flick of his eyebrows.

Marie and Liam saw the sparkle in Fredriksen's eye as he spoke to Isaac. They glanced at each other, smiling slyly.

Isaac only nodded, saying, "I appreciate the vote of confidence."

"I know I'm merely a volcanologist, and not a forensics expert," A.J. said, cutting up a slice of mango, "But even *I* know that identical twins—or triplets like us—have identical DNA. I don't see any way to use that forensically."

"There's a way," Isaac said firmly, "There *has* to be. Think about it, bro. You, Josh, and I are identical triplets, and, yet, although all three of us have green eyes—*vivid* green eyes at that—our eyes are *not* truly 'identical.' My eyes are a 'sea green.' Your eyes are emerald, and Josh's are more of a 'hunter green.' Each of our eyes is a *different* color number on the Pantone scale. Why? Our DNA is identical, so why is it expressed differently in our eyes?"

"Good question," Fredriksen said as everyone else nodded.

"Another question," Isaac said, swallowing some rice, "All three of us are smarter than the average bear. Yet, you, A.J. are a scientist, Josh is obsessed with sports and cars, and I'm a writer, photographer, and generally nosy busybody. If we have the same DNA, and that DNA built three identical bodies, why do we have such wildly different interests?"

"Your suggestion also encompasses another vexing question, Kid Canaveral," A.J. said, nodding. Sitting back, he unconsciously steepled his fingers, looking for all the world like he was doing an impersonation of Mr. Spock as he went on, "Posited as an accepted proposition that our DNA profiles are identical, therefore our physical brains are identical. Josh and I are fully heterosexual. Neither of us ever had even a scintilla of interest in same-sex relationships—"

"As your successful marriages and my four nephews testify to!" Isaac laughed.

"And yet," A.J. went on thoughtfully, *"You* turn out to be as gay as a kite. Since our DNA *is* identical, why? I see the course of your reasoning here, and it's a compelling line of inquiry. Why *are* we three so different if we're identical? When you posit your argument that way, I agree; there *has* to be some data set, some factor, you can use. The two Lýkos brothers who survived into adulthood are another example of this question. Their DNA is identical, yet one brother was a mild-mannered, loving husband and decent human being, while the other is—"

"Utterly evil," Isaac cut in, automatically leaning back, steepling his fingers in yet another unintentional rendition of Mr. Spock. Fredriksen did a double take at the two identical men in identical poses.

"If I'm following you," Maria asked, "Isn't this just the old 'nature vs. nurture' thing?"

"Partly, yes," Isaac nodded over his fingers, "But we have to find something that can be objectively measured. We can't just use some vague statement about differences in personal interests due to some vague environmental stimuli at some vaguely defined time in the past. We have to find an angle in that question that's quantifiable, or else we'll get laughed out of court faster than you can say 'John Q. Arbuckle.'"

"I see the problem," Maria nodded. "I assume you've been doing your homework on this lead?"

"Oh, yes! I've read enough about Boveri-Sutton chromosome theory, multifactorial genetic theory, epigenetics, and Mitochondrial inheritance over the past three days to have me *dreaming* about it," Isaac said, frustration coloring his voice, "I *know* I've seen something that might be relevant, but I've covered so much ground I can't put my finger on whatever it is that's bugging me."

"You've certainly got enough books and papers strewn around your hotel room!" Fredriksen laughed, "You do much more DNA research and you'll qualify for a degree in it!"

"Oh, you saw his hotel room?" Liam asked innocently while giving Maria a distinct glance. She smiled, raising her eyebrows before diving back into her chicken.

"I met him and A.J. there this afternoon," Fredriksen downed a swallow of soda, "And thanks again for letting him invite me since Abe got tied up with those conference calls."

"Our pleasure, honey!" Maria said happily, "We love meeting Isaac's friends. Especially ones as cute as you are!"

"Maria!" Liam exclaimed, nearly spitting out a mouthful of chicken.

"Well, he *is!*" Maria said stubbornly, "Isaac's got good taste in men!"

Isaac's head dropped in abject embarrassment, but not before his face turned as bright red as a fire engine.

Fredriksen suddenly became very interested in his soda.

"So, why did you stick around, A.J.?" Liam asked, steering the conversation back to more neutral waters, "I figured you'd be back with your students now that your car is working again."

A.J. looked green, "Well, after I…"

"He got caught up in the investigation by projectile puking his guts all over the latest crime scene!" Isaac said, his eyes twinkling.

"Isaac!" Maria admonished sternly and swiftly, "This is the dinner table! Please keep your language appropriate!"

"Yes, ma'am," Isaac said, instantly chagrined, "I'm sorry."

"He's right, though," A.J. said, his face turning red, "Sheriff Sigo asked me to stay in the area since I'd…well, 'negatively impacted an active crime scene,' to use her words. My students are fine. They're monitoring thermal readings using portable hidden mass spectrometers to measure dissolved volcanic gasses in the hot springs up in the Olympics. They don't need *me* around for a few more days yet."

"I'm just lucky he doesn't need a CPAP machine," Isaac said. "Otherwise, he'd be snoring up a storm on the sofa in my hotel room!"

"My wife's none too pleased with me," A.J. went on, "She wasn't happy she had to sit through a police interview about me this morning."

"Can't say I blame her," Fredriksen said, "Still, bro, don't sweat it. You're not the first man to puke…er, get ill at a crime scene. We've all been there to one degree or another."

"Even you?!" Isaac asked, startled.

"Oh, yeah," Fredriksen answered while diving into a fluffy pile of steamed rice, "When I was a seaman, just out of Master-at-Arms school, I was stationed aboard *Kitty Hawk.*"

"She's the one mothballed in the shipyard, right?" A.J. asked.

"That's her," Fredriksen nodded, "Anyway, a couple of flight deck rats got into a fight too close to a spinning prop on an E-2 Hawkeye radar plane. Before their chief could break up the fight, one of the guys was shoved back into the prop. I got up there, took one look, and ran straight to one of the catwalks to hurl over the side of the ship. It takes a while to get used to these things."

"I just don't get how you get comfortable with it all," A.J. said.

"There's a quantum difference between getting 'used' to something, and being 'comfortable' with it," Isaac said.

"True," Liam said, recalling his own time as a cop, "I honestly don't know anyone who ever got *comfortable* with crime scenes, especially the messy ones. But you just kind of learn how to compartmentalize it."

"I hope Abe is ok," Maria, not comfortable with the shop talk, firmly changed the subject, "I was looking forward to seeing him again!"

"You will," Isaac reassured her, "Don't worry. Unfortunately, however, between Delores Tate's murder and a couple of cases in Virginia, he wound up having to sit through a full plate of video conferences with the gang back in Norfolk."

"I'm surprised there hasn't been more crap from Washington," Maria said, "What with how that woman, Dana Cremer, was going on every talk show she could. Her crusade seems to have lost some steam after that stupid resolution failed in the Senate."

"She's still pushing it in the House," Isaac said, "But I've got a contact or two in D.C. that managed to slow her down a bit."

"The deer are back!" Maria exclaimed happily, her eyes riveted on a sight just outside their sliding glass door.

The rest of the party swung their heads around to look.

A large, muscular doe stood in the backyard, her ears alert and her eyes scanning the yard. Behind her, two fawns cautiously emerged from the woods separating their property from the nearby house. The fawns had lost most of the speckles from their younger days but were still clearly juveniles.

"Looks like she's got a young buck and one doe there," Fredriksen said, laying a hand casually on Isaac's knee and using his other to draw Isaac's eyes to the tell-tale nubs on the head of one fawn. Those nubs would eventually grow into a full-on rack when the young deer reached adulthood.

"That's pretty damned cool!" Isaac said, standing up to get a better view without ever noticing Fredriksen's hand on his leg, "I didn't think deer would come this close to human habitations."

A.J. and Maria looked at each other, A.J. rolling his eyes in disbelief at his brother's abject cluelessness.

"No one hunts them around here," Liam said, wiping his mouth, "They know they're safe. Terrible for flower beds and vegetable gardens if you don't put up fencing, though!"

"I know," Isaac said, "I saw that fencing around the rose bushes at the Tate house. Still, deer look just so…so *delicate* on those spindly legs. Creates a real optical illusion that belies how strong they are."

Leaving the family of deer to dine outside, the five returned to their meals. The conversation waxed and waned as Fredriksen and A.J. enjoyed hearing numerous stories from Guam over the next hour. Once dinner was finished, the group rose, carrying their plates to the kitchen.

"Out!" Maria commanded once the table was clear and clean. Wielding a wooden spoon like a short sword, she shooshed them away from the cooking area, "Out! I've got this. I don't need you guys messing up my kitchen!"

Liam nodded, "Let's get out of here. She means business!"

Isaac's phone buzzed as they meandered to the TV area. Pulling it out, he saw a text alert flashing. Unlocking the phone, he pulled up the text, his face falling into a mixture of shock and disbelief as he read the short message.

Watch your back. I've got nothing but vague circumstantial evidence, but I fear there's a joker in the deck. Insider threats are real! Be safe, be smart, and be CLEVER.

-L

"Isaac?" Fredriksen laid a hand on his shoulder, "Bad news?"

"Hmm?" Isaac drew himself back to the present, "What? Oh, no. No, not at all. Sorry. Just got distracted. Give me a sec and I'll be with y'all."

Fredriksen headed into the TV area. Isaac forwarded the text to Gray before sending his own message:

Abe, the plot thins. First time I've heard from Mr. 'L' since the middle of last year. Sounds like the Bacon case all over again.

Satisfied he could do no more at the moment, Isaac pocketed the phone. Joining the others in the TV room, he sat down on a sofa.

Fredriksen got up to fetch a glass of water, then sat down next to Isaac. Liam and A.J. shared a glance, each trying to hide a school-boy-like giggle as Liam loaded up a DVD of 1980's *Airplane!*

214

The party finally broke up near 23:30. Isaac, A.J., and Fredriksen began getting their shoes on as Liam and Maria hovered at the front door.

"I'll get on the digital forensics first thing in the morning," Liam said.

"You will *not!*" Maria planted her hands on her hips.

"Oh, right, sorry!" Liam's moon face looked contrite, "I'll get on it after church."

"Better!" Maria said before turning her attention to Fredriksen and Isaac, "Now you two boys make sure you go out to dinner before Isaac leaves the state," She admonished, taking Isaac and Fredriksen's hands and putting them into each other's.

"Maria!" Liam was aghast.

"Don't start, Liam!" Maria said stoutly, "It's clear these two boys like each other, and we're too old to play childish games!"

Eyeballing Isaac's red, flustered face, Maria pulled no punches.

"You've got a nice boy right here who's interested in you, Isaac. Don't blow it!"

"Uh...wow!" Fredriksen said, laughter covering his embarrassment, "You certainly don't mince words."

Maria gave him a piercing look, "I'm a Chamorro woman. We don't play around. Now hurry up and ask Isaac out on a date. And you be nice to him or *else!*"

"Maria!" Liam face-palmed himself.

A.J. managed to get outside the front door before he nearly fell over from laughing so hard.

Fredriksen and Isaac exchanged mortified glances, but Fredriksen couldn't help giving Isaac the tiniest of winks.

"So, when's the first date?" A.J. asked from *Sarah Jane's* back seat. He'd ridden shotgun on the way to the Gumataotao residence, but elected to take the SUV's back seat this time.

It was, of course, totally *not* his intention to have Isaac and Fredriksen sitting next to each other...

"I…uh…" Isaac stammered as he brought *Sarah Jane* to a halt at the intersection of Beaver Valley Road and Highway 104. Turning left on 104, he began the winding drive back to the floating Hood Canal Bridge. "I…well…I mean…Abe and I are busy right now, and besides, Luke, if you don't want to…that is, if you're…I mean, I don't even know…dude, *are* you gay?!"

"Oh, wow!" A.J. face-palmed himself, "Just…wow!"

Fredriksen burst out laughing. It was a deep, staccato guffaw emanating from his deep, muscular chest. His volume rivaled Isaac's famously over-loud laugh.

Isaac's red face morphed into pure crimson.

Fredriksen finally got himself under control, "I'm as gay as you are, dontcha know!"

"Oh, well, then…I guess…I mean…" Isaac spluttered.

"Ok, I'm done!" A.J. declared in pure disbelieving frustration. "Luke, do you want to go out with Isaac?"

Fredriksen laughed again, "I do."

"Isaac, do you want to go out with Luke?"

"Uh…well, I mean…uh…yes, yes, I do…"

"Swell!" A.J. laughed, "I now pronounced you dating! Luke, you may ask my brother out!"

Fredriksen nodded, laughter percolating just below the surface, "Isaac, once this is wrapped up, would you like to go to dinner sometime?'

Sarah Jane's tires hummed as she bounced lightly over the joints where the Hood Canal Bridge connected to the shoreline. Headlights aimed across the waters of Puget Sound, she began the quick journey from the Olympic Peninsula back to the Kitsap Peninsula.

"Uh…I guess…I mean…I…yes. Yes, I would," Isaac said, finally gaining control of his mouth.

"Good," Fredriksen glanced over his shoulder, catching A.J.'s eye. A.J. was doing his best to tamp down his mirth. Fredriksen decided Isaac needed a change of subject.

"Hopefully, you guys *will* be able to bring this one home soon," Fredriksen said. He reckoned Isaac would probably be most comfortable with a bit of shop talk again, "With the obvious exception of the killer, all those with any direct tie to the murder of Young-Saeng Tate are now dead."

"Didn't someone else get killed?" A.J. asked as Isaac drove *Sarah Jane* back up on land, her wheels mounting the pavement on the Kitsap side of the bridge, "I think I remember hearing on the news there was some doofus who leaked crap to the media. Didn't they wind up getting killed?"

"Yeah," Isaac said, turning right to start south out of Port Gamble down along Highway 3, "One of the Kitsap sheriff's interns, a woman named Jane Smith."

"What happened to her?" A.J. asked.

"She lived up here in Port Gamble. Got shot in a hunting accident here about a week…or two ago—*HOLY SHIT!!!!*" Isaac's exclamation startled Fredriksen and A.J. so abruptly they had to peel themselves off the roof. Punching the brakes with his foot, Isaac slid *Sarah Jane* onto the road's shoulder with a minimum of mayhem.

"Isaac, what?" Fredriksen asked, alarmed.

"Oh shit, oh shit, oh shit…" Isaac said, "I'm a screaming idiot!"

"What?!" Fredriksen and A.J. asked in unison.

"Jane *Smith,*" Isaac said, "William *Smith!"*

"I'm not following," Fredriksen said, "Who's Jane Smith?"

"The intern who leaked to the media!" Isaac said, his brain firing so fast sparks nearly flew out of his ears, "And William Smith is the supposed lover of Delores Tate!"

"Ok," A.J. said, "So…?"

"Oh, do try to keep up, A.J.!" Isaac snapped, his panic leading him to forget neither of his passengers had the whole picture as his expression dissolved into a look that was two-parts panic and three-parts boiling introspection.

"Isaac, spit it out!" Fredriksen ordered, "What's the deal?!"

"Jane Smith gets shot in a 'hunting accident' *at long range.* Delores Tate gets shot in a prison yard *at long range.* Crap!" Isaac slammed a hand onto the steering wheel. "Guys, there's still *one* 'principle player' alive! Shit! We have to get to Tacoma *now!* Luke, get my phone and try to call Abe!"

"Isaac," A.J. asked nervously, "I still don't get it. Why do we have to go to Tacoma?"

"To stop William Smith from being killed!"

Chapter 20
Tacoma, Washington
Sunday, September 9, 2018; 01:15 hours

Sarah Jane skidded to a halt in Baker Street Billiards' parking lot. The early morning hour had mostly emptied the area of vehicular denizens. The small, desultory gathering of bikes huddled against the chilly night air in a corner of the lot told Isaac the crowd was so thin as to be zero protection against an assassination attempt.

Where the hell *did everyone go?!* Isaac wondered angrily. *Of course, this would be the* one *weekend this place decides to empty out early!*

"Still nothing," Fredriksen said, handing Isaac his phone back before unbuckling his seatbelt, "I've left voice messages and texts out the wazoo for Abe and Sheriff Sigo…and the Tacoma police flat-out hung up on me!"

"Bloody hell!" Isaac cursed, "Well, come on! If I'm right, William Smith is the next target—and I'll bet dollars to donuts he's Jane Smith's brother!"

"'Dollars to donuts, eh?'" Fredriksen asked as the three men piled out of *Sarah Jane.*

"Old Southern expression," A.J. said, "Isaac, look, I know I'm new to this and all, but just what in the name of John Q. Arbuckle are we doing here? If this man reacted as badly to your presence as you said he did, then how are *two* of us, who are identical, going to defuse the situation?"

Isaac locked *Sarah Jane* before straightening the old windbreaker he wore, "We don't have a choice, Andrew! If I'm right, a man's life is in danger!"

A.J.'s retort was killed aborning when Isaac turned to Fredriksen.

"Luke, watch my back, ok?" Isaac asked as the trio trotted towards the building, "A.J., this time follow my lead! This is not the kind of place you've hung out in before!"

Isaac's hand punching open the door ended all discussion.

The pool hall was quiet. Five bikers, each wearing a heavy-duty leather ensemble, lounged over by one pool table. Numerous empty steins and cans attested to the quantity of alcohol they'd consumed.

Isaac's eyes scanned them: two muscular women in cut-off leather vests hung on two even more muscular men in cut-off leather vests. A third guy, clearly the brother of one of the other men, was taking a shot, the unsteady wobble of his alcohol-infused hands ensuring the cue ball went exactly where he didn't want it to go.

The rest of the place was lost amid darkened lights and the greasy smell of stale beer mixed liberally with the acidic smell of too much liquor. Isaac felt the soles of his sneakers adhering to the mild dusting of spilled libations coating the old linoleum.

Ugh! Worse than a movie theatre! The thought whipped across Isaac's brain before he could stop it.

William Smith stood behind the main bar, wiping down the bar top and looking for all the world like he was ready to throw up. Another barkeep was sliding out from behind the bar, a pile of plates in his hands as he navigated to the kitchen.

"I think they're about to close, 'eh," Fredriksen said to no one in particular.

Isaac took a breath, said the fasted 'Hail Mary' of his life, and marched straight up to the bar.

William Smith looked up from wiping a glass—

—and burped out an incoherent gurgle when he realized who was standing in front of him. A second terrified gurgle erupted when he saw A.J. behind Isaac.

"William, your life is in danger!" Isaac said sharply, "Whoever killed your sister is after you!"

Smith's eyes popped from his head in a passable imitation of a *Looney Tunes* cartoon. The glass fell from Smith's hand, impacting the floor with a shattering crash, "But…but he told me Jane's death was an accident—"

Damn, I knew *I was right!* Isaac thought, "We need to get you to safety! Now!"

"No..." Smith said, backing away, the towel falling from his other hand, "No...I can't..."

"Call the police, and do it now!" Isaac begged emphatically, his hands slapping down on the bar as he shoved aside a barstool to get closer to Smith, "Someone's trying to kill you! Call the police *now!*"

"I can't...I can't talk to you...if he knew..." Smith babbled on, terror clouding his features as his eyes bounced back and forth between Isaac and A.J.'s mirror-like features.

"Dammit, who?! If who knew?!" Isaac asked, desperation raising the volume of his voice.

"He said to back off, fuck face!"

Isaac, A.J., and Fredriksen wheeled around in shock, Fredriksen nearly slipping in a puddle of water on the floor, but managing to retain his footing.

The five aforementioned leather-clad bikers were approaching. One guy was swinging a heavy chain. Isaac saw the chain was attached at one end to his leather belt while the other end held his keys. Those keys were now whistling in a dangerous arc through the air. Isaac labeled the man Tough Guy #1.

Two of the men were holding pool cues but had flipped the long sticks upside down. They slapped the cues' thicker ends menacingly against heavily callused hands.

Tough Guys #2 and #3, Isaac's mind continued cataloging the situation.

One of the women was cracking her knuckles, while the other fidgeted with a folded switchblade. Both women's hands were also callused, and their arms showed considerable muscular definition.

"Hey, we're not here to cause any trouble," Frederiksen said calmly, a friendly smile on his face as he raised his hands in a 'calm down' gesture, "Actually, we think someone's trying to hurt this young man, and—"

221

"Shut your hole, fucktard!" Tough Guy #1 spat, the chain in his hand spinning faster, "He said to leave him 'lone. You bitches needs to get the fuck out of here!"

Isaac's eyes swept back and forth so fast they might have been a blur. He saw A.J. cowering back against the bar, completely out of his league. He noticed the increasing tension in the stance of Tough Guy #1 and the woman with the knife—Tough Girl #1.

"Clean your ears, faggots!" Tough Guy #2 sneered, waggling his pool cue menacingly, "We *said* get da fuck out and leave Billy alone before we beat yo asses!"

Fredriksen backed up a few steps, bringing him shoulder-to-shoulder with Isaac. A.J. tried to disappear into the bar behind them.

Isaac and Fredriksen exchanged brief glances. A.J. could have sworn they shared a 'You've *got* to be kidding me!' look.

"My partner is correct," Isaac said, eyeing Tough Guy #2, but his attention was locked onto Tough Girl #1 (her fingers beginning to flip her blade open and closed), "We were just advising Mr. Smith here to call the police because someone's after him."

The sticky-sweet scent of raging halitosis, mixing with stale sweat emanating from the quintet of inebriated hostiles, hit Isaac's nose like a tsunami.

Swell! Isaac thought bitterly, *These idiots are* way *too drunk to reason with!*

"Is what he sayin' troo, honey?" Tough Girl #2—the one cracking her knuckles—asked Smith. She began to slap a fist into her other hand.

Smith gave a terrified squeak, his eyes still on the back of Isaac's head.

"There, Mr. Hero," Tough Girl #2 said while Tough Girl #1 stopped flipping the switchblade around, instead holding it firmly in her hand, "Get yo faggoty ass out of here!"

A.J. was close to pissing his pants. His mouth dry, he felt his rear end hit the bar, preventing him from backing up any farther.

Why aren't those two idiots afraid?! A.J. thought, looking from his brother's calm demeanor to Tough Girl #1's knife, then to the friendly expression effected by Fredriksen.

This is getting out of control! Isaac thought, forcing the terror in his blood down as he slid a foot carefully under the nearest barstool, *We're here to save this idiot's life!*

Fredriksen maintained his friendly smile, but discreetly shifted his stance to a more defensive posture.

Isaac's keen eyes caught a flash of light as Tough Girl #1 flipped her knife open with a solid *click!* She charged forward, swinging the blade up in one smoothly lethal move.

A.J. gurgled in terror, frozen in sheer surprise as Isaac reacted.

Moving with choreographed precision, Isaac's right foot shot up off the floor, lifting the barstool from the deck. The stool rocketed upward, Isaac's right hand shooting out and catching it just under the seat. Swinging his hips around to lead his shoulders, Isaac's long arm snapped like a whip, letting the chrome-plated projectile fly.

The stool was in the air milliseconds after Tough Girl #1 began her charge through the light brigade. Tough Guys #1 and #3 instinctively stepped aside, meaning Tough Girl #1 took the full force of it in her face.

The impact caught her right across the bridge of her nose and bust line. Blood burst like a volcanic eruption from the wreckage of her nose, a red tide spilling over her Judas Priest shirt while a crimson mist colored the air around her.

Screaming from a mixture of surprise and pain, her head snapped backward as she keeled over, collapsing to the deck in a heap, the stool coming to rest on top of her. Her head thudded on the floor with all the grace of a watermelon tossed off a four-story building, and she lay still.

Everybody froze.

"Nice shot!" Fredriksen said, impressed.

"Mother *fuuuuckerrrr!"* Tough Girl #2 screamed, launching herself forward, a maddened missile intent on bringing the pain.

Fredriksen stepped forward to meet her, his powerful right fist shooting out to strike her as his left hand deftly brushed aside her wild punch.

She'd be dangerous if she weren't drunk off her ass, The idle thought striking Fredriksen as he dropped her like a sack of moldy gourds.

The Tough Guys froze again, stupefied by the sudden defeat of their female compatriots.

Well, only for a moment.

Screaming like an ancient berserker, Tough Guy #1 let fly the chain he'd been swinging around. Isaac and Fredriksen dived to the side, keeping their shoulders together to prevent either one from being flanked.

A.J. squealed in a passable imitation of a piglet getting its tail caught in a dishwasher as the chain whipped through the air toward him with a lethal *whizzzz!* The chain barely missed A.J.'s head, instead smashing into the bar, its keys biting viciously into the wood, tearing a large chunk away as Tough Guy #1 yanked it back.

A.J. dropped like a rock, diving under a nearby table.

Tough Guy #2 swung his pool cue down with all the force he could muster. Isaac saw it coming and threw his left arm up to block, knowing he was about to be in considerable pain. The wooden cue cracked down on his arm, the stick snapping in half across his Ulna as he fired his left foot forward, viciously striking the man's kneecap.

Isaac heard a sickening crunch of bone as Tough Guy #2 folded like a kitten in a tornado, quickly joining Tough Girls #1 and #2 on the deck as useless piles of shapeless pudding.

A.J. watched from under the table in horror as Tough Guys #1 and #3 squared up. Even he could tell these two had proper combat training. Despite the obvious level of alcohol in their systems, they weren't going to fall easily.

The four men fell into a melee. A.J. saw Isaac and Fredriksen deliberately keeping their backs together, preventing their assailants from ganging up on one or the other.

"William, dammit, call the police!" Isaac screamed desperately, blocking a punch, but taking one to the gut as he sought an opening in Tough Guy #3's drunken, but highly effective, fighting style, "Someone's trying to fucking *kill you!*"

Smith screamed and bolted. Skidding a bit on the broken glass from the stein he'd dropped, he fled from behind the bar, his feet taking him towards the front door as fast as he could run.

"Goddammit!" Isaac cursed. Finally seeing an opening, he caught Tough Guy #3's arm. Spinning fast, he used the man's momentum to his advantage. Flipping him over his shoulder, Isaac sent him sailing through the air with the greatest of ease.

A.J. screamed and bolted as Tough Guy #3 landed on the table he'd been hiding under, crushing it to splinters.

"Isaac, *go!*" Fredriksen roared, narrowly avoiding a kick to the groin, "I've got this!"

Isaac ran.

Tough Guy #1 turned to pursue, but Fredriksen wheeled him around by the shoulder, landing a punch to his face.

Tough Guy #3 was back on his feet, his advance forcing the terrified A.J. towards Fredriksen.

"Uh...I...I..." A.J. stammered, his face white as death as he held his hands up in an 'I surrender' gesture.

"Stop sniveling, you coward!" Fredriksen roared as A.J. collided with his back, "Find something to fight with!"

A.J. dived and rolled to avoid Tough Guy #3's fist, nearly dislocating his shoulder in the process.

"Ok...find something, find something, find something," A.J. repeated over and over, his brain jamming up. He noticed an empty beer bottle lying on the floor. Grabbing it, he was getting up when Tough Guy #3 hauled him to his feet by his collar.

Reacting in pure panic, A.J. swung the bottle as hard as he could. Impacting the very top of Tough Guy #3's head, the brown bottle shattered with a horrible crunching crash. Shards rained down around the two men as Tough Guy #3's eyes glazed over. Hands dropping from A.J.'s collar, Tough Guy #3 collapsed like a Ponzi scheme.

A.J. turned just in time to see Fredriksen finally get an opening. The burly sailor got in close, his hands locking onto Tough Guy #1's shoulders. Spinning the biker around, Fredriksen's massive arms snaked around the man's neck, cutting off blood flow to his brain.

Tough Guy #1 was asleep in no time.

Fredriksen dropped him like a bag of broken promises.

"Uh…" A.J. said, still holding the broken bottle, "Is that it?"

"Are you ok?" Fredriksen asked.

A.J. nodded bleakly.

Fredriksen smiled, "Sorry about the coward thing. I was just trying to get you amped up."

Looking around at the pile of human flotsam littering the sticky floor, A.J. dropped the shattered remains of the bottle, "That was my first bar fight."

"Shit!" Fredriksen exclaimed, "Isaac!"

Isaac Shepherd ran as fast as he could. His left knee, injured in a hit-and-run motorcycle accident years ago, screamed in fury, but he pounded the pavement heedless of the pain. Just ahead he saw Smith fly around a corner and down the street.

"William! Stop!" Isaac yelled into the abandoned night, "I'm trying to save your life!"

Squealing something, Smith began running faster. Just not fast enough; Isaac *was* gaining on him.

Lungs cracking, his left knee becoming increasingly unstable, Isaac pressed on with the burning drive of sheer obsession. The street was dark and quiet. Most decent people were already in bed.

Keep going keep going keep going keep going, Isaac repeated the mantra, forcing himself to ignore a horrible stitch deforming

226

the side of his torso. He felt his left leg getting wobbly, but he insisted his nearly crippled knee take the abuse as he pounded nearer and nearer the fleeing man.

"Isaac!"

Isaac heard Fredriksen's voice distantly behind him, but Fredriksen was too far away to catch Smith. Isaac had to be the one to do it.

A...few...more...yards...

Isaac's right hand shot forward, landing on Smith's shoulder. Clamping down hard, he slammed on the brakes. Their combined momentum nearly made him crash into Smith, but the two managed to keep their feet even as Isaac forcibly pulled the panic-riddled man around.

Smith screamed in pure, undiluted terror as he felt Isaac's hand clutch his shoulder.

"William, who the *hell* are you running from?!" Isaac found them spinning slightly as he managed to get the words out.

Smith's face exploded.

Time crashed to a halt as Isaac recoiled.

Smith's visage split apart from the forehead down to the bridge of his nose, ruby red blood and glistening white bone fragments erupting in a pyroclastic flow of gore.

He had a nice nose, Isaac thought dumbly as the proboscis flopped wildly to the left, a sizeable chunk of Smith's brain bursting from his head. A thick geyser of blood painted Isaac in dripping crimson as bits of Smith's skull splattered against him like so many wood splinters.

The act of spinning Smith around forced Isaac to spin slightly as well, meaning he was now at a 45-degree angle to the man as Smith's brain and the bullet inside it thudded into Isaac's chest with a squishy squash. The change in angle saved Isaac's life; the bullet's momentum was largely spent, thus it bounced off him instead of piercing just deep enough to hit his heart.

Smith's brain matter plopped on the pavement with a squelch while the remaining parts of Smith's body—torso, limbs, and legs—collapsed onto the cold sidewalk with a wet thud.

"Isaac!" Fredriksen yelled, watching Isaac step back in horror as Smith fell dead at his feet, *"ISAAC!"*

Spinning around to look at Fredriksen inadvertently saved Isaac's life.

The bullet intended to blow *his* brains out careened instead off his head in a glancing blow.

Isaac grunted in disbelieving shock as he saw a plume of red blood jetting outward from his forehead as his bifocals popped off his face. He felt the weight of a concrete block smashing into his brain.

Isaac's final vision was of a fuzzy Luke Fredriksen racing towards him before he also dropped like roadkill, the consciousness knocked clean out of him.

Chapter 21

"Dude, someone just tried to kill you!" A.J. Shepherd snapped as he followed Isaac into the NCIS building.

"I noticed!" Isaac snapped back. Leaning heavily on a walking stick, he had to resist an impulse to knobble A.J. over the head with it, "I was there, remember?!"

Gray looked up from his newspaper, startled at the vehemence in Isaac's voice. He'd been waiting in the lobby for Isaac, but hadn't expected A.J. to arrive as well.

"Isaac, this isn't some game!" A.J. spouted off, planting himself directly in Isaac's path, "You've been *shot!*"

"I know that, Andrew!" Isaac shouted, unleashing the full fury of his baritone voice. A.J. was nearly knocked back into the wall as the receptionist looked up from behind her bulletproof glass window, her eyes wide.

Pushing back his brown corduroy sport coat, Isaac planted his free hand on his hips, locking his eyes onto his brother's.

"Andrew, this is *not* the first time I've been shot, ok?" Isaac's voice cracked threateningly.

"Say what?!" A.J. blinked, shaking his head in surprise, "You've been *shot* before? Why the hell didn't you say anything to Josh or I?! We're your goddamned *family!*"

"Why the *hell* should I tell you arrogant jackalopes about *anything* I do?!" Isaac snapped, a few decades of suppressed resentment violently erupting under the strain of the past 24 hours, "You jerkwads spent the past *30 years* mocking me because I didn't follow *your* lead like some mindless lemming!" Isaac lost it, his voice roaring into the rafters with such ferocity A.J. stepped backward in shock.

But Isaac wasn't finished.

"You want to be *part* of my life, Andrew?!" Isaac bellowed, "Start showing me *and* Abe some respect, and then I *might* think about talking to you more.   Now, thanks for the lift this morning, but Sheriff Sigo said you're free to head back to Seattle, and I have a job to finish, so *get lost!"*

A.J.'s face creased into a mask of pure shock. Starting to speak, he closed his mouth again, evidently thinking better of whatever he was going to say.

Instead, he sighed, "Look, I'm staying in Silverdale for a few more days. I want to be around just in case…just in case you need my help again."

"Not bloody likely!" Isaac snarled under his breath as A.J. left.

"That went well," Gray said sardonically, standing and folding his newspaper as A.J. stomped out of the building.

"Dammit, I should've been more patient," Shepherd said, a sad countenance darkening his face as he watched A.J. drive off through the glass doors, "The man's in shock."

"So are *you,"* Gray pointed out, laying a hand on Shepherd's shoulder. Studying Shepherd's pale visage, he shook his head. "You look like hell, Isaac. You should take the day off."

"And you know how stubborn I am when someone gets my blood up," Shepherd retorted mulishly, the throbbing in his head mildly distracting, "Any new information on our assassin?"

Gray buttoned his black suit jacket before leading Shepherd through the security door into the depths of NCIS. Shepherd deftly wielded the walking stick with his right hand to compensate for his damaged left leg while clipping his access badge to his lapel with his left hand.

"Where'd you get that cane, anyway?" Gray asked, realizing the walking stick's handle was an old, repurposed doorknob.

"Maine," Shepherd answered, "Bought it from a street vendor in Portland. It's hickory. I just liked the look of it, and right now I'm *really* glad I bought it."

"Luke heard a car start up and speed off almost immediately after you hit the deck, but he didn't *see* anything," Gray said, switching subjects, "That means our shooter was at an extreme range. As to the sibling relationship between our two deceased

Smiths, Denita's running down how Jane was able to keep that omission on her internship application from being flagged—especially since William had two DUIs and one misdemeanor for possession on his record."

"Why do I get the feeling we're looking at yet a *third* cyberattack?"

Gray sighed, blowing his breath out in frustration before nodding, "Probably because we *are* looking at yet a third cyberattack."

"The *gesekgi* is deploying some heavy-duty resources," Shepherd said, "Not to mention some seriously *expensive* resources."

"Now, we just need to figure out how to link Lýkos up forensically with the crime scene at the Tate house," Gray said.

The two men turned a corner, heading past Kerr's office towards their conference room.

"How in the hell did you manage to survive a direct shot to the head?!" David Kerr demanded from his outer office's doorway.

Shepherd grimaced, his gaze distracted by the overhead lights bouncing off the mirror-polished finish glazing the stocks of the two antique sniper rifles visible in the depths of Kerr's inner office, "Just lucky. I guess throwing a quarter in that wishing well in Bozeman worked!"

"Maybe I should go find that well and throw in a quarter myself. Maybe I can make you disappear!" Kerr spat.

Shepherd was in no mood to spar. He smiled pleasantly before limping past Kerr.

Gray gave Kerr a withering look before following Shepherd.

"We're just lucky the security footage from the bar supported your story," Gray said, "Without that evidence proving the three of you *were* acting in self-defense, you'd be sitting in the Tacoma jail right now!"

"They were a bunch of drunken sots, yes," Shepherd said wearily, laying a hand on the doorknob of their makeshift office, "But I have to hand some serious respect to those bikers. They *were* trying to defend a man they thought was under attack, after all."

Opening the door, Shepherd and Gray entered the room to once again find a wholly unexpected person placidly waiting for them.

"Veronica!" Gray exclaimed in complete shock, "What the hell are *you* doing here?!"

NCIS Special Agent Veronica Bale looked up from her seat. The tall, slender African American woman was dressed in a pair of tan slacks, a green blouse, and a dark red blazer. She wore her hair straightened and pulled into a ponytail cinched with a sparkly gold hair band.

Bale had always reminded Shepherd a bit of the elegant actress Angela Bassett. Looking at Bale, he suddenly had a vision of Angela Bassett dressed as a Christmas tree.

"Morning, gentlemen!" Bale smiled, rising to warmly hug them, "I'm on hiatus from my current investigation so I can courier some highly sensitive information a friend of yours asked me to bring over from D.C."

Bale pulled back after hugging Shepherd, her eyes narrowing as she studied the pallor of his face and the bruised, swollen wound hidden under the bandage on his forehead.

"Isaac, you're an idiot!" Bale said sadly, shaking her head, "You should be taking it easy today. I don't care how lucky you were. You're in no shape to be up and about right now!"

"You're wasting your time," Gray said, rolling his eyes, "Isaac's not going to listen to either of us until he collapses."

"Nope," Shepherd piped up, stepping over to the coffee mess to brew himself a cup. "Veronica, you've piqued my interest, however. What's so important you had to courier it personally?"

Bale and Gray exchanged glances. Gray shrugged. They both knew there was no debating Shepherd at a time like this.

"Well, your friend, Senator Alejandro, called me to his office Friday night," Bale said, sitting back down and sliding a locked briefcase across the table to Gray. Tossing him the keys, she continued, "Said Director Belk recommended me as a courier.

There has indeed been chatter over the proverbial airwaves about the Lionfish drone, but it started *after* the murder of Young-Saeng Tate. To be more specific, the chatter started *two weeks* after his death."

The Keurig coffee machine spluttered as it finished filling Shepherd's borrowed mug with its NCIS logo. Pulling the cup free, he opened the mini fridge to retrieve the cream.

"Meaning that we now have firm evidence Delores Tate was simply an innocent victim," Shepherd said, pouring cream into his coffee before returning the carton to the fridge, "If she were trying to steal the Lionfish, then the chatter would have been ongoing long before Young-Saeng's murder."

"Precisely," Gray said, speed-reading the contents of the now-open briefcase, "Damn, Veronica. You're telling me that Senator Alejandro was able to pull all *this* together in the space of 72 hours?! Isaac and I just talked to him and Judge Limbani, what, Friday morning?"

"The senator said he was contacted by a CIA representative Friday evening," Bale said, raising an eyebrow, "What rattled him is that he'd only just started making some discreet inquiries Friday afternoon, and then here comes this CIA spook that night with *exactly* what he was looking for."

Gray and Shepherd stared at each other, eyes wide.

"We're being surveilled," Shepherd stated, his voice thick, "I doubt someone in the agency just *happened* to eavesdrop on the *one* call we'd make that revealed what we needed."

"And, apparently, whoever's watching us wants to help," Gray nodded, thinking of Mr. 'L"s texts. Shaking his head, he dropped the papers he'd been reading, "At least, someone wants to help us to some extent for reasons unknown."

"Sounds like you two impressed someone at Langley," Bale continued, "The dude that approached Senator Alejandro identified himself as Aaron Evers. Ring a bell?"

"Possibly," Gray said, his voice pitching up slightly as he sat down. Leaning his elbows on the table, he explained, "Isaac and I accidentally exposed a CIA operative using the name 'Aaron Seeley' aboard *Ponce* during the Bacon case in 2016."

"We then had to sit through five days of debriefings explaining how we rumbled their operation without even trying," Shepherd said, his face communicating just how boring an experience it had been.

"I heard," Bale said, voice dry, "Charlotte filled me in when I came aboard to help with the manhunt for Gordon Grey last year. From the looks on your faces, I can tell we're all thinking the same thing—that this 'Aaron Evers' and your 'Aaron Seeley' are the same person."

"First rule of good cover names is to keep it simple, and that often means sticking with your own first name," Shepherd said, "Besides, during the Bacon case, I began receiving occasional— but very cryptic—texts from a Mr. 'L.' This Mr. 'L' has been evasive and elusive—and yet every time I get a text from him, it's been both effective and truthful. Abe and I figured he was either CIA or NSA. Looks like he's CIA."

Which means the text I got Saturday is important, indeed. Shepherd thought, sipping his coffee as he watched Gray leaf through the material Bale provided.

"Ziyun!" Gray cursed in Hebrew.

Shepherd nearly spit out his coffee. He knew just enough Hebrew to know he'd barely ever heard Gray use the *English* version of that particular curse, and hearing it in Hebrew was downright shocking.

"Abe?" Bale asked tentatively. She didn't know Hebrew, but the sudden tension infusing Gray's body shocked her.

"Isaac, you've got to see this!" Gray tightly said, "There've been significant feelers extending from an unidentified corporate entity here in the U.S. to Iran, North Korea, Russia, and our old foe, China. Ironically, Russia rejected it outright. Whomever we're pursuing, they're *now* attempting to sell the Lionfish overseas."

"Charlotte and I came to the same conclusion," Bale said, nodding in concurrence with Gray's statement, "She also asked me to catch you two up on the Gordon Grey investigation *and* provide backup here since that doofus, Kerr, sent all his agents off to Timbuktu."

"About that," Gray said, "I'm in the process of throwing a major monkey wrench into his office administration. But, that can wait for the time being. Now, what have you got on the Gordon Grey investigation?"

"Oh, please, do tell," Shepherd said, leaning back in his chair. He still looked a little green under his eyes.

"Well, I've been leading the effort to find out who was 'sponsoring' Gordon Grey during his killing spree last year," Bale said.

"We remember," Gray said, eyes rolling, "Someone bankrolled a small army of helpers to provide him his prescription meds, makeup for disguises, etc."

"And all of them ended up dead by the time he was dead," Shepherd said, "Right up to that hotel manager who tried to help Gordon kill us *and* the Master Chief Petty Officer of the Navy!"

Gray sat forward, his eyes glinting with a sudden thought, "You know, Isaac, *that* pattern of killing everyone who was involved with Gordon last year sounds suspiciously like what we're seeing here."

"Good grief, you're right!" Shepherd said, setting his coffee cup down and pulling out a chair.

"Bingo!" Bale said, "Charlotte wanted me to point that out if you two didn't see it for yourselves."

"Veronica, I have the oddest feeling you're winding us up," Gray said, raising an eyebrow.

"Agreed," Shepherd echoed, picking up his cup and taking a sip. Setting his coffee back down, he crossed his legs and steepled his fingers, "This must be the part where you tell us there's a connection between whoever bankrolled Gordon Grey last year, and whoever's putting feelers out in the international black market this year."

Bale laughed, her hair glittering under the lights, "Isaac, you have a way with words! That is *exactly* what I'm here to brief you two on. Much of the language in these intercepted communications is surprisingly consistent with the language we've encountered with regards to the Lionfish feelers in syntax, phraseology, and even grammar."

"People tend to write with certain styles, the same way they speak with certain styles," Shepherd said.

"Terrific," Gray said, his voice dry and sandy with sarcasm, "Isaac, I don't think we kicked over an anthill as much as knocked down a nest of those 'murder hornets' invading the country."

Shepherd's face blanked momentarily.

"Isaac?" Gray asked.

Shepherd held up a hand, indicating he needed a minute.

Gray and Bale glanced at each other, but then Shepherd spoke.

"Abe, that material from Diego…did you see any connections—of *any* type—that might link this theft of the Lionfish to the attempted theft of the laser weapon *Ponce* tested two years ago? The one Tyler Drummin was trying to steal when he murdered Carl Bacon?"

Gray's spine snapped straight and true. Hands moving swiftly, but assuredly, he flipped open the folders Bale provided and began scanning as fast as he could.

"So," Shepherd said, "We identify and arrest a murderer who was trying to steal new technology aboard *Ponce* in 2016 and get on CIA's radar."

"Then, last year, some benefactor bankrolls Gordon Grey to support his vendetta against you after you nailed him for John Stiles' murder," Bale contributed.

"And *now,*" Gray cut in, "We have a brutal, personal murder *here* that's morphed—after the fact—into another technology theft attempt. Then a CIA operative—likely the same agent we accidentally rumbled aboard *Ponce*—brings this treasure trove of material to Senator Alejandro. James Patterson couldn't have written it better."

"I think we've unearthed both a tidy little money laundering scheme along with a spider's nest on the dark web trying to sell stolen tech," Bale pointed to the files Gray was rifling through, "Several corporate entities suddenly took an interest in Sulfide Services right after you nailed Gordon Grey last March. One of them, Tidy Sweep Industries, bought Sulfide outright in April, and Gordon started working for Sulfide—using a disguise and alias— that very same month."

"So, whoever owns Tidy Sweep bought an *entire company* and used it to set up a support network for Gordon Grey?!" Shepherd asked incredulously, "Just to get at *me and Abe?* The kind of money needed to pull *that* off is astronomical!"

"Agreed," Bale said, "Gordon Grey had a bug up his butt for you, Isaac. But, obviously, so does someone else."

"Well, we've all earned the enmity of own personal Ernst Blofelds," Shepherd asked, "Still, I can't recall anyone with enough wealth to buy up an entire *company* just to use it as a weapon against us. This is beginning to sound less like James Patterson and more like James Bond!"

"Like I said," Bale went on, "There were *several* corporate entities that got unexpectedly interested in Sulfide, so I think they're *all* controlled by one parent company. We're up against some *masters* of corporate and financial misdirection here. Cracking this…this shadow network will take a bit."

"And that *still* leaves us with the mysterious Mr. Aaron Evers…assuming he *is* the 'Aaron Seeley' we met before," Gray said, "You know, there are days when I miss being a simple Atlanta beat cop!"

"Getting back to the Lionfish, how far has our as-yet-unknown thief gotten in selling it?" Shepherd asked.

"That's the strangest part about this," Bale said, shrugging, "The effort to find the 'highest bidder' for the Lionfish has been…I don't know how to put it…well, 'half-assed' is as good a term as any. The attempt to sell *Ponce's* ANQ45 laser two years ago was a master class in persistence and sophistication. That Drummin jerk came *damned* close to succeeding until his murder of OS2 Bacon upended everything."

"So, the Lionfish effort isn't being pursued with the same vigor?" Shepherd asked.

Gray cocked his head, clearly listening as he continued scanning the unending flow of documents spilling out of the briefcase.

"Exactly," Bale said, looking befuddled, "That's one reason the Russians laughed off the offer. And why Iran and North Korea aren't rushing to snap it up. Whoever's trying to hawk it just hasn't been putting in the same level of effort they did when trying to sell the ANQ45 last year. Even China isn't taking this one seriously."

"Sounds like our thief is distracted," Gray said from underneath the avalanche of papers steadily burying him ever deeper, "Which is a very scary thought, seeing as it indicates our targets might be focusing on something bigger—and far more dangerous."

Chapter 22
Silverdale, Washington
Monday, September 10, 2018; 11:13 hours

The three were hip-deep in paperwork when the conference room door blew open. The tornado of one very pissed-off man barged into the room, the purple rage in his face preceding him by several yards.

"GRAY!" David Kerr shouted, eyes bulging in fury and spit flying from his mouth, "What in the *hell*...where do you get off...you son of a bitch, you have *no right...!"*

"Use your words, Mr. Kerr," Shepherd said innocently, "I have the utmost faith in your conversational skills."

"Shut your goddamned mouth, asshole!" Kerr spat at Shepherd before spinning to face Gray as two figures sheepishly entered the room.

"What gives you the right to recall *my* agents?!" Kerr ejaculated with all the finesse of a painter using a potato gun to decorate the side of a barn.

Gray remained seated. Turning the swivel chair slightly, he crossed his legs and straightened his tie. Bale could have sworn she saw a glint of dark amusement in his eyes.

"We can discuss this later, David" Gray said easily, but with a firm voice, "I'm in the middle of something important right now. I'm sorry, but I just don't have time for your complaint at the moment."

"We'll discuss it *now, ass wipe!"* Kerr banged his hand on the conference room table. "I have—I *had*—several important investigations *you* just shut down by recalling these two!"

Gray looked past Kerr, "I assume you two are Special Agents Casey Dobbins and Shelly Kieble?"

The two nodded. Dobbins was a thick-set, heavily bearded man who put Shepherd in mind of Gimli, the dwarf from *The Lord of the Rings* trilogy. Kieble, an athletic, middle-aged woman sported gold star earrings over a dark red blouse and blue skirt. Her proper demeanor and hairstyle reminded Shepherd of Lynda Carter's portrayal of Wonder Woman's alter ego, Diana Prince.

"Never mind who they are!" Kerr yelled, anger tumbling from him like a landslide, "What gives you the right to interfere in *my* operations?!"

"If you recall, my authority comes *directly* from Director Belk," Gray said, calmly, still refusing to rise, "After reviewing the work Dobbins and Kieble were engaged in, I decided to pull them. The caseload here in the northwest has a higher priority."

Shepherd watched with awe. Gray remained sitting casually, and yet he somehow exuded such force of personality that the bombastic Kerr was reduced to a spluttering heap.

"Isaac, why don't we cut out? I'm staying in the same hotel as you two, and I need to check in," Bale said, giving Shepherd a piercing look, "Besides, we both have a lot to read up on. Might as well go to the hotel and be more comfortable."

Shepherd took the hint.

"Abe, I guess I'm catching a lift with Veronica," Shepherd said, pushing his chair back and standing up, his face betraying the pain of his injured knee, "See you later. After I help Veronica settle in, I'll head to that Starbucks by the hotel and do some reading there."

"Sounds good," Gray said, looking over his shoulder to Shepherd, "I'll tidy up some admin work here and catch y'all this evening."

"Get to my office *now,* Gray!" Kerr fairly shouted, his fragile control cracking.

"David, I'll *stop by* your office later," Gray said, the finality in his voice could have halted a runaway freight train, "But, I need to debrief Special Agents Dobbins and Kieble for an hour or so…each. I *do* have a report to send to the director tomorrow, and I need to include these two fine agents' observations."

Plopping his round-rimmed cowboy hat on his head, Shepherd smiled as Gray's calm demeanor and casual dismissal of Kerr sent the agent into a tantrum of boiling curses and blistering threats to Gray's career.

The Starbucks on the corner of Silverdale Parkway and Bucklin Hill Road was typical of the company's architecture. Large windows allowed plenty of natural light (which was good because the Pacific Northwest was being its usual cloudy self). Most of the tables—including the high-top bar along the windows—were equipped with comfortable wooden chairs. A row of padded benches along the wall opposite the windows provided more seating.

His walking stick leaning against the wall, Shepherd leaned back on the padded bench, his sore left leg propped out in front of him on a chair. His table piled high with books, he sipped a cold-brewed coffee, reveling in the silky taste of the cream mingling with the robust flavor of the arabica beans.

Snapping shut the hardback book in his hand, he tossed it on the pile loading down the table. Sliding his bifocals back up his nose, he pulled another sip from the cup.

I've already taken enough ibuprofen to tranquilize an elephant, but my head still freaking hurts! Shepherd grimaced, *Maybe I am being an idiot. I'm pushing 50, after all; maybe I should just go lie down for the rest of the day. Can't just go swanning around like I did when I was 30.*

Breathing deeply and slowly through his nose, he closed his eyes, trying to calm the frenetic hurricane of thoughts churning in his brain. All three Shepherd brothers suffered from brains that incessantly sped along at a frantic pace. Still, A.J. and Joshua didn't seem to have quite the same unpredictably tempestuous cataract of constantly careening mental activity that Isaac lived with.

Most days he could direct its force by working on puzzles, games, conversations, writing; anything to focus his mind. Now, however, the recent pain and fatigue visited upon him eroded his

241

ability to focus. The ambient noise and clatter of the crowd around him only exacerbated the synaptic earthquakes rocking his cerebral world.

Opening his eyes, he flinched so hard his bad knee nearly knocked the table over.

Gippeum Lýkos sat daintily across the table from him. Lýkos' mysterious, dark eyes regarded him with a cool, regal gaze.

"Well, this is an unexpected pleasure, Mr. Shepherd," Lýkos said demurely.

"I very much doubt that, Mr. Lýkos," Shepherd said, feeling for all the world like the proverbial knight who, after having an entire castle fall on him, now faced a rabid dragon.

Lýkos glanced at the books weighing down the table, "Quite a selection. I thought your fortes were history and criminology. Are you considering a shift into genetics research?"

"No, I'm just trying to reckon how current genetic theories can be used to forensically separate identical triplets," Shepherd said, his attempt at casual indifference almost coming off casually. Almost.

"So, you believe I murdered my brother," Lýkos nodded, "I see. Sadly, as part of a set of identical triplets yourself, you should know 'current genetic theories' are a singularly unprofitable tool to employ. Your time would be better spent in pursuit of more logical avenues of inquiry, such as the age-old question of 'Who benefits?' from this crime. I'm afraid I don't benefit at all."

"Oh, you benefit, all right," Shepherd said, trying like mad to find the rapier-like wit he was infamous for. His tired, sluggish brain simply refused to respond.

"Please forgive me for being pedantic," Lýkos said, "But, I must contradict you. My brothers are now both dead. My parents—both birth and adoptive—are dead. Sadly, I'm now alone in this cold, cruel, heartless world."

Shepherd marveled at just how dry Lýkos' voice could be. Despite the cultured, manicured, and even graceful way he carried himself, Lýkos exhibited all the warmth of a malfunctioning animatronic at Disney World, but with none of the potential humor.

Trying to buy time, Shepherd picked up his coffee.

"Chain establishments," Lýkos shook his head, managing to look down his nose at the Starbucks crowd even though he hadn't moved his head, "I prefer to support local businesses."

"Starbucks was founded in Seattle, which is only seven miles *that* way," Shepherd pointed east, "Around here, Starbucks *is* local."

Lýkos blinked, displaying the first emotion Shepherd had seen, "Touché."

"Thanks."

"So, Mr. Shepherd, just how long *are* you planning on futilely tilting at windmills?"

Shepherd blinked, caught off-guard by the seeming irrelevancy, "Beg pardon?"

"I simply don't understand your Quixotic pursuit of me when there are far more realistic suspects to focus on," Lýkos shifted a bit before delicately recrossing his legs, "Even if you intend to continue defending Delores Tate's 'good honor,' surely your time would be better spent investigating the Navy personnel close to my brother and his wife."

"I might not have anything a court would accept—yet, but I've seen enough to convince *me* you're in this up to your eyeballs, Mr. Lýkos," Shepherd responded. His left eye, the one just under the wound on his head, twitched uncomfortably.

"I pity you, you realize," Lýkos said, shaking his head sadly.

"Beg pardon?"

"I fear your 'hero complex' will ultimately lead to your self-destruction, and, just like the sad, old Don Quixote you played in 1990, you'll end up lost in useless misery," Lýkos said, cocking his head to one side. He studied Shepherd with the expression of a behavioral specialist screening a particularly recalcitrant child.

"Excuse me?" Shepherd queried, completely taken off-guard by the change of subject.

"Your brothers excelled in many sports, but you were shunted aside because you only played baseball," Lýkos stated, "Your brothers are Naval Academy graduates. You merely went to Florida State University. Your brother, Andrew, is on the cusp of a Ph.D. in volcanology, and his ground-breaking work on Mount St. Helens will most likely land him a prestigious position with any major university's geology department."

Shepherd's face betrayed his shock. He was simply too fatigued to even pretend casual indifference to the unsettling recitation his cunningly smooth adversary delivered with such brutal grace.

"Your other brother, Joshua, was sadly passed over for head coach of the New Orleans Saints last year, but he's still one of the NFL's most highly regarded offensive coordinators," Lýkos went on, "If he stays the course, he's on track to become a head coach himself sooner than later, and this doesn't even include the three patents he holds for improved knee and elbow brace designs."

Shepherd's brain pushed in the clutch, but his mind remained stubbornly stuck in neutral.

"Both of your brothers are leading highly successful lives in prestigious positions," Lýkos went on quietly, "And yet, here *you* are. Granted, you *did* retire honorably from a military career, but while they build their future, you aimlessly wander the countryside in your vehicle. Your blog and YouTube channel have laughably *few* followers. You keep talking about novels you're writing, and yet no reputable literary agent will touch your manuscript with a ten-foot pole. By my accounting, you're lagging *far* behind your brothers in life."

"I am?" Shepherd mentally kicked himself for the inanity of his response.

"You are," Lýkos said, his dark brown eyes locking onto Shepherd's sea-green orbs, "You were thrust into the 'detective world' by accident in 1999, and I'll concede you acquitted yourself quite admirably helping identify the real miscreant. I believe the adrenalin rush of the game trapped you into an endless cycle of needing to prove you're equal to, if not better than, your brothers by risking your life."

Damn...I have *wondered about that myself,* The thought streaked across Shepherd's mind before he could arrest it. He recognized the manipulative tactics Lýkos was employing, but he couldn't muster the energy or savvy to deflect the attack.

"I fear you may have succumbed to the delusional misconception that your self-worth is based primarily on being a savior," Lýkos said, a feigned look of sadness clouding his face as effectively as any award-winning actor, "A 'hero complex' is a pernicious trap, I caution you. The momentary adulation you receive when you successfully conclude a case makes you feel as high as a narcotic would. And, just like every other addict, you crash when your stimulant is lacking."

Shepherd remained silent, dumbstruck, and frozen.

"I worry about you, Mr. Shepherd," Lýkos' silky voice worming deep into Shepherd's mind, "A man in your position has so much to lose, and I wonder about what your obsession will ultimately cost you."

"Oh, really? Just what will it cost me" Shepherd felt yet again like a child's sandbox being carpet bombed by B-52s, but this time with nuclear weapons.

"You have such a large family and circle of friends," Lýkos said, eyes glinting with cruel humor, "And yet you keep them at arm's length. You remain emotionally stunted, imprisoned by a fear of intimacy...and, I'll wager, by fear the darkness infesting your own heart will consume those around you."

Shepherd blinked, his mouth dry and his tongue sticking to his upper palate. Memories of his powerful temper exploding in a frenzy of kinetic destruction flashed unbidden across his mind...

"Mr. Shepherd, you insist on identifying yourself by the traumas you've experienced instead of moving forward," Lýkos continued the relentless psychological warfare, "You have a man throwing himself at you right now, and yet your relational skills are so immature that you miss even the most patently obvious signals he's telegraphing."

Lýkos shifted his weight slightly. Seeing that his soliloquy had knocked Shepherd into abject silence, he pressed his advantage.

"Your parents are elderly, your brothers and your nephews live active lives—which themselves invite accident and tragedy," Lýkos said, shaking his head with exaggerated sadness.

Lýkos shifted, uncrossing his legs to swing his feet under his chair, "How many enemies have you made? How easy would it be for one of your former foes to attack *them* to get to *you?*"

"Really?" Shepherd's mind floundered in the muddy morass of clouded mendacities Lýkos poured over him.

"The day is coming—and coming very soon—when your obsession will result in your fatality," Lýkos said. "And then where will your family and friends be? Sadly, they'll only be able to mourn over your grave and wonder why you risked so much for so little."

Shepherd's throat closed up tight. He should have been able to fire a few verbal cruise missiles through the holes in Lýkos' logic, but his brain was shutting down under fatigue, guilt, and shock.

"I understand the limited mental abilities you suffer from due to your current injury," Lýkos said, "So I believe the best way to communicate my counsel is to simply recommend you walk away from all of this."

"Walk away?" Shepherd spoke, his voice barely above a whisper, "What do you mean?"

"I mean, dear sir, I'm recommending you employ your considerable talents in reassessing your priorities. Cease this foolhardy line of pursuit. I promise you that *nothing* good will come of it. Well, nothing good for *you.* Return to your road trip and your puerile attempts at literature. I suggest you quit the game now before you—and others close to you—suffer the consequences. There are so many people your activities could expose to…dire threats. I suggest you consider *their* welfare."

Lýkos rose, delicately pushing his chair back under the table. Giving Shepherd a small smile, he sashayed away.

Shepherd wanted to throw up.

"Abe!" The voice preceded the pounding on the door by only milliseconds.

Startled into alertness, Abraham Gray flung the covers off with one hand while grabbing his service-issued 9mm off the nightstand with the other. The shock of the alarum banging through his door drove all thoughts of shirts, socks, and even pants from his mind.

Clicking the safety off, he padded in his underwear to the door. It was shaking under the onslaught of frenzied knocking.

"Abe! He's gone! He vanished! *ABE!!*"

Gray cautiously peeked through the peephole without actually putting his eye to it. He saw Isaac's face outside, nose magnified to ridiculous proportions by the peephole's wide-angle lens. Luke Fredriksen was standing in the background.

Clicking the safety back on, Gray let the weapon fall to his side while he unlocked the door with his right hand. Pulling it open, he ducked to avoid another round of panicked knocking.

"Abe, thank God! He's gone!"

"Isaac, it's four-thirty in the morning!" Gray blustered, his thoughts jumbled by the flash flood of adrenalin crashing through his bloodstream, "What the hell is so wrong that you're...you're not Isaac, are you?"

"No, A.J.," A.J. said, "Isaac's gone! He's vanished!"

"He what?" Gray asked, unconsciously stepping into the hall. He was still playing catch-up to such a degree that he didn't realize he was wearing only a pair of black briefs and holding his 9mm.

"Are you not hearing me?! Isaac's gone!" A.J. blurted, breathless with panic, "I woke up about an hour ago! He's just *gone!*"

"A.J. called me to see if Isaac happened to be at my flat in Bremerton," Fredriksen jumped in, "I came on over and A.J. told me Isaac disappeared. When I asked if you two were working, he told me he hadn't talked to you. So, here we are."

"Wait," Gray shook his head, irritation seeping in over his discombobulation, "Wait, A.J.—are you telling Isaac disappeared at least an *hour ago,* and you didn't think to come get me *first?!* We're on the same bloody damn floor in the same bloody damn hotel!"

"I panicked," A.J. said, "I've seen head wounds make people do some really stupid things!"

"I didn't see him at all yesterday evening," Gray said, voice still carrying a heavy load of irritation, "What was he like before y'all racked out?"

"He was…he was just 'off' ever since he came back from Starbucks but wouldn't tell me much at all except that he'd had a run-in there and that he was tired and just wanted to be left alone so he went to bed and didn't say anything else to me about it," A.J. babbled, speaking at the same Mach 2 rate Isaac used.

Damn, Gray thought absently, *Guess all three brothers are like that.*

A.J. prattled on.

"Isaac said that Lýkos met him at the coffee shop but I honestly didn't think anything of it at the time. Isaac *was* a bit off and I just chalked that up to him being tired and injured but I got up at about three to take a leak and he'd vanished!" A.J.'s breathless recitation finally spluttering out.

"Let's go take a look at your room," Gray said, but Fredriksen cleared his throat, catching Gray's attention.

"Uh, Abe…pants," Fredriksen said delicately, finger pointing downward.

Gray saw a few people were now peeking out their doors to find out what the commotion was. He also realized with embarrassment everything he *wasn't* wearing.

"Oy Gevalt!" Gray muttered, turning to stride back into his room. Grabbing some shorts and a T-shirt, he looked at the clock as he dressed: 04:33. Securing his weapon, he threw on slippers and emerged back into the hallway, locking his door behind him.

"I checked the parking lot on my way in," Fredriksen said as A.J. led them down the hall to his and Isaac's room, "Isaac's car is gone."

The three men entered Isaac's room. A.J. had been crashing on the room's sofa. His blanket and pillow were cast aside in a pile from when he'd gotten up to hit the head.

"Goddammit, I don't need this right now!" Gray seethed through his teeth, "I *never* should have brought him in on this!"

"His teddy bear is still here," Fredriksen's voice brought Gray back to the moment at hand.

Fredriksen was right. Happy Bear sat happily on a well-made bed.

"He made the bed," Gray said thoughtfully, "Hang on…"

Gray ducked into the bathroom, then back out to sniff around inside the room's tiny closet. Hands on his hips, he scanned the room with his eyes, instinctively cataloging everything.

"His daily meds and shaving kit are in the bathroom," Gray said, "His hydropack's missing, too. There's a can of Gatorade powder on the bathroom sink. Was that there earlier?"

"I…I don't know…" A.J. responded with a stammer.

"Well, *think,* dammit!" Gray snapped, "It's important."

A.J. looked like a duck struck on the head with a rock, but Gray's snap re-engaged his brain.

Get a grip on yourself you babbling baboon! A.J. sternly ordered himself. *How would Isaac handle this…?*

A.J. visibly calmed down, clearly forcing himself to throttle back the panic and engage his brain instead.

"Uh…no," A.J. said, pulling the memory up past the discombobulated mess that was his shocked thought process, "No, it was *not* there last night when we crashed. I remember seeing it over in that bin he uses to store his camp kitchen gear. Now that

249

I'm thinking about it, his hiking boots, his walking stick, and one of his hats are also gone."

Gray's eyes narrowed, sweeping the room again, "His phone's gone, but the charging cord's still here. His field jacket's gone, but his camera gear is here—meaning he's not out sightseeing."

"He also left his CPAP machine," A.J. offered, making an obvious effort to be productive and stop behaving like an idiot.

"He left deliberately and has every intention of coming back," Gray said before looking at Fredriksen, "And A.J. called *you* to come from Bremerton before talking to me?!"

Fredriksen nodded.

Gray's temper snapped. Rounding on A.J., he lashed out, "We've already lost over an *hour!* Why didn't come to me first?! Good Lord, Andrew! You used to be a naval *officer!* I sure as hell hope you didn't panic on the bridge like this when your ship was in danger!"

Gray stalked out of the room, a pyroclastic flow of boiling rage.

"I'm sorry…" A.J. squeaked to the spot where Gray had been.

Fredriksen put a steadying hand on A.J.'s shoulder, "Relax; this isn't exactly anything you were trained for. Abe'll be ok. For now, stay in the area in case Isaac comes back. You've got my number, right?"

A.J. nodded.

"Good," Fredriksen said, "We'll be in touch as soon as we know anything."

Leaving the befuddled A.J. behind, Fredriksen headed back to Gray's room. Stepping inside, Fredriksen found Gray already dressed in jeans, a sweatshirt, and a jacket.

"Do you have any idea where he'd go?" Gray asked.

Fredriksen shook his head.

"Damn him!" Gray snarled, "And damn *me!* I *knew* asking for his help was stupid! That Lýkos asshole is dangerous. He found a way to get into Isaac's head. Come on, Luke, I need your help! I'll call your command and get it cleared. Who knows where the hell Isaac's got off to!"

Sarah Jane knew right where the hell Isaac had got off to. He was sitting in her pilot seat, heading to visit a dead man on the slopes of a somnolent volcano.

Chapter 23
Mount Rainier National Park, Washington
Tuesday, September 11, 2018; 10:43 hours

"…Hurricane Florence is rapidly approaching the Carolinas, prompting evacuations as FEMA stages emergency supplies…"

"…Leading indicators predict the NASDAQ and S&P 500 are likely to break a four-day losing streak even as Apple shares are taking a hit. South Korea-based GDI Tech received a boost after announcing the company was finally bringing in a new CEO and COO…"

"…the president refused to comment on accusations leveled by members of Congress against the director of NCIS. Laying a wreath at the Flight 93 memorial in Pennsylvania, the president said he was focused on remembering the victims of the 9/11 terrorist attacks…"

The temperature was heading towards 60° F, which surprised Shepherd since the day was primarily overcast. He assumed it'd be colder as he drove higher into the Cascade Mountains. The thick clouds were threatening to break apart slightly, but that would only allow feeble sunlight to wash the highlands without warming the area any further.

Awakening well before dawn itself thought about getting out of bed, Shepherd bolted. The traumas of the past two days reverberated through him as surely as the mental wounds inflicted by Lýkos. He needed to get away from everything.

Years spent at sea maneuvering quietly around crowded berthing compartments enabled Shepherd to get his hiking kit together while leaving A.J. undisturbed. Gear gathered, he'd silently slipped out.

He sought an early breakfast at an IHOP in Puyallup (which, he was told, was pronounced 'pue-wallop'), a town on the southeastern outskirts of Tacoma. He scanned area trails and parks on his phone during the meal, deciding that Mount Rainier National Park was his best option. He desperately wanted to hike Mount St. Helens, but his injured leg registered an objection to that idea.

Mount Rainier, however, was clear of inclement weather and, more importantly, offered several easy trails he could stroll around in the Paradise area. This would appease his left leg while affording him the solitude he desperately needed.

His journey to the towering volcanic peak was not some great, mystical dawn in which the rising sun inspired spiritual healing. Nope. The Pacific Northwest cloud cover allowed only a subdued light to slowly grow around *Sara Jane* as she trucked along the rural roads.

Shepherd passed under the magnificent wooden archway marking the Nisqually Entrance on the park's southwestern corner. Beginning the slow, winding trek up the mountainside, he passed the Longmire area. His eyes swept up towards the sheer cliffs of Rampart Ridge, a towering lava flow that flooded down from Mount Rainier's summit nearly 400,000 years ago.

A sheer-sided, nearly thousand-foot-high lava flow?! Shepherd marveled as he carefully navigated *Sarah Jane* under Rampart Ridge's shadow. *Really gives you an idea of just how damned* big *the Ice Age glaciers were that covered this area. They were able to hold back a* lava flow *long enough for it to cool into a steep cliff!*

Taking his eyes off the ancient lava formation, he found himself idly comparing how different the lush woods of Washington State were from the long-needle pine and wiregrass forests he'd grown up with in northwest Florida. Tempted to stop and take in the scenery, he had more important things on his mind. Keeping his course, he finally rolled into the large parking lot outside the Henry M. Jackson Visitors Center in the Paradise area nearly 40 minutes after entering the park.

Shepherd was surprised by the number of visitors milling about the elegant A-frame structure despite it being well past the tourist

season. Still, the bustle wasn't anywhere near overwhelming.
Shepherd knew he could find solitude with a minimum of fuss.

Shepherd explained his knee injury to a ranger who helpfully
traced out some easy, paved trails on a map.

Leaving the visitors center behind, Shepherd hoisted his
hydropack onto his shoulders, buckling its waist belt into place.
Still leaning on the hickory, doorknob-handled stick he'd picked
up in Maine, Shepherd lurched his way outside.

Mount Rainier was mostly covered in a vividly deep sea of
green. The emerald needles of cedars, firs, and other high-altitude
trees jealously guarded their lush hues against the encroaching
winter. The ground cover was still green in the bracingly sharp
morning air. The smooth scent of cedar anointed the light
morning breeze with a delicate perfume.

The summit, however, was hidden within thick, fluffy clouds.
A bare hint of the glaciers enveloping Rainier's peak peeked out
from under the clouds.

Walking slowly in deference to his left knee, Shepherd
meandered west along the Avalanche Lily Trail. Marmots poked
their little heads up cautiously from the grass as he passed,
looking for all the world like oversized prairie dogs. Several of
the large, fuzzy rodents trundled through the grass, only their
heads barely visible.

They look like furry little submarines! Shepherd laughed
quietly.

Tiny chipmunks darted about, reminding Shepherd of Florida's
ubiquitous gray squirrels. The little brown and white critters kept
a cautiously hopeful eye on him. He could tell they were
accustomed to getting free food from clueless tourists who fed
wildlife while standing next to a "Don't feed the animals" sign.

"Sorry, fellas. I don't share," Shepherd said quietly to a few of
the chipmunks.

Hooking a right at the intersection with the Alta Vista Trail, he
tenderly climbed higher up the slope until he found a bench along
the trail. Glancing around, he could see no one else.

Dropping the hydropack to the rocky ground under the bench, he zipped his blue field jacket up to stop the gentle breeze from sneaking down his neck. Despite the low cloud coverage and isolated fog down in the valleys, the air around him was absurdly dry.

Well, you are *nearly 5,500 feet above sea level, you nincompoop!* Shepherd thought as he bent to drink from his pack. The sub-alpine air was leeching moisture from his body at an alarming rate.

Shepherd resettled *Ike,* the older of his two round-rimmed cowboy hats, on his head before looking at the broken mountains cascading away below him. Turning again, he stared upwards. Six thousand feet above him, lost in that blank, gray, cloudy vista, was the summit of the largest volcano in the continental United States.

This thing is still alive, Shepherd thought, looking now at the ground as though he could see through it with X-ray vision. *There's a magma chamber nearly five miles beneath my feet. Hot, full, boiling...but asleep. For now.*

One day, Mount Rainier would indeed awaken dramatically once more, but not today. Shepherd was fascinated with volcanoes, just not to the same extent as his brother A.J.

Wish I had more time to look around, Shepherd thought, taking a breath.

Shepherd pulled a towel from his hydropack, dropping it on the ground before dropping his posterior onto it. Leaning against the bench, he stared upwards, trying to imagine the summit.

Closing his eyes, he began breathing slowly through his nose. The air was brisk and clean. He liked clean. He'd felt contaminated ever since Smith's head exploded over him. Clean was nice.

"Dammit, Isaac! You just don't know when to quit, do you?!"

John Stiles sat on the bench above Shepherd. Stiles' crisp, khaki uniform was pressed to perfection—as usual. A tall rack of ribbons adorned his left breast, and his master chief petty officer anchor insignia with its two stars glinted on his collar. The reflected images of clouds drifted lazily in Stiles' mirror-polished shoes, and the combo cover set atop Stiles' head neatly hid the closely shaved high-and-tight the master chief sported.

"John, we're in the middle of a national park," Shepherd said bemusedly, looking up to his former (and former living) mentor, "You could have at least worn NWUs!"

"I'm a master chief *and* a ghost; I'll wear whatever I goddamn want," Stiles said gruffly, his craggy, sun-worn face breaking into a smile with his eyes twinkling, "So, you're up here feeling sorry for yourself."

"You always were a straight shooter," Shepherd said wryly, "But, give me a break! A man's face blew open all over *my* face. I had his *teeth* in my freaking *hair.* Trying to get that image out of my head is hardly 'feeling sorry for myself.'"

Shepherd took a moment, reflecting on how much the deceased master chief's counsel had meant to him during his career, "I've missed talking to you."

Stiles nodded, "Just remember, Isaac—our actions have consequences, even when we're not thinking that far ahead. Keep that in mind, ok?"

"I will," Shepherd sighed.

"Hell, maybe I'd still be alive if I'd been a better husband," Stiles said, reaching down to pick up a rock.

"Oh, sweet cheese and crackers!" Shepherd exclaimed. "Get real! You're *not* responsible for Carolyn shacking up with Gordon Grey and then murdering you! You're a ghost, not God," Shepherd said pointedly. "Carolyn might *still* have traded you in for a boy toy. You can't know one way or the other."

"Ok, ok, you've got a point. Now, why are you out in Washington State? You told me you wanted to stop playing sailor *and* detective," Stiles said, redirecting the conversation, "To find out who you were 'without the uniform.'"

Shepherd remained quiet.

"Well, the uniform's gone, but here you are in the detective role again," Stiles pressed gently, "Why? Why are you *really* here?"

"I honestly don't know anymore," Shepherd said, his voice suddenly guttural and rough.

"Go on."

Shepherd shook his head, putting his fists to his temples, "I can't! I can't *think!* Goddammit, John, I just have this…this noise in my head! I keep seeing…"

"You keep seeing Smith dying," Stile said.

"I was two seconds from getting him to safety!" Shepherd blurted, "Two fucking *seconds!* And they killed him right in my goddamned *face!"*

The dam broke.

Shepherd's form crumpled into a heap of jilting, spasming muscles as the rage, fear, horror, and grief tore away the final shreds of his control. The emotional magma chamber, over-pressurized for days, erupted in spectacular fashion. Tears spilled hot down Shepherd's face as his lungs seized, convulsing in a burping, hiccupping weeping that scared a nearby chipmunk near to death.

Two marmots popped their periscope-like heads up from the grass in alarm. The animals began to slink away from the noise.

Stiles waited patiently as Shepherd wept, a supportively spectral hand on the younger man's shoulder.

The eruption slowly subsided, punctuated by an occasional burping cry as the psychological lahar drained away, taking the poison of the past 48 hours with it.

Rummaging in his hydropack, Shepherd began pulling out items until he found a bandana he could blow his nose in.

"You needed that, Isaac," Stiles said simply, "The fastest way to get rid of pain is to move *through* it, not around it. How do you feel?"

"Like shit," Shepherd said, "But, you're right, though. I do feel…cleaner. But, damn…now I'm hungry!"

"Well, it's been nearly six hours since you had breakfast!" Stiles said wryly as Shepherd pulled more items out of his back, building a small pile as he sought a trail bar. Finding one, he tore open the wrapper and tore into the bar.

Stiles idly picked up Shepherd's epinephrine injector, "I'd forgotten you're allergic to bee stings. Keeping this is smart, but I don't think you'll need it this late in the year."

"Probably not," Shepherd laughed before taking a bite and savoring the savory blend of raisins, nuts, and nougat.

"Isaac," Stiles said, setting the injector back on the pile of gear, "What was the first lesson I taught you when you made chief petty officer back in 2012?"

"We're the masters of tradition, not its slaves," Shepherd answered promptly.

Stiles paused, "Not the lesson I meant. Sorry…though you *have* taken that one on board nicely. No, what was the second lesson I taught you?"

"Don't make promises you can't keep."

Stiles dropped his head in frustration, "Jeez…ok, one more try. What was the *third* lesson I taught you?"

"Act, don't react. Look at the big picture first and don't let emotion push you into kneejerk reactions."

"Fucking-A! That's the one!" Stiles slapped his knee in triumph, "Guess I taught you better than I remembered. Now, do you remember *why* I told you to 'step back?'"

"Of course," Shepherd said, watching a chipmunk nose its way cautiously out of a bush to sniff at something on the trail, "Our emotions can lead us into ill-conceived reactions that potentially threaten the interests of the Navy, our ship, and our sailors."

"Damn near verbatim," Stiles nodded approvingly before shifting rudder with such speed Shepherd was nearly thrown overboard.

"You walked away from the Navy *and* detective work because it was the right thing to do, and the right time to do it," Stiles said, "But then you assisted that sheriff in Kentucky and now you're here helping Abraham Gray. You *have* moved beyond wearing the uniform, but *twice* now you've gone back to being a working detective. Why?"

"I don't know," Shepherd said, dejection coloring his words as he began returning the pile of gear to his pack, "I thought I did, but maybe the *gesekgi* was right. Maybe I'm just playing hero because it makes me feel important, especially when measured against my brothers."

"Well, for one thing, there isn't a human being alive with brothers or sisters who doesn't have to deal with *some* level of sibling rivalry," Stiles stated, his voice flat and unemotional, "Even so, if you *were* trying to define yourself by competition with your brothers, you'd have become an officer. So, let's just knock that shit off, ok?"

"Good point," Shepherd said, nodding, "But the fact is that I *do* like being the hero. I like being the one stopping monsters and saving people."

"Of course, you do, but so the fuck what?" Stiles asked as he casually dismissed Shepherd's statement, "Your friend, Abraham Gray, is a special agent. Clearly, 'playing hero' makes him feel important as well, but you're not getting all butt-hurt over *his* motivations."

Shepherd froze, his hand holding the epinephrine injector in mid-air as he continued restocking his pack.

Stiles reached down, taking the epinephrine injector from Shepherd's immobile hand. Dropping it into Shepherd's bag, he continued rolling around the rock in his hands.

"That Lýkos bastard is the *epitome* of a cold, evil bastard. He's a master strategist and a master of psychological warfare. He chose his target well by taking *one* of your motivations and turning it on its head," Stiles said, "And *you're* getting trapped in an epicycle around his manipulations because you're reacting emotionally; you're not seeing the bigger picture."

Shepherd looked up at Stiles, eyes crinkled thoughtfully.

"Isaac, you're an extremely emotional individual," Stiles said, "I'll admit I used to think that was a liability, but over time I realized your passion is one of your strengths…although it's a volatile strength you have to manage carefully."

"John, I love compliments as much as anyone, but even *I'll* say my ego is big enough as it is," Shepherd said with a laugh.

Stiles refused to be deflected from his point, "This isn't about your ego, dummy. This is about letting that…what was it you called him?"

"Gesekgi," Shepherd said, "Korean for 'son of a bitch.'"

"Thanks," Stiles nodded, "This is about you *letting* that *gesekgi* live rent-free inside your thick skull. He's good, but he's only an epigone of you. *His* advantage is his lack of empathy. *Your* advantage is your very big heart. Sadly, however, that also creates the very epitome of an unstable vulnerability in you, and he exploited it in an epic fashion. However, you're the one with the *real* power here, Chief. Not him. You decide if he wins or loses. Not him. *You.*"

Shepherd turned, looking back over the cloud-draped peaks of the Cascades as Stiles went on.

"It's easy for you to get overwhelmed emotionally because your emotions *are* so powerful," Stiles pointed out, "And you're particularly susceptible to attack when you're fatigued. Still, you've had enough time to recover. His epigonus success is only possible if *you* allow him to set the terms of the conflict, and *I* think you're *way* too smart to do *that.*"

Shepherd cocked his head, considering Stiles' words.

Stiles went on, "You're the epitome of a man who knows how it feels to lose people, so it's no wonder you'd choose to fight murderers. You only feel like a failure because you were at the epicenter of William Smith's death."

"I wasn't busted up like *this* when that hag Melody Rhyme killed Yvonne Jenny right in front of me on *Eisenhower* last year," Shepherd said, throwing his hands in the air, "And *I* was Rhyme's target, not Jenny! I'm only alive because of dumb luck!"

Stiles shook his head, his face cracking into a sea-worn, leathery smile, "Compartmentalizing that one was relatively easy compared to this. You only went through *survivor's guilt* because you felt you had no *responsibility* for the tragedy, save for being alive."

"I'm not seeing your point," Shepherd said, sounding for all the world like a man lost in a cave whose final match just burnt out. "I'm not responsible for what happened to Smith, either."

"No, but you *feel* responsible because you were only seconds away from saving him. *That's* what's got your anchor all fouled up," Stiles said pointedly, but kindly. Idly tossing the rock back and forth, he regarded Shepherd shrewdly. "Here's an epiphany for you, Isaac: we can do our goddamn *best* and still come up short. That's not a failure; that's just *life.*"

Shepherd froze as Stiles' words struck home.

"I'm also struck by just how much effort this psychotic bastard put into stalking you," Stiles pointed out, "He didn't research Abe Gray's life history; he's been epistemically stalking *you.* Why does he consider *you* so important that he went through all that trouble?"

Shepherd's eyes blinked as he pulled in a sharp breath, clearly on the verge of a revolution in the head.

"I knew you'd get there," Stiles nodded, "You should consider the question of *why* this epicene asshole is so freaking desperate to remove you from the situation."

"Son of a bitch…!" Shepherd muttered in a low-level guttural growl of triumph mingled with genuine laughter at his obtuseness.

"Let that sink in for a while," Stiles said warmly, rising to his feet, "I'll bet it clears your mind up so fast the answer hits you like a shot."

Stiles adjusted his cover slightly, straightened his shirt, and began to stride away up the mountain's emerald slopes.

"Oh, wait—Isaac, here!" Stiles turned, tossing the rock he'd been holding to Shepherd.

Shepherd's right hand shot into the air, catching the stone.

"Hey, dude! Uh…are you ok?"

The voice snapped Shepherd back to the present. Opening his eyes, he saw two hikers looking at him quizzically.

"I…uh…what?" Shepherd asked. Realizing he was sitting there with his right hand stuck up in the air, he lowered his arm, "Yeah, I'm fine. Just…just thinking. Thanks!"

The hikers glanced at each other, shrugging before resuming their course back towards the visitors center.

Opening his right hand, the gravity of the discussion hit him anew as he saw he was holding the rock Stiles had tossed him.

Eyes narrowing in confusion, Shepherd rose, his bad left knee creaking as he regained a standing position. He ignored the complaining joint.

Turning the rock over in his hand, he looked up, eyes scanning the surrounding landscape. He was quite alone.

Tossing the rock back to the ground, he pulled Albert the Crab from inside his pack.

"Well, buddy," Shepherd said to Albert, "I *feel* better, so that's a start. But I still need to figure out *how* to prove it all forensically!"

Albert looked back quietly, unable to offer anything useful at the moment.

"Don't worry. I'll get there, Albert," Shepherd said, "I have to. Letting that *mi-chin-nom* get away is *not* an option!"

Sliding Albert back into his pack, Shepherd picked up his hydropack. Looking inside it, he saw the epinephrine injector laying on top of the pile of equipment.

Oh, that's right, John put it in here…in here…in…here…

The answer hit him like a shot.

The impact of revelation was so powerful Shepherd's knees buckled. Collapsing onto the bench, the clarity of thought he'd long sought burst upon him like a flood from a collapsing glacial dam. His mind began shuffling puzzle pieces around so fast that even he was hard-pressed to keep up.

Epinephrine…! His thoughts became a raging torrent, *Epi…! Shit! That's it! That's what I've been looking for! That's it! That's freaking IT!*

"Wait… stop *reacting,* Isaac…think it through," Shepherd admonished himself, "You've got the forensics for the first murder, but the gunshots…the *gesekgi* is no marksman. So, who…?"

Abruptly the cryptic text from Mr. 'L' flashed across his mental screen, followed closely by the image of two items that were supposed to be three…

"Oh, *shit!"* Shepherd yelped, horrified at his leap of logic. "Still, that makes sense…a *lot* of sense! But now…the safe…how does the ransacked safe…"

"No, stop!" Shepherd commanded himself, "The safe is secondary. The *gesekgi* and his accomplice are the primary threat! Crap! I need to text Abe!"

Shepherd pulled out his phone and beat out a fast text using a coding system for unsecured com lines that he and Gray had worked out years before:

Abe, code blue! I've got it, but watch your back!

Hitting 'send,' Shepherd groaned, realizing he had no signal here on Mount Rainier's slopes.

"Crap!" Shepherd scrambled, shoving the phone back into his pocket. Securing the pack on his back, he retrieved his walking stick, "It'll take me at least two hours to get far enough back down to have any cell service!"

Shepherd forced himself to stop. *Calm down, Isaac. It's a long way back to Silverdale. Rushing off in a panic's only going to get you in trouble.*

Shepherd once again swung his gaze out over the broken mountains cascading away under him.

"Thanks, John," Shepherd nodded, quietly speaking to the dead, "The *gesekgi's* gaslighting me, but no more. He thinks his big brain gives him superiority over the rest of the human race, does he? Well, *I* think it's high time I go nuclear on him and let him find out what a *real* genius can do!"

Shepherd felt his spirit reinflating as his metaphorical feet once again found their metaphorical footing.

"Ok, you bastard, it's game on!" Shepherd said in a ringing declaration that sailed over the mountains, "Or, to put it more poetically—and so it begins!"

Chapter 24

Port Orchard, Washington
Friday, September 14, 2018; 11:21 hours

"David, you can make a formal complaint to the director," Gray said into his phone, his inhuman patience buttressed by the miles separating him and David Kerr, "However, if you think I'm afraid of you, then you're exceptionally naive."

Gray stood outside the conference room at the Kitsap County Sheriff's Office. The NCIS building felt oddly crowded now that Gray had recalled nearly all the agents Kerr deployed to other states. Gray informed Kerr this glut of personnel was why he'd moved his meetings to the Sheriff's Office. It wasn't the real reason, of course, but Gray happily took the excuse to put some space between him and Kerr.

"Just because your stupid little 'consultant' decided to run away with his tail between his legs doesn't mean you haven't already jeopardized multiple investigations, including one in Nevada with *major* security implications!" Kerr seethed, his voice dripping demonically through the phone.

"Not according to your own agents," Gray said firmly, yet almost lazily, "Now, I've wasted enough time this morning correcting your egregiously dysfunctional management. I've got a meeting about the investigation I *was* sent here to conduct. We can talk about this later when it's more convenient for me. Goodbye!"

Gray ended the call with an emphatic jab of his thumb. Setting the phone to silent mode, he stepped into the conference room. Closing the door, he smiled at Sheriff Sigo.

"Denita, I owe you more than I can ever repay for the patience you've shown NCIS during this fiasco," Gray said, taking off his blue suit jacket and hanging it on the back of a chair, his shoulder holster swinging slightly at his side.

Sigo smiled wryly as she walked over to the coffee pot, "You know, most people use belt-mounted holsters these days."

"Just call me old-fashioned," Gray joked, "Makes me feel like James Bond."

"Well, you'd need some 'Just For Men' to get the hair color right if you want *that* part!" Sigo said, a puckish look on her face as she poured a cup of coffee.

"Touché!" Gray laughed, his eyes instinctively counting the room. In addition to himself and Sigo, Bale, Fredriksen, and Shepherd occupied the space.

Sigo pulled out a chair next to Fredriksen. Swinging her heavy boots up on the table, she crossed her feet and looked expectantly at Gray.

"Ok, let's get to work," Gray said, taking a seat at the head of the long conference table, Shepherd facing him from the opposite end. Veronica Bale and Luke Fredriksen were occupying chairs in the middle. The piles of papers and books pouring off the table and across the floor were almost deep enough to be classified as a mountain range.

"First off," Gray said, leaning back in his chair, "Everyone over at NCIS now thinks Isaac's pulled chocks and left town. Secondly, Chief Fredriksen is now on TAD orders to our team. Chief, I'm grateful for your time and assistance."

"No problem," Fredriksen said. Bale suppressed a smile when she saw Fredriksen's eyes unconsciously flick towards Shepherd.

Gray clicked a remote control. The room's projector flashed into life, shooting a graph onto the screen at the head of the room, "Between data accrued from William Smith's fatal injuries, the non-fatal injuries sustained by Isaac, and the rounds we recovered, we now have a preliminary ballistics profile of our shooter."

Gray rose, clicking the remote to change the image to a map.

"The fact that Chief Fredriksen and Isaac both remember *hearing* the shot that killed Smith *after* he was hit—and that Chief Fredriksen heard the shot that hit Isaac *after* Isaac had already been struck—is an obvious indicator the shooter was firing from an extremely long range."

Gray clicked the remote again, the map now displaying directional arrows, "The shooter was close enough for the initial shot to cause catastrophic damage to Smith's head, but the projectile's momentum was completely spent after punching through Smith's cranium, so it only bounced off Isaac's chest."

Gray continued staring at the map, "The round that struck Isaac *would* have been fatal, but Isaac was already turning as he grabbed Smith's shoulder immediately before Smith was struck. That turning movement continued when Isaac jerked his arm back in surprise at Smith's death, and then further rotated his body in response to Chief Fredriksen calling for him."

Fredriksen glanced at Shepherd again. Shepherd still sported a small bandage covering the stitches in his forehead.

Gray continued his summation.

"This turning movement resulted in the presentation of Isaac's forehead to the shooter at an acute angle the moment the second shot hit. The angle of impact resulted in the round glancing his off skull, instead of hitting him directly and causing fatal damage. Had the shooter been just a few yards closer, or had Isaac *not* turned to that *exact* angle at that *exact* moment, he'd be dead."

Gray turned, meeting Shepherd's eyes with his own, "You've had more than a few lucky shaves in your day, Isaac, but this takes the biscuit. I think we can all agree God still wants you alive, though, at the moment, I can't fathom why."

Shepherd blinked, startled by the barb. Gray had been oddly distant the past few days. Shepherd chalked it up to Gray's attention being divided between the Tate investigation and David Kerr's unpleasant personage, but this time the coldness was personal. He was pissed, but Shepherd was at a loss to understand why.

"I sent the information about the two rounds to an FBI colleague," Gray continued, "I rousted him out of bed the other night, but he owed me a favor. The bullets are Russian in origin."

"Russian?!" Fredriksen blurted.

"Russian," Shepherd affirmed, "And *that* brings us to an interesting factoid. The bullets are antique 7N1 shells. The 7N1 bullet was designed in 1966 by Russian arms manufacturers V. M. Sabelnikov, Pyotr Sazonov, and V. M. Dvorianinov as a new round for Soviet snipers."

Despite his immediate grudge against Shepherd, Gray was still impressed by the sheer amount of information Shepherd could retain and rattle off so casually.

"The 7N1 was similar in specs to the modern American M118LR round," Shepherd was saying, "However, it was replaced by the Russians with the 7N14 back in '99. This new version changed the penetrator to a hardened-steel design in response to body armor. Currently, we don't know if the rounds used are actual antiques, or were specially made by a modern manufacturer, but our shooter most likely used a Soviet-era sniper rifle."

Fredriksen and Sigo looked at each other in shock before looking toward Shepherd. Even though Fredriksen had worked with Shepherd and Gray years before, he had yet to experience the informational waterfall Shepherd could regurgitate with such ease.

"The fact the rounds are of an antique design narrows the field significantly," Gray picked up the exposition without pause. Pointing to the map on the screen, Gray traced the red line denoting the bullets' flight paths.

"The shooter had a direct line of sight to Smith's apartment building. Based on velocity, wind speed, and impact damage, this puts the shooter at a range of about 890 yards, which locates the shooter *here,*" Gray pointed to a spot on the map, "Our research into Cold War Soviet-era weapons led us to a few contenders effective at that range, even though the distance is at the *extreme* edge of the possibility for a fatal hit."

Gray paused, "Before anyone asks, the round that killed Delores Tate shattered into a few hundred fragments after it passed through her head and impacted the pavement. The ballistics team are still reconstructing it, but I'm confident it'll match up with the rounds we recovered from the strikes at Smith and Isaac."

"The analysis of the Bremerton strike means our shooter's aim was *perfect,"* Bale said, "So we *are* dealing with a professional here."

"I gotta ask," Fredriksen piped up, staring at Shepherd, "When did you two become experts on antique Soviet weapons, 'eh?!"

"The past two days," Shepherd said, "The internet and the full force of NCIS, the FBI, and local collectors like Denita here helped considerably."

"You collect Soviet weapons?" Fredriksen asked the sheriff.

"Personally, I prefer 19th century American firearms," Sigo said, "But my grandfather brought back a few Nazi Lugers whose owners…didn't need them anymore after the Battle of the Bulge. He also brought back a beautiful Tokarev TT-30 pistol he traded a Soviet soldier one of the Lugers for back in 1945. That started him collecting Soviet weapons when he could," She dropped her feet to the floor, sitting up straight as she met Fredriksen's eyes, "He had a few rifles in his collection when he passed, including a Tokarev SVT-40 sniper rifle. He and my dad taught me to shoot them."

"Brilliant!" Fredriksen smiled, "I need to start hanging out with you! I've got a small collection of Vietnam-era pistols myself."

"If the discussion about personal gun collections is over, can we get back on topic?" Bale asked, clicking her sparkly green nails on the table. Her eyes, however, glinted with amusement. "Our shooter was already lying in wait for Smith that night. I'd say the shooter was watching through their scope when they saw Isaac chasing him."

Fredriksen pointed up at the map, "There're two ATMs and three apartment buildings in that part of Tacoma. All have security cameras—the base JAG subpoenaed their footage last year for evidence in a robbery case. You're saying those cameras showed *no one* with a gun?"

"No one," Gray confirmed before clicking the remote again. The projector now displayed a grainy photo of a nondescript brown sedan parked by the curb near a convenience store, "However, we have this car parked here at 23:00. Late 1970s or early '80s-model sedan, brown, and in decent shape. No one got out, but you can see the outline of the driver inside. He sits there until he vanishes at 00:30. Shortly after the shootings, he shows up again in the driver's seat, and the car leaves."

"Wait," Bale said, her forehead furrowing as she digested Gray's narrative, "The driver 'disappears' during the time of the shootings, but there's no footage of him getting *out* of the car? Maybe…maybe the driver just lay down to sleep a bit in the front seat?"

"Possible," Gray acknowledged, "But the salient point here is that this car is *exactly* where the shooter would have to be for the fatal strike on Smith."

"People don't just vanish into thin air," Fredriksen said, "Is it possible the ATM camera from the store malfunctioned?"

"Explored and disproven," Gray said, frustration bubbling over in his voice, "That was my first question, but all the cameras in the area are functioning. I don't know; maybe this turkey put on some super-secret 'active camouflage' suit like they do in the movies."

"Is it possible the driver was able to sneak out by hiding on the car's far side?" Sigo asked, "The side the camera didn't see?"

"Good theory," Gray said, "Except there's a security camera on *this* building across the street."

Gray pulled up another photo bearing nearly the same time stamp as the first, "But, as you can see, no one got out of the car on *either* side. The driver just…disappears. Then reappears *after* the shooting and drives away."

Shepherd cocked his head to the side, listening to Gray's narration. He could feel an idea sneaking around the back of his mind.

"Is it possible our shooter was actually *inside* one of the buildings?" Fredriksen was asking.

"The D.C. Snipers!" Shepherd ejaculated, jumping to his feet as inspiration struck his brain like lightning.

Everyone in the room jumped, but Sigo recovered her wits first.

"The who?" Sigo asked.

"The D.C. Snipers—those two evil twerps shooting people around D.C., northern Virginia, and south-central Maryland in late '02!" Shepherd explained, his rate of speech increasing as his excitement grew, "They modified a car so they could crawl into the trunk space through the back seat and fire through holes cut in the car's exterior. That prevented witnesses from actually *seeing* them fire. I'll bet Luke's retirement pay *our* shooter copied their style!"

"That certainly *would* explain the 'how' of the shooting," Gray said, once again not looking at Shepherd, "And why we didn't find any shell casings in the area—they'd have been contained inside the vehicle."

"*My* pay?" Fredriksen gave Shepherd a bemused look.

"I'm lousy at gambling," Shepherd said, a coy smile on his face. Fredriksen rolled his eyes, returning Shepherd's look with a sly smile of his own.

"I've got my people looking for that car here in Kitsap in case our shooter came back across the Narrows, and the Tacoma police are searching on their side," Sigo cut off the banter, but she was smiling, "It's a long shot—no pun intended—but the fact that the car is a late 1970s or early '80s model should help us locate it."

"Shifting subjects momentarily," Gray said, "Based on Isaac's theory for differentiating Young-Saeng's DNA from that of his brother, I've got our local forensics lab working overtime on reexamining the DNA sequences," Gray went on.

"Do you *trust* the local lab?" Shepherd asked pointedly.

"No," Gray said, avoiding eye contact with Shepherd, "Not with the Code Blue you called in. Liam hooked me up with one of his forensics lab contacts in Seattle, and I also overnighted several samples to Charlotte in Virginia. That's three labs looking at the same material, two of which are independent of normal channels, so I think we're inoculated against evidence tampering."

"What about the safe?' Fredriksen asked, "The one ransacked in the Tates' study? How was that accessed?"

"Still working on that one," Bale said, "However, I'm running down a hunch Isaac had about how Lýkos has been able to get back and forth from the East Coast to here without being detected by TSA or any other competent authority."

"The cell phone aspect of this is an old trick," Shepherd said, "Lýkos likely gave his phone to his friend, Daniel Murgatroyd, who used it to send texts to himself and others whenever Lýkos was *supposed* to be with him on a trip. That ensured Lýkos' phone was recorded pinging cell towers on the East Coast. However, something from the news the other day triggered a thought about how the *gesekgi* is traveling, and Veronica took point on that question."

"That might explain things to us, but we don't have anything that'll hold up in court," Fredriksen said.

"Not yet, but I'm working on the issue," Bale said, reassuring him with confident eyes.

"We're close to nailing this one down," Gray said, "But it all hinges on whether the DNA and the travel aspect pan out. Frankly, I think both *will* bear fruit, but I don't want us getting excited and losing situational awareness. We still have a *lot* of evidence to amass if we're going to prove any of this. We've all seen 'slam-dunk' cases get shot down by a lack of real-world evidence."

"Can anyone say, 'Weapons of Mass Destruction?'" Fredriksen asked sardonically, referencing a massive U.S. intelligence failure in 2002.

"Exactly," Gray nodded.

The phone on the table next to Gray rang. He reached down, picking up.

"Charlotte!" Gray said, recognizing the voice, "What's wrong? You're kidding?! Ah, crap!... Well, that wasn't unexpected. I'm more surprised by the timing of it...Ok, thanks for the head's up!"

Gray hung the phone up, "That was Charlotte in Virginia. Congresswoman Cremer's non-binding resolution passed the House. It was on a straight-party line vote, but you all know very well the news media is fanatically hostile to the president. They'll use this to batter him over the head on top of the Russia hoax being pushed."

"And the hits just keep on coming!" Shepherd said, irritated.

Gray turned to Fredriksen, "You, Denita, and Isaac are responsible for getting Dr. Donna Pounder into protective custody as quietly and quickly as you can. We all thought William Smith was the last living person with a direct connection to this case. However, Denita did point out this morning that Pounder is in as much danger as Smith was. We're not in panic mode because I *do* know right where the likely shooter is at this time, but that doesn't mean Lýkos won't find some other means of silencing the doctor. Veronica and I'll go take down our shooter."

"No problem, dontcha know," Fredriksen said easily.

"We'll get Donna to safety, don't worry," Sigo assured Gray.

"Ok, if I can kick you all out for a moment, I need to hammer out a couple of details with Isaac before we get on with it," Gray smiled pleasantly, but Shepherd noted a coldly hostile glint in the agent's blue-gray eyes.

Sigo, Bale, and Fredriksen got up. The scraping of chairs and chatter of unfocused conversation waltzed around the room as they left, snapping the door closed behind them.

"What's up?" Shepherd rose, stretching and straightening his old, brown, corduroy sport coat, "Are you ok? You've been awfully quiet the past couple of days."

"Listen to me, you narcissistic, pompous, cold-hearted *paskudnik!*"

Gray's voice lashed across the room like a sonic bullwhip as his fist slammed down hard on the tabletop, "If you *ever* pull another goddamned selfish, stupid, bone-headed shit-show stunt like you did the other day, I swear I'll break your fucking neck *myself!"*

Gray's anger slammed into Shepherd's chest with the force of a bomb. The shock of the rebuke, coupled with the venom lacing the words, surprised Shepherd so badly that his knees buckled.

Falling hard back into his seat, Shepherd's eyes popped out of his skull. Quickly retrieving them, he snapped them back into their sockets before finding his voice.

"Abe…?" Shepherd ventured, "What did I do?"

"Are you fucking *kidding* me, you clueless idiot?!" Gray bellowed, "You run off like some fucking goddamned snowflake without telling anyone where you were going, and you wonder what the fuck's wrong?! That's *bullshit,* Isaac!!"

*Ok…he just said more swear words in two minutes than I've heard him say in twenty years…*Shepherd thought dumbly, his brain screeching to a halt under Gray's relentless assault.

Gray marched around the table, an unstoppable avalanche of violent rage. Halting just in front of Shepherd, he leaned forward, hands pressed so hard on the tabletop that his knuckles were white. Shepherd shrunk back in the chair, staring up at Gray's twisted, furious countenance.

"Do you have *any* idea how terrified I was, you self-absorbed *putz?!"* Gray bellowed, "What about your *brother,* huh? You terrified him to *death!* We all know you wrestle with PTSD, *and* you already have one suicide attempt in your past! But there you go, swanning off on your own without a word or note or text letting anyone know that you're ok! Isaac, that. Is. *Bullshit!"*

"I…I'm sorry…I didn't think—"

"That's obvious, your arrogant *beheyme!"* Gray roared, slamming a fist against the tabletop again. The impact was so loud it caused Shepherd to flinch as Gray's volcanic rage explode over him.

"I asked for your help out here—and that makes you *my* responsibility!" Gray seethed, struggling to speak now through clenched teeth. "How do you think *I* felt wondering if you hadn't

274

jumped off a fucking cliff because you were so broken by what happened with Smith?! I was scared *shitless!!*"

*I always said Abraham Gray was the one person I didn't ever want angry with me...*Shepherd thought in a distant part of his mind as Gray hovered over him like a demon from hell, a finger now in Shepherd's face.

"Let me make this very, *very* clear for you since you're too stupid to work it out on your own," Gray spat, *"Partners* don't pull this kind of bullshit on each other! *Partners* don't disappear from an ongoing investigation without a word! *Friends* don't let friends think they're *dead!* If you need space and time, that's fine. But next time you *will* let me know what's up! Is. That. *CLEAR?!"*

"Yes," Shepherd said meekly, finding himself unable to meet Gray's eyes, "I'm...I'm sorry."

"Goddamned right you're sorry, you whiny little *oysshteler!"* Gray seethed before wheeling around on one heel. Exiting the room with all the grace and certainty of an angry rhinoceros, Gray vanished as the door slammed closed behind him.

Finally remembering to breathe, Shepherd remained seated.

I'm going to have to look up some of those Jewish curses he threw at me, Shepherd thought dumbly, still in shock. *Still, now I know what John Stiles meant by 'all' our actions having consequences...*

Chapter 25

Bremerton, Washington
Friday, September 14, 2018; 12:53 hours

"…looking to international business news, South Korean officials announced they're taking a renewed look into the recent deaths of Jung-Hoon and Hae-Won Chul, founders and joint CEOs of GDI Tech. Information obtained by the *Honolulu Gazette-Beacon* indicates the Chuls' death is now being viewed as a possible homicide…"

"…Pope Francis ordered the investigation of West Virginia Bishop Michael Bransfield in connection with the ongoing church-abuse scandal. However, the Vatican did not address calls for an investigation of Rhode Island Bishop Archibald Cremer. Cremer is accused of covering up sexual abuse by discreetly transferring priests while also coercing alleged victims into silence…"

"…Hurricane Florence impacted the North Carolina coast today as a Category 1 storm, and meteorologists warn it'll remain a deadly threat for days to come due to heavy rains and widespread flooding…"

The day featured occasional glimpses of a cheerful yellow sun peeking through the gray clouds lining the Pacific Northwest sky. Temperatures hovered in the mid-60s, but the ubiquitous rain held off yet again.

Isaac, Sigo, and Fredriksen exited the sheriff's office into the cool day. A.J. was waiting outside for them.

"Don't have time right now, bro," Isaac said as the three headed towards Sigo's departmental SUV.

"Wherever you're going, I'm coming," A.J. said with concrete finality, falling into formation next to his brother.

"No, you're not," Isaac said firmly, "This isn't your concern."

"Bullshit it isn't!" A.J. snapped, "That fucker made it my concern when he dragged me and Josh into this—and tried to have my brother shot. I'm coming with you."

Sigo and Fredriksen exchanged weary looks as she clicked the key fob, unlocking the SUV. The forest green vehicle bore the logo 'Sheriff' in bright white letters across its side. Fredriksen piled into the back seat as Isaac opened the passenger door.

"A.J., go home!" Isaac said, getting in.

Snapping the door shut, Isaac was buckling his seat belt into place when A.J. hopped into the back seat next to Fredriksen.

"I'm coming!" A.J. declared, buckling himself in.

Isaac let out an exasperated growl before checking his watch, "Dammit, we have to go! A.J...."

"I'm coming!" A.J. said mulishly.

Sigo fired up the engine, slipping the SUV into reverse. Glancing at Isaac, she smiled, "Well, he's certainly as stubborn as you!"

"You should see our other brother!" Isaac and A.J. replied in unison, still eyeballing each other edgily.

Fredriksen laughed.

Sigo shook her head. Pulling into traffic, she looked in the rearview mirror at A.J., "If you puke on *anything* this time, I'm going to kick your ass into the next time zone. Clear?"

"As crystal!" A.J. said solemnly, "I had a light breakfast anyway. So, now that I'm here, where exactly *are* we going?"

"Bremerton Free Clinic," Isaac answered, shaking his head irritably, "We have to get a witness into protective custody before the *gesekgi* kills her!"

Fifteen minutes later, Sigo applied the brakes with little subtly as the SUV careened into the clinic parking lot. Shutting down the engine, she exited the vehicle before pulling the other three into a huddle.

277

"Ok, I'm taking point," Sigo directed, leaving no opportunity for objections, "Luke, you're the biggest guy here; I want you on our six. Watch our backs. Our suspect might be forced into action if they realize we're closing their window of opportunity."

Turning to the Shepherd brothers, Sigo adjusted her weapons belt, "Isaac, you're still injured, so be doubly careful. A.J., the *only* reason you're not locked up in the back seat of my vehicle right now is that *you* are responsible for assisting your brother if things get hot. Isaac knows Dr. Pounder, so he'll be helping me talk to her. In the meantime, A.J., help Luke watch our backs. Everyone clear?"

The three men nodded before falling into a diamond formation with Sigo at the head. The foursome marched into the King Building's run-down clinic.

Focused on ensuring Doctor Pounder was kept alive to enjoy the rest of her life, Isaac wasn't ensnared by a sense of sadness this time. The same crowd of poor and needy people waited in the cracked and chipped plastic chairs. A few looked up in alarm at Sigo's uniform, but most were caught up in their ailments.

"Denita! It's been a few weeks since you popped by," The nurse at the desk looked up, surprised, "What's up today?"

Makes sense she'd maintain a relationship with the local clinic, Isaac thought.

"I know this is going to royally foul up your day," Sigo said, "But I need to see Donna *now.* I can't go into details, but, rest assured, this *is* an emergency."

Isaac was impressed by the level of immovable steel in Sigo's voice.

The nurse nodded, offering no resistance. Rather the reverse.

"Doctor Pounder's in her office. She's doing admin work right now. Head on back. I'm assuming these gentlemen are…oh, there's two of you! Well, hello again…uh, which of you is the Mr. Shepherd who was here the other week?"

Isaac smiled, always amused by people's confusion when they discovered he had identical brothers, "That's me. This is my brother, A.J. And, yes, we're with the sheriff."

Sigo led them back behind the counter, her boots thudding definitively on the floor as she led the way to Pounder's office.

"Luke, A.J., you two stay in the hallway. Keep alert!" Sigo ordered, "Isaac, you're with me."

Sigo knocked on the door, then proceeded to open it before Pounder could respond.

Stepping in behind the sheriff, Isaac saw Pounder sitting at her desk, pen held in mid-air as she stared up in shock. He guessed most people didn't just walk into her office as though they owned it.

"Denita, Mr. Shepherd," Pounder said, surprise coloring her words, "What's wrong?"

"Donna, we don't have time to explain," Sigo said quickly, "I need you to come with us right now."

"I beg your pardon," Pounder rose, her 6'9" frame unfolding until her head was nearly touching the water-stained ceiling tiles, "I can't just leave. I have patients in half an hour."

"Doctor," Isaac launched into his spiel with a remarkably smooth voice, "You treated a man *calling* himself Young-Saeng Tate on numerous occasions. However, the man you treated was *not* Young-Saeng, but his identical twin, Gippeum Lýkos. We have evidence that Gippeum killed his brother and his sister-in-law. Gippeum is also linked to two other deaths and an attempt on *my* life. You're quite literally the only living person left with a direct connection to the events of this case, which makes you the next likely target."

Pounder looked dumbstruck, "I'm...what? Mr. Shepherd, the patient I treated *was* Young-Saeng Tate. I even have documentation from him proving it. I understand you're investigating the Tate murder, but do you expect me to abandon my patients based on this fish tale of yours?"

"Donna, he's *not* lying!" Sigo shot back emphatically, "That's one reason I came along. You know me. Your *life* is in danger…and so are the lives of everyone in this clinic as long as you're here. We need to get you into protective custody *now.*"

Pounder stared at Sigo, her brain trying to get up to speed as she processed the extraordinary story she'd just been handed.

"I…" Pounder's voice trailed off. Staring hard into Sigo's eyes, she finally nodded, "All right, Denita. Let me get my purse…and I *have* to stop at the front desk and let the nurses know I'll be out on an emergency call for some time."

"Fair enough," Sigo nodded.

Pounder shucked her white coat, walking to the threadbare wardrobe in the corner to hang it up and retrieve her brown leather purse. The purse was old, but, like her clothes, it was well cared for.

Following Sigo and Isaac into the hall, Pounder locked her office door before turning around. Abruptly confronted by the two identical faces looking back at her, she took a breath in surprise.

"Your brother, I assume?" She looked at Isaac, mouth quirking slightly despite the tense atmosphere.

"Yes, this is A.J.," Isaac introduced his brother before gesturing to Fredriksen, "And is this Chief Luke Fredriksen."

She nodded politely to Fredriksen, who was doing his best to look intimidating. His green uniform's tightly rolled sleeves reinforced the impression because his massive arms threatened to explode the fabric.

Sigo preceded Pounder as the group headed back to the front desk.

"Alice, an emergency's come up that requires my presence," Pounder said to the nurse once they reached the front, "I'm sorry, but I have to leave immediately. Please see if our friends at the Tacoma and Seattle clinics can't squeeze in a rotation over here. Dr. Penny over in Seattle owes me a favor anyway. Give her a call first."

"Yes, Doctor," Alice said, scribbling notes down onto a scrap of paper, "I'll take care of it."

The group departed the building, the people in the waiting room staring at them. Isaac could imagine how the scene must have looked: three big men and one female sheriff escorting the clinic director out like that. No matter how strategically sound it was, the optics just plain stank.

"My car is over there," Pounder pointed to a nondescript brown sedan in the corner of the lot.

"Keep an eye out for threats; we're way too exposed here," Isaac said under his breath to Fredriksen.

A.J. heard Isaac's quiet comment. He kicked his own senses into a heightened state of alert and began trying to imagine all the ways someone could attack the doctor.

Fredriksen nodded. He was just as uncomfortably aware as Isaac was of all the upper-floor windows lining the street, as well as the numerous corners and alleys around them. The environment was an assassin's dream, providing plenty of spaces in which a killer could easily hide.

A.J. had a sudden flash of horrified inspiration. Although he felt a bit silly for being a worrywart, he couldn't help remembering how wildly *unexpected* the attack on William Smith had been. Surrendering to his paranoia, he crouched down, pretending to adjust the lace on his shoe while staring intently at Pounder's car. He had no idea what he was looking for, but he looked anyway.

"I've got some files in the trunk I need to get out," Pounder was telling Sigo as she dug around inside her purse, looking for her keys, "I need to take them in and drop them off at the front desk. Been meaning to do it all day."

A.J.'s eyes carefully scanned under the vehicle.

"One second," Pounder said, her face red with frustration as she continued digging in her purse. The stress of the unexpected moment was getting to her.

Well, who can blame her? Isaac thought sympathetically, eyes suspiciously scanning the pedestrians along the sidewalks. *We just upended her whole world.*

"Here we go!" Pounder said, holding up the key fob. Her thumb began descending towards the 'unlock' button.

Andrew Anthony and Elizabeth Jane Shepherd had made sure all three of their boys understood the basics of automobile maintenance. A.J. might not be a mechanic, but he sure as hell knew what should *not* be under a car. His eyes narrowed as he peered through his bifocals.

The tiniest strand of wire dipping down from the car's fuel tank stopped his heart and caused his stomach to cramp.

"DOWN!" A.J. roared, launching himself towards the group even as Pounder's thumb hit the button.

Although he now only coached the game for his boys, his years playing football had not been wasted. A.J.'s body was still trained, strong, and fast. His virtuoso performances as both quarterback and defensive tackle had developed his legs and reflexes to a hair-trigger level.

The 252 lbs. man threw his arms out as he shot forward. His wingspan caught the tall Pounder full in the stomach and the shorter Sigo full across the breasts. The three of them lurched backward, colliding with Fredriksen. Knocked off his feet, Fredriksen crumpled, the dead weight of Sigo, Pounder, and A.J. crushing the wind out of him as they landed on top of him.

Out of the corner of his eye, A.J. saw Isaac throw himself to the ground even as the car lit up with a bright, weirdly cheerful light.

The shockwave smothered them milliseconds later as a cloud of smoke and debris whizzed lethally above their heads. The clinic's front windows shattered as shrapnel violently pierced the glass. Screams boiled up inside the stricken building.

Ears crying out in pain from the noise of the explosion, Isaac watched in disbelief as the vehicle soared fifteen feet into the air while the detonation ripped the doors open and tore the trunk lid clean off. The ruptured gas tank's contents spilled downward, igniting as they went. The burning fuel created a lake of fire even as the car's charred, broken remains fell back to earth, landing in the fiery puddle. The trunk lid wafted down almost gently, like a leaf.

Screams continued to echo from inside the clinic. Still lying on the pavement, Sigo yanked her radio from her belt. She began barking orders into it with ruthless efficiency even as the car fell back to earth.

"Stay down!" Fredriksen ordered Pounder as she tried to rise, "You're the target, Doc!"

Isaac jumped to his feet. His injured knee was not happy about having to take up his weight again, but he insisted the joint do its job regardless.

Eyes scanning the scene with rapid precision, he saw the damage to the clinic's facade and windows. Nurses scrambled inside to attend to people hit by shards of flying glass and debris. Still, he couldn't see any indications of fatal injuries to anyone in the clinic or on the street.

Traffic screeched to a halt as burning fuel trickled into the road, creating a barrier of flame. The streetlight the car had been parked under was leaning at a crazy angle. As Isaac watched, its bent, crinkled form buckled, the light collapsing into the street. Fortunately, traffic had already stopped, meaning the light landed on unoccupied asphalt instead of a speeding car.

Years of photojournalism training kicked Isaac's hands into autopilot. He wasn't even consciously aware he'd pulled his phone from his pocket as the light pole slowly began to topple over. His hand moved of their own accord, snapping several (if slightly awkward) images of the burning vista as A.J. and Fredriksen helped Pounder back to her feet. Both men closed in tight around her, doing their best to keep their bodies between her and any possible harm.

"Doc, keep your head down and follow me!" Sigo ordered, back on her feet and leading a charge to her SUV. Reaching the vehicle, she did a quick inspection before opening the door and unceremoniously shoving Pounder inside.

"Luke, protective detail!" Sigo ordered.

"On it!" Fredriksen jumped inside next to Pounder, doing his best to shield her body with his.

Sigo turned, "You two, in! Now!"

A.J. dived in, instinctively adding his bulk to Fredriksen's to further shield Pounder. Isaac leaped into the front passenger seat as Sigo sprinted to the driver's side. Firing up the engine, she slammed her door shut and peeled out in reverse, the tires leaving long black streaks on the pavement as she blasted out of the parking lot. Grabbing the radio, Sigo barked several orders over the airwaves, calling in the cavalry.

Isaac realized he was holding his phone. Shaking his head, he pulled up his text app, but almost dropped the device as Sigo frantically maneuvered the big SUV around. Securing his grip, he managed to get a fast text to Abe:

Doc's safe. Bomb in her car. Car destroyed; clinic damaged. Multiple injuries inside, no idea of deaths. Taking Pounder to a safe house. Denita, Luke, A.J. and I are ok. Good luck on your end!

Isaac blinked in surprise when he saw the photos of the burning mess. His conscious mind didn't even remember documenting the scene during the panicked seconds between the detonation and the dive into Sigo's vehicle. He sent the images to Gray.

Spinning the wheel and shifting into drive, Sigo mashed the accelerator down while turning on the lights and siren.

"I…I…" Pounder was breathing heavily as terrified disbelief settled in.

Fredriksen realized the slightly squashed doctor was beginning to hyperventilate. Sweat poured off her forehead as her eyes dilated with shock. Shivers down her spine threatened to spiral into full-blown convulsions.

"We've got your back, Doc. Just breathe slowly," Fredriksen spoke soothingly to Pounder, trying to calm her down "You're ok. Breathe slow."

"Where…where are we going?" Pounder squeaked, slowly retrieving her wits.

"My folks' place in Suquamish, Donna," Sigo said, "Safest place there is!"

"Goddammit!" Isaac smashed his fist on his leg, "It never occurred to me the *gesekgi* would change his modus operandi so radically as to use a car bomb!"

Bremerton screeched past in a blur. Sigo took a corner as if the SUV were on rails. The sheriff kept her eyes on high alert as they approached the most dangerous choke point on their route: the Warren Avenue bridge across the Port Washington Narrows. Fortunately, they cleared the bridge and were speeding steadily up Highway 303 without incident.

Relaxing her alert status ever so slightly, Sigo glanced at A.J. in her rearview mirror, "A.J., *great* work back there! Just so you know, any and all *alleged* puking incidents are forgotten!"

Chapter 26
Silverdale, Washington
Friday, September 14, 2018; 16:18 hours

"…turning to the civil war raging in Syria, residents of Idlib, the last territory held by opposition forces, protested against Syrian President Bashar Assad today…"

"…while Hurricane Florence batters the East Coast, the Philippines are preparing for Super Typhoon Mangkhut's impending landfall. The storm is already on track to be one of the strongest typhoons to threaten the island nation in its history…"

"Helllllooooo, Seattle! Tricky Ricky Ray here on WAXE, heralding headlines and slinging songs for the start of afternoon drivetime! A car bomb exploded outside the Bremerton Free Clinic today, damaging the building and causing minor injuries. Local authorities are asking anyone with any information to please contact the Kitsap County Sheriff's office. As of yet, no motive has been identified..."

Abraham Gray was forced to admit Denita Sigo did have a point: it *was* rather comfortable to lean back in a chair with his crossed feet up on the desk. The fact he was relaxing in David Kerr's chair and his feet were up on David Kerr's desk was all the more rewarding. Glancing around the room, he noted everything from the two antique rifles atop the bookcase to the numerous medals and awards Kerr displayed from his Army Ranger days.

Still, Gray was positioned casually for more reasons than mere personal comfort. He could have affected the confrontation more conventionally, but he thought a little showmanship would add a touch of panache to the proceedings.

I've been hanging around Isaac way too long if I'm starting to think in terms of panache!

Gray's mood, already grim, had devolved into sheer darkness over the last couple of hours. Pulling his phone from his pocket, he checked Shepherd's text and photos yet again. He'd already repeatedly read the terse message, but seeing it one more time reinforced his inner serenity. He knew Sigo wouldn't contact him until she was dead sure Pounder was as safe as humanly possible, and that might take a few more hours.

Doc's safe. Bomb in her car. Car destroyed; clinic damaged. Multiple injuries inside, no idea of deaths. Taking Pounder to a safe house. Denita, Luke, A.J. and I are ok. Good luck on your end!

"Just what in the *hell* was *A.J.* doing there?" Gray asked out loud.

"Just what in the *hell* are you doing in *my* chair with your feet on *my* desk?!" Kerr's voice blew aside the quiet in the room from the doorway.

"Ah, David!" Gray said, casually sliding his phone back into his pants. He deliberately didn't rise, "You'll be unhappy to know we got Dr. Pounder to safety before the car bomb could kill her."

"Who?" Kerr demanded, slamming the door behind him.

"Dr. Donna Pounder, Director of the Bremerton Free Clinic," Gray replied, "The last living witness to the activities of Gippeum Lýkos. I'll admit Lýkos' been several steps ahead of us this whole time, but we finally got an edge and prevented Dr. Pounder's murder."

"What are you talking about, Gray?!" Kerr demanded, hands on his hips, "And *get out of my chair!*"

"*I'm* talking about the incredibly sophisticated game Gippeum Lýkos has been playing," Gray said, now putting his hands behind his head. Kerr's eyes blazed red as they popped from their sockets. Gray smirked, continuing his monologue.

"Lýkos developed and executed a very sophisticated plan to murder his brother and then kill the three other people with a *direct* connection to the case," Gray went on as smoothly as if he were delivering a classroom lecture, "You know, Delores Tate, William Smith and his sister, Jane."

"Jane Smith?!" Kerr blurted with obvious shock, "I mean—who the hell is *that?!*"

"She was Sheriff Sigo's intern, as you already well know," Gray said, eyes narrowing, "Her brother, William, was part of a plot to frame Delores Tate as a serial adulterer and domestic abuser. Granted, this is somewhat speculative right now, you understand, but I'm guessing William pumped Jane for information about the case. From what I've learned about Jane, her ego inflated once she became a police intern."

"So what?!"

"So, it wouldn't be hard for her brother to get her to spill information about the case," Gray said, "I think it went to her head. Jane started leaking info to the media, possibly to establish herself as a 'reliable source.' However, her information was too specific and led right back to her...so Jane Smith was killed with a long-range shot to the head while she was driving up in Port Gamble. The type of shot only a trained sniper could pull off."

Kerr's face froze, but he recovered, "I told you to get out of my seat, asshole!"

"Young-Saeng Tate was accosted in his home by two intruders who beat, mutilated, and killed him in his own bed," Gray continued ignoring Kerr's demands, "Clearly an act done out of hatred for him and his wife. Delores Tate was framed and then shot—again at long range—while walking in the prison yard down in Port Orchard."

Gray shifted, removing his hands from behind his head, folding them on his lap, "Now, as to William Smith. We realized he was a target, but Isaac and his group sadly arrived too late. They almost had him, but then *he* was shot at an extremely long range by a *master* sniper who could hit a literal one-in-a-thousand shot. Isaac was targeted as well, but a little luck saved Isaac's life."

"And you're telling me this *why?!*" Kerr's neck muscled bulged.

"Silver Star. Bronze Star. Army Commendation Medal. Multiple combat action ribbons," Gray said, changing the subject so fast Kerr froze in confusion.

"What are you talking about?!" Kerr interrupted, cocking his head to one side.

"Your awards from your Ranger days in Afghanistan and Iraq," Gray said, pointing lazily to one of the shadow boxes on Kerr's wall, "Impressive. Didn't you set the Army record for longest-range kill *twice?* What was your kill count in the desert, anyway, David?"

"What does this have to do with anything" Kerr spat, tension beginning to snap his neck muscles into sharp relief.

"You see, the ballistics that killed Jane Smith were singularly unremarkable. Standard 5.56mm rounds, the kind U.S. and NATO commonly use, so we didn't think to dig deeper than 'a long-range rifle,'" Gray said, enjoying the growing elation he felt as he observed Kerr start to glisten with sweat even as his face grew paler.

"However, the shots that killed Delores and William—and the shot which nearly killed Isaac—were done with *Russian* shells developed for a 1960s *Russian* sniper rifle. And those shots were fired from a ridiculously long range. Don't you find that interesting?"

"Why would I find that interesting?" Kerr demanded, his voice slipping a note higher. His began to turn a slight shade of green as he put his hands behind his back.

Clumsy idiot! Gray thought, keeping his poker face intact, *Like I didn't just hear you lock that door!*

"Well, the actions against Jane and Delores were meticulously planned," Gray said lightly, "However, your assault on William Smith must have been as much of a last-minute move of desperation as was *our* attempt to save his life."

"What do you mean, *my* assault?!" Kerr seethed, sweat beading across his brow.

"I mean that you had *three* antique rifles up there last week," Gray pointed offhandedly to the display rack atop the bookcase, "And now you only have two. The Soviet rifle is missing."

"I took it home to clean, you idiot!" Kerr snapped, sliding his hands ever so slightly back on his hips.

Jeez, this turkey is so damned obvious! Gray thought, "Of course, you had to clean it, David. You *did* just fire it the other night. Your involvement in this also explains how Lýkos was able to stay several steps ahead of us. Let me guess—he's paying you a fortune worthy of the ancient pharaohs, or else he's banging you and leading you to think he's in love with you. Or is it both?"

"*I* ain't no queer, Gray! You've slipped a screw!" Kerr bellowed, "Ok, so what? I own a 1963 Russian SVD sniper rifle. Big deal! I'm hardly the only person who collects Russian weapons!"

"Correct," Gray said, leaning forward slightly to pick up a manila folder. Opening it, he began casually tossing out various security camera photos, "But you *also* own a brown 1973 Plymouth sedan, Washington license plate HGH-4567. Putting your name on the title of a vehicle you didn't want associated with you was stupid."

Kerr's eyes snapped downward, taking in the photos Gray was scattering on the desk. The photos showed a brown car. The license plate was clearly visible in several pictures. Two images showed the unmistakable form of Kerr getting into and out of the vehicle.

"Sheriff Sigo's team found the car up in Poulsbo two hours ago," Gray went on easily, "Have to admit her people are some of the most *efficient* investigators I've ever seen! Anyway, I *do* like how you parked it in the outer reaches of the Walmart parking lot. Pretty damned big lot; easy to keep a nondescript car concealed by occasionally moving it to different spots while keeping it away from the store. Unfortunately for you, Walmart's got a *ton* of security cameras all around the area."

Gray found himself enjoying the arrested look of shock dominating Kerr's face. Sounding as casual as if he were ordering a steak, he continued.

"Once we had an image of the car from security cameras near William Smith's apartment, it didn't take long for Sheriff Sigo's people to find it was filmed in the vicinity of Port Gamble the night of Jane Smith's death. They also found it parked on a street thanks to a garage security camera in the hills above the prison in Port Orchard...coincidentally parked in a direct line-of-sight with the prison where Delores Tate was the night *she* died."

Gray tossed the folder back on the desk before picking up a piece of paper with numerous numbers scattered about it, "A bit of financial excavation uncovered several recent—and unusually *large*—deposits to your personal checking account. These deposits were then withdrawn and invested in several mutual funds under your name. Now, *where* did that monetary windfall come from, hmmm?"

Gray looked up when he heard the distinct metallic *click* of a round being chambered.

Kerr's pistol was steady in his hand, its barrel aimed squarely between Gray's eyes.

Gray sighed, his voice almost bored, "David, do you *really* think you're going to win this one?"

"I know you, Gray," Kerr said, venom coloring his voice, "You're famous for being cool under pressure. But you're bluffing. The door's locked. It's just you and me in here. Now, *get out of my chair.*"

"As you wish," Gray said lightly, slowly dropping his feet to the floor. Carefully pushing the chair far back from the desk, he rose deliberately, arching his back, "I needed to stretch my legs anyway."

"Be my guest," Kerr snarled dangerously.

"Now, the Lionfish angle is the only part of this I'm unsure about," Gray said, continuing his slow stretch. "The timeline indicates you and Lýkos targeted Young-Saeng, *not* the Lionfish. So, why did you rifle the safe several days later?"

Kerr smirked, "The Lionfish was only a diversion, you idiot! A pretty good one, too, don't you think?"

"Really? A diversion?" *Isaac and I were right!*

Kerr nodded, "I've known what that Tate twat was working on for years. I've been to plenty of briefings at Keyport since we provide security for the project. We snuffed Tate, and then I went back four days later to crack the safe."

"I see," Gray nodded, looking for all the world like a man concentrating on a particularly interesting crossword puzzle, "You jacked up the timeline *and* discredited the Kitsap police in one move. Have to admit that was a good plan…except for the part where it all failed, of course."

Kerr cackled, his face beginning to look as if a mask was dropping away. The truly ghastly expression of glee was downright shocking, "The Lionfish is meaningless, anyway. My partner and I have a much bigger objective than a stupid underwater drone. We did just enough to get everyone's eyes on it…and, despite your bravado, the plan worked."

"Just how *did* you crack the safe, anyway?" Gray persisted, "I'm man enough to admit I can't figure it out at all."

"You're an idiot," Kerr said viciously, "You've seen your fair share of companies selling shit to the Navy! Those safes have 'backdoor' codes the company can use to gain access if the authorized users are ever…unavailable."

"Ok. I *am* impressed. But, now the *big* question," Gray asked, slowly moving from behind the desk to the bookshelf where he could look up at the two remaining rifles. Kerr turned with him, the weapon leveled as Gray shrugged, "How much *did* it cost to buy David Kerr?"

"More than you can imagine!" Kerr sneered, clearly over the moon now that he could drop his 'professional' façade, "Do you have any idea the shit they put me through in the sandbox, Gray?! How many back-to-back deployments I made in that shithole?!

And for what? So rich people in Washington and New York could get richer while our boys and girls were dying in the desert?!"

Gray stood quietly, listening as Kerr spewed forth the sum of all the rage and pain haunting his nightmares.

"We snapped tall, saluted the colors, and flew to those fucking cesspools, just so Wall Street bankers and Washington politicians could get fat and happy while *we* lived with scorpions, sandstorms, heat, IEDs, and local *informants* who carried bombs into our lines! And then us 'heroes' were shoved into fucked up places like Walter Reed to rot while they forgot about us!"

"I *am* sorry you were one of the servicemembers shoved into, shall we say, inadequate conditions by the Army," Gray said, a hint of sympathy in his voice, "Even so, how does that justify you becoming a murderer and traitor? Care to enlighten me?"

"You weren't there, you self-righteous prick!" Kerr's voice slashed the air, spittle flying from his mouth as his eyes bulged. *"You* try living with black mold on the ceiling and walls and rats crawling all over while you try to sleep! *You* live with cockroaches trying to eat the dried blood those assholes left all over you and toilets backing up with shit spilling out while the brass screeches at you to shut up and salute and be quiet!"

Gray listened, appalled at both what Kerr had endured and what Kerr had become.

"I was threatened with a *court martial* for simply reporting that shit to my *congressman!"* Kerr bellowed savagely. Even so, his weapon remained steadily trained on Gray. "This country doesn't give a *shit* about us, Gray! They sent me to the desert to kill ragheads. When I came home a war hero, they shoved me into a rotting coffin and then tried to hang me for complaining! I don't give a shit about this country!"

"I noticed," Gray responded wryly.

"Besides," Kerr spat, "I can guarantee nobody'll be able to connect any of the rifles I own with the shots that killed that William Smith asshole. And there's no way to prove Gippeum had anything to do with his brother's death. They're identical twins, you twit! Their genetic profiles are the same, so *no* court in the land would take the case!"

"Do you think I can't *forensically* link you and Gippeum to the Tate house the night of Young-Saeng's murder?" Gray asked.

"I don't give a shit what you think you can do!" Kerr cackled, a look of unhinged fury now twisting his face, "You're bluffing because you *can't* prove anything!"

"You *do* realize I'm wired and recording this, don't you?" Gray said idly, now leaning on the bookcase. Kerr turned further away from the desk to keep Gray covered.

"Irrelevant," Kerr said.

"Not really," Gray said, boredom now in his voice, "We were told by a whistleblower there might be a 'joker' in the deck. Have to admit that one was so vague even Isaac didn't pick up on it at first, and he's a *master* at puns. A *joker* in the deck. David *Joseph Kerr.* Nice. But, it was only a hint. Your confession is what I needed. Thanks for obliging!"

Kerr smiled, an evil light glinting in his wicked eyes, "Look around, you moron! This room is soundproof and hardened against EMF waves!"

"So what?" Gray yawned.

"You're recording this, *not* transmitting it," Kerr's lip curled happily, a snake about to strike, "That means no one will hear the shot, and your 'recorded' evidence dies with you. Hope you updated your will with some posthumous protection clauses because Sarah is going to need all the help she can get."

"Oh, so now you're going to drag my *wife* into this?" Gray's voice betrayed the first hint of steel-edged fury.

"Of course!" Kerr smiled darkly again, "For one thing, it's fun to watch people beg and plead and piss themselves as you slowly kill them. I did it all the time in the desert to those ragheads! Tie them down and push a knife in through the ribs until you pierce the heart, but do it slowly so you can see them plead and cry and piss themselves. Do it right and you can even feel the heartbeat through the knife…and feel it stop!"

Gray forced himself to keep his utter disgust for Kerr's story from showing on his face.

"But, more importantly," Kerr kept rattling on, "Taking out the family and friends of nosy bastards like you sends a very clear message to anyone else to stay out of our way!"

"You're a real piece of work, David," Gray said, overwhelmed by a crushing sense of sadness, "I remember back when you signed on with NCIS. Sarah and I even had you over for lunch a few times. My God; what a freaking waste."

"No, the waste is all the effort you put into this, you moron!" Kerr chortled, "What kind of an *idiot* are you, anyway? You're all alone here!"

"Who said he's all alone here?"

The mild, easy voice startled Kerr so much he nearly dropped his weapon as he spun on his heel.

Veronica Bale had materialized behind the desk, her weapon held rock-steady level with Kerr's eye.

"What—?!"

Gray surged forward, his powerful legs launching him at Kerr with blinding speed.

Kerr hadn't even fully turned his head towards Bale when Gray swept Kerr's feet out from under him. Gravity yanked Kerr to the floor as Gray snatched the weapon from Kerr's hand before dropping his weight mercilessly atop the disgraced agent.

Kerr's scream of pain was truncated into a choking gurgle of spit as Gray pile-drove a rage-filled elbow deep into Kerr's solar plexus. Rolling Kerr over in one, smoothly vicious movement, Gray ruthlessly yanked Kerr's arms behind his back. Gray snapped handcuffs around Kerr's wrists with metallic efficiency.

"Before you ask, she was hiding *under* your desk," Gray said with dark glee, "That's why I kept my feet up *on* the desk. Get up, you piece of shit!"

Gray hauled Kerr to his feet. Swiftly reading him his rights as Bale holstered her weapon, the two took up post on either side of Kerr.

"Now, let's go," Gray said, voice as cold as ice. "We need to talk, but not here. Shelley Kieble and Casey Dobbins will sweep this building for the concealed microphones and cameras I'm sure you and Lýkos may have installed around here."

Chapter 27
Port Orchard, Washington
Friday, September 14, 2018; 21:43 hours

"Abraham!" Shepherd blasted down the corridor of the Kitsap County Sheriff's Office with all the grace of an exuberant St. Bernard knocking aside lesser mortals around him in his over-charged haste, "Veronica just called me on the Bat-Phone! She was right, and Liam proved it! They know how the *gesekgi's* been getting back and forth without being tracked!"

"Isaac..." Gray held up a hand, starting to speak, but Shepherd's verbal tsunami drowned his voice into powder.

"They've also nailed down the money angle!! What contacts do you have in South Korea?!" Shepherd prattled on, his sea-green eyes blazing like two intense suns, "This whole damned thing's going international! This puts a whole new twist on a crap load of casework we've done over the past two years!"

"Isaac, hang on a second—" Gray tried again, stepping aside to let a county police officer pass.

"My God, Abe!" Shepherd zipped onward, heedless of anything save the copious amounts of information bursting his skull at the seams, "We've got to revisit *everything* back to *Ponce!* I can't believe that bastard's been able to pull off something this *huge!* It's like something out of a *Jason Borne* movie, and I'll bet you guys—!"

"Isaac!" Gray cut in, stopping Shepherd's monologue like a train slamming into a brick wall, "I'm sure what you're saying is critical, but you need to slow up and listen to me for a minute!"

"Sorry," Shepherd stammered, "I...uh...what's up?"

Turning, Gray gestured Shepherd to follow him to the conference room Sigo had allowed them to use as an impromptu office, "Look, when we got the evidence implicating Kerr, I...made a call."

"Ok…?" Shepherd said, shifting his brown corduroy sport on his shoulders, "I'm proud you figured out how to use that wonderful 21st century device—the cell phone. But…so what?"

Gray grimaced, bracing himself as they reached the door, "The 'so what' is that I'm throwing a *huge* Hail Mary pass to keep David Kerr alive. You know as well as I do that everyone connected to Lýkos has ended up dead—"

"Or nearly dead," Shepherd nodded, his hand automatically reaching up to brush the bandage still taped over the stitches in his forehead.

Gray noted Shepherd's breathing had slowed considerably, and now resembled something akin to normal human respiration.

"Exactly," Gray said, "I can't trust NCIS; Kerr proves we've got snakes in the ranks. Charlotte and I talked late last night, and she backed my play for keeping him alive now that he's been processed and booked. To ensure he *stays* alive, I called in some…outside help."

"So far, so good," Shepherd nodded, at a loss to explain Gray's unease, "I don't see a problem here."

"I'm glad you agree," Gray said, nervously reaching up to straighten his tie as they stopped outside the conference room, "Because it involves someone you might find…problematic."

"I get the feeling you're winding me up for something rather unpleasant, but, come on! Dude, I know you; how bad could anyone be if *you* called them for help?" Shepherd said lightly, a friendly hand on Gray's shoulder.

Before Gray could say another word, Shepherd opened the door, boldly striding into the conference room—

—and screeching to a halt as surely as if he'd run headlong into a telephone pole at 85 miles an hour. Gray could hear Shepherd's expression collapse from out in the hall.

"Isaac," Gray said cautiously, entering the room, "I believe you know FBI Special Agent Shey Cremer."

Shey Cremer was seated at the conference table with Sheriff Sigo. A short, muscular bald man, his arms stretched the seams of his FBI polo shirt. The squat man's round face crinkled ever so slightly as his eyes fell on Shepherd.

"Mr. Cremer," Shepherd said, his voice sepulchral. Despite his extreme displeasure at seeing Cremer, he couldn't help but suddenly have a vision of Mr. Clean sitting there wearing an FBI polo shirt.

"Chief Shepherd," Cremer's voice was equally icy.

Sigo stared between the two antagonists. The palpable hostility was so egregious it nearly knocked her out of her chair. Although he remained still, Shepherd's jaw muscles clenched in tightly controlled spasms while his left hand cramped into a fist.

Gray closed the door behind him, "Isaac, please have seat."

Shepherd and Cremer did not take their eyes off each other as Shepherd reached out his right hand to pull out a chair. As he sat, Sigo noted his left hand remained curled into a fist.

Gray pulled out a chair. Falling into it, he unbuttoned his suit coat before picking up a manila file folder, "Shey, here's the paperwork from Charlotte. Transfer of custody, authority from Sheriff Sigo and the local county court to take the prisoner out of state...everything you need."

Cremer took the folder. Opening it, he rifled through the contents, "Ok, Abe. This looks to be in order. I've got a safe location already lined up to keep Kerr in custody—and a few backups in case our security is compromised. I presume you still want the location of these sites kept on the down low?"

"Correct," Gray said, shooting an apologetic look to Sigo, "My team's already found half a dozen listening devices planted in the Bangor NCIS building. We just got lucky he hadn't put any devices into the conference room *we* were using. Anyway, I wouldn't put it past Kerr to have bugged this office as well. Until the sheriff's team can complete their sweep of this building, I think it's best you keep Kerr's location secret."

"Agreed," Cremer nodded, closing the folder, "So, just for my clarification, everyone who has a direct connection to your primary suspect is dead except for Kerr and this Doctor Pounder you mentioned?"

"Isaac's the third survivor," Gray said, glancing at Shepherd.

Sigo glanced at Shepherd. His jaw continued twitching.

Cremer looked at Shepherd. Nodding to the bandage on his head, Cremer's voice was still cold, "Looks like you narrowly avoided that shot."

"Disappointed?" Shepherd asked, face tight with open hostility.

Gray seemed ready to jump in, but Cremer's reply precluded him from acting.

"No," Cremer said with a casual air, but there was no missing the undercurrent of hatred just beneath the surface, "I always knew you were a hard-headed bastard."

Shepherd raised a single eyebrow but didn't respond.

"Shey," Gray said, redirecting the conversation, "Thank you for getting out here so fast. I know from experience that jet lag is hell, but I needed someone I can trust to take custody of Kerr."

Cremer nodded, rising, "No problem, Abe. I owe you one or two anyway. I've got my people supervising Kerr now. I'll round them up and we'll get moving. Sheriff Sigo, thank you for your cooperation. The bureau owes you one!"

"No problem, Special Agent Cremer," Sigo smiled, still inwardly waiting for him and Shepherd to launch themselves at each other.

Cremer and Gray rose, shaking hands.

Picking up the folder, Cremer strode to the door. Laying a hand on the knob, he looked back to Shepherd, "What? Nothing to say?"

Sigo was shocked to see Gray tense in anticipation, but Shepherd's soft answer froze him in his tracks.

"That behavioral profile you provided the other week was immensely helpful," Shepherd nodded, neck muscles still taut, but his voice still level, "Thank you."

Cremer grunted, snapping the door shut behind him as he left.

"Ok…" Sigo exhaled slowly, "Might I inquire…?"

"That son of a bitch tried to pin a murder on me back in '99 because I'm gay," Shepherd's voice becoming overtly bitter and hateful, "And then he spent the next twenty years making my life a living hell. Considering I'm the reason he got fired from NCIS, I'm surprised he agreed to help at all!"

"He got *fired* from NCIS?" Sigo asked, looking stunned. After the briefest of pauses, her eyes suddenly widened, "Oh, wait—I *knew* I'd heard his name before! Wasn't he caught on camera making gay slurs or something like that?"

"And threatening Isaac," Gray nodded.

Shepherd leaned forward in his chair, "Why in the *hell* did you call *that* jerkwad?!"

"Because NCIS is compromised and I need someone I can trust," Gray flatly responded.

"Say *what?!*" Shepherd flew to his feet.

"Isaac, please," Gray said, sitting back down and gesturing for Shepherd to do the same. Shepherd slowly lowered himself back into his seat.

"Isaac, I'm *never* going to pretend what he did to you in '99 was ok, nor will I defend the harassment he subjected you to after that," Gray said, leaning forward on his elbows to meet Shepherd's eyes, "I don't blame you for being angry, and I'm *extremely* grateful you didn't jump him, but I need you to please calm down for a moment and let me explain. You owe me that much."

A huge, deep breath rattled out of Shepherd's lungs. Sigo saw his left hand finally unclench and his jaw muscles stop twitching.

"You're right," Shepherd conceded, nodding slightly as he calmed down, "Please, go on."

"Cremer *did* learn something from that fiasco in Spain," Gray said calmly, "Ironically enough, he finally learned the *first* lesson I ever taught you."

"Don't twist facts to fit theories," Shepherd rattled off before realizing he was even speaking, "Adjust theories to fit facts."

"Exactly," Gray nodded, "Even when we partnered in Norfolk years later, he still had a bug up his ass about LGBTQ sailors and Marines, but he never let his prejudices bring him to the brink of professional suicide again. I won't lie; I didn't like working with him in Spain and I *sure* as hell didn't like having to partner with him again in Norfolk. But, overall, he's a top-flight agent who brought down more threats to the Navy and Marine Corps than you can imagine."

Shepherd listened quietly.

"He even helped *stop* the wrongful prosecution of a gay sailor in Bahrain back in '14," Gray said.

Shepherd's jaw bounced off the table in utter surprise.

"Yep; had a captain who was frankly so anti-gay he made Cremer look like the soul of inclusivity," Gray explained, "The jerk tried to destroy a second-class culinary specialist just because the sailor was gay and the captain was a fundamentalist Jew who wanted the kid stoned."

"Wait—the captain was *Jewish?!*" Sigo blurted in surprise.

Gray nodded, "Unfortunately, there're bigots in all faiths, Denita, mine included."

"Cremer led the charge to save this guy?!" Shepherd's voice pitched up into a falsetto dripping with disbelief.

"Yes…Cremer led the charge to save that guy," Gray responded, "As you would say, he wasn't exactly peaches and cream towards the kid, but he saved the sailor's career *and* ensured the captain got to…'enjoy' an early retirement."

Shepherd opened his mouth, but Gray held up a hand to quiet him.

"Before you bring up the Bacon case, yes, he *did* go after OS2 Cline like a zealot because Bacon and Cline were gay," Gray said, holding Shepherd's gaze, "His myopic viewpoint got him in the shorts again on that one. However, after *we* proved Cline's innocence, Cremer changed course big time."

"That's only because Charlotte tore him a new one and filed yet *another* reprimand in his record!" Shepherd said.

302

"Partly, yes," Gray admitted, "But, think about it. With the political connections that man has, do you think Charlotte's reprimand would hurt him in the long term? He learned his lesson back in '99. That's why he backed off so fast after we uncovered empirical evidence of Cline's innocence. He was always willing to correct himself after coming to work for Charlotte again."

Shepherd's face was impassive, but his eyes telegraphed disbelief.

"He came to me after Charlotte was done ripping his face off and apologized...well, apologized as much as I think he's capable of," Gray said. "After that...well, who do you think did all the paperwork for me while *we* were aboard *Ponce* ruining Tyler Drummin's life? He built the case file I handed to the prosecutor—and his paperwork, plus our evidence, was what convicted Drummin."

"Ok," Shepherd grudgingly acknowledged, "Just don't expect *me* to partner up with him anytime this century!"

Gray nodded, feeling a certain trepidation lifting from his mind, "Cremer was never able to get past his personal animosity towards you, but he's proven to be a champion for the wrongfully accused, and, more importantly, he's a patriot. A very flawed man, yes, but a holy *terror* against insider threats. Now that he's FBI, he has access and resources we need—and...well, he's saved my life and career a few times. It's 'realpolitik' in action—I don't have to *like* him to trust him."

"I've got to ask," Sigo interrupted, "If Cremer was so bad, why did your boss let him work for her again, and why did *he* want to work for someone he already knew didn't like him much? Assuming I'm following you two correctly."

"I don't know, honestly," Gray shrugged. "He's got some powerful political contacts that pretty much allowed him to get any job he wanted. Neither Charlotte nor I *ever* put up with his crap or let him get away with anything, but he wanted Norfolk."

Shepherd suddenly inhaled through his nose, the sharp sound causing both Sigo and Gray to look at him.

"I think *I* know why he wanted the Norfolk job," Shepherd said, still staring at the table, "I mean, I've wondered about that for years myself considering that meant he wasn't just around you and Charlotte, but also *me.*"

"Care to share your insight?" Gray asked, mouth quirking in amusement.

"Abe, you and Charlotte were the *only* people who ever called him on his crap."

"I'm not following," Gray said.

"Of all the 'friends' he has, politically and professionally, I think you and Charlotte are the only people he felt safe around because he *always* knew where he stood with the two of you," Shepherd explained, "Neither of you ever backed down from a line in the proverbial sand, and you both maintain high—but realistic—expectations."

"You know, that actually kind of makes sense," Sigo said, cottoning on to Shepherd's rationale, "People generally respond positively to consistent boundaries and expectations from colleagues and leadership."

"Terrific," Gray pretended to grouse, "Charlotte and I are dysfunctional colleagues magnets! Not like I have any in this room at the moment…"

Gray and Shepherd locked eyes for a moment before both broke out laughing. Gray's laugh was a solid sound of mirth from a man with a solid chest, but Sigo was caught off guard by the atomic bomb of Shepherd's infamously loud staccato guffaw.

Recovering himself, Shepherd nodded, "Ok, ok—I concede the logic of your argument, Counselor. I guess even *I* have to concede Cremer's not *that* much of an—"

"Evil bastard?" Sigo suggested, unable to resist.

Shepherd burst out laughing again, dust rattling down from the ceiling.

"Damn, Abe!" Shepherd spluttered through his laughter, "Why does it suddenly feel like Dionne Robertson's here in the room?!"

Gray also began laughing, again "Now that you mention it, there *is* a certain similarity of personality!"

Shepherd looked at Sigo, getting his laughter under control. Noticing her look of confusion, he explained, "Dionne Robertson used to work for me. She also helped Abe and I on a few cases. Amazing sailor!"

Sigo chuckled, her tension easing, "I guess I'll take that as a compliment, then! Still," Sigo shook her head, "I have to admit your compliment to Cremer about the behavioral profile was a very gracious thing to say, Isaac."

Shepherd grimaced a bit, "Well, intellectual honesty required me to give credit where due, and his profile *was* shipshape in Bristol fashion. Besides, deep down I reckoned Abe had a valid reason for bringing him in. So, I thought it best to try and calm the waters a bit and batten down my gun ports."

"Thank you for that," Gray smiled, leaning back in his chair. "Now, unless Denita can't be privy to what Veronica and Liam found, what's up?"

"Actually, we *will* need your help again, Denita," Shepherd said, "Hold onto your socks, kiddos; this is going to be a bumpy ride!"

Shepherd required an hour to eagerly lay out all the findings Bale and Gumataotao uncovered. Sigo's eyes widened with every paragraph—and only *part* of her disbelief was at Shepherd's Mach 2 rate of speech.

"My God!" Sigo, explained, shaking her head, "I've seen things like this in the movies, but I never thought these kind of…of plots were really *real.*"

"I can see why you wanted Denita here," Gray said, his voice dark, "Denita, assuming Isaac's information is correct, we have less than 24 hours to move."

"On it!" Sigo rose smartly, "Let me make a few calls over to Seattle and Sea-Tac. Give me an hour or so, gentlemen."

Sigo swept from the room so fast the dust didn't have time to settle before the door shut behind her.

"Well, that *wasn't* how I'd planned it, but I'm glad she took off," Shepherd said, "We need to talk about the elephant in the room."

"What's up?" Gray's voice was tired, *Dammit! He's pissed about me losing my temper the other day. I* knew *I went too far!*

"That *mi-chin-nom's* killed his entire family, accomplices, and possibly people over in South Korea," Shepherd charged down a completely unexpected path.

"The 'Mee-chee-*what?!'"*

"Sorry," Shepherd said, "Korean again. *'Mi-chin-nom'* roughly translates as 'crazy bastard.' Anyway, legal consequences don't mean *crap* to him. Our friends and families are in danger. *Real* danger. Not to mention you and I as well."

"I know," Gray nodded, his eyes rolling in frustration as he ran a hand over his stubbled face, "I've already talked to Charlotte about protective details for both of our social circles. Sadly, beyond that, there's not a lot we can do."

"You know damn well that's *hysterically* insufficient," Shepherd's voice was hard, "Unless the *gesekgi* feels *personally* threatened, he won't care. His power and wealth can buy him freedom faster than we can say 'John Q. Arbuckle' backward."

Gray shifted, uncomfortable with Shepherd's apparent direction, "Isaac, I feel you; I really do. But, come on—you know there's only so much we can do. We're bound by the law."

"The only law I care about right now is survival."

"Isaac, don't go there!" Gray held up a hand, his eyes cold, "I will *not* cross that line! I *know* the danger he presents, but I won't tolerate any action that violates my oath to the Constitution of the United States!"

Shepherd folded his hands on the table, his eyes as steely as Gray's, "Abe, I *get* where you're coming from, and, in the course of normal events, I'd be right there with you. Unfortunately, we're so far out of 'normal events' here that we're on a completely different continent! We *have* to do something radical and entirely unexpected."

"Isaac, the moment we cross that line, we're no better than David Kerr!" Gray's voice was flat as his fist slammed down on the table.

"Sarah's *dead* unless we cross *some* sort of line, Abraham!" Shepherd shot back, smacking his hand down on the table, "Get your head out of your ass! Do you *really* believe NCIS can protect our loved ones, *especially* considering it's compromised?! And don't even get me *started* about corruption in the FBI!"

Gray closed his eyes, forcing himself to control his breathing. The conversation had veered into an area he never imagined going…but here he was. Worse, he knew Shepherd was right.

Still, Gray was log-jammed by one immovable point.

"Isaac," Gray said, his voice slow and thick with repressed anger, "Even if—just for argument's sake—even if I agree with you, there are some things I just can't do. I'm a *federal agent.*"

"I'm not."

"What?"

Shepherd raised his eyebrows, "I'm a free agent. Now that I'm out of uniform, I'm not bound by the UCMJ or Navy regulations—or a specific oath to the Constitution—anymore. I've got an idea that'll keep your hands clean *and* neutralize the threat, but it does require you to…momentarily look in another direction."

Gray's head dropped in exasperation as he stared at the table.

"What have you got?" Gray finally asked, voice weary as he looked back up.

Shepherd laid out his idea. Gray's eyes widened and his face went pale.

"Ben-zona!" Gray cursed in surprise, shock coloring his complexion a dusky red hue, "Ok, I admit that likely *will* work…but, Isaac, think beyond the next 24 hours. Are you *sure* you'll be able to live with yourself after this?"

Shepherd leaned back, "You'd be surprised what I can live with when it's necessary, and this is *necessary.*"

"But you're *retired* now," Gray retorted, desperately trying to find a way out of the logical trap Shepherd had boxed him into.

"Officially, yes," Shepherd nodded, "But you've heard me recite the Chief Petty Officer's Creed plenty of times. A chief never takes off the anchors, even after retirement. I've been a warrior ever since I enlisted back in '97, and formal retirement can't change that."

"Dammit," Gray sighed, deflating in defeat, "I suppose there's no talking you out of this, is there?"

"Face it, retired or not, Abe, I'm a sailor, a chief, *and* the Accidental Detective," Shepherd said determinedly, "This is the *only* move we have that'll get through that *mi-chin-nom's* thick skull. It's time *we* set the rules and show this motherfucker just how dangerous *I* can be!"

Chapter 28
Seattle, Washington
Saturday, September 15, 2018; 13:00 hours

Seattle-Tacoma International Airport's 2,500-acre campus was a bit smaller than the area occupied by other airports with similar passenger loads. However, Sea-Tac bustled with aerodynamic efficiency, its concourses coursing with throngs of air travelers as its long runways catapulted and caught hundreds of planes every day.

Safely ensconced away from the muddy, sweaty mass of rabble jostling about for a low-rent plastic seat in the low-rent common areas, Gippeum Lýkos enjoyed the plush armchair enveloping his reclining body. The comfortable, plush chair was located next to a tinted window in the Gold Star Lounge for members of Pacific World Airways' exclusive Executive Club.

Sipping a cocktail, Lýkos sighed, crossing his legs delicately. He was *almost* content. Very soon now he would forever drop the horrid, mousy little surname his plebian Greek adoptive family had imposed on him. He was also finally free to stop flying economy. *So* beneath him.

A Boeing 737 painted in the bright greens and blues of Alaskan Air trotted by, intent on reaching its gate.

Lýkos smirked, unbuttoning the coat of his $10,000.00 Ginko Illustradé suit (Armani and Versace were *so* two years ago!). He could *finally* start enjoying the benefits of the very long game he'd been playing for many very long years. He'd decided to enjoy a quiet, personal 'coming out' party as a rich magnate by donning the Illustradé ensemble in silk and rayon, pinstripes and all, while enjoying the Gold Star Lounge.

He might be flying back to North Carolina, but that empty backwater of North Carolina was soon to be part of his past.

About damn time, too, Lýkos thought, setting the empty cocktail glass on a sleek table. Looking around at his fellow lounge occupants, he took note of their suits and ties and jewelry.

309

This was the world he belonged in. Smirking privately, he noticed he was the only one who could apparently afford a Ginko Illustradé suit.

"Ex-excuse me, M-Mr. Lýkos?"

Lýkos turned slightly, looking up at the source of the tremulous voice. A young man in blue slacks and a dark blue blazer, a Pac World badge clipped to his lapel, stood trembling with barely repressed excitement.

"Yes?" He said in a bored voice, his eyes surreptitiously undressing the young, boy-faced man.

Not bad, Lýkos savored the privacy of his thoughts, *I wonder how he'd sound under my…personal tutelage?*

"Sir, I'm *so* sorry to bother you, but I've been asked to escort you to the gate counter," The young man said breathlessly, "There's a problem with your boarding pass, and they need to print you a new one. Unfortunately, our computer here in the lounge is broken, and TSA regulations require you to be present for this correction. Again, I'm sorry to have bothered you, sir!"

Lýkos smiled pleasantly. No need to badger a hapless peasant, after all. Especially one who knew his place.

"It is no trouble at all," Lýkos replied smoothly, "I admire Pac World's strict adherence to such regulations. Please, lead the way."

The eager young man offered to carry Lýkos' bag for him. Lýkos, enjoying the privileges of wealth, accepted.

Exiting the lounge, Lýkos buttoned his suit coat as they traversed the long Pac World concourse. Posters extolling the virtues of Washington State adorned the walls next to advertisements for products and services ranging from alcohol to pedicures.

"Sir, I sincerely hope I'm not out of line, but I wanted to offer my condolences for your brother and sister-in-law!" The young man jabbered, "It's all so horrible! How you've been able to be so…so *strong* on the news, fighting for justice, has been simply *amazing!*"

Lýkos smiled indulgently, "Thank you for your sympathy. Sadly, my brother and I were estranged for many years, but he *was* my brother. Family is very important in Korean culture, so I was merely fulfilling my familial duty."

"I know, but I don't think I'd be as strong as you were, and if I or Pac World can do *anything* for you, please, *please* let me know!" The cherub-faced man rambled on.

Lýkos smiled, surreptitiously reading the man's name badge.

"You are too kind, Edgar," Lýkos said as they maneuvered around a corner where two janitors were hunched over, evidently fighting a stubborn spill on the waxed tile floor.

I wonder how young Edgar would respond to leather restraints and judiciously applied electrostimulation, Lýkos internally mused, *I think such an adventure would be fascinating...*

A knot of people pushed past, running to catch their connections. Further groups, occupying the seating around the gate, stared blankly at their phones or paperback books. The atmosphere reeked of commoners trying to fill meaningless time in their meaningless lives.

Life is wasted on the living! Lýkos thought contemptuously, *Most of the living, anyway. I certainly haven't wasted my life or my talents.*

"Here we are," Edgar said, setting Lýkos' bag on the floor by the desk, "The desk agent here will take care of you. Again, I'm so sorry to have bothered you!"

Before Lýkos could reply, the breathless young sycophant was gone. The desk agent, wearing a dark blue sport coat over tan slacks, stood with his back to Lýkos at the far side of his little workstation. Beyond him, massive windows showcased a Boeing 747 in the blue and red Pac World livery sitting idle at the gate. Ground crews scurried about the aircraft, conducting pre-flight maintenance.

After waiting a few moments for the desk agent to turn around, Lýkos cleared his throat.

The man didn't respond, instead continuing his intense staring match with a computer monitor.

"Excuse me!" Lýkos said imperiously, "I believe you needed me here for a new boarding pass."

"No, I just needed *you*, you diabolical *gesekgi.*"

Lýkos blinked in surprise, rage boiling up his spine, "I beg your pardon; how dare *you* speak to me like that! I'll have you fired for showing such disrespect!"

"You can't have *me* fired, jerkwad," The man still didn't turn.

Lýkos' eyes blazed into full fury, "You're nothing but a fucking little clerk! I can have you thrown out of this airport like *that!*" Lýkos barked, snapping his fingers.

"No, you can't, but it's *loads* of fun listening to you bluster on about it," The man replied in a voice dripping with sarcastic boredom.

"And just what makes you think I have no power over your pitiful little job, you discourteous cretin?!" Lýkos' voice was bitter acid.

"Because I don't work for you, you dumb asshat," Isaac Shepherd turned to face Lýkos.

Lýkos' jaw bounced off the countertop in abject shock. Shepherd thought it made a rather satisfying *thunk!* as it did.

Smirking, Shepherd cocked his head slightly to the side, "Have to admit, it's nice to render *you* speechless for a change. You nailed me pretty good a few times there over the past couple of days."

Grabbing his door-knob-handled cane, Shepherd steadied himself as he unsteadily tottered across the small work area to the customer service desk opposite his discombobulated foe.

Lýkos' mouth continued to hang open in disbelief.

"You look like a dead halibut, Mr. Lýkos," Shepherd said in the friendliest of deadly voices, "You might want to close your mouth before you start catching flies."

Still processing the shocking revenant appearing before him, Lýkos unconsciously obeyed, snapping his mouth closed.

312

"You're slipping," Shepherd taunted in a casual voice as he shucked the blue jacket. He retrieved his brown corduroy sport coat from under the desk, "You, of *all* people, should've realized I wasn't wearing the correct uniform, even when my back was turned. Pac World employees wear blue slacks or skirts under their dark blue jackets."

Lýkos' face flashed into a stunned expression, but he covered it with such speed an Academy Award-winning actor would have been jealous.

Realizing he'd irretrievably lost the opening move, Lýkos sighed, letting go of his momentary observational lapse. Shepherd could enjoy the small victory; after all, Lýkos knew his foe was on the verge of abject defeat.

This sad man has no idea just how deeply he's immersed himself into a game he cannot win, Lýkos thought, his shoulders relaxing further as he geared up for the fun of once more locking horns with Shepherd, *Still, this will be a diverting few minutes...even if Mr. Shepherd only has a few minutes left alive in which to be diverting.*

Lýkos cocked his head a bit, a pleased expression softening his features, "To be honest, I *am* surprised to see you here, Mr. Shepherd. I honestly thought you had conceded the game and retired from the field. Still, I prefer this outcome; victory in the game is much more satisfying this way."

This screaming idiot has no idea just how deep a pile of shit he's in, Shepherd thought, a pleasant smile softening his features as well, *I'm going to enjoy every minute it takes to destroy your entire life, you evil troll. Unfortunately, it's only going to take a very few minutes to do so, but, hey, them's the breaks!*

"That's because you're an amoral psychopath with *zero* understanding of humanity, Mr. Lýkos," Shepherd responded pleasantly. "You're a dangerous *mi-chin-nom,* but I've seen worse than you."

"You have?"

313

"Try standing in your underwear at boot camp facing a screaming senior chief petty officer beating a metal trash can lid in your face at 04:30 on a 45° morning in a berthing compartment while you have to piss so bad your bladder's about to explode all over your shipmates," Shepherd responded evenly in one long breath.

"You paint a very vivid picture," Lýkos responded dryly, "No, I must admit I have never experienced that particular…situation."

"Well, if you had, you might understand the *real* definition of dangerous, because it sure ain't *you,* you nefarious hack," Shepherd's words were all the more cutting because his voice was smoothly conversational, "To put it in chess terms, Mr. Lýkos, this is 'discovered check' and 'mate.'"

"I fail to see how, Mr. Shepherd," Lýkos said, eyes firing up with enthusiasm, "The woman who murdered my brother is dead, and you have no evidence placing me anywhere near any of the crime scenes. Therefore, you have no case. I suspect this is but a final desperate attempt to shock me into some sort of ill-conceived confession. I believe the football term is a 'Hail Mary' play."

"Not at all. I might be given to a bit of theatrics, but even *I'd* never do anything so trite and predictable," Shepherd said, leaning his cane against the back of the desk before resting his weight atop the counter on his elbows, "Mr. Lýkos, I said a minute ago you're a psychopath who doesn't understand humanity. Aside from the fact that you're an evil murdering asshat, and, well, I'm not, do you know what the *real* difference between us is?"

Lýkos' eyebrows twitched in amusement, "Please enlighten me."

"You're alone," Shepherd said, a note of real sadness in his voice, "You're utterly alone in the world. You're as lost a soul as the Good Lord Jesus ever lamented in the Gospels."

"That was prosaic, Mr. Shepherd," Lýkos laughed lightly, "In fact, I would almost accuse you of waxing poetic, but I don't believe your miniature soliloquy quite rises to that level of

314

elegance. Besides, I would dare say I'm far from being 'lost' in any sense of the word, religious or otherwise."

"That's because you're a murdering moron who steadfastly refuses to get off his gilded high horse and *see* what's around you," Shepherd said, "Or, to be more accurate, *who's* around you."

"I confess I don't understand," Lýkos' said, his movements fluid to the point of effeminate, yet Shepherd could see underlying steel camouflaged by the seemingly airy gestures.

"You look out there and only see tools you can use to your advantage," Shepherd said, gesturing to the crowded terminal with his chin, "I look out there and I see *people.* People with hopes and dreams and fears and pain just as valid and real as my own. Mr. Lýkos, you're dancing along the shores of the lake of fire because you reject all *real* connections with other people. You *choose* to be what you are—a diabolical mastermind caught up in his own sense of grandiosity. And that's why you're going to lose."

"Oh, come now, Mr. Shepherd," Lýkos retorted smoothly, "These populist opinions are beneath you! We two are superior in every way. People like you and I look at the world from above these...these animals. We create opportunities and build empires while they're trapped within the vagaries of their herds. We see *everything.* We see possibilities, we see power...well, at least *I* do."

"You see *nothing,* and that's what makes you careless," Shepherd countered, voice still as genteel as if he were attending afternoon tea at Buckingham Palace. "You're aware the authorities are investigating the deaths of your parents, aren't you?"

Lýkos sighed impatiently, "Mr. Shepherd, the North Carolina authorities already ruled my parents' deaths as suicide."

"That's not what I mean, you myopic buffoon," Shepherd said impatiently.

Lýkos snickered, "I have to admit, your ability to craft amusing insults is quite witty."

"Don't change the subject," Shepherd said, voice taking on the first hint of a hard edge. "I wasn't referring to the authorities in Durham—although they *have* reopened the investigation into the deaths of your adoptive parents. Nor am I referring to the authorities in south Florida who've reopened the investigation into the suspicious Merritt Island car wreck that killed your other brother, Su-Jin, when you guys were 13."

Lýkos glanced down at his elegantly manicured nails, bored.

"I'm referring to the *South Korean* authorities," Shepherd went on, "They were quite interested in your *birth* parents after we provided them evidence indicating your parents were murdered a few *years* ago. You know, the Chuls—the people who gave you up for adoption forty-some-odd years ago when they were dirt-poor and living on the street so you and Young-Saeng and Su-Jin could have a shot at a decent life? *That's* who I'm referring to."

Lýkos found himself speechless for the second time in the conversation.

"Oh, yes, I know who you are, Mr. Lýkos," Shepherd said pleasantly, "But, I *do* have to admit your choice of the name Chul Kyung-Joon was clever. 'Gippeum' translates as 'happy,' and Kyung-Joon translates in several ways, one of which is 'happy, powerful man.' Nice little parallel there between your new name and your original one."

"I was unaware you spoke Korean," Lýkos' voice was even, but Shepherd caught the hint of surprised unease in his eyes.

"I don't," Shepherd admitted, "But you don't have to speak a language to become familiar with its foundations, or its insults, you *byeonshin,*" Shepherd said, employing one of the more vulgar Korean insults he'd recently learned, "Still, it was an excellent way to divert attention from the fact you're now the new CEO and COO of GDI Tech, Mr. Lýkos."

"Since you know my true name, I would prefer you address me as 'Mr. Chul."

"And *I'd* prefer your brothers to be alive and you, well, dead, but it looks like neither of us is going to get what we want today, Mr. Lýkos," Shepherd said lightly, "Anyway, this brings me to an interesting point. The Chuls ostensibly went into seclusion back in early 2016. What's interesting is that *you* started attending regular meetings with the South Korean consulate in late 2014."

Lýkos' expression snapped back into a look of mild shock as Shepherd rattled on.

"Since you kept your adoptive name, 'Lýkos,' it was easy for the Chuls to find you. Su-Jin died when y'all were 13—and your adoptive mother nearly died with him—but, anyway, you took him out of the picture some 35 years ago. Young-Saeng had married, and I bet you neglected to tell the Chuls that Young-Saeng took his wife's name in a bid to get some distance from you."

"Very good, Mr. Shepherd," Lýkos looked genuinely impressed, "I was beginning to worry that you weren't equal to the game."

"You call it a game," Shepherd said, all pretense of his pleasant façade dropping away, "I call it mass murder. You and your now-deceased friend, Murgatroyd, went on vacation to Japan in late 2015…but there's *no* record of *you* in Japan, just him and your cell phone pinging international towers. I'll wager *you* took a trip to Seoul to meet your birth parents. They were last seen publicly in January of 2016, so I'm guessing you made another trip or two and killed them so you could ascend the GDI throne."

"Perhaps," Lýkos said, smiling, "You *are* good at this, aren't you?"

Shepherd glanced over at the janitors as they began laying wax on the area they'd been cleaning, "Oh, it gets better. There was a little dust-up aboard my old ship, USS *Ponce,* back in 2016. A GDI Tech employee was trying to steal a prototype weapon system the ship was testing. And then, *last* year, that nitwit Gordon Grey went on a murder spree to get at me while being sponsored by someone else."

Lýkos raised an eyebrow while reaching up to straighten his $700 blue silk necktie.

Shepherd sighed impatiently, "You know very well where I'm going with this, but I'll keep on dumping exposition if you wish."

"Of course, I know where you're going" Lýkos nodded, "You believe I was the sponsor of this… what was his name? Gordon Drey?"

"Cute," Shepherd said, "I don't just 'believe' it, I can *prove* it. Just like I can *prove* you enticed David Kerr into your little scheme by playing on his sense of betrayal and outrage at our government, and by paying him a *crapload* of money. I can *prove* you and Kerr killed Young-Saeng, and that Kerr killed Delores Tate, Jane and William Smith, and made the attempt on my life. I *will* however admit we're still unsure who you hired to bomb Dr. Pounder's car, but she's safe, just so you know."

"I'm delighted to hear that, whomever this 'Dr. Pounder' is."

"Nice try," Shepherd said, "Aren't you the *least* bit interested in how I came by all this information?"

"I am, but not so much that I care a great deal," Lýkos said, "You see, despite the diversion you've proven to be, the game is mine. The 'checkmate' is mine. While I *am* grateful to speak with you one more time, you *will* be dead quite soon. I assure you that I'll be very creative—and deliberate—in addressing the issue of your family. I *did* warn you that you have much to lose, Mr. Shepherd. You should've heeded me."

"Why kill my family after I'm dead?"

"It sends a clear message to anyone who might wish to challenge me," Lýkos said casually.

"That's what Kerr said when he threatened Sarah Gray," Shepherd nodded, evidently deep in thought.

"I suppose you have him in custody?" Lýkos asked.

"Why waste time asking questions when you already know the answer?" Shepherd inquired, a single eyebrow hiking up into his hairline.

"He won't be alive very long, either," Lýkos said, boredom creeping into his voice, "But, even so, there's nothing he can say, no evidence he can provide, that will tie me to him. I don't think you need to be told that I am *very* good at keeping myself in the clear, Mr. Shepherd."

"I believe you're mistaken, Mr. Lýkos," Shepherd said lightly.

Lýkos was puzzled. Shepherd was behaving in an unexpectedly cavalier fashion. *Perhaps he hasn't foreseen enough moves ahead to realize his predicament...?*

"I am never mistaken, Mr. Shepherd," Lýkos finally replied.

"That's what George Custer said right before the Battle of the Little Bighorn," Shepherd retorted sharply.

Lýkos shook his head. He felt sadness at the fall of so engaging a foe, but the game was over. *Alas, all good things must come to an end...*

"You're tragically uninformed about your immediate situation, Mr. Shepherd," Lýkos said before nodding to a nearby security guard.

The man jumped to life as if by magic. Striding quickly behind the desk, he took up position behind Shepherd. The soft click of metal on metal told Shepherd a round had been chambered in the man's gun.

"You see, Mr. Shepherd, I am not, as you so colorfully put it, 'alone' at all."

"This is a major airline's concourse," Shepherd pointed out, "Security cameras are everywhere. Even this meeting is being recorded, as is the fact this turkey has a gun on me. I'm giving you fair warning there's more in play here than you realize. Are you *absolutely* sure you wish to make this move?"

"Ah, but *you* have failed to make the most basic of deductions, Mr. Shepherd," Lýkos countered, his blood beginning to course in excitement as he closed the trap, "You see, GDI Tech is a vast, multi-national corporation. I own numerous subsidiaries, including Pacific World Airways. This is *my* terminal. I own it."

Lýkos snapped his fingers. Numerous security guards materialized as if teleported in. Joining the first guard, they formed a tight circle around Shepherd and Lýkos, every weapon they had pointed at Shepherd.

Shepherd noticed the passengers in the waiting area looking over nervously at the spectacle.

Lýkos could not prevent a triumphant smirk from anointing his face with glee.

"The security cameras in this entire wing have been inoperative for days now," Lýkos effected a fake sigh, "I'm sure I'll have to fire someone for such a deplorable lapse in maintenance, especially as it will significantly disable the investigation into your death."

Well, that *certainly makes things easier for Abe and I!* Shepherd fought to keep his poker face intact.

Lýkos stepped forward, folding his fine-boned hands elegantly on the customer counter as he looked Shepherd in the eye.

"You *should* have quit when I gave you the opportunity, Mr. Shepherd," Lýkos said quietly, "You were a very welcome diversion. Most of the time I go through life feeling like I'm stuck in line behind someone who doesn't know how to work an ATM. You provided a welcome level of mental stimulation. Sadly, the game will end along with your life." Lýkos shook his head sadly, "You had so much potential. Such a waste."

Chapter 29
Seattle, Washington
Saturday, September 15, 2018; 13:36 hours

Shepherd glanced around, mentally counting the number of guns behind him. He then scanned the crowd of security guards forming the other half of the ring behind Lýkos.

"Yeah, I guess I'm royally screwed now, huh?" Shepherd said with as much concern as a man discussing the scores of a football game he didn't particularly care about, "Looks like you win, and I lose. Oh, the shame. My teddy bear will be so distraught."

"I confess I don't understand your cavalier attitude," Lýkos said, the slightest hesitation of uncertainty in his voice, "Unless simply wish to die with more dignity than most people effuse, of course."

"No, it's not that at all," Shepherd responded, shaking his head, "It's just that you're making the same dumb mistake David Kerr made. I have to ask, what makes you think *I'm* alone? Don't you know what this moment *actually* is?"

"No," Lýkos said, real confusion now coloring his face, "What is it?"

"This is the moment you pucker up and kiss my ass!" Shepherd spat, hateful venom turning his voice into a lethal torrent, "Abe! Veronica!"

Ripping the caps from their heads, the two janitors threw down their mops and turned. Abraham Gray and Veronica Bale swung their weapons up even as badges materialized in their hands.

"Federal agents!" They bellowed in unison, "Drop your weapons!"

Before Lýkos could fully process this turn of events, a human tsunami swamped them. The laconic, bored crowds of supposed air travelers shot to their feet producing weapons and badges from handbags, hidden holsters, and carry-on luggage. The small army of federal agents surrounded the counter, out-numbering Lýkos' forces three-to-one.

Lýkos' head swiveled violently around, eyes wide as he took in the scene.

"There's an old Korean proverb, 'kick a rock and you injure your own foot,'" Shepherd said breezily, "Or, as Shakespeare wrote, 'Heat not a furnace for thy foe so hot / That it do singe thyself.'"

Shepherd shared a glance with Gray, "I'd advise you to have your people lower their weapons. Otherwise, the combined forces of NCIS and the FBI will kill every...single...one...of...you."

Lýkos gestured to his people. The guns dropped as the mass of Pac World security guards stared about in abject confusion. Weren't *they* the ones who were supposed to have the upper hand?!

"You just couldn't resist, could you?" Shepherd asked, "You could have just killed Young-Saeng quietly and gotten away with everything you've been working towards for the past four or five years. But you just *had* to go for overkill. You had to suborn an entire NCIS field office—which raised a number of suspicions—and you had to *brutalize* Young-Saeng. You let your hatred of him 'heat the furnace' so much that it burned you, you ridiculous moron."

"There is *no* evidence placing me at my brother's death, Mr. Shepherd," Lýkos spat, stubborn rage fueling his voice, "And don't threaten me with DNA evidence. We share the same—!"

"You share the same DNA, blah, blah, blah. I know, you dimwitted troll!" Shepherd interrupted impatiently, "Ever heard of a little thing called *epigenetics?* No? Well, to put it in a *very* rough verbal shorthand, epigenes are markers that control *how* genes are expressed. This is why my brothers and I all have different *shades* of green in our eyes. We have the same DNA, but our epigenes determine the unique ways each of our bodies express those genes."

Lýkos' mouth fell open, once again hitting the counter with another determined *thunk!*

"The genetic material found under Young-Saeng's fingernails did *not* match his epigenetic profile. Since Su-Jin died when you were kids, you're the *only* person on the entire planet with a DNA sample containing those particular epigenes."

Lýkos' mouth began unconsciously opening and closing, his eyes bugging out in shocked disbelief. He reminded Shepherd of a gasping fish flopping in the bottom of an empty fish tank.

"I also knew you own Pac World, Mr. Lýkos," Shepherd went on, "It took a fair bit of digging, but we were able to trace the money trail you left in your wake. Getting Pac World under the GDI Tech umbrella was strategically brilliant. You can pull corporate rank and hop a cross-country flight without being on the official aircraft manifest, or just use Pac World private jets. Either way, it was a slick idea to keep both the TSA and the FAA off your trail."

Lýkos closed his mouth, but his eyes were as wide as the backside of an overweight elephant chowing down on a few birthday cakes.

"Your money-laundering techniques are good," Shepherd continued pleasantly, "But it was Tidy Sweep's acquisition of Sulfide Services in Norfolk in late '16 that was your Achilles' Heel. Tidy Sweep is ostensibly independent, but our investigation showed it's secretly owned by Cable Partridge Enterprises, which itself is a subsidiary of Mammoth Holdings and Investments. Mammoth just happens to be Pac World's immediate corporate parent. Interestingly enough, Mammoth itself was brought under GDI Tech's control in a hostile takeover two years ago."

Lýkos remained frozen, utterly unable to comprehend the fall of his house of cards.

"Additionally, your money trail provided the break we needed in tracing the cyberattacks on the Naval Hospital in Bremerton, the Tates' financial institutions, and even the Kitsap County Police. There were enough coding similarities between both efforts that our team was able to trace the hack to a certain David Kerr. Very sneaky how you secretly trained him in cyberwarfare over the past few years, but you shouldn't have left so many lovely digital fingerprints."

Lýkos again opened his mouth but again emitted no sound.

"And *that,* I believe, is check and mate!" Shepherd leaned in close, his nose nearly touching Lýkos', "Or, as we say in the Navy: 'Boom, bitch!'"

Gray stepped forward, "Looks like your empire is crumbling, Mr. Lýkos.

Gray then spun right into reciting Lýkos' Miranda rights but noticed the suspect was ignoring him.

"Do you understand these rights?" Gray asked.

Lýkos continued to ignore him. His gaze was a burning, rage-filled silent screed directed at Shepherd's serenely smiling face.

"I *said,"* Gray jerked Lýkos' arms slightly as he snapped on handcuffs, "Do you understand these rights"

"Of course, I do, you idiot!" Lýkos spit back at him.

"Good!" Gray nodded in vicious satisfaction, "Veronica, would you contact our Sea-Tac liaison? I'm afraid this gate will be shut down for some time."

"On it!" Bale said, holstering her weapon and pulling out her phone.

"Shey!" Gray looked around.

Shey Cremer, now sporting a windbreaker emblazoned with "FBI" on it, materialized, "Abe?"

"We're going need to get this crowd processed. Can you and the other FBI personnel do a sweep of the rest of Pac World security?" Gray asked, "I'm pretty sure this piece of crap has more hired goons in his pocket than just these yahoos."

"We've got your back," Cremer said gruffly. His eyes briefly flicked to Shepherd's face, but uncharacteristically, he said nothing. Instead, he pulled out a radio and began barking instructions into it as he walked off.

"You think this is over, don't you, Mr. Shepherd?" Lýkos said quietly, "You believe the swift hand of impartial justice will inflict righteous punishment on me, whatever the charges may be? You truly think you've won the game, don't you?"

"Don't believe in remaining silent, do you?" Gray asked.

"Oh, do shut up!" Lýkos ordered.

Gray's eyebrows shot up in mild surprise.

Lýkos redirected his ire to Shepherd, "I concede this match, but I still own one of the largest multinational tech companies in the world. I'm also one of the biggest contributors to numerous American *and* South Korean officials. I have allies all over the world—including in nations who wish to see United States interests damaged."

Shepherd yawned, "And you're monologuing like a bad *Austin Powers* villain *why?* I mean, come on! Why can't diabolical masterminds like you ever just *shut up?"*

"Let's take a walk, Mr. Lýkos," Gray said, his eyes locking on Shepherd's for a moment.

Gray began leading Lýkos away from the crowd slightly, Shepherd tottering along with them on his cane.

Lýkos laughed, "My governmental contacts, both here and in South Korea, will ensure I am not overly inconvenienced by these events. Nor will my power or reach be curtailed."

"Let me guess, you're about to tell me that your power far exceeds mine," Shepherd said, "And that you'll dust me like a bug sooner than I think."

"Oh, not you, no," Lýkos said breezily, "At least, not for a long time. I find it quite edifying this encounter resulted in this outcome."

"And why is that?" Gray asked.

Lýkos ignored him, looking instead to Shepherd, "Are you the least bit curious as to why, Mr. Shepherd?"

"I'm breathless with anticipation," Shepherd's voice was all honey and sarcasm, "Please, enlighten me."

"As I said earlier, you have so much to lose!" Lýkos laughed, "Sentiment. Such a defect."

"Really?"

"Of course," Lýkos nodded, "That's the *real* difference between us. I will always do what's necessary to advance my interests. Between your parents and brothers, that's four Shepherds I'm sure will be considered a tragic statistical coincidence when they all succumb to some form of violence. And your nephews and stepdaughter…you *are* aware that privileged little white children get trafficked into sexual slavery every day, aren't you?"

"You just don't know when to shut up, do you?" Gray snapped.

Lýkos finally condescended to look at him, "You're even *more* ridiculous, Mr. Gray. Doesn't your younger daughter, Rachel, live in Israel? Such a violent part of the world. I also have contacts there, you know. I could always have them…keep an eye on her, if you wish. And your *poor* wife, Sarah, all alone and surrounded by the violent miscreants of Virginia Beach."

Gray's neck stiffened, his jaw muscled clenching so hard Shepherd was surprised his teeth didn't shatter.

"Just *had* to go *there,* didn't you?" Gray asked, his countenance hardening so quickly one might have thought he'd had an unfortunate encounter with Medusa.

Lýkos smirked, pleased his barb had landed with such exquisite precision. Turning back to Shepherd, he sighed pleasantly, a man who knew he'd won, "Please, enjoy your momentary victory. Savor it, even, because you won't be enjoying the next few years very much."

Lýkos looked away, allowing his eyes to serenely take in the view of the bustling airport outside the gate's picture windows.

Gray and Shepherd locked eyes again. Shepherd, caught up in steeling his nerves, was startled to see a depth of murderous rage flaring from Gray's eyes. It was something Shepherd had never seen in those blue-gray eyes before.

Gray raised a single eyebrow.

Shepherd nodded imperceptibly.

Gray turned his head, sneezing loudly and violently. His hand on Lýkos' arm slipped.

Shepherd's tottering gate vanished, his walking stick dropping to the floor even as his right foot shot out, sweeping Lýkos feet from under him.

Lýkos began falling, his brain registering the drop as Shepherd's hand snaked forward, grabbing Lýkos' cuffed left hand and twisting violently.

The snap of Lýkos' wrist shattering like glass echoed off the tile floor; a visceral gunshot report of bones being smashed into multiple pieces.

Shepherd allowed himself to topple downward while releasing Lýkos' wrist. Shifting his arm, Shepherd swung an elbow into position, pile-driving his full 247 lbs. into Lýkos' side as they tumbled. The falling mass of Shepherd's body, concentrated in the point of his elbow, snapped two of Lýkos' ribs with ruthless efficiency.

Lýkos screamed as blinding pain tore through his arm and side, careening into his brain with caustic efficiency.

Before he could react further, Shepherd's weight crushed the wind from him, silencing any further cries.

Shepherd's left hand shot upwards, fingers closing about Lýkos' throat and squeezing violently. Lýkos couldn't cry out now even if he wanted to.

"Listen carefully, you twisted troll," Shepherd's voice was carbonic acid burning through Lýkos' ears, "You're free to come at *me* all the live-long day, but if anything—and I mean *anything*—happens to my family and friends, or Abe's family and friends, I'll find you and I *will* kill you as slowly and painfully as humanly possible. This is *my* game now, you bastard. My game and *my* rules. *Do you understand?"*

Lýkos peered at Shepherd, stunned into silence. Inside those sea-green eyes, Lýkos saw rage and blood-curdling fury erupting like a deranged volcano. Inside those eyes, he saw violence born of an explosive temper kept in check by rigidly maintained constraints. The whimsical, slightly ridiculous buffoon was gone; Lýkos was pinned underneath a man exuding searing hatred.

Shepherd's rough hand continued to slowly, relentlessly, and mercilessly crush his larynx.

For the first time in his life, Gippeum Lýkos knew fear.

Speechless, he could only stare back at the demon pinning his broken body to the floor. Spit bubbled from Lýkos' mouth as he gasped for air. He felt his bladder unexpectedly spasm, soaking his expensive pants in his own urine. Lýkos' skin was the pale white of a dying fungus as he summoned up enough energy to nod.

"Good!" Shepherd hissed.

Untangling himself, Shepherd looked up, his face the picture of innocent horror, "Abe! Quick! Help! He tripped and injured himself!"

"Damn!" Gray responded, all sugar and concern, "I need help! Someone call the EMTs! The prisoner tripped and fell! He's injured. Isaac, are you ok, or do you need medical attention too?"

"No, no, I'm fine," Shepherd said, rising to his feet. Looking down at Lýkos, he hitched a sickly-sweet look on his face, "Mr. Lýkos, the EMTs will be here shortly. Just stay there and lie quietly. I promise we *will* take care of you!"

Shepherd 'accidentally' kicked Lýkos' broken wrist as he 'stumbled' while reaching down to get his walking stick. Lýkos whimpered like a whipped puppy.

Two EMTs materialized, a stretcher laden with medical equipment between them. They examined Lýkos with remarkable speed as Gray filled them in on 'what' had happened.

"I heard his wrist snap, but the way he landed might have caused further injury to his hand," Gray said.

"He tripped me when he fell, and I went down on top of him," Shepherd said, breathless with feigned concern, "I think I might have broken his ribs! I weigh over 240 pounds!"

Shepherd met Lýkos' eyes, his voice rising to ensure everyone nearby heard his next sentence, "Oh, and watch it; the suspect pissed himself when we fell!"

Lýkos' eyes, wide with terror, now took on a humiliated look as his broken wrist was splinted before the EMTs hoisted him onto the stretcher.

Veronica Bale returned, "Airport security's in place with our people. The concourse won't be shut down, but they're working with us to cordon off this gate." She wrinkled her nose at the smell emanating from Lýkos' pants, "Oooh, did we have a widdle accident?"

Bale's voice carried absolutely no hint of concern.

"The poor dear tripped," Gray said hatefully, "Broke his wrist and some ribs, I think. Even pissed himself like a four-year-old. Veronica, would you mind staying with him? I'm on-scene commander, so I need to stay here."

"I've got it," Bale said, "Go do what you need to do. This creep ain't anything special."

"While you're waiting for trial, you ought to look up the story of *Janghwa and Hongryeon,*" Shepherd said to Lýkos, "Your own culture teaches us the dead *do* speak to the living who listen."

Lýkos, still silent with terror and humiliation, stared at Shepherd as he was wheeled away, Bale firmly at his side.

Shepherd stared back, making sure Lýkos saw the unadulterated violence in his evil smile until the last.

"Ok, Isaac," Gray said quietly, "I have to admit you were right. I about broke his neck when he mentioned Sarah and the girls...Isaac? Are you ok?"

"I'll be back in a minute," Shepherd said, eyeballing a nearby men's room, "I have to go powder my nose."

Shepherd headed towards the restroom; his gait not nearly as unsteady as he'd been affecting.

Concerned that Shepherd was looking increasingly green, Gray hesitated for a moment. Worry won out. Signaling to another agent to momentarily take charge, Gray swiftly strode to the men's room.

He found Shepherd standing in a stall, leaning over a toilet and puking his guts out.

Chapter 30
Port Ludlow, Washington
Monday, September 17, 2018; 17:51 hours

"…this is nothing but another salacious attempt by white supremacists to silence a prominent man of color!" Rhode Island Congresswoman Dana Cremer bleated on a talk show, "The very idea that Gippeum Lýkos…excuse me, I should have used Kyung-Joon Chul, his chosen name; anyway, that Mr. Chul is a killer and architect of this insane conspiracy only proves that toxic, radical, right-wing extremists are threatened by powerful people of color…"

"…the distinguished representative from Rhode Island might do well to review the facts of the case," Florida Senator Diego Alejandro said on a later news program, "I applaud her zeal in advocating for the marginalized in our society, but I suggest she familiarize herself with the incredible forensics work by NCIS during this tragic case before she makes another statement that might be construed as ill-informed…"

The sun was falling, but the late afternoon light wafted peacefully through the cedars and firs surrounding the Gumataotao's spacious backyard.

Maria Gumataotao stepped out onto the back porch, wiping her hands on a dish towel as she scanned the massive spread threatening to topple the picnic table. The feast she'd spearheaded was already partially demolished, but enough food remained to feed one small army and two small towns.

"…I'm *telling* you we *both* need to reassess our opinions of Isaac! He's not the loser dork we thought he was!" Maria heard a voice emanating from around the side of the house.

Poking her head around the corner, she saw A.J. Shepherd deep in conversation, his cell phone glued to his ear.

"Josh, dude, I was *there*. All these years we gave Isaac crap for being a second-rate wannabe...well, we were wrong...No, I'm not exaggerating!" A.J. said emphatically, "First off, he can *fight!* I'm talking about a full-on bar fight like in *Road House! And* he shrugged off a bullet wound to his *head!* Josh...hang on; let me finish! I'm telling you, keep talking down to him at your own peril, but he's done a shit-ton more than we ever thought..."

Smiling, Maria quietly moved away, sidling back towards the fire pit just off the porch. Liam sat in one of the numerous Adirondack chairs, his feet up on a stool as the fire crackled merrily. Luke Fredriksen reclined in another Adirondack, a beer in his hand. Isaac, who had been unusually quiet that night, sat next to Fredriksen.

"Dude, the way you were able to track down those bank records and make the connections between that Lýkos bitch and the funding to Gordon Grey in Norfolk last year was amazing!" Fredriksen was saying to Liam as Maria sat down next to her husband.

Liam shrugged, his moon face breaking into a smile, "I was only able to make the connection after Veronica supplied the key data while I fired up some new decryption software I've been working on with Sarah. Those two factors let me connect the coding in the cyberattacks with Kerr's office computer."

"Nicely done!" Fredriksen said.

"One question, Isaac," Liam spoke up again, "You said you and Abe ensured this jerk won't bother your friends and all while you're alive. How do you know he won't just have you shot and then go on a rampage?"

"It's a gamble," Isaac said, shrugging, "But one based in pretty well-documented psychology. This *gesekgi* is a raving egotist. Although Abe and I took him down along with a team of agents, he sees *me* as the cause of his downfall. In his mind, I defeated and humiliated him...and quite publicly, at that," Isaac answered, "His ego won't be satisfied by merely killing me. He's trapped in a mindset requiring him to take me down in an equally public fashion to assuage the insult he suffered at 'my' hands. Therefore, when he does come after me, it'll most likely be in a rather publicly spectacular fashion."

"That's a pretty big gamble, Isaac," Maria said.

"It is, but that's just part of this business," Isaac said, "Sometimes you have to risk big if you want to win big."

Fredriksen raised his eyebrows, "I know that jerk thinks of this as a game, but I'm surprised to hear *you* say something like that."

"Don't misunderstand me," Isaac said, shaking his head, "I'm just constrained by the limitations of the language. The *gesekgi* considers this a game, yes. But Abe and I are doing what we have to in order to finish the *job.*"

"So, when are you two boys going out to dinner?" Maria asked, changing the subject as she looked pointedly at Fredriksen and Isaac.

"When he gets back from his week up in Alaska," Fredriksen responded promptly, shifting his right leg, which had gone to sleep below the knee. "I've got a couple of places in Seattle I'd like Aegir here to try out."

Aegir? Isaac quizzically wondered, making a note to look it up later as Liam caught his attention.

"Isaac, you going to make your 50-state deadline by the end of November?" Liam asked.

"I should," Isaac said, a slight decrease in his usual energy level noticeable in his speech, "I'll be staying with A.J.'s family in Seattle for a week or so when I get back. I'll be here another week, maybe ten days, then back on the road."

A.J. sauntered back over, stuffing his phone into his pocket, "Well, dinner was terrific. But, unfortunately, I need to go. I've got to get back to Port Angeles and tie up some things with my students over the next few days."

"I'll walk you out," Isaac rose.

"Where's Abe?" A.J. asked as everyone rose to shake his hand. Maria gave him a big hug.

"He said he wanted some quiet for a bit," Liam answered, jerking a thumb over his shoulder, "He's hanging out in the swing near the fence."

"Let me go say goodbye," A.J. said, "One sec."

A.J. was gone only a few minutes before he returned, "Ok, time for me to run. Oh, yeah, by the way, Kid Canaveral—I've got something for you in my jacket."

"Cool. I like free stuff," Isaac smiled, but A.J. noticed a certain lack of light in his eyes.

Cutting through the house to the front door, Isaac and A.J. shifted through the pile of jackets for a moment before finding A.J.'s bright red wool jacket. Rummaging in it, A.J. pulled out a small package wrapped in brown paper.

"Here you go," A.J. said, "I found it the other day in a local artist's shop over in Poulsbo. Hope you like it."

Isaac noticed A.J. looked intensely uncomfortable.

Unwrapping the oddly lumpy parcel, he revealed a rather unusual magnifying glass. The lens was held in a standard shiny brass frame while the handle was made from a curved piece of antler.

"It's elk antler," A.J. explained, "I was killing some time while you were working and…well…it made me think of you."

Isaac stared at the beautiful piece of craftsmanship in his hand. Oddly enough, he *knew* he'd seen it before, if only he could remember where…

"It's beautiful!" Isaac finally said, coming back from the brief fugue caused by the combination of déjà vu and affection for his brother, "Thanks, Space Cadet!"

A.J. smiled, "Josh and I never really gave you the time of day about the choices you've made in your life, Isaac. But, going through this…'adventure,' for lack of a better word, …you're a good man, Charlie Brown. You really do make a difference in the world."

"You're going to make me cry!" Isaac laughed out loud, "Go on! Get out of here! I'll see you guys in a week!"

The brothers embraced one last time before A.J. clambered into his jacket, heading out into the falling evening.

Wow! I honestly never thought I'd ever hear either one of them say anything like that. Isaac smiled, studying the magnifying glass in his hand.

Re-wrapping the gift in its paper before picking up his jacket, Isaac carefully slid the magnifying glass into a pocket before laying the garment back down.

Isaac found the Gumataotaos and Fredriksen deep in a fervent discussion around the firepit about the Seahawks' chances for a Super Bowl run that season.

"Abe still sitting out there?" Isaac asked, pointing to the grove of trees hiding the agent.

"Yep," Fredriksen said, "I'm starting to get worried, 'eh. He's been off on his own for 45 minutes now."

"I'll go check on him," Isaac said, his voice ever-so-slightly listless.

Crossing the lush grass, Isaac found Gray sitting in a bench swing the Gumataotaos had installed in a small grove of cedars.

"Dining on ashes?" Isaac asked, sitting down next to Gray.

Gray smiled a little, "Just…just thinking. I'm sorry I got you involved in this."

"Why?"

Gray looked over, eyes wide in disbelief, "Isaac, you got shot and had a man's brains blown out all over you. *And* you physically assaulted a suspect. That's a huge jump across the…well, 'a' line."

"Better I live with *that* than go to Marth's funeral," Isaac responded flatly, "You know full well Lýkos is a full-blown psychopath *and* a full-blown genius. What he can't think his way out of, he buys his way out of. The *only* method of stopping him was to make him personally afraid of *me.*"

"I…I still should've been able to bring this one home without dragging you into it," Gray persisted, voice breaking, "I spent *twenty years* trying to get you to *stop* playing detective…and yet, there I go, calling you in the first time I have a major snafu in a case. Hell, I didn't even *ask*. I *told* you to come to Silverdale."

"Yes…yes, you did," Isaac nodded, "And because you *didn't* phrase it as a 'proper' request, I, of course, couldn't decide *for myself* to come."

Gray's eyes roamed up to the darkening sky before the import of Isaac's sentence penetrated his brain.

Head swinging over to look at Isaac, Gray's eyes narrowed, "Say that again?"

Isaac shook his head, "I could easily have said no. To be honest, I *was* two seconds from refusing, believe it or not. You were closer to being a solo act than you realize."

"I see."

"Do you?" Isaac pushed on, "We had this same conversation last year after that dust-up on the *Dwight D. Eisenhower.* Remember how you were feeling guilty for bringing me and Dionne into the investigation to help?"

"Yeah, and the killer nearly killed *you* in the process," Gray said grimly, "This was the second time I ever called you in on a case, and for a second time you nearly got killed. I'm sensing a pattern here."

"Oh, you magnificent idiot!" Isaac laughed. Shaking his head, he caught his breath, "Abe, how many times over the past twenty years did *you* get threatened or injured after *I* called you for help? You don't see *me* getting my propeller fouled up by that, do you?"

Gray sat back, mildly stunned as Isaac's point hit home.

"Besides," Isaac went on, "That *gesekgi's* been gunning for me ever since we thwarted his attempt to steal the ANQ45 two years ago. That's why Smith was terrified when he saw me; he knew that *mi-chin-nom* had a vendetta against me."

"And by bringing you in on this case, I put a target on your back!" Gray said mulishly.

"Abraham, knock off the martyr act, ok? There's a quantum difference between working through guilt and wallowing in self-pity. Stop wallowing; you're boring me."

Gray's head shot around, mouth hanging open.

Isaac, however, was smiling with gentle concern, "You *asked* me for help. I made my own choice to give it, consciously, freely, and for a reason. I grew up a long time ago. I can make my own choices and accept my own consequences."

"If you were so close to refusing to come out here," Gray asked, confusion in his voice, "Then why *did* you come?"

Isaac's smile widened, looking out over the yard, "Remember needling me about that murder down in Kentucky earlier this year? Know how I got *into* that one? I overheard the sheriff talking in a diner while having lunch. I didn't even think about it; I just stuck my nose in because I knew I could make a difference, and I did."

Gray thought about that, "That's a great response, but, as I heard *you* once say, not all responses are *answers.* I still don't understand why you stopped a major road trip to help with *this* case if you were so close to declining."

Isaac dropped his head in amused exasperation, "Jeez, and you think *I'm* dense where people are concerned? Abraham Gray, you lovable, adorably obtuse dork! Are you *really* that clueless as to *why* I'd drop everything to come help you?"

Gray shrugged, clearly lost.

Isaac sighed, closing his eyes for a moment to get his throat around the words that meant so much, but were so hard to say for reasons he still couldn't understand.

"You're one of two men in the world I refer to as my 'other brother.'" Isaac said tightly, "I came to help *you.*"

Gray sighed, unable to figure out what to say.

"Abe, do you know why we get on so well?"

"Because I'm willing to put up with your atrocious ideas of humor when most everyone else would just chuck you into one of the volcanoes around here?" Gray said in a dry voice.

"Other than that, yes!" Isaac laughed, "Deep down we're very much alike. We take what we do seriously, we share similar ethics, and we generally have the same outlook on life. But we also share a few shortcomings, one of the biggest being a tendency to shoulder responsibilities that aren't ours."

Gray cocked his head, listening as the night grew darker.

"That was one the *hardest* lessons I had to learn when I picked up chief petty officer," Isaac said, "It took me a long time to get past feeling like a failure if my sailors did something stupid. But, you know what?"

"What?"

"As long as I'd ensured my sailors were trained, equipped, mentored, informed of schedules and requirements, etc...well, then it *wasn't* on me if they did something dumb like missing ship's movement. I might *officially* accept responsibility since I was the chief, but there's a difference between taking *official* responsibility and being *personally* responsible."

"Good point, but I have to change the subject for a minute," Gray said, apparently forcing himself to address a sensitive issue, "I owe you an apology for going off on you so hard."

"I deserved it," Isaac said, rueful amusement coloring his voice, "I *was* pretty damned selfish just swanning off like that without letting anyone know I was ok. I'm sorry I put you in that position."

"You *were* selfish, yes," Gray agreed, "But, in my stressed-out mindset, I failed to consider that you were both physically and mentally traumatized, so you weren't thinking as clearly as you might otherwise have been. I should have addressed the issue more constructively, and, for that, I apologize."

Isaac laughed, "Oh, my! Are you saying the great Abraham Gray is a *human being* after all?! Oh, dear, I think I might faint. Break out the smelling salts!"

Gray rolled his eyes as Isaac put a hand to his forehead, feigning a fainting spell.

"*You* are a galactic-level *dork,* Isaac!" Gray said, slapping his knee as laughter finally dispelled his clouds of depression, "I hope you know that!"

"Know it...I *embrace* it!" Isaac smiled, puckish merriment shining in his eyes.

"Now, do me a favor and answer me this, Mr. Psychological Expert," Gray said.

"Shoot fire!"

"I've been on several details away from home before, so why have I been so off-kilter this whole time?" Gray asked, "I treated you like a rank newbie, lost my temper when I shouldn't have...I feel like I'm losing my edge."

"You aren't," Isaac said, "You're simply reacting to the fact everything's changed now."

"Not following."

"For twenty years I was in uniform and constrained by the UCMJ, Navy regulations, and military customs and courtesies," Isaac said, *"And* most all of our cases were on the East Coast. *This* is the first time you've worked with me when I'm not bound by those professional restrictions...and this was a case in a completely new geographic setting to boot. It's no wonder *both* of us have been off our game a bit. Many of the 'old rules' we used to operate under are no longer in force."

"You have a point," Gray said, comprehension brightening up his eyes, "Kind of reminds me of how much Sarah and I had to adjust once the girls were grown up and married. We were used to dealing with our *little* girls. It was hard relating to our adult, independent daughters. Took us quite a while to get used to it."

"Same thing," Isaac said, "Only, I've had the advantage of being on my own for the best part of a year now on my Grand Tour, so I've had time to get used to being 'free,' if you will. You didn't."

"I'll still be here when you get back from Alaska," Gray said, changing the subject again. His eyes, however, were brighter, as if a weight had been lifted from his shoulders. "When you get to Anchorage, tell 'Hazy' Payne I said hi. Seems like he's done pretty good for himself."

"Considering he owns one of Anchorage's most successful back-country air services, I'd say he's done *damned* good!" Shepherd said, "Now, are you going to come join us by the firepit voluntarily, or do I have to knobble you over the head and drag you? It's getting chilly out here."

Gray laughed uproariously this time, slapping his knee, "I'll come, I'll come...if only to watch Maria play match-maker between you and Luke!"

Isaac rolled his eyes, "Tell me about it!"

"Isaac, maybe there's something there," Gray said sternly, "Don't cavalierly dismiss any possibilities."

"Oh, not again!" Isaac said, exasperation coloring his voice. Getting to his feet, he stretched his back, "Please, spare me!"

Gray rose, "I mean it! Look, you know how you got me and Sarah into *Babylon 5,* right?"

"Uh, yeah, I think I remember that," Isaac said, quizzically cocking his head, "Considering I brought the DVDs over for a *Babylon 5* binge night once a week for, what, three years? Why?"

"There's a line from the show coming to mind, though I might butcher it a bit," Gray said, "Isaac, touch passion when you can. It's rare enough in this world. Don't be a fool and ignore it when it calls you *by name.*"

Chapter 31
Silverdale, Washington
Tuesday, September 18, 2018; 09:30 hours

Broken clouds obscured the sun, but the star's flowing radiance raised the temperature to 61 °F. A light breeze smoothly whispered through the trees as Shepherd exited *Sarah Jane's* cockpit outside the NCIS building.

Striding to the passenger-side door, he opened it, retrieving his brown corduroy sport jacket. Sliding his arms into it, he jiggled the jacket straight before reaching back into the car for *Montana*, plopping the hat on his head. The 'eccentric writer' look was completed by his doorknob-topped cane. The cane wasn't merely an affectation; his sore left knee was still slightly wobbly.

"Isaac, good morning!"

Turning, Shepherd saw Veronica Bale exiting her rental car, "Morning, Veronica!"

Bale smiled, buttoning up her green blazer over her slacks, "I'm sorry I missed dinner last night, but I had a *mountain* of paperwork I had to get done. I told Abe I'd cover some of it for him because, well, he looked like he *really* needed the night off!"

"He did," Shepherd said, a puckish look on his face, "He fell asleep around the fire pit last night, and his snoring triggered seismographs all the way down in New Mexico!"

The two laughed as Shepherd grasped the door handle, pulling it open. Stepping back, he let Bale precede him into the lobby.

"I heard from Chief Dionne last night," Bale said, referring to Shepherd's former protégé.

"Chief Robertson," Shepherd corrected her, "You use last names, not first, with the rank."

"I know; I just wanted to see if you'd turned into a landlubber!" Bale playfully punched Shepherd's shoulder.

Once their laughter subsided, Bale went on.

"She told me she's got tentative orders to Pensacola as the PAO for the Aviation Systems Maintenance Command," Bale nodded as Shepherd followed her into the building, the door closing automatically behind them.

"I thought she was heading to Bahrain next year?" Shepherd said as they strode across the lobby.

"That was the plan, but the Navy switched her orders," Bale replied, "The PAO chief at ASMC got a DUI, so they need someone to replace him fast."

Carol Keeters was talking to the receptionist. Seeing Shepherd and Bale, Keeters smiled warmly, buzzing them through the security door. She wore a bright, cheerful yellow skirt and matching blouse with a white jacket. Her hair was held by two clips with tiny sparkling roses. Her attire was completely professional, but there was no hiding the fact she was no longer under a very dark shadow.

"Good morning, Carol!" Bale said cheerfully.

Keeters smiled, "Good morning! I'm glad I caught you both here. Isaac, I heard you're off to Alaska. When do you leave?"

"Tomorrow morning," Shepherd repeated pleasantly, "Need to finish up some paperwork today before I abscond for a bit."

"Well, good. Abe and the director are waiting for you two in Mr. Kerr's...I mean, in Abe's office," Keeters said, her mood airy.

"The director?" Shepherd and Bale said in perfect synch, shock coloring their faces as their eyes widened.

Keeters nodded, "Director Belk flew in on the red eye early this morning. That man drinks more coffee than anyone I've ever seen! He's already gone through *two* urns. Anyway, he and Abe are waiting in Abe's office."

"Ok, we're on our way!" Bale said, slightly breathless in anticipation of the unexpected meeting with The Big Boss.

Shepherd still marveled at how crowded the building felt now that Gray had repopulated it with the agents and staff Kerr deployed on futile pursuits of untamed waterfowl from the family Anatidae. He and Bale had to stop every few feet to return the greetings of people who seemed to materialize out of the wallpaper.

It took them a good few minutes to disengage from Dr. Albert Nguyen. Nguyen stood only 4'2" tall, but his force of personality took over the corridor as he introduced himself to them. The short Vietnamese man was one of NCIS' top forensics experts, and his testimony had incarcerated many a nefarious evildoer.

"I only returned from New Mexico last night," Nguyen said, "I'm more fortunate than most. I was able to provide vital information that advanced several *real* cases. I'm *very* grateful to you both for getting Kerr out of this building!"

"Thank you," Bale said, beaming with pride, "But, unfortunately, we have to excuse ourselves, Doctor Nguyen. The director is waiting for us."

Nguyen's eyes widened, "I had no idea the director was *here!* Forgive me; I'll talk to you more later when you both have time."

Nguyen smiled one last time before heading off.

Bale led Shepherd down the hall, threading the needle through more greetings and introductions until they reached the Special Agent in Charge's outer office. Crossing it, they found the door to the inner office closed.

Shepherd raised an eyebrow wryly, noticing someone had stuck a sticky note reading "Under New Management" over David Kerr's brass nameplate.

"Under new management, indeed!" Shepherd muttered to himself.

Bale knocked lightly.

Gray opened the door, smiling.

"Good morning! Come on in! We have a *lot* to talk about!"

Bale and Shepherd stepped past him into the office.

"Veronica, Isaac—Kirby Belk, Director of NCIS," Gray said closing the door.

Belk was a reedy, thin man with skin nearly as dark as Bale's. Shepherd had seen him numerous times on TV, of course, but was struck by how hollow the man's face looked. Empty skin hung over dry bones, and arms as thin as a skeleton's were lost in the blue suit and green tie he wore. Cresting at an altitude of five feet, Belk did not possess any sort of imposing physicality.

That is, until he strode across the room with his hand out.

"Veronica, it's good to see you again!" Belk's voice was a powerful baritone filling the room with strength, grace, and the unshakeable conclusion that he was, indeed, in charge.

"And you! It's been quite a few years since we partnered in the DEA." Bale said, taking his hand, "I didn't expect you to come out here."

Belk's energy filled in the missing body mass, his face losing its resemblance to an emaciated corpse as he spoke, "Normally I wouldn't be here, but David Kerr's criminal activities stained our organization, and that requires my attention. I'm in Abraham's debt for the damage control he's done, but *my* job is to repair shit, not hide behind my desk in Washington like some asshole politician."

Shepherd was still processing the limitless energy pulsating from Kirby Belk when the director turned his way with all the fanaticism of a 1960s teenager attending a Beatles concert.

"The Accidental Detective!" Belk said, the hurricane of goodwill and enthusiasm breaking over Shepherd, "I must say, this is a true honor, Chief Shepherd! Kirby Belk, NCIS. You're something of an urban legend, you know! Half of NCIS wants to shoot you, and half wants to hire you!"

"The honor's mine, sir," Shepherd said, taking Belk's proffered hand, the skinny appendage surprisingly strong, "How was your flight?"

"Long, tiring, boring, and fucking *loud,*" Belk said, "Had a baby crying behind me the whole way. Typical. But, shit happens. I can't complain too much, not after the cluster fuck of deranged assholes you people untangled out here!"

Shepherd's face betrayed his surprise.

"Are you ok, Chief?" Belk asked.

"I'm sorry, sir," Shepherd laughed, "I'm no wilting flower, but I'm not used to executives at your level using such 'colorful metaphors' so freely!"

Belk returned the laugh, "I'm an old Jarhead; you're an old airdale. The language just kind of sticks with you like a tick hooked into your cock!"

Bale and Gray exploded with laughter as the office was filled with merriment. The dark cloud infesting the building was well and truly gone.

"It does, indeed, sir!" Shepherd chuckled, nodding.

"Sit your asses down and relax," Belk gestured to the sofa.

Shepherd noticed Belk nod at Gray as Gray sat behind the Special Agent in Charge's desk, while he took one of the chairs across from the sofa. Another sticky note covered Kerr's garish nameplate. The note read simply, "The new management."

"Do you want some coffee?" Gray asked Shepherd and Bale.

"No, thank you," Bale said.

"I'm good," Shepherd shook his head, "Had some already."

"Yeah…" Gray shook his head, "We don't need to peel you off the overhead. I've seen him on too much caffeine, Director. It's not a pretty picture!"

Belk chuckled, "I can imagine."

"Would you care for another cup yourself?" Gray asked Belk.

"Hell no!" Belk shook his head, "I'm already shaking harder than a Chihuahua with an electrical cord jammed up its butt!"

The four shared another laugh before Belk brought them back to the subject at hand.

"Now, to business. I came out here because I need to undo Kerr's shit show. However, I also wanted to see the three of you together. I'm sure none of you missed the connections between Gippeum Lýkos and the Bacon case."

"No sir, we didn't miss it at all," Gray said.

"Granted my predecessor was still in office when you and the Accidental Detective here arrested that Drummin fucktard aboard *Ponce,*" Belk said, his eyes squarely on Shepherd, "So, we now also know that Lýkos was bankrolling Gordon Grey's killing spree in Norfolk last year, but what *you* need to know is just where Senator Alejandro got his information."

"He said he was briefed by the CIA," Shepherd said, "He was surprised he was contacted so quickly."

"Does the name Aaron Seeley ring a bell?" Belk asked.

Gray and Shepherd both sat bolt upright.

"I see it does," Belk said, reading the stunned expressions on their faces.

"He was aboard *Ponce* investigating a CIA lead on Drummin's attempt to steal the laser," Gray said, "We listed him as a suspect in the murder until we cleared him from that...but we learned his company, Smith-Table Electronics—"

"Was a fraud," Belk nodded, crossing his thin legs, "Correct. Smith-Table Electronics, and its parent company, Dolus Holdings, are both fronts for CIA operations."

"Well, that explains how Dolus Holdings was 'hoodwinked' by Seeley," Shepherd said.

"His real name is Aaron Evers," Belk said.

"We figured that out, as well, sir," Gray said.

"I'm sure you did," Belk said, "What you two don't know is that there's someone—and I honestly do *not* know whom—in the CIA who has their eye on you. The reason Senator Alejandro got the information so bleeping *fast* was because the two of you are one of Evers' projects."

Belk's eyes linked Shepherd and Gray as he spoke, "Turns out he's had orders from on high to keep an eye on both of you."

"I'm not sure whether to be flattered or frightened," Shepherd said, shaking his head while sharing a glance with Gray.

Belk laughed, "I'd be pissing my pants if I were you, Chief! I mean, the IRS is the only agency that scares me more than the CIA!"

The four broke into laughter before Belk got back to business.

"I'm assuming you weren't given some formal briefing," Gray said, a shrewd look in his eye, "I'm guessing our Mr. Evers just walked into your office and spilled all this?"

"That about surrounds it," Belk said, "The international implications of Lýkos' activities are too big for Langley to ignore. As I said, though, Evers is only part of the equation where the CIA's concerned. You two have a guardian angel…or, perhaps, 'guardian spook' is a better term."

"I always said we were special!" Shepherd couldn't resist. Although he sat casually relaxed, he noticed just how intently, if unobtrusively, Belk was studying him.

"That's *one* way to put it!" Belk's laugh was loud, strong, and infectious, "Still, there's a bigger picture we—the CIA, FBI, and NCIS—are only now just starting to put together."

Bale nodded, "That also explains the speed with which I was able to begin piecing together the money laundering aspects. I had a feeling that things were coming a bit easier to me than normal. What put me over the top was a conversation with… wait a minute, what does this Aaron Evers look like?"

Belk pulled out his phone and called up a photo showing a slender, Caucasian man with light sandy brown hair.

"Wow," Bale said, sitting back, "Ok…we *are* in something now. Your Aaron Evers is my 'Aaron Corrigan, Vice President of Investments from Fiduciary Financial Services. I interviewed him at great length, and that helped me link up the money trail undergirding Gordon Grey's rampage last year."

"FFS is another CIA front, of course," Belk nodded, putting his phone away "I can't tell you three everything because, frankly, *no one* in NCIS, the CIA, or FBI, knows everything, but all three agencies suspect a link between Gippeum Lýkos, GDI Tech, and an operation the CIA's been running for a few years regarding threats against *something* the U.S. is currently developing."

"Years?" Shepherd blurted out, surprised.

"Years," Belk nodded, "Chief, I do applaud you for your record for speed. It's frankly so great as to be almost un-fucking-believable. But I don't think your brief time in the intel community prepared you for the long game we often have to play."

"No, sir," Shepherd shook his head, crossing his legs and sharing a look with Gray.

"You've mastered the art of criminal investigations, but when you operate at this level in the intelligence sphere, you often get only one shot at your target," Belk explained, "Operations can take years to plan and bring to fruition. Both the CIA and FBI have separately tracked some kind of ill-defined threat, but no one's been able to determine the 'who' or 'what' of it all...much less *what* tech is being targeted. Well, now we know one of the 'who's' involved."

"Which is the *big* reason you're here," Shepherd deduced.

Ok, it's obvious he wants something from me, and it doesn't *take Hercule Poirot to figure out what he's fishing for,* Shepherd thought. *Still, I'm happy to let him drive this train and see where it goes.*

"Whatever's going on, you three are on the periphery of it," Belk went on, "I believe you played baseball, correct, Chief? Pitcher?"

"Yes, sir," Shepherd nodded, "High school and college."

"Then, to use a baseball analogy, you three might be the pinch hitters we need to distract the targets enough to allow us an opportunity to close the trap," Belk stated.

"Wow," Shepherd said, "That's heavy."

"Very," Belk said, "Obviously, Abraham and Veronica are players. *You,* Chief Shepherd, are the wild card. I'm depending on you for your special brand of assistance when we need you—if you're willing to give it. And let's not shit ourselves; everyone in this room knows we'll need your help before this is over."

"I'm just a phone call away, Mr. Director," Shepherd said without hesitation, hiding the uncomfortable backflips his stomach was doing.

Belk's face melted into a relieved smile, "Thank you. Now, I know you're on a road trip and all, and you've earned every minute of it, but be careful. You *have* made some powerful enemies, so watch your ass. We've got your six, and, apparently, so does the CIA. But, if I were you, I'd keep your head down a bit until we figure out the best way to deploy your talents."

"Understood," Shepherd nodded.

Belk glanced at his watch, "I'm sorry to cut this short, but Abraham and I have a meeting with Sheriff Sigo in thirty minutes. Veronica, I need you to head back to Quantico and 'continue' the Gordon Grey investigation. We'll use that as a cover so you can get on with the *real* work. I want to keep things close to the chest until I get a better picture of the big picture."

"Will do," Bale nodded.

"Chief," Belk rose, holding out his hand again, "You've gone above and beyond your assigned duties for a long time…and often in the face of a great deal of abuse. As a fellow veteran, thank you."

Shepherd rose, taking the director's hand, "No problem, sir. I'm here when you need me."

Belk suddenly let out an unexpected guffaw. Gathering his breath, his eyes crinkled as he glanced sideways at Gray, still holding Shepherd's hand.

"Shit, I feel like I just swore him back in!"

Five hours later, Gray and Shepherd were sipping coffee in *Sarah Jane*. Parked outside the Starbucks on the corner of Bucklin Hill Road and Silverdale Parkway, the two used the vehicle for an impromptu meeting.

Traffic zipped by on Silverdale Parkway as Gray enjoyed the aroma of a steaming mug of Americano, while Shepherd happily attacked his cold brew.

"I never thought I'd get used to coffee without sugar," Shepherd said, "Took four years, but I'm down to cream only."

"You want to go healthy—take it black," Gray said, his own coffee black as night, "There's still too much sugar and fat in the cream alone for my taste."

"You're a stronger man than I am, Abe!" Shepherd laughed, "Well, that was one *hell* of an unexpected meeting this morning. I don't envy the clean-up Belk has to do."

"Neither do I," Gray said, "Now, let's address the elephant in the room."

"Good idea," Shepherd said, "Hang on, I've got a pen and some stamps here in *Sarah Jane's* glove compartment.*"*

"I—what?" Gray asked, confused. Seeing Shepherd's cat-ate-the-canary grin, Gray found himself suddenly fighting an urge to use his firearm. "Ha, ha. Seriously, so, do you think Aaron Evers and our mysterious Mr. 'L' are the same person?"

"No," Shepherd shook his head.

"I tend to agree," Gray nodded, setting his coffee down, "Timing's wrong, for a start. We met Evers in 2016, yet our Mr. 'L' said we saved his life *years* before that. So, it seems Evers is keeping an eye on us as part of *his* assigned duties."

"Looks like it," Shepherd said, sipping his coffee again.

Gray sighed, "Well, there's nothing we can do right now. You're flying to Alaska tomorrow morning and I want you to have some good R&R. In the meantime, I'm going dig around and see if I can't find out a bit more about what Mr. Evers is working on."

"Already on it," Shepherd said, holding up the Bat Phone, "I texted Aidan and asked him to poke around a bit after Linda gets back to Ohio. I also talked to Diego while you were finishing up with the director. He said he'll also keep poking around a bit and let us know what he finds. I'm as curious as you are."

"You do realize we'll be running into Mr. 'L' sooner or later, don't you?" Gray asked.

Shepherd sighed, glancing to the side before looking back at Gray, "Eventually, yes. But I don't think Mr. 'L' will appear on stage until we're well into the final act of this drama."

Gray inhaled a deep breath, "Based on what we know so far, I've got a bad feeling about how big that 'final act' is going be. We're *way* beyond stopping murderers here Isaac; now we really *are* fighting monsters!"

"That we are," Shepherd said, but then his mouth quirked into a smile, "I'm in a bit of shock, to be honest. I thought I was just a detective now, but it seems we've *both* stumbled into the big show! Still, we *should* write this case down in our respective diaries!"

"Might as well get it over with," Gray said with a resigned sigh, sensing the coming joke, "And why is that?"

"Because we *were* right," Shepherd began laughing, "The Lionfish really *was* a red herring!"

Gray face-palmed himself.

Denouement

Seward, Alaska
Friday, September 21, 2018; 11:32 hours

With highs in the mid-50s, the building clouds were a beautiful, fluffy ornament in the azure blue sky...for now. The sky was expected to be overcast by early afternoon, but that was commonplace for Alaska this time of year.

"Good grief, Hazy!" Shepherd blurted as the two walked towards the Seward marina, "You never said you and your wife know Peter Clemp! I mean, well, jeez! His Neon Flamingo Group owns some of the biggest travel and vacation companies in the world. Ocean Adventure Cruises, Skyline Airways, American Classic Hotels. You never mentioned you're such a mover and shaker yourself!"

Bradley 'Hazy' Payne laughed as the two Navy veterans sauntered along the quiet street. Both had been skinny, eager young men just starting out on the adventure of life twenty years prior. Today, while Shepherd had filled out into a barrel-chested bear of a man, Payne largely retained his slender form. His face, so angular years ago, was rounder now, but he still sported a skin tone making him look like a misplaced California surfer.

"I was at another restaurant here in Seward with Ginger back in 2009. The bank had denied our small business loan because of the economic crisis in '08," Payne responded. "This old guy overheard us and struck up a conversation about our business plans. Damn, we must have talked for over two hours before he told us who he was. After that, he called his assistant to set up a loan for me."

"Just like that?"

"Just like that," Payne nodded, looking up at the bright yellow leaves on the trees, "Oh, and he also cautioned Ginger and I about revealing business plans to strangers in the future in case some jerk wanted to steal our ideas."

"So that's how you financed Glacier Air Pilots," Shepherd said, his voice sounding genuinely impressed, "And now you two just routinely catch up with one of the 20 richest men in the world for lunch since he keeps a vacation home here in Seward. Damn, Hazy—you've done well! I hope you're proud of everything you've accomplished."

"I am, Sparkiopolis," Payne said happily, using a Greek-esque variation of 'Sparky,' Shepherd's old Navy nickname.

The pair turned down a walkway leading to the floating pier where Payne's floatplane was tied up, "Hey—changing subjects, you got lucky—normally the leaves are down by now, but this year they've held on."

The deciduous trees around them were, indeed, still blanketed in a cacophony of gold and red leaves. Seward looked like a Bill Alexander painting come to life.

"It's been a lovely autumn up here, all right," Shepherd agreed, shifting the laptop knapsack on his shoulder, "I think I could live up here someday!"

"I'm *really* glad you brought the computer to the restaurant, dude!" Payne said, the floating pier's resin planks creaking and shifting slightly under their feet, "Those shots of Denali you got after we took off from Anchorage were off the *hook!* That mountain's nearly 140 miles north of Anchorage, but you got it clear as a bell!"

"Helps that I rented a high-def camera and long lens," Shepherd said, "Remember, I *was* a professional photographer for most of my career."

"You impressed Peter with your work," Payne said, "Who knows? Maybe he'll finance you if you want to start up a photography business. He gave you his card, after all—and, trust me, when he says to give him a call if you need anything, he *means* it!"

"I appreciate that, but I'm taking my shot at being a novelist," Shepherd said, "I think I'll keep photography as a hobby for a while."

"Ok, give me a minute to get this baby prepped," Payne smiled as they reached the bobbing float plane. The icy blue 'Glacier Air Pilots' livery on the vertical stabilizer surmounted a fuselage done in blue and white stripes. This particular aircraft bore the name *Purple Haze* in a fancy script on the nose.

"This was the first plane I bought after we paid off Peter's loan," Payne said, "So it's *my* plane. My other pilots don't get to fly this one!"

Shepherd felt his phone vibrate in his pocket as Payne stepped onto the nearest float, opening the cabin door.

Putting down his backpack, Shepherd retrieved his phone.

"Abe!" Shepherd answered brightly, "What's up?"

"I've been promoted," Abraham Gray said disgustedly, his disgruntled voice drifting out of the phone's small speaker.

"Say again?"

"I've been promoted!" Gray snapped, sounding as if he were suffering the greatest insult of his life, "Wanted to let you know personally. Anyway, the director flew back to Washington today after naming *me* the new Special Agent in Charge of the Northwest Field Office. I start in January."

"Congratulations...?" Shepherd offered carefully. *Not like I didn't see this coming a mile off, even if Abe didn't!*

Payne glanced out of the plane with a curious expression on his face. Shepherd held up a hand to let Payne know he'd explain in a moment.

"Isaac, you damned well know I never wanted to be anything but a field agent!" Gray blustered, "I'm a detective, not a bureaucrat!"

"Well, *you* know I never wanted to be anything but an F-14 Tomcat tech and a combat photographer," Shepherd countered, gazing east across the water to the jagged peak of Mount Alice, "But, it happens to all of us. I *do* know how you feel, though, and I *do* empathize. Still, I honestly can't imagine a better man for the job. I'm just surprised you accepted the offer."

"There was no 'offer' to accept!" Gray shot back, "When we had breakfast at Sea-Tac before his flight, he *told* me I could either take it or resign from NCIS. He was nice as can be about it—even a bit sympathetic—but he made it crystal clear this was an 'offer' I'm not allowed to refuse."

"Well, you *could* leave NCIS," Shepherd pointed out.

"Just walk away and not finish the job?" Gray's voice was incredulous, "Yeah, like I'm going to do *that!*"

"How'd Sarah take it?" Shepherd asked, his eyes studying the nearby boats. A desultory seagull cawed overhead.

"She's…stunned," Gray said, "But she said *exactly* what you just said. So, it looks like we're moving to Washington State in December. Isaac, what the *hell* am I going to do?! I've been in charge of details before, but I have *no* experience in the kind of leadership this job requires!"

"Make it up as you go along, just like the rest of us!" Shepherd said lightly before catching himself, "I'm sorry, Abe; I shouldn't be so glib. I had a similar conversation with John Stiles back in 2012 when I was selected for chief. Unfortunately, there's no easy answer. Leadership is as much an art as anything else. All I can do is reassure you that I think you'll do fine…though I understand that statement does nothing to actually *help* you."

"Yeah…about that," Gray said, hesitation in his voice, "Isaac, it turns out Kerr's also implicated in the 'Big Mitch' scandal in addition to his involvement with Lýkos."

"Doesn't surprise me," Shepherd said, "But I have a feeling Kerr wasn't content just getting bribed, was he?"

"Nope," Gray said, "He's admitted to obstructing that investigation while he worked with Lýkos."

"Yikes!" Shepherd said, "Is Kerr still alive?"

"Oh, yes," Gray said, "Cremer's team already thwarted one assassination attempt. Cremer's assured me not *everyone* in the FBI is trying to frame the president with a bogus hoax. Lýkos is still in custody. But, trust me, he's pulling out all the stops. That man has power, all right."

"I bet."

"So, anyway," Gray said, his voice carrying a 'get back to business' tone, "That's why I needed to talk to you. Aside from sharing my 'good' news, that is."

"Oh?" Shepherd saw Payne leaning back, snoozing in the pilot's seat. Shepherd knew what was coming, but held his peace.

"Yes," Gray said, hesitation in his voice. He seemed to be steeling himself up to say something, "Look, do you *really* miss working with me?"

"Of course," Shepherd said, leaning on a piling, smiling as his suspicions were confirmed.

Glancing down at a nearby boat, he chuckled as he read its name: *She Said Yes!*

"The director's giving me a budget to hire a part-time consultant," Gray said, "I need to find a candidate with 20 years' Navy experience in intelligence, and/or instructor duty, and/or public affairs. The candidate must have interned in a police department forensic lab, possess a master's degree in history and/or criminology, and be Navy paygrade of E7 or above on the enlisted side, or O5 or above on the officer side…" Gray's voice trailed off.

Shepherd was stone-cold silent, but his smile was huge.

"Isaac?"

"I'm here," Shepherd shook his head, "Gee, Abe, I have *no* idea who that might describe!"

"I know, right!" Gray chuckled, "Director Belk told me to do *whatever* I have to in order to officially get you aboard NCIS. He knows you're not going to accept a full-time gig, but he did make a few good points."

"Such as?"

"For one, if you're on the payroll, we can avoid all the logistical gymnastics we've had to do in the past to get you on a case," Gray responded, "Second, since you're as hip-deep in this as I am, you might as well be part of the solution. Third, we can extend greater protection to you with much more efficiency."

"Wow," Shepherd felt his chest tighten with…what?

"'Wow?'" Gray asked, "That's all you, the great Isaac Shepherd, have to say?"

Shepherd took a breath, the rattle of tumbling tension dancing on his sternum making him giddy, "Can't pretend I didn't see this coming. But, I have to ask—what do *you* want?"

"Isaac, you're an idiot!" Gray laughed with a light, ringing tone Shepherd hadn't heard in a while, "Of course, I want you here! Consider this the formal interview."

"You start in January, right?" Shepherd asked.

"I do," Gray said, "Director Belk wanted me to start sooner, but he knows Sarah and I have to get packed and move across the country in just over three months. So…when I can have your answer? I imagine you'll need a few days to think about it."

Payne, awake again after his brief nap, was climbing out of the plane.

Shepherd smiled again, his thoughts returning to Big Sky Country, *Well, here we go again! The Accidental Detective is back!*

A cloud shifted, allowing bright sunlight to fall unobstructed on the pier Shepherd stood upon. The sudden bright warmth echoed the comprehension of just *what* that sense of tension dub-stepping along his chest was. It was the fires of incipient adventure…with all the good and bad the word 'adventure' implies.

"I'm in," Shepherd said definitively, "But I won't be out until January myself. I have a few more states to see by November, and I promised my folks I'd be home in Niceville for the holidays."

"Fair enough," Gray said, "I'll have Carol email you the paperwork. Welcome aboard NCIS, Isaac! What's that line the Borg always say in *Star Trek?* 'Resistance is futile, you will be assimilated?'"

"Close enough!" Shepherd chortled, "Ok, I've got to get going. Hazy and I are in Seward, but we need to take off for Anchorage before the weather gets funky later this afternoon."

"Ok, I'll talk to you later," Gray said, "And, Isaac, one more thing."

"Shoot fire!"

"I might bend your ear now and then for leadership advice once I take over out here."

"With pleasure, Abe," Shepherd said, "I'll catch you in a couple of more days when I get back to Seattle."

"Later!"

"What's up?" Payne asked, zipping up his jacket.

"I just got hired," Shepherd said, putting his phone away.

Payne smiled, "Congratulations, Sparky! Uh...what job?"

Shepherd laughed, "I'll tell you about it on the flight back to Anchorage."

"No problem," Payne said, "We've still got a couple of hours before the weather would make me hesitate to fly, so I figured I'd take us back the long way around. Here, I'll put your bag in the back."

Payne took Shepherd's computer knapsack and headed back to the float plane as Shepherd shoved his phone back into his pocket.

Payne settled himself into the pilot's seat, starting the engine. The Cessna 185 coughed and spluttered before roaring to life. Shepherd untied the aircraft from the pier, then clambered aboard, buckling himself into the copilot's seat.

Payne gently taxied the plane away from the pier with such a deft hand the pontoons left but the slightest hint of a wake.

"Ready?" Payne said into his microphone as Shepherd settled his headset over his ears.

"Punch it, Chewie!" Shepherd said happily as he reached down, picking up his rented high-def camera from the floor under his legs.

Payne laughed, "Sparky, *you're* the hairy Wookie; not me!"

Pushing the throttle forward, Payne kept the stick steady as the diminutive aircraft sprinted across the waters of Resurrection Bay. Gaining speed, the Cessna wobbled a bit before her wings bit into the air, lifting her pontoons from the water as she hurtled skyward.

Shepherd gazed over the untamable Alaskan wilderness, his heart racing as Payne took them higher.

He didn't look back; his future lay ahead.

<u>Fantail</u>

Grand Canyon Village, Arizona
Friday, December 21, 2018; 09:05 hours

The bright desert sun swiftly raised the ambient temperature from the 20s to the balmy 50s. The golden orb's radiance lit up Sarah Gray's face as Abraham framed her in the camera…without her realizing it.

Sarah gazed north across the Grand Canyon from the Bright Angel Trailhead, the striking reds, oranges, browns, and other desert hues dazzling her eyes. The air was clear, dry, crisp, and almost painful to breathe. She smiled, hugging herself as sheer wonder overwhelmed her ability to truly understand the vista spread below her.

The two were taking the long way to Washington State. Seizing the unique opportunity for an extended road trip, they were finally seeing many of the sites they'd only read about for years.

Now, Abraham caught Sarah in that candid moment, the smile of pure bliss reminding him of the way she smiled at him at their wedding so many years and so many miles ago. The sun's pure light gave her dark skin a ruddy, attractive glow even as her expression conveyed beatific serenity. Her graying hair blazed with a fiery glow of purity, making her look like an angel come to Earth.

Snapping the exposure, Abraham lowered the camera, gazing at her before letting his own eyes travel over the breathtaking landscape.

No wonder Isaac said this is one of his favorite places on Earth! Abraham thought, recalling an entry in Shepherd's travel blog from the previous October.

The Grays had splurged, deciding to stay an extra couple of days at the Canyon. Their first few nights had been down in historic Williams along old Route 66. However, taking advantage of their flexible timetable and the low rates available in the off-season, they'd booked a room in the Bright Angel Lodge, located in Grand Canyon Village right on the canyon's south rim, for a few more days.

"You're looking happy," Abraham said, coming up next to his wife, "And I mean *really* happy. First time you've seemed at ease since we got the news about my promotion."

Sarah smiled, snuggling into Abraham as a chilly breeze pricked her exposed skin into goosebumps, "I don't know. Something about the canyon gives you a new perspective. Something about the vastness of it conveys a sense of serenity I never found on the ocean."

"I know what you mean," Abraham nodded, wrapping his arms protectively around Sarah, "The ocean is a restless, relentless place. This place is just as relentless, but it's not restless. Out here you can *taste* the quiet. So, what conclusions have you reached?"

Sarah sighed peacefully, "It's not so much that I've reached any conclusions; it's more that I've reached a state of mind, I think."

"Oh? Do tell."

Sarah looked up at her husband, her face taking on an earnest expression, "It's going to take me a while to get over missing Chesapeake, what with the house and all."

"Me too."

"But, you know what? God's handed us a remarkable opportunity," Sarah said, "Think about it. We've had a very successful life together. We've traveled extensively, raised two girls—"

"Survived cancer," Abraham cut in.

"Yes," Sarah nodded, "We've done well together. But now we have a chance for a whole *new* start, a whole new adventure. How many people does the Lord hand such things to, especially middle-aged people like us? I'm getting more and more excited as we drive across country and I see—and I mean *see* with my own eyes—what's out here."

"So am I," Abraham said, "And I'll confess my mind's been a lot more at ease about taking over the Northwest Field Office since Isaac accepted the consultant job."

"We're starting on something wonderful, Matok Sheli," Sarah said, "But I have the oddest feeling this is...well, to borrow Churchill's phrase, this is the end of the beginning."

"Excuse me?"

"Oh...I don't know how else to put it," Sarah said, frustrated by her inability to better articulate her thoughts, "It just feels like, however big a move this is for us, this is only the first...whisper of something even bigger. I guess I feel like God's positioning us for something greater, and this move is just the prologue."

"Time will tell, Balibte," Abraham said, "But you might be right."

"I think I'm beginning to understand Isaac a little better as well," Sarah said, "I've never quite grasped the wanderlust that keeps him moving so much, especially when everything he's been through makes him yearn to find a safe, quiet place to live. Now, however, I think I'm beginning to understand why. Once you taste the excitement of finding out what's over that next horizon, it's hard to stop."

"It is," Abraham said, checking his watch, "But, sadly, we've already been here two extra days; we *do* need to get on the road. My report-no-later-than-date is January 5th, and we still need time up in Silverdale to find a house and all."

"Yes, we do," Sarah agreed, "Oddly enough, although we're not near the ocean, this place makes me think of a line from one of the pirate movies we've watched over the past few days."

"We watched a *lot* of pirate movies over the past few days," Abraham said, "Which one? *Curse of the Black Pearl? Cutthroat Island? The Buccaneer?*"

"*Curse of the Black Pearl*—that's the one," Sarah said, "Jack Sparrow has a line at the end of the movie that's coming to mind."

"What's that?" Abraham asked.

Sarah leaned her head on Abraham's chest. Reaching out with her hand, she gestured to the distant meeting of sky and land beyond the great canyon.

"Matok Sheli," She said, excitement in her voice, her hand reaching toward the future, "Bring me that horizon!"

The Accidental Detective will return in
Northwest Ordnance

Selected Letters

Letter from Isaac Shepherd to Robert G. Wilson

Sept. 21, 2018

Hello from Anchorage, Alaska, bro!

I'm *finally* in Alaska! I've only been going on about getting up here since we were in high school, but I made it!

Visited Seward today. Flew over with my friend Brad 'Hazy' Payne. He said to say hi, and he still has fond memories our trip to Paris with you and Cody Rupp in February of 2000. Oh, yeah—to answer your question, Hazy *still* refuses to say what he was drinking back in April of '98 when he earned the nickname 'Hazy.' Still, whatever it was must have been pretty good considering he spent two whole days going on about 'purple lobsters on roller skates...'

I know this is a hard time for you, and I'm sorry my own struggle to come to grips with it has kept me silent. Well, that and a rather nasty case I took up in Washington State. I'm sure you saw it on the news—that Lýkos bastard we arrested in Seattle. Dude, that shithead is the most *evil* fucker I've ever met!

I don't know what to say, Bob. I don't know how to help, but I'm smart enough to ask you outright what you need or want me to do (or not do) over the next couple of years. You've got to drive this train, but I'm on board with you as much as you need or want me.

I know Eric's still a sore spot for you, but I hope you've come to a place where you can give yourself a bit of grace. He was only six when Elena died. You got thrust into being a single dad while trying to handle your own grief *and* be a full-time firefighter—*and* you also got caught up in 9/11 since you were on

Staten Island. Yes, it's easy to admit all the mistakes you made, but what I find intriguing in your last email is the fact you don't mention anything you did *right.*

I'm not going to blow smoke up your ass and say you were perfect, but give yourself credit where it's due. You kept a roof over Eric's head and food on the table. You moved up to Tampa and got him into a better school system even though that forced you into fire investigation instead of actively knocking them down.

I know this does little to help ease the pain of his estrangement, but it's not easy handling your own grief while trying to help a six-year-old boy deal with losing his mother. There's no shame in not performing such a painful balancing act imperfectly. As an old friend recently reminded *me,* we can all do our best and still fall short. That's not a 'failure,' that's just life. Still, it sounds like Eric's starting to warm up considering he asked you to go to the Daytona 500 with him next year. Forgive yourself for being human.

I landed a job in Washington State, so I'm upending 20 years' worth of plans about moving home to Florida. Before you ask, yes, it's as a consultant with NCIS. I'm making the leap and full-on embracing the Accidental Detective. I'm sorry I won't be close by like we'd talked about, but I'm only one phone call and one flight away when you need me.

You've always been one of my heroes. You're the one who deliberately rushed into burning buildings—including the wreckage of the Twin Towers. You were also the best father you could be through some truly horrible circumstances. You're a good man, Bob, and that's the best that can be said for any of us.

I'll be swinging down to Tampa in November as I wrap up the Grand Tour, so I'll see you then.

Love you, bro!

Isaac

Letter from Peter Godfrey Clemp to Isaac Shepherd

368

Sept. 30, 2018

Dear Isaac,

   Forgive me for writing you through your parent's address, but it was the only one Bradley had for you since you're still on your, I believe you called it your "Grand Tour," correct? I applaud you for seizing such a unique opportunity, and I've enjoyed following your blog and YouTube channel!
   Donna and I've visited all 50 states in the course of our business, but we've never explored them the way you are now. I've been fascinated by the sites you show and the stories you find. Perhaps you should consider starting up your own guided tour business; you'd be a natural! (Your video on the Serpent Mound was incredible; I'd never even heard of the place until seeing your program!)
   Bradley and his wife are quite the savvy businesspeople. Although Donna and I started the Peter and Donna Clemp Foundation specifically to support start-ups, neither of us are in the habit of just randomly talking to strangers in restaurants. However, I admittedly began to eavesdrop that particular day. I was dining alone when they were seated next to me and began discussing the denial of their start-up loan.
   You see, the higher you go in the corporate food chain, the more isolated you get from the small business owners who make up the backbone of our economy. I'm sure you experienced something similar in the Navy; the higher you go, the harder it is to relate to your very junior people.
   I began to eavesdrop because I was afforded an unexpectedly candid window into the real effects of the 2009 downturn. What led me to introduce myself was hearing Bradley and Ginger discussing strategies to ultimately secure a loan. They were clever, resourceful, innovative, and, most importantly, legal. I don't say that in jest; I'm often discouraged by the number of

369

businesspeople I run into who find very clever—but illegal—ways to overcome obstacles.

Their efforts in building Glacier Air Pilots have been nothing short of remarkable. The only reason GAP is not a bigger firm is that they don't want it to be. Bradley and Ginger are both fully capable of growing the air service, and both are confident enough to do it. However, they have what they wanted—a solid local company (for Ginger it was the desire to own her own business, regardless of what it was; for Bradley, as you probably already knew, it was to run a back-country air service).

The reason I'm writing is because I wanted to make sure you understand that I <u>MEANT</u> it when I said to get in touch with me if you ever need anything. I'm sure we both have experienced those who hand you a card and say "Contact me" only as a cheap way to make themselves look good, but never mean it.

I mean it, but I also confess to an ulterior motive. Bradley shared your employment news with me (and assured me he had your permission to tell me you're going to be a part-time consultant with NCIS). This is where I might be of service to you. The Neon Flamingo Group was drug into the OSSC scandal earlier this year when our newly hired Vice President of Operations, Kyle Bartlett, was indicted for taking bribes from 'Big Mitch' when Bartlett was still a captain in the Navy stationed at Yokosuka in 2016.

The fallout significantly damaged the Neon Flamingo Group's earnings for the first half of last year, and the ongoing bad press (always insinuating we were part of the bribes) nearly derailed our acquisition of Ocean Adventure Cruises. Had NFG not gained control of Ocean Adventures Cruises, OAC would have gone under (no pun intended) and the 110,000 people employed by OAC would be out of work.

Besides, one of <u>my</u> long-running dreams is to own and operate a fleet of cruise ships. This is what we call a 'win-win' in business!

I seem to recall a quote of Jefferson's that fits here. Something to the effect of, "I apologize this letter is so long; I didn't have time to shorten it." I need to wrap up and get this in the mail before Donna and I fly out to Paris (not on vacation, sadly; a conference with European Union leaders to negotiate new port concessions for OAC).

The Neon Flamingo Group—and Donna's and I's personal reputations—have suffered because of the OSSC scandal. If I can ever be of assistance to you in your new capacity, let me know! If my experience in the corporate world can offer guidance, insight, or contacts with other leading business figures, I'd be pleased to offer it.

I've made inquiries into your background and service (both naval and investigative). I'm satisfied your integrity is above reproach, and that I can trust your discretion with this offer. I'm also intelligent enough to know you're probably extremely suspicious of me right now. However, I'm confident your background checks on Donna and I will assure you I'm making a good faith offer and not trying to coopt you to cover for my own sins. (Just putting all my cards on the table.)

Even if you don't avail yourself of this offer, Donna and I both genuinely want you to stay in touch. Perhaps I can introduce you to her next time you come up to visit Bradley and Ginger?

I must close this out and get it in the mail. Be safe on your journey, and keep up the great travel blogging!

Yours sincerely,

Peter G. Clemp

Photo Gallery

A 2008 aerial photograph looking north over Bremerton with Naval Base Kitsap, Bremerton (home of the Puget Sound Naval Shipyard) occupying the southern third of the image. The waterway at bottom is Sinclair Inlet, while Dyes Inlet curves north up the right side of the photo. Silverdale is out of the photo to the north at the very top of Dyes Inlet.

By 2018, the former USS Kitty Hawk (CV 63) was the only aircraft carrier left in mothballs with the other ships of the Bremerton ghost fleet. The ghost fleet is housed along the piers to the left in this picture.

Bremerton, Washington. (Public domain by Dcoetzee. October 26, 2008)

The former USS Kitty Hawk (CV 63) in storage at the Naval Inactive Ship Facility as seen from across Sinclair Inlet in Port Orchard. Kitty Hawk served from 1961 - 2009, and was finally towed to Brownsville, Texas, for scrapping in January 2020. This is the view of Kitty Hawk Abraham Gray and Isaac Shepherd had as they drove north along Highway 16 towards Silverdale. Port Orchard, Washington. (Nathanael Miller, September 9, 2018)

The ferry Tacoma *approaches the Seattle Ferry Terminal. This image is looking west, with Bainbridge Island and the Kitsap Peninsula in the background. Ferries like the* Tacoma *provide water transportation to multiple points around Puget Sound. Seattle, Washington. (Nathanael Miller, Oct. 13, 2019)*

The Great Seattle Wheel and the distant Space Needle are two of the Emerald City's most famous landmarks greeting visitors as the Seattle Ferry approaches the terminal. Opened in 2012, the 175-foot-tall Great Seattle Wheel is the tallest Ferris wheel on the West Coast. The flying saucer of the Space Needle soars 605 five into the air, and was built for the 1962 World's Fair. Today, the Space Needle is Seattle's most notable icon.
Seattle, Washington. (Nathanael Miller, August 30, 2018)

Albus the Crab checks out the statue of Ivar Haglund outside Ivar's on Seattle's Alaskan Way. This is the statue Abraham Gray and Isaac Shepherd were admiring when they ran into A.J. and his students. Ivar Haglund founded an aquarium and, later, several eateries that are still famous today. Ivar was truly one of Seattle's more colorful characters during the mid-20th century. Seattle, Washington. (Nathanael Miller, September 30, 2018)

Albus is the real-life inspiration for Isaac Shepherd's Albert the Crab. The adventures of the real-world Albus can be seen on my Instagram feed: @sparks1524.

Mount Rainier rises above the horizon like the ghost of a mythic leviathan emerging from the deep. The tallest volcano in the Cascades Range, Mount Rainier is 14, 411 feet above sea level and is visible from nearly every part of Washington State. The great mountain dominates the landscape even when seen from 75 miles away in Poulsbo (pronounced "Paul's bow"). Poulsbo, Washington. (Nathanael Miller, September 28, 2018)

Mount Rainier's southern face seen from near Paradise in Mount Rainier National Park. Paradise is located at 5,400 feet above sea level, but the volcano's summit rises more than 9,000 feet higher into the sky. This is the view of Mount Rainier Isaac Shepherd would have had if the weather had been clear. The height of the mountain often means its summit is lost in cloud cover during the autumn and winter months. Paradise, Mount Rainier National Park. (Nathanael Miller, August 5, 2020)

Gillian and Fraternity Halls are the two most famous buildings in the Montana ghost town of Elkhorn. In fact, these two structures on the only buildings protected by the tiny Elkhorn State Park. Founded in 1872, Elkhorn was a boom town that thrived until the silver minds played out, leading to the town's eventual abandonment in the late 20th century. Elkhorn is mostly forgotten today, but about a dozen people still call this quiet corner of Big Sky Country home, so be careful and respectful as you explore. Elkhorn, Montana. (Nathanael Miller, August 21, 2018)

The grave of Thomas John Willey visited by Isaac Shepherd in the tiny boot hill cemetery above the ghost town of Elkhorn. Elkhorn, Montana. (Nathanael Miller, August 21, 2018)

*The wooden grave maker for young Elisya Stevens
visited by Isaac Shepherd in Elkhorn's boot hill.
Elkhorn, Montana. (Nathanael Miller August 21, 2018)*

Beginning life as a Russian fur trading post in 1793, Seward is a hub for seasonal tourism and one of the most lucrative commercial fisheries ports in the United States according to the National Marine Fisheries Service. Seward is only 120 miles south of Anchorage, making it an easy day trip by car...or via a float plane piloted by Isaac Shepherd's old buddy, Bradley 'Hazy' Payne. Seward, Alaska. (Nathanael Miller, October 5, 2018)

Denali, the tallest mountain in North America, soars to a height of 20,310 feet above sea level. Formerly known as Mt. McKinley, Denali rises so high that it bursts through the clouds even when seen from ground level over 130 miles away in Anchorage. The name 'Denali' was given to the mountain centuries ago by the indigenous Kuyukon people. The federal government recognized this by officially renaming the peak from Mt. McKinley back to Denali in 2015. Anchorage, Alaska. (Nathanael Miller, October 5, 2018)

This magnificent wooden Thunderbird in the lobby of the Bright Angel Lodge greeted Abraham and Sarah Gray when they checked in. Opening in 1905, the Bright Angel Lodge was designed by Mary Jane Coulter for Grand Canyon Village along the canyon's south rim. Coulter often called this Thunderbird her 'bright angel.' Grand Canyon Village, Arizona. (Nathanael Miller, May 15, 2021)

Visitors marvel at the Grand Canyon from the Bright Angel Trailhead along the canyon's southern rim. This is where Abraham and Sarah Gray took in their final views of the canyon before getting back on the road for Washington State. Grand Canyon Village began life in 1901 as a stop for the Atchison, Topeka, and Santa Fe Railroad in order to bring visitors directly to the edge of the canyon. Grand Canyon Village, Arizona.
(Nathanael Miller, May 15, 2021)

Fictional Corporate Logos

Acronym and Nickname Dictionary

The Department of Defense uses a unique lexicon. The following terms are used throughout this book.

List 1: Naval and Legal Terminology

Airdale
An old, informal term for Department of the Navy personnel who work in the aviation field (both aircrew and maintenance personnel). Originally applied to both officers and enlisted, today the term predominantly refers to enlisted personnel.

AOR
Area of responsibility. The geographic area in which a combatant commander is responsible for operations.

CMC
Command Master Chief (senior enlisted advisor to a CO).

CNO
Chief of Naval Operations.

CO
Commanding Officer.

DoD
Department of Defense.

FUBAR
'Fucked up beyond all recognition.' An informal military term used when things get out of control or fouled up.

JAG
Judge Advocate General (the military law office division).

MA
Master-at-Arms (enlisted active duty security personnel).

Naval Working Uniform (NWU)
The 'digicam' uniform worn by Navy sailors. The current version in use is the green 'Type III" uniform.

NSF
Naval Security Forces (amalgamation of active duty Masters-at-Arms, civilian naval police, and other assigned security personnel).

Port
The left side of a ship when facing forward. The term derives from Middle English (11th to 15th centuries) denoting the side of a ship where it was tied up since the old steering oars predating below-water rudders were mounted on the right (starboard) side of the hull. Modern ships and airplanes use red navigation lights to denote their port side at night.

PTSD
Post-Traumatic Stress Disorder.

Quarters
The formation of a workcenter's personnel for muster, instruction, and inspection. During Quarters, administrative issues are discussed, work assignments and progress reported on, and personal grooming standards inspected. Quarters are held every workday morning, and many commands also hold evening Quarters to wrap up the day's efforts and prepare for the next workday, or hand off current work assignments to the night check if applicable.

Starboard
The right side of a ship when facing forward. Derived from Old English (5th to 11th centuries) when ships commonly used large oars as rudders. These steering oars were typically mounted on the right side of the hull, called the 'steobord' side. Modern ships and airplanes use green navigation lights to denote their starboard side at night.

TAD
Temporary Additional Duty. The short-term assignment of a sailor or Marine to another command or line of profession within the same

command. Commonly called 'TDY' for 'Temporary Duty' in the Army of Air Force.

TRIAD
Delineation of the top three senior leaders within an organization. Commonly used in the Navy to refer to the commanding officer, executive officer, and senior enlisted leader.

UCMJ
Uniform Code of Military Justice (laws and regulations governing military members).

XO
Executive Officer.

List 2: Fictional Naval and Legal Terminology Used Within this Book

AEL
Autonomous Electronics Lab. A laboratory operated by the Puget Sound Naval Shipyard to facilitate cooperation with research at NASED Keyport.

NASED
Naval Subsurface Experimentation and Development Command. Located aboard Naval Station Kitsap – Keyport in Keyport, Washington. NASED exists to develop and refine new technologies for the Navy and other military branches.

NEPAC
Naval Expeditionary Public Affairs Command. Fictitious command inspired by the real-life Navy Public Affairs Support Element (NPASE). NEPAC exists to augment ship-board public affairs media support by deploying public affairs officers and enlisted Mass Communication Specialists to deployed ships and other Navy / DoD requirements. NEPAC is broken into three centers: Norfolk, San Diego, and Japan.

This Page Intentionally Left Blank
(Navy veterans will get the joke!)

Writer's Notebook

Welcome to the Pacific Northwest, land of ancient peoples, great mountains, powerful volcanoes, and, ultimately, adventure!

First off, please remember this is a work of *fiction.* Events often happen quicker in fictitious investigations than they do in real life. This is done for dramatic purposes and story pacing, but it *is* fiction nonetheless.

Isaac Shepherd and Abraham Gray's relationship, both personal and professional, underwent a profound change when Shepherd retired from active duty service. The relational dynamic and boundaries they operated within for twenty years came to a dramatic conclusion at the end of *The Norfolk Murders.* The characters are now moving into a new chapter of their lives and friendship, so how better to represent the unfamiliar relational territory these two men now occupy than by moving the whole shebang to the opposite side of the country?

Relocating the narrative to Washington State puts both men into unfamiliar territory (metaphorically *and* literally). They have to learn how the Pacific Northwest 'operates,' both socially and legally, while also navigating the extensive changes in their relationship. Gray has always been the senior partner and mentor to the younger, somewhat volatile Shepherd...until now.

Suddenly, the roles are oddly reversed in several ways. Life may not be *about* change, but our lives are lived in a constant state of change. We're generally comfortable when change is gradual because we have plenty of time to easily adjust and adapt.

However, adapting to a large and sudden change is a much more difficult proposition. When the 'signposts' providing security and guidance in our lives are upended, tension grows because we no longer know what to expect or just how to react.

I became fascinated with the detective genre as a young boy when I discovered *Encyclopedia Brown* novels. Now, four books into the Accidental Detective's adventures, I found I wanted to shake up the tropes a bit.

I've already turned quite a few detective-story tropes on their head. Yes, the Accidental Detective is the quintessential amateur. However, his partner is a highly successful federal agent. My amateur detective is a genius, but reveled in his blue-collar life as an enlisted Navy sailor before he retired. However, in writing as in life, there are always new waters to chart and new horizons to chase.

The experience of writing the previous three books brought me to the point where I was ready to attempt the next-level challenge in my growth as a writer. This new level is the expansion of 'simple' murder mysteries into a larger narrative with more horrific implications. The murders are still the heart of the narrative, but our characters must now adapt to a world they never expected to be in.

In other words, they're going through what we go through in real life when something major shatters the peace of our normal routines.

I've waited *five years* to get to the point where I can start revealing how the previous three books fit into a larger narrative no one outside my editor (and parents!) knew I was crafting. The goal is to keep the larger story woven tightly together while ensuring each novel is an easy on-ramp for a first-time reader. This challenge is faced by *every* writer who wishes to develop a multi-book arc, and now it's my turn to grapple with it.

Jerry Foltz, my old friend, faithful editor, and hard-nosed coach once again came through for me. We've fine-tuned our working relationship and workflow over the past few years. This allowed him more time to push, cajole, recommend, and argue with me about the story mechanics, and I can see significant improvement in my writing.

I've said it before, and I'll say it again, I can't thank him enough for his work, his time, and his investment in my dreams. He's most certainly the Tom Landry to my Roger Staubach. My debt to him can never be repaid.

I also wish to recognize Eric Butler for a fourth *incredible* cover! I came up with a design embodying the Pacific Northwest setting behind the lionfish silhouette, but then Eric turned that sketchy idea into *art.* I'm as blessed to have Eric ensuring my covers are evocative and high-quality works as I am to have Jerry ensuring my prose is tightly woven and my narrative exciting.

Also, while I design most of the logos and graphics (such as the Glacier Air Pilots logo), then send them to Eric for professional-level execution, there is an exception this time around. The red-and-blue logo for the fictitious Pacific World Airways was designed by Eric from the ground up. The only directions I gave him were the colors to use and to give it a classic aviation art deco vibe. The PWA logo he created is a stunning piece of work I'm proud to have in the world of the Accidental Detective! If you're interested in offering him a commission, hit me up through my blog (www.sparks1524.com), and I'll pass on your contact information to him in case he has the time to take on the job.

Just for the record, the GDITech logo is mine from start to finish. It's a matter of personal pride in my own background as a Navy graphic artist that I designed *and* executed the final form of at least *one* of the major graphic elements in these adventures! Most of the rest I design, but leave to Eric's good offices to bring to life.

A writer could *not* ask for a better team! I craft the stories and I write the books, but I'd be *dead* in the literary waters if not for Jerry and Eric's support, effort, encouragement, and suggestions.

The adventure continues!

About the Author

Nathanael Miller exploring Seward, Alaska. (October 5, 2018.)

Nathanael Miller is a retired U.S. Navy Chief Mass Communication Specialist who enjoyed a rich and wildly varied career. Born in Texas to an Air Force family, Nathanael graduated from Niceville High School in Niceville, Florida, in 1990. He earned a bachelor's degree in American history from Florida State University in 1995 before working as a curator's assistant at the Museum of Florida History. State budget cuts eliminated this position, leading him to enlist in the Navy in September 1997.

Nathanael's first assignment was as a yeoman assigned to Fleet Air Reconnaissance Squadron Two (VQ-2)'s administration department in Rota, Spain. From VQ-2, Nathanael attended the Defense Information School (DINFOS), becoming a naval photographer in August 2000. This led to an assignment as a reconnaissance camera technician working on F-14D Tomcats with the Black Lions of Fighter Squadron 213 (VF-213). Nathanael was later stationed on Guam, taught at DINFOS, and served aboard USS *Ponce* (LPD 15) before taking over the Training Department at the Navy Public Affairs Support Element (NPASE) East aboard Naval Station Norfolk in Virginia. Nathanael completed his master's degree in 2016 while developing a new Navy training program for public affairs specialists at NPASE East.

Nathanael became NPASE East's Operations and Production Manager after he was advanced to chief petty officer before ultimately retiring from active duty in late 2017. He would accept an 18-month term position as staff writer for the public affairs team at the Naval Undersea Warfare Center Division, Keyport in Washington State in 2019. Nathanael went independent after he published his first novel, *Proud Lion*, in 2020.

397